THE BEST HONOLULU FICTION

STORIES FROM THE *Honolulu* MAGAZINE FICTION CONTEST

EDITED BY
ERIC CHOCK &
DARRELL LUM

BAMBOO RIDGE PRESS
1999

ISBN 0-910043-57-4
Copyright © 1999 Bamboo Ridge Press
Published by Bamboo Ridge Press
Indexed in the American Humanities Index
Bamboo Ridge Press is a member of the Council of Literary
    Magazines and Presses (CLMP).

This is issue #74 of *Bamboo Ridge, Journal of Hawai'i Literature and Arts*
(ISSN 0733-0308).

Cover: "writer" by Jason Nobriga. Oil on illustration board, 6" x 15", 1999.
Cover design and graphics: Michel V.M. Lê
Typesetting and production: Wayne Kawamoto

"Hanalei" by John Heckathorn was previously published in *HONOLULU
Magazine*, September 1984 and in *Passages to the Dream Shore*, UH Press, 1987.

"The Resurrection Man" by Craig Howes was previously published in
Passages to the Dream Shore: Short Stories of Contemporary Hawaii. Frank Stewart,
ed. Honolulu: U of Hawaii, 1987. 50–61.

"The Brilliance of Diamonds" copyright © 1999 by Nora Okja Keller.
Reprinted by permission of Susan Bergholz Literary Services, New York. All rights
reserved.

"Gau" by Laureen Kwock was previously published in *Aloha Magazine*,
February 1995.

"Day's Work" by Chris Planas was previously published in *Mānoa*, Vol. 3,
No. 2, Fall 1991.

"Wordsworth and Dr. Wang" by Peter Van Dyke was previously published in
HONOLULU Magazine, April 1991.

"Unstill Life With Mangos" by John Wythe White will also be published in
Hybolics (forthcoming).

"Sunnyside Up" from *WILD MEAT AND THE BULLY BURGERS*. Copyright
© 1996 by Lois-Ann Yamanaka. Published in paperback by Harvest Books; first
published in hardcover by Farrar, Straus & Giroux. Reprinted by permission of Susan
Bergholz Literary Services, New York. All rights reserved.

Bamboo Ridge Press is a nonprofit, tax-exempt corporation formed in 1978 to
foster the appreciation, understanding, and creation of literary, visual, or performing
arts by, for, or about Hawaii's people. This project is supported in part by grants from
the National Endowment for the Arts (NEA), the Hawai'i Community Foundation,
and the State Foundation on Culture and the Arts (SFCA) celebrating over thirty
years of culture and the arts in Hawai'i. The SFCA is funded by appropriations from
the Hawai'i State Legislature and by grants from the NEA.

Bamboo Ridge is published twice a year. For subscription information, direct
mail orders, or a catalog please contact:

Bamboo Ridge Press
P. O. Box 61781
Honolulu, HI 96839-1781
(808) 626-1481
brinfo@bambooridge.com
www.bambooridge.com

10   9   8   7   6   5   4   3   2   1   99   00   01   02   03

Contents

JOHN HECKATHORN
7 INTRODUCTION

ALAN AOKI
15 ONE FISH STORY

ALANI APIO
21 KA HO'I 'ANA (THE RETURNING)

PAMELA BALL
32 THE CENTIPEDE OF ATTRACTION

STUART CHING
38 HOUSE OF BONES

DAVID CHOO
49 AKIKO BURIES HER SON

WANDA DIAL
55 ROM BORI

MARIE HARA
60 OLD KIMONO

MAVIS HARA
66 CHEMOTHERAPY

JIM HARSTAD
78 THE BLACK AND YELLOW RAFT

JOHN HECKATHORN
90 HANALEI

CRAIG HOWES
107 THE RESURRECTION MAN

YOKANAAN KEARNS
119 CONFESSIONS OF A STUPID HAOLE

NORA OKJA KELLER
132 THE BRILLIANCE OF DIAMONDS

LAUREEN KWOCK
140 GAU

R. ZAMORA LINMARK
147 FROM THE STONE THE VIRGIN MARY SEES EVERYTHING:
    A TRILOGY

MARY LOMBARD
159 THE SILVER PATH

DARRELL H.Y. LUM
169 WHAT SCHOOL YOU WENT?

GEORGIA K. McMILLEN
177 THE NAME

WENDY MIYAKE
188 MOON PEOPLE

GARY PAK
194 HAE SOON'S SONG

CHRIS PLANAS
205 DAY'S WORK

GRAHAM SALISBURY
216 WHY WE HAVE RAIN
234 THE YEAR OF THE BLACK WIDOWS

WILLIAM D. STEINHOFF
253 HONOLULU HAND GRENADE R AND R

CATHERINE BRIDGES TARLETON
266 THE FISHING CLUB

BILL TETER
282 HA'INA KA PUANA

LEE A. TONOUCHI
286 WHERE TO PUT YOUR HANDS

PETER VAN DYKE
294 WORDSWORTH AND DR. WANG

JOHN WYTHE WHITE
309 UNSTILL LIFE WITH MANGOS

CEDRIC YAMANAKA
316 BENNY'S BACHELOR CUISINE
323 OZ KALANI, PERSONAL TRAINER

LOIS-ANN YAMANAKA
332 SUNNYSIDE UP

LUE ZIMMELMAN
336 END ZONE

347 CONTRIBUTORS

Illustrations

Jason Nobriga

13   CHAINED, Oil on Illustration Board, 20' x 16", 1999

105   WIZARD, Oil on Illustration Board, 14' x 11", 1999

167   BULLIES, Oil on Illustration Board, 14' x 11", 1997

251   COUNT TO TEN, Oil on Illustration Board, 12' x 9", 1998

307   HELPER, Oil on Illustration Board, 12' x 9", 1998

345   TEETH, Oil on Illustration Board, 14' x 11", 1999

BY JOHN HECKATHORN

INTRODUCTION

In the summer of 1983, *HONOLULU Magazine* announced its "first annual" fiction contest. It offered $500 plus publication in the magazine for the winning story, a princely $50 for four runners-up. The requirements were pretty simple: Stories had to be previously unpublished, typed double-spaced (remember typewriters?) and have "a Hawai'i theme, setting and/or characters."

The contest was Brian Nicol's idea. Nicol, who edited *HONOLULU Magazine* from 1982 to 1990, was constantly looking for ways to add interest to its pages. "Way back in the old days, the magazine used to publish fiction—legends of the Hawaiian gods, that sort of thing," he recalls. "We didn't want to do 'Maui captures the sun' any more, but we thought short stories—if they were contemporary, if they were about Hawai'i—would be a fun addition to the mix."

The contest was a gamble. The "first annual" business was, at the time, bravado. Would readers hate the stories? Would writers take a city magazine seriously? "I saw it as a way of reaching out mainly to the academic community, which is where I thought all the creative writers were," says Nicol. "It was a not too subtle way of pointing out the magazine valued writing, was full of good writing already."

But were there enough good writers in Hawai'i to justify a fiction contest? Would anyone enter? At first, the answer seemed to be no. Six weeks went by after the initial call for entries. There were only 11 stories, eight of which seemed to be about Menehune. "Our grim office joke was, 'What if we gave a fiction contest and no one came?'" says Nicol, ruefully.

The magazine had forgotten that writers procrastinate—they can't seem to finish anything without a deadline looming. On the last few days before the contest ended, a blizzard of manila envelopes hit the magazine offices, more than 200 entries. At the last minute, everyone wanted to come to the party.

This pattern never changes. Every year we're gnawed with anxiety, *where are the entrants?* Every year, 80 percent to 90 percent of the stories show up the last week, most the last few days, many the last hour. You'd think we'd stop worrying; we never do.

Nicol's worries about the contest didn't end until the first grand prize winner appeared in print. Then he threw one of *HONOLULU Magazine*'s famous courtyard parties and invited everyone who had placed in the contest.

"That was the moment I knew we'd done the right thing," says Nicol. "The winners' faces just glowed, not just the grand prize winner, but the honorable mentions, the runners-up. They were delighted and there was almost a kind of awe that somebody cared enough to throw a party for them. There was finally public recognition of their private talent and passion."

He's right. I ought to know. I was there—as one of the guests.

Except as a reader, it was my first contact with the magazine. At the time, I taught in the UH English Department. I'd heard through a member of my writers' group that nobody was entering the contest.

That was just fine with me. I dusted off the beginning of a novel I'd started and abandoned. I stayed up late on hot sticky Kuliʻouʻou nights, swatting swarming termites and pounding out draft after draft on a Smith-Corona portable, recrafting the piece into a short story called "Hanalei."

I thought I'd win. At the very last moment, I stuck my entry into a manila envelope and thought, *Try to beat that.*

I didn't win.

"Hanalei" was a runner-up to a short story called "Choice of Crack Seed" by a Chinese-American doctor named Terry Tom Gerritsen. Terry Tom and I, having met at the party, became friends. About a decade ago, she moved with her husband and two sons to New England. Now writing as Tess Gerritsen, she has become a *New York Times* bestselling writer (*Harvest*, *Life Support*) and gotten her picture (quite stunning) in *People* magazine.

As a first winner of the contest, you couldn't top Gerritsen. But in many ways, I felt I won as well. At that first party, I met Brian Nicol. Within a couple of months, I was writing a column for *HONOLULU*. Within a couple of years, I came to work full-time for the magazine. In 1993, I became *HONOLULU*'s 20th editor in its 111-year history.

And from the beginning of my time at the magazine, I've felt a sense of responsibility for the contest. I always wanted to make sure we took good care of it—because I knew it changed lives. Mine, anyway.

That knowledge over the years has kept me from that "oh, here we go again" tendency to take the contest for granted. Associate Editor Kam

Napier now handles the contest details, as I used to do, making sure that the integrity of the contest isn't breached. Since the beginning, all the entries have been judged anonymously. The only person who knows who wrote which story is our receptionist Brita Chilecki, who keeps the secret list, giving the judges only numbered manuscripts.

Every year, every judge reads every story—no small amount of labor. Over the years, the judges have added up to a distinguished group—Ian MacMillan, Lois-Ann Yamanaka, Nora Okja Keller, Walt Novak, Robbie Shapard, Cathy Song, Steven Goldsberry, Darrell Lum, to name just a handful. For us at the magazine, working with such people is part of the pleasure.

Sometimes, the judging is tendentious—at one of the early judges' meetings, one distinguished judge invited another equally distinguished judge to settle their differences outside on the sidewalk. Most of the time, however, the judges have managed to accommodate each other's aesthetic sensibilities without rancor.

I have taken to scheduling judges' meetings right before a meal at a good restaurant. I figure hunger will push the judges toward consensus. At the meal, we unveil the list and the judges learn who won. Every year the judges think they know who wrote this or that story. Almost invariably, they are wrong.

And, of course, the entries are not all of the same quality, and even the kindest judge will raise his or her eyebrows at some stories. When I was a judge, I used to keep a list of bad opening sentences. My candidate for all-time worst lead, from 1985: "Sitting on the beach in Ka'anapali, Marion looked at the island of Moloka'i across the channel and saw the ridges of a huge mauve tooth."

But, remarkably, the level of effort every year is quite high. The contest has become an incentive to many Island writers to produce a new story each year. Award-winning KITV reporter Cedric Yamanaka, for instance, has entered a fresh story almost every year of the contest. He's represented in this anthology by two stories. But really his entries for the *HONOLULU* fiction contest—plus his other creative work—deserve a volume all their own.

No one keeps writing without a passion for it. It's too hard. But we've hoped that our generous yearly prize is a spur to hunker down at the word processor. The prizes have become increasingly generous over the years, thanks to our sponsors. From 1988 to 1994, Michael Hinderlie of Parker Pen Company. supported the contest, doubling the original cash prizes, giving stunning limited edition fountain pens to the grand prize winners and personalized pens to everyone who placed.

When in a meeting, his local distributor questioned whether the contest sold any pens for Parker, Hinderlie said, "We don't support this contest to sell pens, we support it because it's the right thing to do. It's something I'm proud to be associated with."

When Parker Pen was bought by Gillette, we lost that sponsor, only to have others step forward. The Maui Writers' Conference has been providing a free admission to that event to each year's winner, thanks to founders John and Shannon Tullius' devotion to cultivating Hawai'i writers. The major cash prizes are now provided by Borders Books and Music.

One year not so long ago, the grand prize winning story had a stronger sexual content than usual. I'd been at the judges' meeting, and the judges had, to their credit, asked if the magazine could publish the story if they chose it as winner. I said yes. If they thought the story was the winner, I'd publish it and live with the controversy.

Even in-house at the magazine, there was some criticism of my judgment. And some real apprehension at "how the sponsor might react." I faxed the story to Borders and set up a meeting for the end of the day. I was feeling more than a little beat up by the time I got there; one of the hazards of being an editor is how many people can be counted on to tell you you're an idiot.

I walked into a small back office with Joe Tosney, Borders regional manager; Cynthia Latish, then manager of the Ward Centre Borders store; and Borders community affairs liaison, Les Honda. And Tosney said, "We read the story. We like it. People are always trying to tell us what we can sell and can't sell, and the way we see it, we're about freedom of expression."

One could not ask for better corporate sponsor.

All that said, *HONOLULU Magazine* and its various sponsors can claim only partial credit for the book you have in your hand.

This is a Bamboo Ridge book. Not ours. Our major contribution was allowing Bamboo Ridge access to the white boxes of winning stories that have been accumulating all these years in the credenza in our editorial offices.

Bamboo Ridge and its founders Darrell Lum and Eric Chock have long had our respect. In the past 20 years, they not only have put together the most distinguished nonprofit literary publication in Hawai'i, they've also created a local literature, where one hardly existed before. Look at the writers they have launched onto the national stage—Lois-Ann Yamanaka, Nora Okja Keller, and more, we're sure, to follow.

Had *HONOLULU Magazine* done the book, it would be the 16 years of grand prize winners. But to make this truly a Bamboo Ridge book, we agreed that Lum and Chock could reselect from the whole pool of winning stories—the honorable mentions and runners-up each year included. Only three of the 33 stories in this collection—Lue Zimmelman's "End Zone," Peter Van Dyke's "Wordsworth and Dr. Wang," David Choo's "Akiko Buries Her Son"—won the grand prize in the original contest.

I have mixed feelings about this. On the one hand, I would like to remind people of all the winners, would have liked to see such stories as Terry Tom Gerritsen's original winner.

On the other hand, the grand prize winners have already been published. Every year, readers ask us to publish the runners-up and honorable mentions. Some years, as space allows, we publish a few. But most of these stories in this collection are seeing print for the first time.

Some of these stories are by winning writers—Mary Lombard, Cedric Yamanaka, Pamela Ball—but these aren't the stories they won the grand prize with. Instead, they are runners-up and honorable mentions from other years.

The stories here also include a number I've always wished we'd published. Laureen Kwock's "Gau" is the single best "passing on of local traditions" story I have ever read. R. Zamora Linmark's powerful "From the Stone the Virgin Mary Sees Everything," almost won one year. I'm glad to see it find readers. Years ago, Brian Nicol thought a story called "Honolulu Hand Grenade R and R" was the best story entered in 1987, even though it didn't win. It's included in this collection.

Also included is my story, "Hanalei," which almost made it the first year. And there's Darrell Lum's charming story, "What School You Went." Neither Lum nor I ever won the contest—which may explain why we became editors. Lum was a runner-up so many times, he used to joke he had Honolulu's largest collection of Parker Pens. So the both of us knew, first hand, there were stories in those white boxes that perhaps deserved a second chance.

I'm pleased Bamboo Ridge has given so many of those stories the opportunity to find an audience. The contest is enriched by this volume.

CHAINED

1999, oil on illustration board

BY ALAN AOKI

ONE FISH STORY

DEDICATED TO THE MEMORY OF RYAN Y., FISHERMAN AND FRIEND.

We was going climb da mountain. But was so hot and da stream by da trail look so good, dat we started fo' fool around. Everybody was splashing water on everybody else li' dat and I went chase Bobby up da stream. Den all of a sudden he went stop and stare at da water. I was going dunk him one good one but den I went stop fo' see what he staring at.

You know what? Was one fish. One beeg fish. Not da small manini kine like guppy or mosquito fish li' dat, da kine you see in da stream all da time, but da kine beeg kine. Da kine you catch with fishing pole. I only went see um fo' couple seconds, cuz da buggah look kinda shock, like he nevah see one people before or like he just went wake up from one nap. But den, with one flick of his tail, da buggah was gone. Me and Bobby was standing there, 'cuz we was all shock li' dat. But den finally he went say:

"You seen dat?"

"Yah, look like one *pāpio*," I went say. I nevah know what else fo' say at da time. I just went say da first fish I went think of. I nevah like look stupid, eh.

"Stupid. *Pāpio* is one saltwater fish. Da kine dat live in da ocean."

"Den what he doing up here?"

"He not doing anything up here. Dat was one bass. One smallmouth bass."

"Not. How you know was one bass? Only get dat kine up in da mainland." I figgah, how Bobby know what kine was? He always act like he smart.

"Get dat kine here. Up Lake Wilson. I know, 'cuz my uncle went take me fishing in his boat Wahiawā side."

"I thought you said you only went catch tilapia?"

Bobby went give me stink eye. "At least I know wasn't one *pāpio*."

I just went ignore him. "And if get in Lake Wilson, how da bass went swim all da way here?"

"I dunno. Maybe da thing connect." Bobby went scratch his chin fo' make like he thinking. "Maybe dey was here in da first place."

I guess I just went believe him at da time, 'cuz I nevah believe how beeg da fish was. I nevah care what kine was, so long as was beeg. "But how you know was one smallmouth and not one largemouth?" I went ask, 'cuz he think he know everything.

"'Cuz his mouth mo' small den yours."

Bobby went go home soaking wet dat day and I went get busted 'cuz his maddah went call my maddah 'cuz he went blame me.

We nevah told da oddah guys who was at da stream with us dat day. We figgah dey wasn't interested. Besides, would have mo' fish fo' us, eh? So da next day after school, we went go back to da stream. I went borrow my faddah's pole, even though was da cheap kine he went buy when was on sale at Longs. You know da kine dey sell in da plastic bag? Come with one free reel. Bobby had his own pole. Was real nice. One "professional" one he went say. Da kine you buy from one real fishing store, like Charley's. I figgah he just bring um fo' show off, 'cuz he know I nevah have my own. But da thing stay real nice eh, and I figgah I going save my allowance fo' buy one just li' dat.

We even went borrow one book from da library with pictures in um so we could figgah out fo' sure what kine fish was. Could just have been one regular fish fo' all we know.

We was fishing fo' about one hour but only whitewash even though Bobby said his Rapalas was guaranteed fo' catch bass. He said da lures was supposed fo' look like stuff da bass grind. I was little bit jealous, 'cuz da rubbah strip tease I was using nevah look like nothing—dey just look like saimin. But even with his Rapalas we still nevah have strike.

"Eh, we supposed to whip or dunk?"

Bobby nevah even went look up from his pole. "I dunno. No make difference."

"Maybe we supposed to troll."

"Stupid. We no mo' boat."

Half an hour went pass. Den Bobby went try use one crayfish he went catch in da stream instead of da lures we was using, 'cuz da book went say da bass like fo' eat crayfish li' dat. So he went poke da crayfish through the tail but even dat nevah work. I nevah have luck with da rubbah stuff, so I went sit down and pull out one bag licorice. Bobby went hog-cheese all da good red ones. Only had da junk black ones left.

I went bite one black licorice and spit um out 'cuz da thing taste junk. "Eh, go put this on," I went say, wiggling da licorice. "Look like one worm, eh. Maybe da bass like candy."

"Stupid. Dat not going work. Da bass mo' smart den you."

But I guess Bobby was desperate like me so he went grab half and put da piece on with da crayfish tail. He went cast into da water by one log. At first da thing went hang on top da water like da crayfish stay floating, and den da thing went sink slowly. And den bam! This thing went fly out da water like one marlin I went see on "Let's Go Fishing." Was one fish! Look like was beeg but not as beeg as da one we went see da day before, but still was nice size. We was so excited we forgot fo' unhook um when Bobby went reel um in and just threw um inside da bucket with da hook still in da mouth.

We went open da book fo' compare da fish, fo' make sure was da right kine. 'Cuz we figgah shame, eh, if we brag to da boys and da thing only one tilapia.

I went pull out da string I went use fo' mark da page with da picture of da smallmouth bass. You know what? Da picture went look almost da same.

"So what you think?" I went say. Looked like one smallmouth bass to me.

Bobby went squint his eyes at da book, den at da fish, den at da book and den at da fish. Den he went stick out his thumb and close one eye. Just like he one painter or something. He went point his thumb at da picture and den at da fish. I was thinking, he mento or what? He must think he Harry Kojima. I was about fo' say something when he went say:

"Yup." He went smile. "Das one smallmouth bass all right." Den he went hook his thumb in his shorts and went say: "A big ol' hog." I think he was trying fo' make like he from da South, like he from New Jersey or something.

"What you mean hog? Das one fish. Not one pig." And he telling me I stupid.

"Das what dey call um on da mainland. One hog is one beeg bass. I know, 'cuz I went read um in da book."

"You was only able fo' read um 'cuz you went hog um from me. I went point at da fish. "Das not one hog, da thing manini." I went pull da fish out of da bucket and went hold um up next to his mouth. "Yup, smaller den yours. Must be one smallmouth."

Bobby went push me and I went drop da book in da water and da thing went get all wet! We figgah Mrs. Fujita da librarian going get pissed, but we nevah care 'cuz was one bass, one real live bass, just like on da mainland! But we went let um go anyways, 'cuz we went make like we was real sportsmen like Harry dem.

But da licorice was da secret. After that, Bobby went catch three more bass, all about da same size. He went use all da licorice up. But I nevah care, 'cuz taste junk anyway.

Me, I nevah have any luck. I think was da junk pole das why. But just when I was about fo' give up 'cuz Bobby having all da fun, I went feel one pull. I was so excited, I went yank um as hard as I could and da buggah went shoot out of da water, over my head, and into da bamboo trees in da back. I was scared fo' check um, 'cuz I figgah maybe I went pull da lips off da fish. 'Cuz one time I went *'oama* fishing with my faddah and I went pull da line so hard, only had da fish lips left on da hook. I no joke you.

Anyways, I seen da fish flop on da ground so I went check um out. My line was all tangle up in da trees, so I just went leave my pole by da stream. I was so happy, I nevah care. When I got there, da fish was on da ground and was breathing real slow. But was real nice. Just like da picture in da book. I thought was bigger than da fish Bobby caught but he said wasn't.

I nevah went notice um before from da ones Bobby went catch, but da bass get beeg eyes. Just like da thing stay looking at you. I figgah I better put um back in da water, otherwise the thing going *make*. So I went put um in da water but da thing just went float there. I went get rocks and went build one pond around um so da buggah could rest while we went clean up. I figgah, if I let um go, da thing might not make it. I was thinking da oddah fish might eat um das why. And den would be my fault, eh?

By da time we was ready fo' go, da fish look better, but was still floating around, like was weak. Since we had da bucket, I figgah I better take um home. 'Cuz just like he stay my responsibility, eh? On da way back, we was talking about da Flintstones dat was on dat morning, so right den I decided fo' name um Fred. Fred da fish. Sound good, eh?

When June came and school was pau, we used to go stream almost every day. Almost every day we would catch bass, too. I kept Fred in one old 20 gallon tank my faddah went give me, even though he joke that he going make sashimi out of Fred when I not looking. I always went say dat I was going let Fred go, but I nevah could. I nevah could. Just like I went get attached, eh? But Fred nevah seem fo' mind, 'cuz he just went cruise around da tank and went get biggah and biggah. I think 'cuz was da black licorice I went sneak um.

There was like one endless supply of fish in da stream. It was like da mountain—she take care us, eh? Like when you hot and da wind come down fo' cool you off and da bamboo make music, it's like da mountain, she whispering, "Take care me, and I take care you." I nevah hear um exactly like dat at da time, but now dat I think of dat, dat must be what she saying.

Anyway, when you get older, things change. We grew up, went high school and got interested in other things we would try fish fo'. When I was one senior dey went announce dat dey was going build one golf course at da base of da mountain. Da developers went say dey going try keep da area "as natural as possible." Dey went say dey not going touch da stream or da mountain li' dat, but dey was all *shibai*. Look just like somebody went take one knife and went cut da mountain. Just like all da bulldozers went leave one big scar.

One day after school pau, us guys was sitting in da back of Bobby's bus' up Toyota 4x4 in da parking lot. Bobby went spit out da side of da truck. "Eh, you guys went hear that they starting fo' build da golf course already?"

"Not? I thought they nevah start yet," I went say.

"Stupid. You no read newspaper or what? Dey went start fo' build um already. Even had um on da news. Joe Moore was talking about um last night."

I nevah say nothing 'cuz I figgah Bobby still salty 'cuz I went ask Lisa to da prom last night and "beeg Shelly," da catcher fo' da softball team, went ask him fo' go.

I almost went forget about da stream and da new golf course. We nevah go there long time. I went put Fred in one bigger tank and my fad-dah still threatened fo' make sashimi out of him whenever I nevah mow da lawn.

"Ah. No matter," I went say. "You nevah going catch up to how much bass I went catch, anyways." Me and da other guys went laugh.

Bobby nevah say nothing. He was looking towards da mountain. "Eh, we should go, brah." Bobby was looking all serious kine. "Before da stream stay gone." Then he went hop in da cab and went start da truck. Us guys just went look at each other like Bobby stay crazy or something and just all jumped in da truck. I went up in da front with Bobby. I figgah he must be all pissed off. Besides, I nevah like walk home.

When we pulled off da highway, we went fly down da gravel access road which led to da stream, past da bulldozers, and da beeg piles of dirt and da construction workers who went look at us like we stay nuts. When we went reach da stream, Bobby went slam on his brakes. We nevah could believe our eyes. Da part of da stream we used to fish was small. Da grass was gone, da bamboo trees was gone, everything was gone. I went look at da stream. Used to be clear, but was mo' dirty now. I think da bass was gone too. No way dey could survive in this part of da stream, unless dey went swim up da stream, deeper into da mountains. On da side had one sign dat said: "NO TRESPASSING."

Da construction guys went come and one thick local guy, I think he was da foreman, went tell us dat we nevah belong there. He went say was private property li' dat and dat if we wanted fo' hike up da mountain we would need fo' get one permit from da owners. We couldn't believe dat. One permit fo' go hike. As if somebody could own one mountain. We was so pissed off, we just went shake our heads and leave. Bobby went burn out and went leave da foreman in da dust. Da construction workers just went give us stink eye as we went fly away.

Early da next morning, Bobby and me, we went drive up da construction road in Bobby's truck with some shovels and picks banging around in da back. Was still dark, and we figgah was even too early fo' da construction guys li' dat. We went drive straight up to da "NO TRESPASSING" sign and Bobby went run um over. We got out, and went dig up da rest of da sign and threw um in da stream. We knew dey going make one noddah sign for replace um, but we never care, we just went watch um float down da stream.

As da sun was starting fo' rise Bobby started fo' load da truck back up. I went take out da bucket I went bring with me and walked up da stream past da bulldozers where da water was wider and mo' clear. Bobby went follow me quietly and stopped when I went kneel down. I went open da cover. Fred was floating inside da bucket like he still sleeping. I went look at Bobby. He nevah say nothing. But I think he went nod. I went tilt da bucket to let Fred swim into da stream, back to his home. Fred went swim out of da bucket real slow and went look around, almost as if he nevah know where he stay, but knew he was home even though not da same. He went swim for a while, looking around, just like he stay waking up from one long nap. Den finally, with one flick of his tail, he went swim slowly up da stream. I went watch and squint my eyes 'til I nevah see him no mo'. Then I went sit back on da mud with Bobby and went dig my hands into da earth. I went close my eyes and tried hard fo' listen to da mountain whisper.

BY ALANI APIO

KA HO'I 'ANA
THE RETURNING

eat waves piled slowly on top of each other as the morning rolled in, surrounding the old house like a warm pool. In them lay a lifetime of memories. It was possible, at times like this, to scoop up the layers of heat and feel days of fishing flow over your body. Or, walking quietly through the yard, hear children playing in the mango tree from years ago. One could even smell curry, or fried *weke* cooking on the old gas stove, if the hands poured the layers of heat over one's face.

Into all this entered Alan. Out of his air-conditioned rental he stepped, knowing only that he was hot. He took his bags out of the trunk and walked up the stairs. Paint from the railings flicked off at his touch. He knocked at the screen door once, then entered.

"Hello, Grandma."

Sitting on her *pūne'e*, she was quite startled. "Ku'uleialoha?" she reached for her glasses, "Ku'ulei! Come in!"

He put his bags down, then hugged and kissed her warmly.

"Oh, my boy, Grandma wasn't expecting you. How are you! When did you come in? How come you never call me to let me know you were coming?" The old lady took his hands and clasped them warmly. "It's been such a long time, my boy. You're so grown up already...." Before he could answer, she had already grabbed a bag and was heading for the parlor, "Well, come in, come in."

Alan sat down smiling, dust rose from the couch in the light that flooded through the doorway. "I wanted to surprise you," he said, "I just got in. I've only got a week and I wanted to come stay with you."

She smiled and leaned back on the couch. "That's so nice of you, Ku'ulei. Grandma misses you plenty."

"Grandma, nobody calls me Ku'ulei anymore.... I don't know, it just doesn't sound like me, you know...."

The old lady smiled awkwardly, stared at the floor, then out the window.

"Anyway, I miss you too. I brought my scuba gear, figured I could do some diving while I have the chance."

"The water's been just beautiful all summer. You'll have a nice time." She got up and walked into the kitchen, "Can I fix you something? I made a pot of beef stew."

Alan chuckled. Grandma always had good food around. "Sure."

"And how are your parents doing?"

"Oh, they're okay. Mom's having a nervous breakdown waiting for her final grades. With my study habits, I should be the one worrying. . . ." Chickens in the front yard caught his attention. They scratched around in the sparse grass. "She studied twice as hard as me."

"And your father?"

"Dad—I don't know. He works constantly. I figured he'd say something if he wanted to, but he doesn't, so I don't bother him."

She placed a bowl of stew on the table. The steam filled the room with its earthy smell. "Eat," she said, and went off into her bedroom.

Alan fingered the ceramic bowl with painted dragons running around the sides. It had been his Bak Po's. He remembered the set from that even older house in Kalihi, on Oʻahu. Thick curls of steam rose above the table, drawing his eyes to a collage of pictures that hung on the wall. All of his cousins, all of his grandmother's grandchildren, were pictured there. Some were graduation pictures, some were candids, and some were of cousins that had died in childhood. Alan could not remember all their names.

"Good?" she asked, as she entered the parlor carrying her knitting. Alan could only nod and smile, his mouth full of the sweet meat. "Good," she said, and sat down on her *pūneʻe*.

"Ho, your Grandma's getting old, my boy. This *hāliʻi* . . ." she held up a brightly colored patchwork quilt. "Take me almost three months now." She smiled, and Alan noticed the heaviness of her skin upon her. Over the years, the strength of the sea and the warmth of the sun had saturated her old body.

She sighed and took out a needle, "One month used to be . . . one month I *pau* make one."

Alan filled himself with another scoop. Nothing, he thought, could satisfy like Grandma's food. Could he market it in L.A.? He was sure his classmates, his dorm-mates especially, would die for it.

"This one's for Kuʻuipo's son," she said, and began to sew.

"Kuʻuipo?"

"Uncle Larry's youngest girl."

"I didn't even know she was married."

"She's not. This is her second son. Keʻala's almost two now."

Alan looked at the pictures, trying to place the face with the name. He could only remember instances; playing chase-master with a picture of two boys whose front teeth were missing. From a school photo he heard an older girl calling him inside. His eyes stopped at the picture of a young boy, almost a mirror of himself at that age; that was Kevin, who had died of a brain tumor.

"Grandma, do you have a recipe for this?"

"What?" She looked at him from over her glasses. "Oh, that. Well, I guess so—Um . . . you use how much you need for make 'em taste good."

Alan stood up to get another bowl. "You can't get anything like this at U.C.L.A. They have good food there, but there's something about your cooking. . . ." He sat down and watched her hands work the needle through the fabric: Though slow, they moved with the strength and accuracy of a guitar player's hands.

From across the waves of heat came the deep assertion of the surf. This reached his ears, though he was not conscious of it. And along with the warm food in his 'ōpū, and along with the heat that gives life to old wood, he felt himself being pulled to the floor, stretched out on a mat that smelled of the ocean, sinking into a deep slumber.

* * *

A dog barked, the sound finding its way into his dreams of big cars and fast houses. The dog barked again, as if to say, "I am in the present!" and Alan woke up. The afternoon sun danced on his toes, spreading threads of smiles through him. He looked around and his grandmother was gone. He got up to wash his face, and passing through the hallway, found her napping in her bedroom, Bible lying at her side.

Through the venetian blinds that hung on the windows, warm air mixed with warm light and swirled lonely dots of dust through a room that could have been the universe. Alan went to the bathroom and cleaned up quickly, filled with anticipation for the dive.

Once outside, he took his scuba gear out from the trunk. Everything gleamed with newness: bright steel tanks, a vivid neon wet suit, matching fins and mask, and a jet-black spear gun with a gold-tipped shaft that nothing could say "no" to.

There were sharks in these waters, he knew that. His grandmother's house sat on a promontory that bordered the great bay. At the end, where she sat, the cliffs dropped straight down into water that was deep and haunting. At the other end of the bay, the shallows created tide pools where she would gather 'ōpae, limu, and strength. Alan started along the trail through the kiawe trees that led to the cliffs.

Since his childhood, he had always dreamed of diving off Grandma's cliffs. He had watched his father pull great *ulua* out of the water with his Hawaiian sling. He remembered his father grinning proudly as his arms and chest rippled with the weight of a fish made out of quicksilver and lead. He remembered also, with pain, the gaping hole in his father's calf, the blood that ran down it, and the ragged fish head he had held up to his family. His father laughed at his missing calf.

"He was jus' like one pussycat, dat *manō*. He said to me, 'Hey, whea you goin' wit my fish!' Cannot help my leg got in da way, hah?"

Grandma had wrapped both the fish head and his father's leg in *ti* leaves, then thrown the head back in the ocean.

That hadn't changed anything, Alan thought. His father had continued to dive. What had changed everything was his mother's desire to succeed in L.A. His father's love for his mother was like the wind against the Pali; constant, supporting, unconditional. They moved to California when he was five.

At this point Alan found himself coming through the growth of *kiawe* trees. Their massive trunks reached up from the ground like the arms of old warriors; spears were now crooked branches, blades had become quiet leaves.

His mind raced; he fantasized about killing a shark. For some reason that he was not totally conscious of, he had made the connection that as a man of Hawaiian ancestry, he could kill sharks—he had to kill them. Besides, his schoolmates expected him to, just like they expected him to know Tom Selleck.

How would he kill it? Maybe he would take his tank off, and just when the shark came in close, shove it in its mouth. He saw himself on the evening news, explaining nonchalantly how he had managed to kill the thirteen-foot beast. Or, would he shoot it? His gun, aptly named "The Californian," could pierce aircraft steel at close range, or so he thought. He hummed and smiled in his confidence. During the past two years he had done a lot of diving off Catalina Island, but never had he seen a shark, and he was dying to brag to his friends about his Hawaiian Shark Kill.

The ocean sat calm and innocent in front of him, stretching out into that ancient past from where his ancestors had sailed. He stood on the plateau between the trees and the cliff, and as the sun dropped lower, the water became darker. He walked to the edge. A fifteen-foot drop. He decided that climbing down with his gear on would be cumbersome, so he would jump in from the top, then climb out afterwards. Peering into the water, he saw flashes of color peppering the coral heads that grew out at ninety degrees from the steep wall.

Alan looked down the shoreline towards the setting sun. Figures moved on the sand at the far end of the beach. They might as well have been on the moon. This is where he would prove himself, he thought. He wanted to be a man. He wanted to be his father. Alan lifted the tank to his back, put on his fins, held the mask tightly to his face, cleared the regulator, and jumped.

The bubbles from his splash blocked his view and he instinctively pulled himself down to clear them and see below. A dark circus appeared before him. A school of yellow tang raced along the wall, looking quite odd swimming perpendicular to the ocean floor. Three-spot damsels, their white patches shining against their black bodies, and the even blacker rock behind them, alternately exploded and contracted from a head of staghorn coral.

Alan gripped the coral heads with his stainless white gloves, pulling himself straight down. The effect was immediate vertigo, and he had to steady himself to control his breathing. His gun and his depth gauge hung down in front of him, banging on the rocks and coral heads. Wrasses and butterflies skittered out of reach. The bottom, now only ten feet away, was an endless plain of sand. He slowed up and twisted his body so that he landed gently on his feet. *Weke* grazed off the bottom to his right, the wall on his left. He peered out into the emptiness, the darkness and immensity making him feel like he was in space. Underneath his mask he began to perspire—the isolation was intense.

Immediately, he took off his gun and loaded it. As he forced the shaft down into the barrel, he did one thing differently: he did not attach the end of the shaft rope to the gun. That meant that anything he shot could not be pulled in.

Over his head glided a shadow. He looked up to see a long, solid belly flow over him. His knees went weak and he choked on his own saliva. Oh, Jesus Christ! This can't be happening! His mind screamed for control and understanding. Not yet! Not yet! He did not really, truly, want to see a shark. His bowels spasmed as the great animal turned away from the wall and circled slowly back towards him. His mouth went dry. He stared in abject fear at the dark stripes that lined the sides of the *manō*. Tiger! He crammed himself into the narrow crevice that undercut the cliff side at its base. He felt himself urinate and defecate in his suit. The *manō* cut the water like a streamlined cement truck.

"You stupid fool! You silly, stupid fool!" He could not believe his own arrogance and stupidity. "Stick a tank in its mouth? Dumb. Dumb, stupid fool!"

The *manō* made a wide sweep to the back of Alan, turning again to follow the wall about thirty feet behind him. His right hand held the gun; it was shaking so much he had to take his finger off of the trigger for fear of misfiring it.

As the *manō* approached, it swung out away from the wall so that it was not directly over the boy, but to his right side. He lifted the gun towards the animal, which made no adjustment for the hand coming out of the wall. As it approached, he tried to follow its gill slits with the gun shaft. When it passed directly to his side he squeezed, he squeezed so hard that his arm cramped. Nothing happened. The *manō* rolled on ahead. He had forgotten to re-grip the trigger! His finger pressed inanely on the outside guard. Oh, God! Help me, please help me!

Alan looked at his gun; the safety was still on. He pushed the button violently to "fire." The shark turned back quickly and circled to his rear. Little fish were darting around his buttocks, attracted to the scent of his own defecation. The air he was sucking on was getting harder to pull. He glanced down quickly at his gauges; depth, forty-five; pounds of pressure, one hundred! He had already sucked his whole tank. Alan knew he had only seconds of air left. The *manō* surged towards him; he could see the jagged teeth cemented into place in its gaping mouth. It hugged the wall, trying to force him out. Alan curled up desperately. The thing pounded by him, so huge it blocked his view. He lifted his gun—in a blur he saw the gills, and in a blur he fired.

The *manō* froze for a twisted instant. Then its huge tail swung violently, smashing Alan into the wall. He cried out in pain as his head slammed against a rock. The regulator was blown from his mouth, sand covered everything. His lungs burned and his skull pounded. He reached for something, anything, pulling himself blindly up the wall. His left hand struck a sea urchin and was filled with spines. He cleared the cloud of sand and looked down. The *manō* was gone. A trail of green spun around lazily in the water—he had hit it. His head was dizzy, his body limp. Seventeen feet from the surface, he floated slowly, painfully, up. He finally made it, grabbed a rock, lifted his head out of the water, and gasped.

Alan heaved and choked, trying to catch his breath. Tears came silently as he felt a large bump growing on his crown. Blood trickled down the side of his face. He took off his tank and threw it on a ledge near the surface. He searched the water constantly for fear of the shark's return. Finally, he got his fins off and pulled himself onto the ledge. Immediately, waves of pain shot through his left hand and up his arm. Alan buckled and fell on his elbow. He winced in agony. His left glove was checkered with the thin, black spines of the *wana,* some of which stuck out from the material almost three inches. He slowly broke away the remaining spines and pulled the glove off. Fat, tender, red, and laced with countless black dots, the flesh throbbed with each pump of blood.

Alan stood up. Slowly, with much difficulty, he unzipped his wet suit, took off his trunks, and rinsed them both in the water. The ocean below lay like a pool of India ink. He threw on his gear and shorts as best he could, then started up the wall.

As he climbed up he realized his gun was missing. Shame pricked at his face; he had lost his gun and crapped in his pants. Reaching the top, he looked up to find his grandmother standing only a few feet away.

"What'd you come here for, Alan?"

He pulled himself up.

"What'd you come here for! What'd you do down there!"

Alan was stunned. He had never seen his grandmother look so severe. Her hands, clenched tightly, screamed out at him from her sides.

"Grandma, wait! You don't understand! I was almost killed!"

"By what?"

"A huge shark!"

"Why'd you come here, Alan, answer me!"

"I—I—" He could not admit to what he had planned to do. Alan dropped his head and stared at the ground. He had not felt so much shame since he had been caught taking money from his father's drawer when he was five. Still staring at the ground, he asked, "But Grandma, what did I do? I don't know what I did wrong!"

The old lady just stood there. He could feel her eyes burning into him, though he dared not look at her, or even move.

"Who you think you are, Alan?" she asked, "You think that shark was just some stupid monster swimming around, waiting to get shot? Where you think you come from?"

He made no attempt to reply.

Finally, she turned and walked back to the house.

Alan watched her walk slowly through the understory of *kiawe* trees. Her skin blended in with the coming darkness, and only her vividly colored *muʻumuʻu* shone through, like a beautiful ghost in the dim light. Against that dark background, the sun set.

Alan got up, his body aching, his head pounding, and sat on a near-by rock. He looked down into the black calm of the sea, which mirrored the universe above him. A gust blew through his wet body and he shivered.

*   *   *

Nothing was said all evening. Alan sat at the small table, finishing a bowl of chicken *lūʻau*. He hadn't wanted dinner, but she had put it out for him anyway, and to reject it would have been even worse, so he ate the bowl of guilt quickly. Everything around him screamed with accusations. The bare bulb that hung above his head exposed him, yelling, "You did wrong!" From the collage on the wall his cousins mumbled about how stupid he was. Every move he made was an invasion of his grandmother's world. Every mouthful he took felt like stealing.

She sat reading from her Bible in the light from the driftwood lamp his father had made for her years ago. After he finished eating he slipped quietly out the back door.

Alan sat on the steps, not wanting to go in until she had gone to sleep. His head still ached. Mosquitoes bit indiscriminately, and he took it as a form of self-punishment. But for what? As the cold ocean wind added to his discomfort, he wondered why she was so upset. Somewhere between mosquito bites, the cold, and her anger, he fell asleep. A man of almost twenty-one, he lay curled on the steps, hoping for pity.

Sometime in the night the cold drove him inside. When he awoke to the first crow of the cock, he found himself on the *lau hala* mats, covered by a *hāliʻi* his grandmother had laid on him. His first thought was to steal out like a dog with his tail tucked under him. That idea was checked by the kitchen light being flipped on. Alan looked up to see his grandmother putting the kettle on to boil. He rubbed the *maka piapia* from his eyes.

"Get ready, I want you come with me today." She set the table without any more of an acknowledgment. Alan sat with his head lowered and his body tightly drawn in while she served *poi*, eggs, Portuguese sausage, and silence.

Halfway through the meal the sun came in, laughing through the window, sitting down at the table like a familiar guest. But instead of warming him, it only served to make Alan more uneasy; the sun belonged here, he did not.

After finishing his meal, he tried to clean up. The old lady grabbed the dishes from him and pointed to the *pūneʻe*. Alan's discomfort grew with this rebuff, but it soon turned to irritation as he waited for her to finish.

Enough is enough! he thought, his L.A. haughtiness returning to him. He did not deserve to be treated like this. What did she know? As far as she was concerned, he could have been hunting for anything, *ulua* maybe. Besides, it wasn't his fault that the shark had attacked him. For Christ's sake, he had almost been killed, gotten his hands filled with *wana* spines, and at twenty-one been made to sleep outside like a dog! He decided to tell the old lady, as politely as possible, that an explanation for her behavior was necessary.

After coming to this conclusion, he sat back and relaxed. The old lady went to her room. He heard drawers opening and closing. Presently she reappeared. She had on her beach hat and an old *mu'umu'u*. She took a bag off the table and headed for the door.

"Grandma, I'd like to have a word with you." She paused for a second, then went outside, not even bothering to look back.

Damn! he thought. What to do now? Man-Alan said to pack up and leave, since he was obviously not welcome here any more. Grandson-Alan felt compelled to obey. He groaned in frustration and headed for the door.

Outside, the sun had tickled everything awake, making the *'ilima* plants, *kiawe* trees, even the chickens, smile with the warm gold of morning. His grandmother walked down the road that ran along the beach. As he followed her, wearing his designer clothes, he felt distinctly out of place and time. It was like walking through home movies that had been made years ago. Alan caught up with her quickly, but stayed a few feet behind.

They walked down the hill, coming into the wide stretch that made up the bay. Here and there sat other homesteads. On the breeze came a vaguely familiar stink. Alan stopped and peered into the growth. An old pigpen sat a few yards in from the road. From in between the wooden slats he could see heavy bodies lying in the mud. Water splattered suddenly, waking the pigs, then an old, wooden man appeared from behind the shed. He smiled at Alan, then called out something to his grandmother in Hawaiian. She raised her hand, then continued on. Alan hurried after her.

Coming to the end of the dirt road, and the beginning of the paved one, she walked into the yard of a house that fronted the beach. A chubby, brown child sat splashing water on herself in a metal vat. The child stopped playing and asked something of his grandmother, again in Hawaiian. She answered soothingly, then continued on through the garage. The child addressed Alan, who for lack of understanding just smiled nervously and followed.

In the garage hung fishnets, almost filling the space. They smelled faintly of dried *limu*. Fish tails were tacked up on the walls. Fish scales crinkled as he walked over them. But there was something wrong, Alan sensed a strange oldness to this place too. The nets had not been used in quite a while; the eyes of the nets gave way like cobwebs when he touched them. The fish tails had long lost their vigor; they were twisted and dried to the point of sadness. Alan was startled by a large lady holding a bucket of wash.

"Youa Granmadda stay on da beach." She walked on into the front yard.

The beach was a wide strip of sorrow. Here and there lay beer bottles, degradation, used condoms, and shame. The old lady stopped to collect them into her bag. He would have liked to help, but this was her beach. Instead, he followed silently behind her.

As they walked along, Alan remembered coming down there years before to collect *limu, ʻōpae,* and *heʻe* in the shallows that made up the other end of the bay. He noticed that something was wrong with the beach, something even more serious than the garbage. The water was becoming murkier, the sand darker. He looked down towards the end of the bay: the water ran red with mud. Alan stopped and stared. The womb of his childhood looked like a big, rotting sore—filth and garbage everywhere. The old lady stepped slowly through the muck and silt of the tide pools, collecting plastic can rings. And as if that were not enough, she scooped up something from the water and turned to stare at Alan with a handful of shit.

Realization came to him like a punch in the face, knuckles massive with the old lady's anger. He slumped down in the sand and hid his face. Behind them a whistle blew, men shouted, and engines screamed with inhuman delight; the workday had begun.

*   *   *

The wind whispered gently across the faces of seashells that hung from a chime on the *lānai.* Inside, the old lady read from the Bible in her rocking chair, Alan sat on the floor next to her. As they rested under his father's light, Alan looked up to see a face carved with hurt, age, quiet defiance. She looked like the driftwood behind her.

The old lady caught his eye, smiled, and put the Bible away. She ran her fingers through his hair, humming an old tune that he could not remember the words to.

A bright moon had risen above the protective skirt of *kiawe* trees, its light filling the room with the ageless gaze of all their ancestors. She clicked off the lamp. They sat and listened as the surf massaged the earth. After a while she spoke.

"You know why you're here, Alan?"

He hesitated, knowing full well she did not want to hear that he had come to kill a shark: "I needed a vacation."

The old lady shook her head. "You came 'cause when you were a boy, you and me used to talk to the ocean. You remember that, don't you?"

"I remember picking *limu* with you."

She lowered her head and closed her eyes tightly. The old lady said nothing for a very long time and Alan began to worry for her. Finally, she looked up, Alan could see that she was on the verge of tears. She gazed out at the moonlight as it glittered on the ocean. "You remember telling me what your *'aumakua* was?"

Alan sat momentarily stunned, the word had triggered something lost deep inside him. He stared blankly at the floor. His scalp began to feel icy, his fingertips tingled and fear shot into him, piercing his heart with its gold-tipped shaft until he could barely breathe. He nodded slowly and looked up at her. "'*Ae, Tūtū. 'O ka manō ko'u 'aumakua*. The shark is my *'aumakua.*"

From across the ancient mother ocean, he heard his soul call out for him, call out from broken nets, coral, and old boats, from tired women, dead *manō,* and *kūpuna* he had never known.

Alan watched tears roll down the old lady's cheeks; filled with the light of the moon, they looked like pearls.

"Ku'uleialoha, my dear boy, don't you know who you are?"

Alan K. Robbins, Dean's List pre-med student at U.C.L.A., owner of a vintage powder-blue Mustang convertible with matching scuba gear, President of Phi Sigma Epsilon, clutched his grandmother's handmade *mu'umu'u*, and cried. Ku'uleialoha came down from the mango tree in the back yard, forgotten and ignored for so many years. He skipped up the steps, laughing with delight, and rushed in to comfort himself. Outside, on the front porch, a *mo'o* ate termites off the wall.

BY PAMELA BALL

THE CENTIPEDE OF ATTRACTION

In Hilo, there were dead sharks hanging on hooks under the rafters of the small wooden buildings. Within days the line of gray flesh multiplied, and when no one was looking, I put my hands out and touched the hard, rubbery skin. The blood pooled on the ground and the fishermen gathered in circles around the edges of the blood and later their slippers left tracks down the sidewalk, mixing the blood of one dead shark with another. The fishing supply store ran out of gaffs and marlin hooks and rope, and the shoe store ran out of the high wooden getas that would keep people's feet away from the blood. It was like nothing I'd ever seen.

It was all due to the boy. I couldn't even get used to the idea of the boy, never mind that he wasn't a boy really, but a young man named Nicholas, my ex-husband's stepson.

A week ago, Nicholas had come to the Big Island and had looked me up. He was proud of the fact that he'd found me; I didn't point out that any fool could have found me; I'd been in one town my whole life. I was irritated that he was so large; so fully grown. The idea of him would have been much easier to deal with in a smaller, less-finished form.

Nicholas said he needed work, so I drove him down to the harbor in my small truck that had to be left running or kickstarted, and I sat in the cab with the engine idling, pointing out different boats that I knew were hiring.

It was early in the morning, and the flat side of the mountain behind us was a soft pink, the same color that was reflected on the water, and by the time I'd rolled a cigarette the water had turned metal colored, the rain started, and Nicholas was halfway out of the harbor in a flag line boat.

Later, the fishermen said that Nicholas had worked hard for a haole boy from the Mainland. Later they said a lot of things, but on the way back in, on his very first day, Nicholas decided to jump off the boat before they came around the breakwater. He yelled that he would swim in from there, after being warned not to, but he was from somewhere with lakes, not an ocean, and the boat was too far out. Before they could turn the boat around to pick him up, the high fin of a shark was already coming from the opposite direction, heading for Nicholas faster than the boat with the engine at full throttle. He had his arm up, waving; he never saw what was behind him, and his arm twirled in the air as the shark attacked, and he yelled, just once.

I had to call Ivan and tell him that his stepson was dead. I sat in front of the phone, not wanting to call him, waiting for it to ring instead, for Ivan to have been told by someone else.

But the phone didn't ring, and when I called him I said, "Nicholas's dead, Ivan, and I'm so sorry." I didn't know how to warm people up to bad news. I didn't know how to gently lead anyone anywhere.

"Why?" Ivan asked, after a moment.

Which why, I wondered. Why was I sorry, or why was Nicholas dead.

"Loss of blood," I said finally. "He died from loss of blood."

"What the hell does that mean?" Ivan whispered, and I told him all of it, all except the scream and the waving.

I wanted to leave it at that but Ivan wanted more. I hadn't heard him crying like that since he'd left me, fifteen years earlier, for Nicholas's mother. I wanted him to hang up and do his crying with her.

Ivan was incoherent for days. Though he called me constantly from his home in California, all he did was rave once he got me on the phone. He blamed himself, he blamed Nicholas. After that, he blamed me because I was the one who put the boy on the boat.

Several days after Nicholas's death, Ivan got an idea that made his voice clear on the line. I knew that tone of voice well enough to be wary of it, his voice pulling like a strong tide.

His idea was to put a bounty on sharks. Cash, so much per foot. Ivan still knew a lot of people in Hilo, and before the end of the day the word was out, and the fishermen came from as far away as Kona and down the mountain from Kamuela, to make extra money. A few days later Ivan called back raising the price on pregnant sharks.

"Now, why didn't I think of that," I said, and from then on I quit answering the phone.

I drove slowly through the streets in town, the same town that Ivan and I had both been raised in. Hilo had shrunk down since Nicholas had died. A young boy dying made me feel suddenly old, as if my body had stiffened overnight. I turned into the park and drove under the monkeypod trees that threw dark shadows of lace onto the sky, and I looked up and thought of reefs, of dense clumps of coralhead, of places that were safe and places that weren't.

Then I turned down toward the bay, drawn there like everyone else, and idled in the loading zone that no one had ever dared ask me to move out of, not even when I was an underage kid driving my father's old Nash, and definitely not now that I was fifty-five years old.

I rolled a cigarette and watched the boats, and the point farther out, where the water was metal colored, where the boy had died, and I thought surely a landscape must be worn down by what happens in it.

I wanted to think of Nicholas as a man now that he was dead. I wanted to remember something particular about him. The way he carried himself, whether or not he was at ease in the world. To somehow know that he'd had his time on earth. He had a faint safari tinge to his clothing, I recalled that much. But I hadn't wanted to spend a lot of time on a boy whose mother had taken Ivan from me.

Years earlier, Ivan left me for Nicholas's mother, a woman who need-ed rescuing from a stalled elevator in the hotel where Ivan was in charge of maintenance and emergencies. Even I could see the humor in that. We never love anyone as much as someone needing rescue. He was the first person that she saw after the hours it took to fix the elevator, and she must have seen Ivan the way I always had. For me, Ivan was a reward with his black hair the color of split-open coal, and long boat-shaped eyes that went from brown to gold. To me, he was the center of attention. The centipede of attraction I used to call him. You can wait a whole lifetime to feel its bite.

Still, I liked to think of Nicholas's mother as a kind of gosling, hatching after an hour in an elevator, and following forever the first face she saw.

I wondered if the fishermen moved closer to the boy when they killed a shark. I understood that kind of vengeance as well as anyone, and when I saw my friend Alapai down at the dock, getting ready to go out, I turned the engine off, got out of the truck and ran past the ice house, flagging down his boat before it left the pier.

Alapai's boat had the sampan hull that was favored on the Big Island. It was a shape I'd known all my life, a shape I was at ease in. I'd been friends with Alapai since we were kids, and I didn't have to explain anything, just hold onto the fishing pole that he gave me.

To attract sharks we poured a gallon of slaughterhouse blood over the side of the boat. I knew I was basically an eye-for-an-eye kind of per-son, but that was before I saw the blood spreading in the water like a reef, like the canopy of a monkeypod tree. It was a smell that I couldn't get away from, a smell that rose up off the wet streets and followed me home and now it mixed in with the smell of the diesel. I felt queasy, but it was the wrong boat ride to be throwing up on.

We went farther out, where the waves turned into swells and the color of the sea went from metal to turquoise to navy blue. I felt like a complete fool, not knowing if I was on the boat for the boy, or for Ivan, or for myself. I looked back at the island whose shape was tattooed across my memory, and Ivan's memory too, because the island wasn't a thing you could let go of. It let go of you. I knew that it hadn't let go of Ivan, that somewhere in the corner of whatever he was looking at now, on the mainland, there was this same dark shape. Why else would his stepson have come?

My line started whining, running out so fast that I got nervous and almost gave up my seat to Alapai, but I stayed in the chair and worked the shark, and Alapai pretended that he hadn't seen me waver. After about twenty minutes Alapai came over and massaged my shoulders, and I felt like a damn tourist in a marlin tournament, and that made me laugh. Once I started, there was no stopping but Alapai just ignored it and told me a story about when we were kids.

"Do you remember," he said, "when we were six or seven years old and we went around town and made all the men lift up their shirts so that we could see whether they had a shark jaw buried in the middle of their back?"

I did remember, and after a while I quit laughing and thought of that god who was a shark, who came on land in the shape of a man, always a beautiful man, but he couldn't hide the shark mouth that was in his back. While some men had pulled their shirts up voluntarily, others refused, and we followed those men home and spied on them.

I was still working the line when we turned the boat around and headed back in toward the island. The swells disappeared into waves and the water turned metal colored again, and it seemed a long journey for just one small shark. I heard Alapai yell for the captain's gaff, and then the gun went off and the shark was brought in over the side of the boat.

A few minutes later, the shark suddenly flipped itself over next to where I was standing. I jumped up onto the hold and found Alapai's baseball bat tucked behind the tackle box, and I clubbed the shark on the head, again and again, until I was sure it was dead and I could breathe again.

It was as scary looking dead as it had been alive, with its fake looking skin and face wound up tight like I'd seen on certain people when they were getting ready to do something really crazy.

While Alapai was congratulating me on my mighty swing, and predicting our welcome back at the dock, I wondered if the whole point of a bounty was to show you that you didn't know anything at all. If so, I'd learned it.

Ivan raised his prices again halfway through the second week, when he thought interest was lagging. Soon a whole hierarchy was established, from the person who measured the length of each shark, down to the man who had the job of gutting them. I had no idea how he had been picked. He was a truck gardener. I had never even seen him near a boat, though I recognized his new prestige, I could see it in the small of his back, and in the way that he shuffled in his fake leather slippers with the small toes hanging out at each side, lightly grazing the sidewalk. Each time he gutted a shark, the crowd went into automatic pilot while buoys and beer cans and clorox bottles spilled out with the stomach. My job, I realized suddenly, was to witness it.

I went home. I stood naked in front of the mirror and brushed my long coarse hair. I looked at my body, registering the changes that had taken place over the last fifteen years. I looked like I'd been through it and I had. It was better, I decided, than looking untouched like what's-her-name, better than looking like a vacant building that no one had even moved into.

I found myself circling the wet streets in Hilo like a teenager, eating from an okazu plate on my lap, and a six pack of beer in the backseat. Once I even drove up to Volcano and sat for a while in the mist, pretending that there was nothing going on down in Hilo, but even up in Volcano the mist was shark colored.

I thought of Ivan, that his idea of the perfect life was like one of those drive-in movie theaters that they had on the Mainland, where there were three screens and three movies running simultaneously, and all a person like Ivan had to do was turn his head and he'd be in another movie, another life, and the one he'd turned away from would keep on going, it would turn out the same whether he was in it or not.

I found myself hanging out in the loading zone, probably the safest place on the island. I got out my papers and rolled a couple of cigarettes, lining them up neatly across the dash, and watched a cop walk back and forth in front of my truck, getting himself all wound up about my truck being parked in the loading zone. He was new to the police force, and I could tell that he wasn't sure whether I mattered or not. I pulled the chopsticks out of my bun, and my long white hair fell around my shoulders. Read that, I thought.

Watching the cop made me think of Alapai's story about the shark god. What if he had a twisted sense of tradition? What if he came to land as a young haole cop from the Mainland? I wondered how he would feel about lifting up his shirt, but then we were both distracted by a boat coming in.

I didn't recognize either the boat or the men. One of the men held up three fingers. Three sharks. They took their boat up the ramp, and pushed it onto a trailer. Their swim trunks were wet, but they were dry from the waist up. I saw each man's strong back in the center of a circle of people, and though I was too far away to hear, I watched their hands telling the same story that every other pair of hands had been telling. A new boat came in, just minutes after the first, and the center changed as the people moved onto the next group, discarding their previous excitement the way spectators left the scene of an accident that didn't pan out.

There could have been a shave ice stand, things were that weirdly festive. The fish were dead, but everything else was fresh. People talked more than they had in years, rival shopkeepers nodding over the same dead shark.

I believed that each fisherman wanted to kill that first shark, the one which had attacked the boy, and then each man was secretly relieved that it didn't turn out that way.

Still, the boy would be remembered in ways that would give no comfort. The children in town would remember him as a haole boy from the Mainland who hadn't listened. The children themselves were sick of listening, and followed those fishermen who didn't lecture them on safety, jostling to be nearest to those men who were just inside the circle of blood. The kids were having the time of their lives, though at night their dreams were something physical that they had to pass through.

I couldn't remember a peaceful day with Ivan, though there must have been a few somewhere. We yelled, we raved, one of us always threw something, and the other one always laughed, and we would fight over the car keys because the victor was the one who got to drive away, who could lay a patch in the crab grass that grew down the drive.

By the time I had truly learned how to burn rubber down the length of the drive, not losing momentum even while sideswiping a few tree ferns, Ivan was gone.

When I drove down to Hilo I couldn't even find a parking space, with all the pickups backed in sideways. The sharks that had been dead for a day were being hauled off in the beds of some trucks while the newly dead sharks were being carefully unloaded off the beds of other trucks. Not even the fishermen themselves could say why the newly dead sharks should be treated more carefully. It was just past training, the kind none of us could get away from.

I decided I might never forgive Ivan, but that wasn't exactly a new thought. By my reckoning, Ivan had a bill the size of which he could never pay off, and sometimes I thought that I liked it that way. Watching the sharks and the men and the wet money changing hands, I thought maybe I still wanted him.

BY STUART CHING

HOUSE OF BONES

In the darkening yard, Uncle Manny thrust his arms forward, his fists striking the tree like wooden mallets. He hit ten times with each fist, one mango fell to the grass like a stone, and I felt the concussions in Manny's hands and forearms, his biceps, even his shoulders—as if the leather wraps padding his knuckles weren't even there. He breathed silently through his nostrils, not letting one sound, not even a hiss, escape from his mouth. I wondered if he knew I had come around the side of the house and was watching from the patio.

The floodlight mounted on one of the patio's flimsy eaves illuminated the yard, the screen door opened, and my brother, Bobby, stepped out. He walked into the yard, nodded at Manny, took off his shirt and swung his arms in circles, rotated his hips, paused and measured his physique—the thin waist and broad chest, the arms more like cannons. He hopped, doing an imaginary jump rope, and then he began shadow boxing.

"You was watching?" said Manny. "Maybe you learn something."

"The tree no hit back," said Bobby. He was several inches taller than Manny and built like a middleweight. Manny pointed to the duffel bag on the grass.

"Put on the gloves," he said. "Three rounds, if you can last."

Bobby opened his eyes and looked up at the dark, blue sky. His mouthpiece was in my pocket, and I was kneeling at his side, holding smelling salts to his nose. He winced and pushed my hand away.

"You okay?" I said. "Your nose."

Bobby had circled Manny, peppering Manny's face with jabs. "Sissy punches," Manny had said. Bobby threw the overhand right. Manny ducked and countered to the body. Bobby slumped to one knee. "One punch, fight over!" said Manny. Bobby struggled to his feet. "You too pretty," Manny said. "I give you face job." He'd punched Bobby's nose three times, then struck his chin with an uppercut.

Now Bobby sat up, rose to his feet, and stripped off the gloves. "Beat it, Domingo," he said. I followed him into the house. In the kitchen, he grabbed the ice tray from the freezer and spread a dish towel on the counter. He bundled the ice in the towel and pressed the cold pack on his nose. I followed him into the bathroom. He removed the compress and looked in the mirror.

"Holy shit," he said. The skin beneath his eyes and across the bridge of his nose was taut and plum colored.

Through the bathroom wall we heard Aunty Pua and Uncle Manny talking in the bedroom.

"You too hard on him," she said.

"He act like big shot, so I teach him."

"He taught you good," I said to Bobby.

"Domingo, you open your mouth one more time I going give you slaps," Bobby said.

"You better go doctor," I said. Bobby tried to swat my face with his open hand. I leaned back—Manny had already taught me how to slip punches. The tip of Bobby's finger clipped my forehead.

"For real," I said. "Look broken." I stared up at his nose. "What if you sneeze?"

Bobby swung again, this time too quickly for me to react. His palm struck the side of my head, and the force of his hand rang deep in my left ear. I had learned from watching the amateur boxing matches at Pālolo Gym how to absorb a blow stoically—with dignity. I said nothing and looked at Bobby. He placed the ice pack on his nose again and looked in the mirror.

"Achooo!" I said, and ran away.

Aunty Pua and Uncle Manny lived in Pālolo Valley. We were their *hānai* children, adopted without legal paper work. Their only daughter, Kehaulani, had moved to California, and because there was plenty of room in the house, it was the understanding among family members that we should live with them. Pua and Manny told us that our father and mother, Luis and Ana Sanchez, lived in 'Ewa, west O'ahu. Ana was mixed, Chinese-Hawaiian. Luis was full-blooded Puerto Rican, the youngest of Manny's siblings. Luis and Manny's grandparents were among the six thousand Puerto Ricans who had crossed the Pacific in 1901 to work on the Hawai'i sugar plantations. Eventually, their grandparents had settled in Waialua on O'ahu's north shore. Two generations later, when Manny turned nineteen, he married Pua Leialoha, and together they set out for Honolulu.

In Honolulu, Manny worked on the docks at Honolulu Harbor, loading and unloading the Matson barges that plied the shipping lines between Hawai'i and California. Boxing had been a family tradition among the men of the family all the way back to Puerto Rico, and so every evening after work, Manny boxed. Bobby and I heard the story many times—how on Manny's twenty-fifth birthday, the day that he turned pro, he mounted a speed bag on the trunk of the mango tree in the back yard. The bag gave him rhythm and timing, but he needed power. Instead of punching a heavy bag, he began punching the tree itself, an exercise he learned at the Nu'uanu YMCA from the Okinawan karate men striking the *makiwara* post—a wooden pole some ten inches in diameter with rope wound tightly around the top. Many years later, when the city parks division had put in the boxing ring at Pālolo Gym, Manny had left the speed bag on the mango tree, and he had even hung a heavy punching bag for Bobby and me.

After dinner that night, Manny called Bobby outside and I saw them facing each other in the backyard, talking. Manny placed his fingers on the bridge of Bobby's nose, checking the cartilage. Eventually they shook hands, and three weeks later, after the swelling disappeared around Bobby's nose, he began training again. One day I came home from Pālolo Elementary to the sound of Bobby's fists thrumming the speed bag. Bobby was wearing shorts and tennis shoes, and he was sweating profusely. Holding the stopwatch, Manny was sitting in his lawn chair beneath the shade of the patio and sipping Coca-Cola. "Time!" Manny called. Bobby walked to the patio, a sheet of corrugated metal supported by several beams and four wooden posts anchored on cement blocks. He took Aunty Pua's dresses and blouses down from the wire clothesline strung between the posts and placed them in the laundry basket, then rolled out his barbell. Bobby gripped the barbell and pressed it over his head ten times, grunting. Setting it on the ground, he reversed his grip, then curled the bar to his chest five times. Next he sat on a wooden stool and secured to his head a strap made of two leather belts. Attached to this strap was a chain, and onto the end, he attached a large tin bucket filled with ten- and five-pound weights, which he motioned up and down with his neck. He repeated these exercises four times.

"Road work," Manny said. "Five miles. Your gas tank is in your legs."

After Bobby left, I walked to the mango tree and pressed my bare knuckles into the bark. I flinched. I turned to the heavy bag. I punched. My wrist hurt. The bag didn't move.

"Here, Domingo," said Manny, motioning me toward the small speed bag mounted on the tree trunk. "Try this." He placed a low, wooden platform on the ground and I stood on it, so that my eyes were even with the speed bag. "Watch," he said, beginning the exercise in slow motion. "One punch, the bag bounce three times. You see. When the bag come back, the third bounce, then you hit again. Tack-tack-tack, tack-tack-tack. You hear the ticking?" I started slowly, and then my punches quickened. "Good," he said. "You learn fast. I teach you how to use your hands. Maybe one day you be the next champion in the family."

When Bobby returned, Manny told him to wipe down with a towel and to get his bag. "We going to the gym," he said. "I asked Tommy Chang to set up one sparring partner."

At Pālolo Gym, we were standing at ringside when Bobby's sparring partner walked out of the locker room. "That's Alex Cabral," said Bobby. "He one pro."

Manny nodded. "Then today you watch, *muchacho*," he said. "Last time I teach you respect. Today I show survival." Manny took off his shirt. The gym manager, Tommy Chang, wrapped Manny's hands, pulled on the gloves and taped Manny's wrists, then strapped on a head-gear. In the ring, Alex Cabral was grinning, springing on his toes. "Pops!" he said, punching his gloves together. Manny opened his mouth and Tommy Chang slipped in the mouthpiece. Alex Cabral was jogging around the ring now. "Pops!" he shouted. Then Manny climbed onto the ring mat.

And Manny did survive—three rounds of jabbing and clinching. Trapped in the corner in the third round, he punched low, one tremendous crack to the balls. The fight was over. After, we drove all the way to Makapuʻu Beach, and there in the glow of the lighthouse and in the cradle of the Koʻolau, where mountain falls into sea, Bobby trained. Manny barked commands. Bobby sprinted up and down the powdered sand. Then Manny ordered Bobby into the ocean. The water swelled and collapsed, pitching forward with tremendous sound. Bobby, standing thigh-deep amid the boiling foam, thrust his forearms into the waves threatening to crush him into the sand. When one wave took him down, he rode the current into the deep water, floating on his back like a seal, barely visible from shore, and having drifted out some one hundred yards, he began stroking in diagonally toward the far corner of the beach. When he reached shore, gasping frantically, Manny dragged him up the sand and laid him down, pressed his fingers into Bobby's back, working his healing magic all the way to the bone.

Two weeks later on the swimming pool bleachers at Pālolo District Park, I saw Elena Clemente touching Bobby the same way. And so for the next three months, they swam every day after school, not like lovers, but like athletes. He trained in intervals, throttling the water with clumsy strokes; she, an accomplished canoe paddler, now a solitary swimmer in the lane beside him, cut the water, her long, slim body always pulling away.

Within weeks, it seemed, Bobby's chest broadened. Sometimes after swimming, Bobby and Elena would sun themselves on the bleachers. From afar, I saw Bobby with his eyes closed and his mouth curved in a closed smile as though he were feeling her beside him without even touching—the curve of her body. Sometimes she came to the house and lifted weights with him, she herself able to curl a forty-pound barbell twenty times.

But despite their afternoons together, they remained apart from each other. Bobby spent long hours alone at night, brooding out back behind the house, his silhouette visible in the moonlight. Then, even after the house was dark and we'd gone to bed, I sometimes heard the sound of his fists striking the tree like an ax. I asked him once, "What you thinking when you punch the tree?"

"I picture one face," he said, "*his* face, and I punch 'em. I blast 'em. I blast 'em hard. You remember what Dad look like, Domingo?"

"No," I said.

"I remember," said Bobby. "Every time I look in the mirror, I remember. I see him."

Eventually, Elena stopped coming around. Bobby went to the barber and came home with a severe crew cut. "Better for training," he said.

I have this memory of Bobby. At night, he runs beneath the street light of our cul-de-sac in Pālolo Valley. The perspiration on his bare back glistens. His head, nearly bald, is smooth. On one of the balconies two houses up the street, one of the Alama sisters, Lisa, is smoking a cigarette and watching him. Bobby doesn't look up as he passes. He runs until he vanishes around the corner. Now Lisa is looking up into the sky. The smoke leaving her mouth blows a kiss at the moon.

Then one evening, near midnight, I left my bedroom, walked to the living room, and watched him from behind the sliding glass door. He was a shadow in the moonlight. I heard the sound of tired hands drubbing wood, then the hands quickened, singing a sweet rhythm, a cadence that was almost music. And when he was done and started walking toward the house, I saw that his hands were bleeding, that he had been hitting the tree with his bare fists. Tears were streaming down his face.

Around November, one Sunday afternoon when Bobby and Manny were training at the gym, a handsome woman appeared at the front door. She wore a printed dress and three plumerias pinned in her hair. She was perhaps six feet tall with her high heels. Aunty Pua gasped and opened the screen door. "I wanted to surprise you," the woman said. She stepped in and hugged Pua, and then she touched my face gently. Her hands smelled of flowers. And though she was much taller than Aunty Pua and more youthful, I saw in her face the slant of Aunty Pua's nose, the curve of her cheekbones. "You must be Domingo," the woman said. She had beautiful hands, a dancer's hands. Her large brown eyes looked at me affectionately. She wore no make-up; her skin was unblemished. She was the woman in the pictures in the living room, Pua and Manny's daughter Kehaulani. I recalled her vaguely, though her last visit home had been years before. Then Pua hugged Kehau again and touched her face.

"How long you home this time?" Pua asked.

"Two weeks."

"My goodness, so short!" She hugged her again. "I wish you home for good."

On the way to the guest room, Kehau entered my room and sat on the bed. She looked at the walls as though my posters were not there, and I could see that she was remembering.

When Manny and Bobby came home, Manny hugged Kehau. During Kehau's stay, the house took on the scent of flowers. In the evenings, after dinner, Pua, Manny, and Kehau would sit out back in the patio, talking into the dusk and then into the warm, still fall night with the tropical bugs ticking against the patio light. I sat with them and listened. Inside the house, Bobby busied himself with homework—he was a junior at Kaimukī High School at the time—and after he finished his work, he would walk to the gym.

It was during one of these evenings that I learned Kehau was now a high school history teacher in California. She had taken leave for half a year to work on her doctoral degree at Berkeley, and she was gathering family stories for an oral history project. And so that night while Kehau listened and wrote in her notebook, Aunty Pua recalled the old stories—piecing together a family memory, and even a history before that memory—the ways of combat and war in ancient times, warriors wielding clubs much larger than a bat. She recounted, as though she had lived these experiences, the arrival of whalers, the devastation of sandalwood, the tumultuous plantation strikes, the overthrow of Queen Liliʻuokalani. Pua said that her great-grandparents, after the land-dispossession known as the Great Māhele, had been swept by the island's economic and political tides into plantation labor. Two generations later, Pua had been born into this same labor system. "But the day we leave Waialua," she said, "I tell myself, 'Now you free.' And I promise myself that I leave the plantation forever."

Like Pua, Kehau was fluent in the native Hawaiian tongue. She had founded a *hula hālau*, a *hula* dance troop, in San Francisco. Mrs. Oligario, the Filipino-Hawaiian *kupuna* in our cul-de-sac in Pālolo Valley, visited daily, and sometimes I heard the three women talking in Hawaiian, a language I could only mimic when I sang with the radio. When Manny was there, he would smile and sip his Coca-Cola. In college, Kehau had also studied abroad in Mexico and Puerto Rico. She could speak Manny's Puerto Rican Spanish, and she would describe to him his *patria*, his homeland, which he had yet to see. Those nights in the patio, their private languages drew them together.

Even a week after Kehau had gone, her beautiful scent stayed in the walls of the house, even in my bed, where she had sat one last time before leaving. At night, unable to sleep while I lay in bed, I heard in my memory the Hawaiian syllables rolling so fluently from Kehau's tongue and Aunty Pua and Mrs. Oligario responding, the three of them sharing the intimacy of language. These memories were painful. Seeing their intimacy made me feel my own distance. One evening, for a reason I couldn't understand at the time, I removed all of my sheets and the bedspread and placed them in the hamper, then asked Pua for fresh bedding.

It was December, Christmas Eve, and from around mid-afternoon, family members began arriving at Aunty Pua and Uncle Manny's house for the annual get-together. Manny's mother and father drove in from Waialua, and Pua's parents came from Pearl City. Manny's younger sister, Yolanda, and her husband, Keoki, a Chinese-Hawaiian, drove in all the way from Mākaha. Pua's two brothers, Gilbert and Kamuela, who now lived in Kapahulu, arrived with their families.

In the front yard, I saw my cousins Sammy and Jason, Uncle Keoki's sons, holding a pair of boxing gloves. Like Manny, Uncle Keoki was legendary in local boxing. Sammy, the elder of Keoki's two sons, was eleven years old. His shoulders filled out his T-shirt, and when he put on the gloves and posed in a fighting stance, his biceps balled up like a man's.

"Domingo! Domingo you like spar with Sammy?" said Jason.

"Nah," I said, waving him away.

"You scared?" said Jason.

"No," I said.

"No lie," said Jason. "Everybody scared of Sammy. You chicken."

"No be chicken, Domingo," Sammy said, grinning. "Only soft kind."

I took the gloves from Jason and put them on. The entire lawn was our ring, and Jason was our timer.

"Ding-ding!" he said.

Sammy and I squared off in the center of the front yard. He threw wide, looping punches. I ducked, bobbing and weaving beneath his gloves. When I straightened again, I saw his elbows high, his ribs exposed. I threw a left hook to his ribs. He buckled and dropped to the grass. "Hnnnh . . . hnnnnh," he wheezed. His eyes bulged. "Hnnnnh."

"Sammy!" Jason said. "Sammy, get up!"

"Hnnnnnh," Sammy groaned.

With my gloves still on, I rolled Sammy on his back. Jason grabbed Sammy's arms and raised them over his head, and I pushed Sammy's knees down, stretching out his solar plexus and stomach.

When Sammy regained his breath, he stood up. "I told you only soft kind," he said. "You lucky I never go all out."

"You wish," I said. "Try it."

"No act, you *hānai* bastard," he said.

Not knowing how to respond, I said weakly, "Get plenty people *hānai*."

"Not like you," he said. "You *hānai* cause . . . I not supposed to tell."

"What you trying for say?" I said.

"*Hānai*! *Hānai*!" Jason said.

"Shut up!" I said. "I not adopted. I get one father."

"*Hānai*," Sammy said again. I wanted to hit something—anything. I wanted to punch the tree. I wanted to punch my own face on the tree trunk. But the tree was in the back yard. In front of me, Sammy was grinning. "*Hānai*," he repeated. I stepped forward, centered my weight, and then threw my straight right hand. Sammy's head popped back. Blood blossomed around his nose. He cupped his gloves to his face.

Jason yelled, "You cheat. You went false-crack Sammy!" I turned to him and cocked my right hand again. Jason began to cry. I punched him anyway. I lowered my hands, stripped off the gloves, and shoved them into Jason's chest.

"Here, wimp," I said. "And next time I not going hold back." I walked back to the patio and joined the men.

The men were sitting on folding metal chairs. Gathered around a table, they were eating boiled peanuts; dried *aku*, or skipjack tuna; and *poke*, or raw fish mixed with seaweed, chili pepper water, and *shōyu*. Kamuela, a fisherman, had brought quarter-sized raw 'opihi. He said that he'd picked these mollusks from the rugged coastline beyond Yokohama. The surf there was tremendous, and we all knew the risk involved—Kamuela scurrying to the edge of the rocks between the intervals of crashing waves, working his hands into the jagged crevices, dislodging the mollusks with his old, dented butter knife, and then shoveling them into his canvas pouch before the next wave rolled in. Now Manny's two younger brothers, Ernesto and Jessie, both fighters, and some of Manny's uncles, also boxers from the old days, were savoring the 'opihi, poking them with toothpicks and dipping them in a *shōyu*-and-ginger sauce and then swallowing them whole.

Manny's father, Paulo Sanchez, my grandfather, sat quietly at the table. With silver hair and dark eyes, thin skin about a hard face and knuckles still calloused from occasional bouts with the heavy punching bag, he usually said little at family parties and was content to eat raw fish and drink Primo Beer. He usually took pleasure in patting the heads of the little nieces and nephews chasing each other around the yard.

But this Christmas he was talking about Bobby. I sat down beside him.

"I hear the boy punches hard," Grandpa Paulo said.

"As hard as his father?" said Ernesto.

"Harder," said Jessie. "Like his grandfather."

"Manny, how hard does the boy punch?" said Ernesto.

"He punches the tree," said Manny. "When he punches the tree, the branches shake, the mangos fall."

"The Golden Gloves," said Jessie. "He going fight this year?"

"Maybe you should take him to New Mexico," said Paulo. "Ignacio at Waipahu Gym said New Mexico get one good fighting circuit, good experience for young fighters." Paulo said that the desert burned a certain toughness into the fighters. The boxers there, mostly Mexicans, were solitary, religious Catholic men who habitually crossed themselves and had the severe reputation of boxing with ferocity and abandon.

"Maybe," said Manny. "When he ready to turn pro, maybe I take him."

"When he ready you take him," said Paulo. "I work his corner. I can be the cut man. . . ." His voice trailed off. He looked at the far end of the yard near the old wooden gate, at a sturdy man in a T-shirt and trousers and a slender woman in a black dress. As they approached the table, the woman smiled slightly. The man remained stoic. His face was tanned, scarred above the eyes. His nose was flat, and he had a thick, dark mustache. His hair was buzzed close to the sides and flat on top. All the men at the table had placed their forks and beer bottles down and were looking at the man and woman who had entered the yard quietly, probably from around the side of the house, and, up to this point, had said nothing.

"Luis," said Manny. "Luis . . . Ana . . . come sit down, sit down. Domingo, do you remember your mother and father?"

I shook my head, no. The woman sat down beside me and kissed my cheek and embraced me gently with one arm. She smelled of wine and smoke. I pulled away. The man remained standing. Then he reached down and shook my hand. His hands were calloused, hard. So was his gaze. I looked down at the ground, and when I tried to meet his eyes again, he was already looking beyond me into the yard. I leaned into Grandpa Paulo, and he put his hand on my shoulder.

"Good to see you, Luis," Paulo said.

The man named Luis nodded, then walked out to the yard. He walked up to Bobby, who was beneath the mango tree, amid a crowd of young nephews and nieces. Luis extended his hand, but Bobby didn't take it. They faced each other, their heights nearly even, their physiques compact and muscular. Bobby's face was red as though swollen with wine. I couldn't hear what Bobby said then, but Luis nodded abruptly and began walking back toward us.

"Who told you for come anyway!" shouted Bobby. "You think I like see you? Only one jackass would think that! You think . . . after all this time . . . you think I like one ex-convict for be my father? Go home. Get the hell out of here, you damn loser!"

Aunty Pua came out into the patio and grabbed my arm. "Come here," she said.

"Oww!" I said.

"Did you hit Sammy and Jason?"

"They was teasing me!"

"I don't care what they was doing. You no go punching people."

"They called me 'hānai,'" I said. "They call me one 'hānai bastard.'"

Pua glanced at Ana, then at Luis. She looked at me in the eyes. Then she said, "That's still not one excuse. You don't hit your cousins!" She dragged me into the house, made me apologize to Sammy and Jason, pinched Sammy's and Jason's cheeks until both boys cried, and then sent me to my bedroom.

That Christmas Eve, after most of the guests were gone and as I lay in bed and I could hear only hushed voices out back—Bobby's voice and the voice of a man and a woman, strange voices struggling out of long breaths of silence—Aunty Pua came to my room and told me a story. She told me about the great chief Kahekili's house. Its ancient posts and rafters, bound with sennit, were the bones of more than a thousand slain warriors. The great chief built the house so that the spirit could pass from the bone of the dead to the bone of the living. "Your father and mother have their troubles," she said. "You understand, Domingo? But they came tonight to see you and Bobby. Parents need that sometimes. To set things straight. No matter how hard. They're in your bones. That's where you remember them. You cannot change that."

I nodded, mimicking understanding, but not really understanding at the time, no, not at all. I was only eleven, too young to understand what it means to come from a family of fighters, Puerto Ricans who have been fighting for generations, Hawaiians who have been fighting for their land since the 1840s. A few years later, when I myself took up boxing, I realized that in my hands are the hands of others—Paulo's, Kehau's, Manny's, Luis's, Pua Leialoha's, Ana's. But that night I could only receive Aunty Pua's story as a much-needed gift—she was now giving to me the kind of story that she had passed on to Kehau, and somehow the story moved me closer to her. And I knew only that the man, Luis, and the woman, Ana, were strangers come from a place faraway—and that I had looked at the man Luis and felt the hands of the woman Ana, and I had been afraid. Later, Ana entered my bedroom and kissed my forehead, thinking I was asleep. I knew her touch already, her hand combing gently through my hair, her smell of smoke and wine, as though they had been called up from somewhere before memory. When I felt her rise from the bedside and move toward the door, I peeked and saw Luis standing outside in the hall, his face clear in the light. He was looking directly at me, and I was afraid that he'd seen me stir. Then Ana shut the door and I closed my eyes, her face and Luis's already vanishing in the black space between us.

I stayed awake for a long time that night, trying to forget and tossing restlessly in bed. Then I began imagining that I was the final sentry at the house of bones's entrance. I was dressed in a *malo*, a loincloth wrapped around my waist. I held in my fists a spear. My body from head to foot was divided, the skin on one side bronze and smooth, the other side darkened by the tattoos of an ancient warrior. My physique—long arms, broad shoulders, a thin waist, and sturdy legs—was that of a fighter. Eventually, I must have slipped into dream. And when a stranger approached me in front of the house of bones and I spoke, I could not understand the language that left my tongue. Neither could the man asking to enter, my father. But still he came forward, and, in the way dreams show us sometimes what we cannot yet articulate, I stepped aside that night without questioning, and let him in.

AKIKO BURIES HER SON

oji, the smooth-faced dog-boy, was run over by the vegetable man and died in his mother's arms. Before then the townspeople had thought that "the wishing" was only a rumor, but that day they saw Akiko Higa hold her once-retarded son and stroke his gray fur as he bled. Some say Koji had been chasing butterflies, leaping high into the air trying to taste them.

The vegetable man never saw him. His pickup swerved and lost half its load. Two crates of tomatoes bounced down the street and into the gutter, twenty pounds of tofu crumbled and six dozen eggs broiled in the sun. In her kitchen, with her hands in a ball of banana bread dough, Akiko heard the scream. She wiped her hands on her pink hibiscus dress that attracted bees, then ran out the door.

Koji's flattened body lay in the middle of the street. He was surrounded by tomatoes. "Don't touch him, he might bite," a witness said. "He's in shock, you know."

"All you women, take your children and go to your kitchens," said Masa. The potbellied vegetable man raised his arms to calm the crowd. "This isn't anything to worry about. Go home now."

"Shut up, old man," the women answered.

To get to her son, Akiko pushed Masa to the ground. She knelt next to Koji and ran her hand down his smooth fur, across his taut neck to his smashed hips. "I had . . . I have such a beautiful son." His tail shook, and the crowd gasped.

"Koji turned into a dog," someone in the crowd said.

"A greyhound, I think," another whispered.

"No, a shepherd."

Akiko brought her son's head to her chest and cleared the mucus from his eyes. "No, no . . . you beautiful boy." She rocked him slowly. "You dream too well, look what happens." The blood ran out of Koji and down her hibiscus dress, making a small pool in her lap.

Koji had been born two months after his father had burned in a cane fire while making love to a 13-year-old girl he had dreamt about. A cane worker had found the black, tangled bodies in the mud. At first he thought he was pulling on roots until he saw fingers and arms. He knelt beside the couple and touched them again, this time lightly, afraid that they might disintegrate. The lovers must have held each other in the last moments, he thought. They had lain in the dry earth and watched their sky burn orange, then flake.

When the crew foreman saw the pair, he thought that they should be separated. "It's the most decent thing to do," he said. He grabbed hold of Koji's father. The worker held the girl and they pulled. Nothing. He thought he'd try a chisel. "I think one good hit by the torso will free them."

The cane worker stepped away and folded his arms. The foreman wiped his brow with his sleeve. "Maybe you're right." He turned and shook his head. "Lucky bastard," he mumbled.

When Akiko heard about Koji's father, she held on to herself and said nothing. She remembered the night at the social, the time they danced till the band stopped playing, then danced again, outside by the sugar cane. She thought about their love, but then her room was filled with the familiar odor of smoke.

When Koji was born, Akiko had noticed that her son had a smooth face like a vegetable, and he was silent with an empty look in his eyes. She touched his head and kissed his cheek, but he still had the vacant stare. She pinched his heel. He didn't cry. She didn't need to count his fingers or toes.

"I think he's a greyhound," said someone in the crowd.

"Nah, a pointer!" said another.

"He would have probably been a good pig dog."

Akiko stroked her son's fur, looked into his eyes and saw them turn into cold stones. She gripped him tighter and tighter, then smelled the smoke.

"Go home . . . please," said Akiko. She stood up and carried her son's body home.

Some say that Koji felt himself turning back into a retarded boy and when the chill of solitude went through his body, he ran into the street and under the wheels of the vegetable man's truck.

Every year, during the first full moon after *Obon*, the village celebrated the lantern festival. Eligible men took a flute and lantern and in a clearing where there was soft ground, they played under the light of the moon. From miles away the music of bamboo flutes could be heard. If a woman heard a song that was particularly touching, she went to the lantern and they would talk and dance.

Fourteen years earlier, when her phoenix kimono was not yet torn, Akiko Higa was told about her mother's Chinese lover.

"I met a man there," her mother began. "The song on his flute was so sad. It was hollow and sorrowful, like love. I never knew who he was. He was part of the crew that built the hauling road to the mill. He had rough hands and his face was wide and his eyebrows were sharp. They say he was Chinese." She drew circles in the air. "He ran his finger down my body and talked about flying. He wanted to be an aviator. When we made love, he had me blow in his face. After, I wrapped myself in my kimono, and when I turned to face him he blew out his lantern and was gone. I never saw him again. He smelled like motor oil."

A week later, they found the *Pākē*, whom they called Li Luang, at the bottom of the quarry, at the foot of the cliff. His body was soft and broken. His flesh was white and puckered. When they lifted his arm, a thin membrane of skin spread out from his elbow to his side. Thick shafts of white hair were attached like quills.

"Feathers," they said.

Yukio Abe, the priest, was called. When he arrived, he picked up the arm and dropped it in horror.

"The wishing," he said. He shook a charm at the dead man. "These pagan gods. They give these men their dreams."

Under the direction of the priest, they buried Li Luang at night in the cane field, not twenty yards from his road. They made the grave deep and laid a heavy rock on his body.

"Promise me that you will not tell a soul," said the priest. "What you have seen tonight is blasphemous."

Thereafter, whenever Akiko's mother heard a combustion engine, she thought of her Chinese lover. When the vegetable man raced down the road in his pickup and its engine coughed, she imagined her lover high above Shanghai. When the foreman started his generator, the flier was over Guam and on his way to Honolulu. Sometimes she would walk down the middle of the hauling road and notice how the cane, in certain spots, would grow tall and green. In his grave, under a flat rock, Li Luang struggled to fly.

Akiko buried her face in her son's fur and smelled him one last time. She laid him on the porch and cleaned his body of the blood. From her trunk she pulled her still torn and stained phoenix kimono and wrapped her son in the silk, and within the folds of blue and silver the dog-boy chased the bird.

At the time of her own lantern festival Akiko's kimono had been too loose. "You don't eat enough rice," her mother had said. "Akiko, hold still." She pulled at the *obi* belt, grabbed hold of the loose silk, and stuffed it into her daughter's side. "Look at the moon, look at the moon!"

The flutes had begun to play. Before she left, her mother slipped a eucalyptus leaf under Akiko's tongue to prevent babies.

The cane sounded as though it would tear in the wind. Akiko stood frozen in the field. She thought of taking off her slippers, running home and hiding underneath the porch. But then she remembered how her mother would jump in anticipation when she smelt gasoline.

Lincoln Takemoto didn't know how to play the flute, but that didn't stop him from taking his lantern and finding a soft spot in the fields. His father had given him a flute that was carved in Japan and had little dragons on its mouthpiece. But Lincoln never bothered to learn. It seemed ancient. Instead, on that night, he took a Coca-Cola bottle and with a delicate lip he blew out a tune.

Lincoln Takemoto had dreamed of grasping the world with his two hands, but he had the stamina to use only one. The last child and only boy in a family of seven, he was born without struggle and lived without fear. Coddled, overfed, and never contradicted, he displayed a boldness and imagination that his sisters were not allowed to cultivate.

From the age of 4, it was decided that he would become a doctor and he was protected from the world of the plantation that anxiously awaited him. His neighbors were described to him with disdain. His parents' work in the fields was shameful. The world they all shared was a blight, a world that he was to deliver them out of. By the age of 6 he was already subject to admiring gazes from relatives, gazes which betrayed their thoughts of an approaching world of wondrous cures and discoveries.

At 8, when he found a small mango tree in the back yard, Lincoln developed an appetite for gluttony. The fruit fit neatly in his hand and tasted vaguely like a flower. He ate two, then three, then another, and another till the tree was stripped bare. He chewed on the dry leaves and gnawed on the thin branches tasting a hint of the edible perfume. He gorged, nibbled, and munched until, several hours later, his mother found him gnawing on a naked stump trying to find the taste of blossoms again.

From then on Lincoln Takemoto ate continuously. He ate sweet mochi and tart Chinese preserves in handfuls. He ate pickles and salted greens faster than his sister could prepare them. He continued to indulge his appetite for wood, preferring the texture of hardwood but the taste of fruit and flower trees. He enjoyed the salty taste of rusted metal, and he even suckled on rocks with delicious shapes. And, of course, there were the mangoes. He consumed them in such quantity that his perspiration resembled thick heavy sap, causing a bothersome acne problem. However, no matter what he ate, Lincoln Takemoto would not gain extra weight. "It is a sure sign of a glutton," his father lamented.

Hoping they were finally launching a fabled medical career, the Takemoto family pooled their resources and sent Lincoln to live with relatives in Japan. Away from the mangoes and in a place of taste and culture, they hoped that Lincoln would lose his enormous cravings and find his destined profession. Instead, he found the countryside's pine and cypress tress, and indulged in the hard resins that oozed out of their trunks. He also never lost his taste for edible foods, keeping his cousins as busy as his sisters. They boiled and baked, peeled and fried until they took up their own collection and sent Lincoln back home to his mangoes and overworked sisters.

Lincoln played his simple tune again, this time louder. He waited. Then again. The Coca-Cola melody reminded Akiko of the loneliness of her grandmother's music. From behind a tree she appeared. She looked at the ground and glanced up quickly. He kicked his Coca-Cola bottle away.

"Hello," said Lincoln.

Akiko nodded nervously. "I heard your music. Where did you learn how to play so well?"

"Japan."

"You're from Japan?"

"Oh no. I just spent a lot of time there," he said.

"My father talks often about returning to Japan. Is it as beautiful as they say it is?"

"It is. Green and fertile with gentle mountains that roll on and on. And the trees, the trees. They are . . . beautiful," he said. "And the food, oh the food!"

He told her of the delicate taste of pine in fresh *matsutake* and of the imperceptible sounds that salmon roe makes as it breaks apart in your mouth. He continued about his love of trees until they both noticed that the other flutes had fallen silent. He bent over and kissed her. They both pulled away and smiled. He kissed her again and held her. She was more delicious than any fruit or tree or rock. They made love standing up, her kimono torn at her ankles. A cold breeze went through the field. It made their skin shrink, and it felt as though they had grown fur.

For the following months they spent nearly every night together. Akiko would sneak out her bedroom window after everyone had fallen asleep and meet him at their spot. He was always there waiting for her. He would tell her stories of his travels through Japan—the steamship voyage to Yokohama, the train trip to Hiroshima, the texture of freshly harvested abalone. Sometimes he would go on about his imminent medical career.

"When do you think you'll start?" she would ask.

"Soon," he would reassure her. "Soon."

Before long, Lincoln lost his appetite for all food. He subsisted on only bowls of clear soup and handfuls of rice, oblivious of the meal's ambiance and texture. His concerned but well-rested sisters would offer him platters of fish and meat, but he would turn them away. They made mango pies and cakes and breads, but he would refuse them. Instead, he would swallow down his meal and head to their clearing, watch the sun go down and wait for her to appear from the trees. He would begin with one of his stories, but eventually their conversations grew shorter and shorter as Lincoln cultivated a taste and stamina for lovemaking.

Two months after their first meeting, Akiko became pregnant.

"Are you sure? Didn't you have a eucalyptus leaf?" Lincoln asked.

"I'm positive."

He told her that he wanted a big wedding, that he wanted to go to Honolulu and begin medical school. He said that he had a strongbox underneath his bed full with money he had earned in Japan. He had enough for a wedding and a honeymoon that would take them away forever.

"I want to see Japan," she said. "I want to see the world with you."

After they buried him, still entangled with the 13-year-old, they took his strongbox from underneath the bed. When they opened it, they found $20, a knife with a broken blade and the branch of a mango tree. One end had been chewed and all the juices had been sucked out.

Akiko dug the grave till she hit rock. It was about four feet deep. She lined it with freshly picked ti leaves, then sprinkled it with water. She laid Koji and the kimono inside, then folded the silk back for one last look at her son. Akiko buried him and sat on her porch and looked out at the road and imagined her son was no longer a dog, but a boy running around in circles.

BY WANDA DIAL

ROM BORI

My name is Yanna. I live at Hanauma Bay on the edge of an island in the Territory of Hawai'i. I want to write down this year to remember. It is 1946, the year I marry and leave my father's camp to live with my new husband's family in town. There are many families in our camp, all brothers and sisters, aunts and uncles, and cousins to each other.

My mother doesn't like it when people in town call us Gypsy. We have names, she says, just like the Hawaiians, the Japanese, the Filipinos, and the Portuguese. The gadje should call us by our name.

It's not yet time, but already I know how much I'll miss this camp. In the day, it's hot inside the wagons and tents, but outside there's shade from tall palm trees, and tradewinds always blowing.

At night when it storms, the high wind sounds like old mulos, ghosts, lost at sea, crying out to their loved ones. I dream that in the morning when I wake, the ocean will be gone, sucked up by the wind. But when the night is over, I wake, and it is still there, shining deep blue and green in the morning sun.

In January, my father sells me to Stilio's father for one thousand dollars. This is my daro, my bride-sale, the money Stilio's father pays for Stilio to marry me. My father wants more for me, maybe as much as two thousand dollars, but now is bad time for fortunetelling business. The war's over, sailors and shipworkers go back to the States or wherever they come from before the bombs at Pearl Harbor. They stop wanting fortunes told.

My father knows families who close their fortunetelling places, go on welfare.

That's why he says he has sold me well. After I marry Stilio, I will tell fortunes at my mother-in-law's ofisa in Chinatown, upstairs on the corner of King and Maunakea streets.

It's God's will that gypsy women be dukkerers, born with the sight. It's the way gypsy women take care of their husbands and children, the way they get money for food and clothes.

Since a little girl in short dresses I know this. I learn the colored stones and how to throw them in a sacred circle. I learn how to read the lines, the shapes, the mounts of the palms. Many times I study these things with my mother and my baba, grandmother. All gypsy girls do this.

Strangers are happy to pay two dollars to have their fortunes told by an important fortuneteller like my mother-in-law. She wears five heavy necklaces of twenty-dollar gold pieces around her neck, and many rings and bracelets of gold. My mother worries a powerful woman like Madam Lena wants a town girl for her daughter-in-law, not a camp girl like me. But father doesn't worry, he says we are all Romani. It's true the Lovaria gypsies are higher than the Kalderash, but we are smarter.

I'm happy my father chose well for me, but I'm scared. When my friend Dotcha's father sold her sister Rava, he sold her to a man she didn't like. So Rava run away, back to her father's house, and refuse to live with her new husband. Her father had to go before the Kris, and the old folks council makes Dotcha's father give back the bride-sale money the husband's family gave in pakiv, respect, for the loss of Rava. They say no more Rava, no more daro. I tell Dotcha even if Stilio be mean to me, I'll not cause my father to give back my daro. I'll not shame my father.

We don't know each other, Stilio and me. He's two years older and pretty smart. He went to school for six years. Gypsy girls don't go to school. But we're smart anyway. We learn everything from our mothers and our aunts and our babas. Mostly we learn how to tell the fortunes. Gypsy boys don't learn this. After they go to school, they go around with their fathers fixing the copper cooking pots, sharpening knives, and looking out for trouble for gypsies.

On my wedding day, I am to meet Stilio for the first time. We never go out together before we marry like the gadje, not even to see a picture at the show house in Kāneʻohe.

This is because a Rom Bori must be a virgin. Baba says if a girl's no good when she lives with her family, she'll be no good when she lives with her husband.

It's the gypsy way to hold an Ascertainment of Virginity ceremony on the third night of the wedding celebration. On this night, the girl is examined by the mother of the boy and the mother of the girl can be there if she wants to. This is how they find out if the bori is a virgin or not: they examine her vagina. If she is not a virgin, the groom's family calls off the wedding. My mother and father think I'm a good girl, a virgin bori for Stilio because I never tell them about Chavaro. Two years pass now since Chavaro and me make love. Can Stilio's mother tell what happened between Chavaro and me two years ago?

Dotcha says don't worry, Stilio's mother not stop the wedding. She won't tell her son's bori not a virgin, look bad for him, maybe he the one, nobody know for sure.

Gypsy mothers-in-law want their daughters-in-law to have many babies. It's good for their old age, plenty of grandchildren to make money for the family when the old mothers get tired. Baba remembers gypsy women with twenty or thirty children in her homeland. My mother had nine babies, and four that died before they were born. Stilio's mother had nine boys and three girls. I don't know if she lost any babies before they were born. I don't know how many children I'll have, but I don't want to lose any before they're born. It's best for gypsy girls to have their first baby soon after they marry. If one year goes by and still no baby, the husband can ditch his wife and go find another wife to have his babies. The Kris tribunal says this is his right as a man.

After eight years, my Aunt Stella and Uncle Tony have only one boy. His name is Johnny, but they call him Koko Head because he was born at their camp in Koko Head crater. Uncle Tony's mother thinks Aunt Stella should have more babies by now, not just Johnny.

Because I marry soon, Aunt Stella cries and tells me she thinks after Johnny was born the doctors fixed her up so she couldn't have no more babies. They did it by scraping inside her with a knife.

She remembers coming out of the ether and hearing the doctors talking about her. They said she was a bad girl, that her baby had no father. This is because when her mother takes Aunt Stella to the clinic on King Street she tells them, take good care of this daughter for her old mother. She thinks if she tells them that, like her daughter has no husband, Aunt Stella will get good care. Her mother doesn't think they say this one is a bad girl, we must fix her so she can't have more babies. The very first time I go to the clinic, I tell the doctors I'm married, my baby has a father, and I want more babies.

Because Aunt Stella tells me her secret, I think maybe I'll tell her about Chavaro and me. How we fell in love when we were thirteen, how we plan to ask our fathers to arrange a marriage for us, but Chavaro's father gets restless, wants to go back to New York. He tells Chavaro three years in one place, even a beautiful place like the islands, is too long. Chavaro says he has to go where his father goes so someday his father will buy him a wife. They go to live in New York City. I bet Chavaro finds plenty gypsy girls in New York City. I don't tell Aunt Stella about Chavaro and me.

Tomorrow's the first day of April, and I marry Stilio in just three weeks. My mother plans a real old-time wedding, and my father spends many dollars more than the thousand dollars Stilio's father pays for my daro. Baba and Aunt Stella stitch a dress for me of white satin with tiny pearls and a long veil. My baba smokes a short brass pipe filled with sweet tobacco as she sews. She tells me funny stories about when she was a child, and sad stories about what happened to her family in the war.

My father wishes for a mandolin and a real gypsy orchestra, but Uncle Tony plays a fine violin, carved from one piece of wood, and my cousin Rupa plays guitar. When they play together the sound is so sweet my father sometimes cries, and even the old and feeble get up to dance.

Today my father sets up a big tent in the curve of the bay, a little way from our camp. He invites all the gypsies on the island and his gadje friends from town to come to the three days of the abiav, over a hundred guests to feed each day. There are no lambs for sale on this island, so he orders three lambs from the island of Maui and builds a pen for them. When he brings the lambs to our camp, he instructs the children to calm them with food and water and petting so their meat won't be tough, but my father says not to name the lambs.

At sunrise on the first day of my wedding festivities, my father and Uncle Tony perform the traditional throat-cutting ritual on the beach in the shallow waters of the ocean. The clear waves turn black with the blood of the no-name lambs. I think of sharks and turn away. I see Stilio watching me. He's tall and looks older than me because he's seventeen. He has a thick mustache I didn't know about. Chavaro had no hair on his mouth. I will practice kissing my hairbrush.

I think Stilio is handsome, but when I tell Dotcha this, she says it's not always good that husbands be handsome. She says handsome husbands stray, find new wives without telling old wives. This is a matter for the Kris, but one time Dotcha knows about, the Kris vote for the husband and left the wife and his three children with nothing.

Tonight I sleep at Stilio's house on Vineyard Boulevard. It's called Doctor's Row because a lot of doctors live on the street. It's on the way to the clinic where Rava had prikaza, bad luck. I'll not sleep with Stilio. I'll be on a camp cot in his sisters' room. I have three sisters-in-law, all younger than me. Ava is the oldest, Mara the youngest, and Sandana in the middle.

At first I cannot think what to say, and they cannot, but then we laugh and they tell me stories about Stilio when he was little. All good things so I know Stilio better. Aunt Stella tells me the bad things a bori finds out by herself after the wedding. But she laughs when she says this.

The third day is here. I wake up in Stilios's house, still sleepy from the long night of talk. When I get back to camp, the bay is bright and beautiful, and I'm wide awake. Many people come today, more than the two days before, all happy smiling cousins, aunts, uncles, and their nieces and nephews, all members of our kumpania. There are some gadje, but all the people I know and love are here. I am a gypsy princess about to marry a gypsy prince and be happy ever after.

When night comes, my stomach hurts. I get sick and throw up. Nerves my mother says. Don't worry, she says, sex is not so bad, maybe not good first time, but gets better. I can't tell her I don't throw up because of sex, I throw up because tonight is the night of the Ascertainment of Virginity.

The guests eat, drink, and enjoy the feast. I cannot. When the plates are finally empty and it's time, mother nods for me to rise and together with Stilio's mother we go down to the small tent at the water's edge. The evening tide cools the sand under my feet, and with each step I pray to Saint Sarah, patron saint of gypsies. I pray to be a virgin.

Stilio's mother lights a candle beside a low cot. This is the moment I fear. My eyes close and in the rhythm of the waves I hear Chavaro's soft voice, as soft as his mouth on my breasts. It's okay, we won't make a baby, I make sure, we just make love. Chavaro's words so clear in my mind are like a smile on a face I trust, and I'm no longer afraid.

I lie there happy, remembering Chavaro, remembering his promise to marry in the Rom way a gypsy girl like me. I promise him, too. Now I keep that promise. My eyes open at the touch of my mother's hand. Yanna is a good girl, she says. I breathe and say thanks to Saint Sarah with all my heart. The three of us return to the laughter and music of the big tent and the waiting guests.

The mothers present me to Stilio. My father places a round loaf of maro with the center scooped out on a wooden plate and sprinkles it with salt. He passes the maro down the long line of guests. Paper money and gold coins fill the hollow and cover the plate. The bread is good health, sprinkled with salt for fertility, and covered with money for prosperity for Stilio and me as we start a new Rom family.

My father unfolds a bright yellow square of silk, the diklo I will wear on my head as a married woman. He holds it on a short stick above our heads, and together we begin the final procession.

My father is proud. I have been tested and found to be a good girl. I have lived as a gypsy, and now I marry as a gypsy. As a Rom wife, I wear the diklo and and never go into the streets of Honolulu without it.

BY MARIE HARA

OLD KIMONO

rom the moment she saw it folded neatly on the top of the pile of old clothing, she was sure it would look good on her.

One of a kind, a perfect find.

The color was right, a sophisticated black crepe. The design was just what she hoped for, *Japanese-y* and clearly ethnic, plus the incredible price. It was second hand, of course, but the jagged scrap of masking tape stuck on to it read three dollars. Three dollars. For something antique and classy. You couldn't go wrong.

People she knew or had heard about, women her age, were using old kimonos in intriguing ways, pleating them for sophisticated skirts and cutting them up for fashionable blouses and vests. If they couldn't sew, they found dressmakers. And why not? Old material turns worthless forgotten in camphor chests or left in closets as termite food. And the patterns . . . you couldn't find that kind of design on bolts anymore . . . they had become priceless. Her own creative idea was simple: this one would be the perfect robe over a silky, black nightgown. No matter whose it had once been, it was destined to be part of her own wardrobe now, finally appreciated for its true worth, its one-of-a-kind lining, its fashion statement, subtle, but bold.

She held it up to the two elderly Japanese women who were tending their booth. The crowd at the Shinshu Mission Bazaar milled through displays of housewares and knickknacks. Most people stepped right past the rack of dark *baba-san* dresses and assorted heaps of cast-off garments.

The annual fair attracted a varied clump of people to the temple on a winding street off the heart of downtown Honolulu. Shoppers moved through tents and stalls. Some waited for the next batch of homemade sushi while a wave of smoke from the huli-huli chicken barbecue next door forced the bystanders to move aside or cover their watering eyes. The temple, a vestige of the 1920s, was bright pink, concrete India Indian style architecture. Easy to spot but hard to figure how it could have been built by Japanese Americans in Hawai'i, the temple now rarely attracted the young, except at Bon Dance time or the fair. So her first reaction whenever she visited was to open her eyes to take it all in once again. Here, lay evidence of good luck, the very blessing she remembered a priest telling her grandmother she would receive for faithfully visiting the memorials to the dead.

The two old ladies saw her growing interest. As the women examined the garment, they noted her enthusiasm by exchanging questioning looks. She ran her hands over the elaborate design one more time. Her action was closely watched by the hunchbacked old lady whose neck was frozen in a perpetual bow.

"Young girlu-san." She got her attention.

"Saah . . . befo' time . . . you know Watanabe-san? Yuriko? The family wen' donate all her clothes after the one-year service." This from the elderly woman with mottled age spots all over her face and arms.

With annoyance at the unasked-for information, the young woman shook her head. "Maybe my grandma might have, but I nevah come to temple nowadays."

"You know how fo' wear dis kind?"

"Sure, but I might change it and maybe cut it all up, too. I don't wanna wear dis kine old-fashion stuff. In Hawai'i, too hot."

As the other one stared, the young woman pressed three bills into the hand of the silent old lady and quickly packed the neat kimono—now a precisely folded rectangle—into her designer-label satchel. Without a word the hunched one handed her a stained cotton obi, more a child's sash than a proper waist piece. She noted also that neither of the two women thanked her, even as they carefully watched her walk away.

Hypocrites. They think they know how to do things right . . . but it's always their way or no way. Typical! In her mind's eye she saw a long line of Japanese mothers, aunties, and other older women lecturing young girls relentlessly about how to do things correctly, what they meant was *perfectly*. Even creasing a line in paper had to be done just so, with the edge of a fingernail. Crazy women. She would never do it their way. Leaving them far behind in her thoughts, she freed the kimono from any further association with such negative types.

No matter what anyone might say—and it would be some old lady for sure—she wouldn't tell where she bought it. This black silk kimono held so many possibilities. Even the glossy satin collar lining was quite elegant in a crisp way; there wasn't a single stain or moth hole. Not a whiff of camphor clung to the garment. Under her stroking touch, as she felt it in her handbag on the bus ride home, the kimono took on the form of a dozen different outfits, all hers.

The frame house on Pua Lane was surrounded by helter-skelter plantings. The varicolored ornamental growth winding along a flourishing garden of rows of green onion and lettuce ruffled out all around the neatly painted building. Vaguely similar to the other homes which formed a short row along the street, the brown cottage could have been a variant of the standard, now vanished plantation house. Littered with assorted slippers and shoes, the front porch where she dashed off her sandals stopped her motion for only the briefest moment.

She stood fixed in front of a full-length mirror. She sighed in satisfaction at the blackness of the top half of the kimono held next to her skin. The mirror gave proof that her choice, the sophisticated black and exquisite design work were exactly right for her. She would look bold and new: Asian, not oriental. Sexy, not cute. The silky fabric confirmed her choice.

Once she turned the garment inside out to satisfy herself, she saw how painstakingly it had been made. Every seam was hidden by a double fold; every visible stitch, each identical to the eye, had been put in with stunning regularity since they were not machine made. Delighted, she said aloud, "My precision kimono!" held it to her chest, then frowned when she rechecked the sewing. She began to turn the kimono rapidly, then frantically. Where would the knots go? They had to be there or the whole thing would have fallen apart. All the finely matched rectangular pieces would break away. She chewed the logic of no anchor knots. Certainly they must be subtly hidden under the precise seams, of course.

At this comforting thought, she caught a glimpse of her mom's arrangement of what she called "boy flawahs," anthuriums, in a blue vase placed on a bureau behind her. The red and pink flowers with their knobby pistils and sturdy stems, seemed—the only word she could call up to fit—crude. Not only were they ordinary and not placed in any particular order, they were also in no way fragile or aesthetic. They were so . . . local. Only hours away from the yard with its motley vegetation, the anthuriums shone out in their robust colors. They had been inserted into the vase for no particular reason, one more thing that her mother did by habit, not design.

By contrast the pattern of cranes and tortoises in a bamboo forest with a garden lantern, wisteria vines, and chrysanthemums worked into a delicate but elaborate balance at the bottom of the kimono, spoke of art. Here lay the world where every fine line of distinguishing detail existed to make a difference. And then the crest needed some accounting for as well. On either breast, at the center back line and at two places below the shoulders, a tiny *mon* had been meticulously embroidered in white-gold thread. Whoever sewed it must have been a red hot seamstress, maybe a professional who had studied hard and aimed for perfection. She couldn't make out what the symbol meant but recognized a flower and the shape of a bird in the quarter of an inch allotted. The beak was sharply delineated.

Considering the imagery as she ran her hand wistfully over the garment now carefully spread out over the bed, she decided wearing it would make her not only look fashionably Japanese but also like someone who was used to wearing one. The only problem was that she'd have to learn all the finer points: what kind of under kimono and undergarments to wear, how to fix her hair just so, how to get her feet to walk together right and maybe even more. The kimono looked like the first step on a tiresome road of tasks to learn.

So she would use it as a simple robe. It looked like something from a fashion magazine. She was flexible. Easy elegance, that was just what she wanted from the moment she saw it. How would it look with a wide open neck and a flowing, loose sash?

When she saw herself in it for the first time, she felt a curious prickle run down her neck. It fit perfectly. That word again. She used the lightweight sash to tie herself in tightly. She wouldn't have to worry about a new hem, since it had been sewn precisely into an expert roll of one-fourth inch at the bottom edge. As she gazed at herself in the long mirror, she saw a young woman who, when she swept her full head of hair upward to form a ponytail, then a tight bun, was transformed into someone very much like a traditional Japanese woman, suddenly more demurely feminine than she had ever looked. Her form was elegantly contained in the decorated kimono column.

Oddly, she had a hard time meeting her own eyes in the mirror. She had to first look up and break out of the posture of her head bowed toward the kimono's border and the floor. She suppressed an impulse to move toward the kitchen to prepare a kettle of green tea.

Mother would bust laughing.

She chuckled too, to think of the necessity to trot absurdly in this tight garment. Hilarious. She positioned her feet slightly inward so that the right pigeon-toed stance greeted her eyes when she admired herself again.

The blackness of the silk crepe glistened under the overhead light. To be so encased began to feel seductive. She could imagine being totally in control of an audience of observers who followed every movement she made . . . as if she were about to demonstrate an important cultural activity, explaining the reasons why people "should choose this way, the proper one. Not that way," and why it looked so much more graceful, "much better" in the way that she had presented the action. What was the action? Just the way, actually the exquisite style with which she lifted her forearm and readied her own now elegant, elongated hand in a formal gesture of pointing to her slender form in the mirror. Her hand looked much longer, the nails subtly and perfectly shaped.

"Simple—absolutely simple—but correct, in fact, perfect." The last word came out in a pronouncement of satisfaction, although whispered.

She gazed at her image in the mirror. The Japanese-looking woman in disarray who returned the glance from the glass was vaguely familiar. With a realignment of her body posture, she saw what she would look like were she more attentive to details. The line of her back now had some starch to it, and her face grew masklike as if dreaming deeply. Erasing her individual expression, she had traded it for something more adequately female. Her eyes looked down.

One hand at her side, she fingered the cranes and tortoises and felt at home, no longer lost somewhere where the symbols meant nothing.

The figure in the sophisticated black kimono stared back at her without curiosity. With every tiny motion, her own breathing became part of a larger rhythm, something as ancient as the pattern on the cloth. She began to think about the Japan she had never seen, tatami mats and courtyards, wet garden stones and bustling street fronts, a Japan which she would never see, since it was all gone anyway. The romance of that charming past, replete with beckoning lanterns grew into colorful sweetmeats for her imagination. Lost in long, pleasant moments of a dream world layered with images from the Japanese movies she had gone to see with her grandma, her body began to fit the old kimono.

Her loyalty would never waver; she would serve her lord courageously. Her training would not let her do anything else. Her face would betray no emotion. Her feelings would be replaced by her purpose. She would learn what the great Lord Buddha taught about equanimity. Only her eyes would express how she regarded the universe: matter-of-factly, steadfastly seeing beauty in nature, in all the simple things, in respectfully acknowledging even bothersome people. She would lead by actions, not words.

The hour went by, the minutes unnoticed as she receded into deep thoughts about her role as a woman who appreciated the aesthetic above all. Beauty and pride, discipline and high endeavor ruled her very being.

When she let down her long hair in a straight mass against the back of the kimono, the black tresses looked like a silky waterfall with the light of the day outside picking up shiny glints in the flowing strands which moved together as one.

She pivoted slowly on one foot just to see if she could move correctly. Her hand daintily tucked back into her sleeve, she minced in tiny steps as if in time to a persistent koto melody. Back and forth, back and forth, she moved. Her face was determined as she disallowed herself a smile at the pleasing image of herself as a dancer, while she hid her hands within the kimono's delicate openings so that she looked more childlike and helpless. She cocked her head just so. No teeth, no fingernails, nothing sharp or jarring, broke her peaceful demeanor or the smooth lines of her softness dancing.

In the mirror someone diminutive and guileless reflected light. Music in her head, ringing with the rollicking cadences of koto and samisen, rushed her into electric motion, back and forth, back and forth, until she collapsed on the bed, giggling at the spectacle.

She caught her breath when she looked backwards at the mirror. The woman in the black kimono was still dancing as if the music had increased its frantic rhythm. Back and forth, back and forth: her motions were hypnotic.

Lifting her face, the dancer, caught in the instance of clapping her hands, froze at the sight of the woman staring at her from the bed.

Both gasped, the young woman and the reflection in the mirror when the bedroom door opened.

Her mother peered in from the darkened hallway.

"Oh. You. I thought I heard music. W'at did you put on? Hmmm . . . nice. But you have it on backwards. You wen' fo'get! Always wrap da kimono left over right or else you gonna look like one dead man. Fo' real! Anybody who know anyt'ing—all da people who see dat—dey gonna laugh at you."

She was ready to explain more and give examples from her experience. Her daughter's face must have discouraged her because she departed without waiting for a response.

The used kimono was left in a heap on the bed.

BY MAVIS HARA

CHEMOTHERAPY

he slightest touch in the shower and my hair pulls out of my scalp, coming out in my fingers in wide black ribbons. The ribbons flow down my back and arms with the warm water. They encircle me, cling to the warmth of my body like a toddler fearful of being left. Finally, curling in tendrils around my ankles, they flow reluctantly toward the drain. There, abandoned by water, and trapped against the silvery round grating, they twist themselves into black balls, hollow worlds, empty nests.

Medical file:

Patient is a 35 y/o who had surgery on July 18 for CA of lt breast. The operative findings showed infiltrating ductile CA w/ productive fibrosis, stage II. Pt is pre menopausal.

"Cancer patients are usually the most agreeable people," the medical social worker informed me before my first chemotherapy session. "They are viewed by their families and co-workers as uncomplaining selfless saints who give up everything for others. Cancer survivors, on the other hand, are difficult," she paused, eyeing me slowly. "They laugh when they need to laugh, cry when they need to cry, demand what they need and don't ask permission."

The chemotherapy agent is a chemical cocktail that goes directly into a vein in my arm. This perverse happy hour will continue weekly for one full year. My cousin Taeko drives me to my first treatment. She is twenty years older than I, a retired accountant. She volunteered for the job. I was never close to her; I ponder the mystery. The nurses in the oncology unit are professionally cheerful; they give me a round yellow pill in a small paper cup. "For the nausea that may come," they explain. I swallow the Compazine, and escape the chemotherapy room which is called a cell. My cousin and I walk across the street to Thomas Square. Under the giant trees, I wait for the tiny sphere of calm to unravel in the pit of my stomach.

"I wanted to drive you because you look like my mother," my cousin, who is old enough to have been my mother, explains. Then I remember. The dark woman in the photo. Thin and fragile, with deep set eyes. The one that all my life people have begun sentences about, "You look just like Big Auntie," before averting their eyes and looking hurriedly away. I want to respond but the Compazine has dissolved. Tranquility has unrolled within me; it spreads out and settles languidly, it weighs down my tongue.

I return to the chemotherapy cell, a bright chamber with impervious surfaces; my thoughts unreel but bypass speech. The nurses swab my arm and in the hollow above the bones of my elbow; they insert a tiny needle that feels like the ember of a strand of spider web singeing the surface of my skin. The kindly faced nurse opens a clamp and I feel a surge of unexpected cool, like the north wind on a summer day, or the bubbling of artesian water out of the mouth of Kunawai Stream.

"First we just run saline through the lines," the nurse is explaining, "to buffer the chemicals." I drift in the cool, thinking of the strands of algae waving at the bottom of the stream bed in Kunawai Park, and I hear the stories about the thin dark woman who was confined at Pālama Settlement with tuberculosis eating away at her lungs. She pounded the heads of her children, saying, "You better be good, you better study, you. . . ." until they no longer wanted to go see her and ran off into the neighboring vegetable gardens on visiting days.

"Here come the chemicals now," comes the announcement, as the nurse inserts a syringe into the plastic tubing connected to the silver metal nozzle that has been installed directly into the my vein. My heart races and beneath the tapestry of Compazine; I prepare for an assault. A cold dark whisper travels up my arm and suddenly a chemical fragrance blooms behind my nose as I exhale, not unpleasant but unexpected: a source of sensation that is totally new. I sit ready to resist any waves of nausea, but nothing stirs in my stomach. Relief circulates through me carried by saline. I sit for thirty minutes, bathed in cool salt water, my veins washed clean, rinsed and preserved; the ordeal is over for today.

In the waiting room, my cousin sits reading. As I walk out of the chemo cell, she rises toward me, magazine in hand, concern in her eyes. "So how was it?" she asks as she embraces me. In her hair I can see the vigorous white roots under the dark dye she uses to conceal them. This is one of the children who endured the head pounding; she has been waiting sixty years for my smile. I try to embrace her with a substitute mother's warmth, I hug her hard; when we break the embrace, Taeko turns away quickly. I think there are tears in her eyes. For the first time, I feel gratitude that in this life, I have no children.

It is not until my cousin has driven me home and I have finished waving good-bye that the lethargy hits. Perhaps it is the Compazine, perhaps the chemotherapy chemicals. I want to lie flat with my face against the cool earth. My mother has been anxiously waiting for me to return.

"You feel like throwing up?" she says following me anxiously. "Take Daddy's throw up bowl." She hands me the gold, plastic, kidney-shaped receptacle that my father, who died of cancer three years ago, used to use.

"I'm fine," I say. "Can I just go to bed now? I feel so sleepy." I change out of my street clothes and into a T-shirt and slide between the sheets of my bed. My mother is anxious and I should talk with her but the need to sleep is too intense. I drift below consciousness and have the dream I used to have just after my father's death. The one where he is smiling at me so warmly that I feel enfolded and secure, the one where I go forward to embrace him then suddenly realize that he is dead. The one where I abandon him again when I tell him I cannot go with him yet.

Surgery

Operative procedure and findings:

The breast was removed from the pectoralis major with the pectoralis major muscle coming off with the breast tissue. An en bloc dissection of all axillary tissue was then performed. . . . All other lymphoareolar and vascular tissue was excised en bloc. Specimen was sent to lab for frozen section. The area was thoroughly lavaged with saline.

With clean gloves and instruments, the wound was then closed with 4-0 Vicryl to the subcuticular tissue, closing the remaining skin with Steri-strips. Prior to that hemovac tubes were inserted. A sterile dressing was applied. The patient tolerated the procedure well. . . .

When I woke up in the hospital after the surgery three weeks ago, I couldn't tell what they had cut out. I was just relieved that they had removed the cancer. I felt pressure across my chest but no pain. I was wrapped from my armpits to my waist in gauze bandages. There were I.V. tubes in my arm and two large tubes coming out from beneath the bandages. Both of the tubes emerging from the white gauze were connected to a plastic squeeze bottle that was fan-folded like the bellows of an accordion.

"It's a drain . . . a hemovac," the nurse explained when she came to inject snake venom called heparin into the I.V. tube in the back of my hand to keep the I.V. line unclotted and freely flowing. "That plastic bottle is squeezed until there is a vacuum. The vacuum drains the blood out of the wound so you don't get an infection." I looked apprehensively at the bright red blood collected in the plastic container. There did not seem to be a lot of blood. It seemed to be seeping out of my chest and not flowing. Each move that I made triggered a spurt of warm liquid somewhere inside the bandages, somewhere inside the tight area in my chest. Warm liquid was moving somewhere between the layers. I could not see any blood flowing beneath the white wall of bandages. I did not feel pain. Nothing spilled out into the plastic accordian-shaped bottle. The drain did not pull a matching spurt of bright, fresh blood out of my chest. It was bewildering. I could not understand what caused the sensations. Perhaps the blood in my body was confused. It used to flow smoothly from heart to muscle to breast but now it was stumbling, trying to find its new path. Perhaps it was crying in frustration. Perhaps it was strange that I was not.

Pathology Report:

The tissue subjacent to the areola contains a stony hard tumor which covers an area measuring approximately 3 x 2.5 x 1.5 cm. Infiltrating Ductile Carcinoma.

This is typed in my medical records. Dictated by a pathologist who probably wore a white smock covered by a black rubber apron. Who, with hands gloved and gloved again to keep out pathogens in dead tissue, probably stood over a stainless steel table looking at a portion of a human breast in a stainless steel basin. The materials of the doctor's work surface are chosen because they will absorb nothing; even the floors are probably concrete poured in a single slab so that they are able to be washed completely clean.

A breast portion in a steel basin, unconnected, an areola and epidermis which temporarily continue to cover a small mound of muscles and glands. Losing warmth, losing elasticity, draining fluid, losing color, it cannot shrink from the glare of the overhead lights as it would invariably have when it was still part of me. It can only sit in its basin, absorbing the cold of the stainless steel, contracting, drying. The areola atop it is a shameless dark brown. A bud that has never bloomed, it has never suckled a baby's hungry mouth. It used to hide dutifully in a white fiberfill bra and refuse to be caressed by any pair of teenaged hands. Now it will offer no reaction to the probing of a scalpel.

Does the doctor pause slightly to inspect the line of demarcation that runs across the skin before drawing his blade through this lump of tissue? Above the areola is a line of demarcation between contrasting hues of light and dark skin. The brown is a sunburn which was at its darkest on the day of the surgery. It is the skin's now useless memory of that day only a week ago when I, thirty-five and invulnerable, washed my car all afternoon wearing a bikini bathing suit top and a pair of jeans shorts under the bright, warm afternoon sun.

Japanese Women Don't Cry

Several days later, when the bandages finally came off I looked curiously at my chest. Where my breast used to be, there was only pale skin which was stretched over a narrow roll of fatty tissue. Beneath that was a white scar held closed by strips of tape pressed up against my ribs. The scar looked tight and bloodless like lips pressed together maybe in fright. Below the scar, there was skin stretched taut across my rib cage and the surprise of motion. I could see the motion of my heartbeat under the skin. There used to be muscles covering my rib cage keeping the secrets deeper in my chest away from observation, but now I could suddenly see the beating of my heart. How odd the pulsating membrane of skin looked as it shuddered rhythmically. Beneath my rib cage, a drain tube emerged from a hole in my skin so matter-of-factly that only red-orange Betadine painted around it gave it fanfare. Another tube emerged from the skin of my back which felt completely numb. The tubes met and emptied into the plastic accordion-shaped hemovac. The color of the liquid in the hemovac had by this time changed from bright red right after the surgery to a calmer more ambiguous bubble gum pink. I looked curiously at my chest. I have read stories that say that this is the point at which most women cry.

Perhaps it was those afternoons in my aunt's kitchen where she served me the previous night's Kokuho rice drenched in strong yellow tea. We ate daikon radishes pickled in brine, vinegar, and sugar; and fish cooked in brown shōyu and grated ginger. She accompanied the astringent tea-soaked rice of each of these lunches with stories about Japanese women who suffered silently through a multitude of terrible things.

"When the samurai wives were captured by the enemy soldiers, they were supposed to commit seppuku, or harakiri. But death is painful and during their suffering they might struggle and fall into a position that was shameful, so before they stabbed themselves with their swords, they would dress in white kimono, tie their legs together at the thighs, then grasp the blades of their short swords and stab themselves in the stomach, turn the sword and cut across their abdomens, all the while not crying out." Japanese women plan ahead for every eventuality.

"When Japanese women have babies, they are silent even during the pain of childbirth. All the other women in the hospital delivery rooms are screaming but the Japanese women are silent." Anyone who would cry out cannot claim to be Japanese.

"There is a ghost story in which a good wife was poisoned by her adulterous husband. She died in agony without crying out, then came back as an obake and gained her revenge on the husband and his mistress." Japanese women have the right to emotional expression only after they are dead.

My aunt is a Japanese School teacher. She paints her face with white foundation, and wears bright red lipstick. Before she draws on her eyebrows with brown pencil, she looks like her head is made of porcelain. She reminds me of one of those life-sized puppets you see in Bunraku theaters with men dressed all in black hovering behind them animating them and giving them their voices.

Medical Report:

Pt. Apparently doing well except for slight anorexia and still w/ postop discomfort, sensation of pulling in left chest.

The scar runs across the left side of my chest and under my arm. The flesh under my arm and the flesh on my back feels as though it has been anesthetized with Novocain. The underside of my left arm and part of my back feel like rubber. They are no longer part of me. When I touch them with my right hand, they feel as though they belong to someone else.

My left breast and the feeling in my upper arm and the upper left back have been removed. But they are not the only things that are missing. The feeling of being safe in my own body has also disappeared. I always felt that I could run and hide if there was danger. I could curl up somewhere, small and tight and close my eyes and stop my breathing and the danger, growling menacingly, would scent my fear but be unable to find me, would pass me by. The danger is inside me now. "Infiltrating ductile carcinoma," means that stray cancer cells circulate in my bloodstream. Each one is able to grow and start whole colonies that can eventually kill me. I cannot run away, but I need to run to feel safe. Safety has been excised with diseased tissue. What's left is a frenzy that eats my energy.

My cousins do not visit. I think it is a protective mechanism. The healthy animals avoiding the sick. Instead, everyone in my family seems to have sent me flowers. There is a basket of lavender roses, arrangements of orchids, large cattleyas and sprays of cymbidiums in white plastic vases, yellow and white chrysanthemums whose petals form frilly spatters or tidy clusters, pikake leis, white ginger leis. Baskets and vases keep coming. They line the counters and congregate on the floors. I sit alone in my room and look at the multitude. The cumulative fragrance weighs down the air around me. I don't have to attend my funeral, I know what it will look like.

Medical Report:

Pt started on chemotherapy last week w/ CMFVP plus tamoxifen and comes in today for her second dose of chemotherapy. Except for slight anorexia, pt. apparently doing well.

There is C which stands for *Cytoxan* which can crystallize in the bladder and make patients urinate blood. The M is *methotrexate* which is also used to treat leukemia and psoriasis and inhibits folic acid. The F stands for *fluorouracil* which sounds like a neon tube for lighting up my bones. The V drug, *vincristine*, is made from the Madagascar periwinkle, and *prednisone* is the P which will make my face swell up like the full moon in August. Last there is *tamoxifen* which except for sterility has no side effects.

Medical Report:

Second chemotherapy treatment. Patient reports she is going crazy.

I know I should speak more to my mother. She asks me continually how I feel. "I'm fine, fine." I tell her. Except when I mention that sounds echo in my ear, so that I feel like I am in a tunnel. Except when I drop my fork when I'm trying to eat because my fingers are getting numb, and I tell her that my shoes feel funny because my toes are also getting numb. Except when she sees the hairballs multiplying in the trash can in the bathroom. And then she asks me how I feel even more and now has taken to standing outside the bathroom door when I am inside chanting an endless stream of advice.

"Don't drink so much Coca-Cola, see, I told you caffeine was bad for you. And you never eat any oranges so you don't have enough vitamin C. Did you remember to drop tissue into the bowl before you go so the water doesn't splash back up on you? Did you remember to wipe yourself from front to back?"

"Ma!" I scream. "Stop it! Stop it!" And I am immediately sorry. I did not scream at her when my father was alive. I think I tried to once when I was thirteen but my father weighed in on her side and yelled at me. Since then I don't remember ever yelling at her until just now. I listen expectantly and half hope to hear my father's angry reaction. But, of course, since he has been dead for three years there is nothing. "Ma, 'nough already," I say in a softer voice. She does not answer but I can hear her quick footsteps echoing down the wooden hallway. The prednisone is affecting my hearing and the sound of her footfalls seems to spiral across the walls and ceiling and echo around me. When I emerge from the bathroom, I walk into the kitchen and sit at the table, my mother looks at me sullenly but does not speak.

"We should talk about how we feel, Ma. That's what the medical social worker said," I claim with authority without apologizing. I know I should be a good daughter and apologize. I know I should stop badgering my mother. But I am driven on and on. Maybe I am getting like big Auntie, and will soon be pounding heads. My mother frowns at me and goes to the sink to wash rice for our dinner.

"Easy for you, we sent you to college so now you know how to talk, talk, talk," she sniffs in irritation. There is a long pause in which the only sound is the rattling of uncooked rice grains against the aluminum sides of the pot in her hands. The metallic patter of rice grains echoes like swirling water in my ears. Then suddenly, "You cried?" she asks without turning toward me.

"About getting cancer?" I ask defensively, thinking she knows that I have so far not shed a single tear.

"No, when Daddy died. You cried?" she asks.

"Only a little at first, but six months afterward I cried when I was driving the car home. I used to cry on the highway all the time when I was driving by myself."

"I never did you know," she reveals. "My friends say that's not good for the body. But I cannot cry. Not even once." She pauses in her rice washing and waits for my reaction.

"You should cry, Ma. That means that you're dealing with your feelings about what happened. It's not good for your health if you don't cry." I try to be sympathetic and hope that she does not sense the irony. She seems to soften at this evidence of my concern and goes on speaking.

"Daddy was different to you, you know. When I had my hysterectomy surgery, he never did take care of me. He never even would wash rice. I had to get up and cook as soon as I came back from the hospital." She inserts the rice pot in the rice cooker and comes to sit next to me at the table. "The social worker who came when Daddy was sick, she told me that at least Daddy told her he appreciated me taking care of him. But I never did cry after he died." She does not look into my eyes and ends up staring at my thinning hair instead. "He never did help me around the house. Men, they all like that, they treat the wife and the daughter different. Everytime you used to get sick he used to blame me. He was really mad the time when you got pneumonia." Suddenly, I have a realization.

"Ma, this is not your fault that I got cancer. It just happened," I say.

"Of course it's my fault, " she says to my surprise. "How can it not be my fault, I'm your mother."

My mother is the oldest daughter in a family of six children. I once saw a picture in a textbook captioned, *Japanese girl, 1920*. It shows an eight- or nine-year-old girl with black hair cut in bangs straight across her forehead. She is wearing a kimono and strapped to her back is an enormous baby. She is the caretaker of this helpless younger sibling. She looks like an ant struggling with a boulder. She wears an expression that is a mixture of fear, grief, and resignation. I have often wondered if it is a picture of my mother.

Mortality

When we are young, our belief in our immortality is thick and durable as denim. We can use it to fashion innumerable futures to wear over ourselves. As we grow older the cloth of our illusion thins gently and inevitably into gossamer transparency.

This is the phone call in which I found out the results of my biopsy.

"Ms. Hayashi, your biopsy. . . ."

"Yes, how bad was it?" I managed to ask through what sounded like the backwash of a jet engine roaring in my ears.

"Well, I don't know—that is to say that there was cancer and it was not cancer from the original site. . . . That is, it has spread."

After a long silence I produced what seemed to be the most logical question. "So how long do I have?"

"The thing is . . . I don't know. It may be a very long time but the point is that it is very serious. It is life threatening. I'm not the one who will deal with this. You need to see an oncologist. . . ."

"So, I'm going to die."

"Well, we are all going to die, Ms. Hayashi, and we cannot know when, but this is very serious. In terms of staging, this is beyond the first stage at this point. But as to how long, I don't know. You need to be evaluated . . . by another doctor, you see . . . soon."

"Today?"

"No . . . but within the week."

This is only the conversation. What is missing in this re-creation is the sound of a raging river of blood rushing in my ears, the roaring of thoughts, the voices urging me to run away, fly away, fly far away. Go now. Run! Run! Run away from the sound of claws tearing through safety. And the smaller voice that is too frightening to listen to. The one that growls that the danger has already invaded my body and is now part of me. I sat on the couch all through that night until the sky lightened into dawn. I sat looking longingly at a bottle full of aspirin, wondering if a whole bottle of little white tablets could become a ticket into oblivion. Japanese women don't cry out in childbirth, they bind their legs together so that they do not fall into a shameful position during suicide. They stare dry-eyed for twelve hours at the possibility of a botched suicide attempt. I sat until the next morning, then, with my belief in immortality and my future shredded into strips around me, picked up the telephone to make an appointment to see the oncologist.

I remember the moment that my mother discovered her own mortality. My mother is putting up the hem on the dress I will wear to my first day in the sixth grade. I make my own clothes but my mother hems them better than I do. She sews with invisible stitches, blind stitches, she calls them. She learned them and drafting, that is creating her own patterns, at sewing school when she was a girl.

"You lucky," she says to me as I sit on the floor where I am laying out the jigsaw puzzle pieces of tissue paper patterns over the long piece of fabric that stretches from the front door to the end of the living room. "You can go to the store and buy the patterns you want nowdays. We had to make our own." My mother frowns as she re-threads her needle. She cuts a new length of thread, moistens one end of the strand in her mouth, then twirls the filaments in the thread together tightly. Holding the thread in one hand and the needle with the other, she attempts to put the end of the thread through the tiny steel eye of the needle. She holds the needle closer to her face then farther away. Blinking in irritation, she removes her bifocals and tries again.

"Getting old . . . ." she sighs.

"How old are you Mommy?" I ask from my seat on the smooth wood floor at the other end of the living room. My mother puts down the needle then thinks out loud and recites the story I have heard many times before.

"You were born when I was thirty-three years old . . . now you are eleven . . . so I'm forty-four. I'm an old lady," she sighs.

"You're not old yet, Mommy. How old was Obachan when she died?" I ask.

"My mother died when she was sixty-nine," my mother muses. "That means I'll be sixty-nine in . . ." she pauses, calculating, then, "in twenty-five years," she exclaims. Then she turns suddenly, her face breaking. "I have only twenty-five years left to live . . . ." Twenty five years. She had married at twenty-seven, she had been married seventeen years, it must suddenly have seemed like the blink of an eye. The stitches unraveling in her lap, her eyes taking me in, she realizes she will abandon me when I am only 36, younger than the age at which her own mother had gone away from her. She wipes her cheeks and turns away from me then stands hurriedly and scurries along the river of fabric that covers the living room floor toward the bathroom at the back of our cottage. Her heels leave little round wrinkled prints on the tissue paper pattern pieces. I can see drops of water where her tears soak into and soften the tissue. Ever since that time, I have often wondered when I would have this same moment of discovery. Until now I have never envied her that moment.

Other Women With Cancer

Saleswomen stare at the wispy strands of my hair and my scalp which is daily becoming more assertive but say nothing. I begin wearing brightly colored scarves to hide my condition. But now in the waiting room of the oncologist's office each week, I am becoming more and more visible. Several old ladies with scarves covering their hair who have ignored me for the last month begin to look at me with interest.

"You picking up your grandma?" asks the little 4'10" woman in the green dress, whose wig is too large and whose lipstick is too red.

"No, I'm going for chemotherapy," I answer. The tiny woman comes to sit next to me, smiles mischievously.

"You going for chemo? What kind of cancer you get?" I am interesting to her. She stares intently into my eyes, her mouth turned up into a grin.

"I have breast cancer," I whisper. She puts a wiry hand on mine. The red, red, nail polish on each of her fingers gleams above her cool, smooth caress. Neither of us is insulated by any illusions and I can feel her vibrant touch against my naked skin.

"Only breast cancer," she beams. "I get liver cancer . . . over three years." She pauses and chortles. "And I went to Las Vegas four times between the chemo you know." She smiles a kiss at me as the nurses call her in for her treatment.

The next week, there is the woman who has multiple swellings on the left side of her skull who struggles to navigate the walkway up to the oncologist's office. She lists to one side, then stumbles toward the railing. I run forward to catch her.

"Why, thank you," she murmurs graciously and I look past the swellings on her skull and directly into her eyes. I am startled that they are still beautiful. She looks at the scarves covering my hair and at the band-aid on the back of my hand, which covers the newest perforation in the green vein that runs across it. She straightens up then caresses my arm.

"You know, I've had this cancer over 14 years. It started as breast cancer then came back and I fought it down," she tells me as she steadies herself. "I had two children to raise you see. And I raised them. But now, well now, I need a little help sometimes." She smiles as she leans into me. I lean back gently, just enough to steady her as I walk her into the oncologist's office.

Then today, there is the tall woman who enters the elevator outside the lab the same time that I do. We both hold our arms bent upward, pressing on the small white squares of gauze taped over the fresh puncture wounds left by the hollow hypodermic needles used to draw blood. She wears a plain cotton dress that looks as if she made it herself. She moves stiffly, as if favoring her left side. She looks apprehensively around the elevator and her eyes come to rest on me. I smile slightly, but it is enough.

"Can you tell me the way to Dr. Ho's office?" she asks hesitantly. Dr. Ho is my oncologist. I look at her face which is ordinary and unadorned by any cosmetics. She would be plain except for her hair, which is long and swept up into a French braid and pinned neatly to the back of her head.

"Yes, you get off on the ground floor and follow the signs to the Palma Building," I instruct her. She manages to look grateful even though it is clear that she is still anxious. I punch the button for the first floor and hold the door open for her as she smiles nervously and begins walking in the direction I have indicated for her. Her hair is the color of garnets and wisps that have escaped the hairpins glow softly in the afternoon sun. I watch her walk down the concrete pathway to the oncologist's office and I cannot make myself leave the elevator to join her. The elevator doors close on me and I find I must ride up to the top floor and back down again before I can see well enough to press any buttons. I cannot make out the numbers through my tears.

BY JIM HARSTAD

THE BLACK AND YELLOW RAFT

ou know why I hate *haoles?*" Hiro Hirata glared at me with a cold intensity I don't usually associate with dark brown eyes.

"No sir," I said.

"It's because every time a *haole* gets a chance . . ."

Waitwaitwait. Let's try again.

This backyard deck where I write sits between two full-grown macadamia nut trees that could make me think I still live out in the country, if I didn't know better. I built it the week after our trip to Japan. It was one of many home-improvement projects inspired by that beautiful family adventure. They reinforced the connection to ancient, rural Nihon I'd felt in the snow-country villages we visited, the feeling that I was almost Japanese.

On a corner of the deck, like a giant's spitout wad of designer gum, lies a deflated black and yellow rubber raft. Beside it are two plastic black and yellow oars, neatly parallel, in contrast to the shapeless lump they were designed to propel. I bought the raft from Ala Moana J C Penney's for less than $30 and used it once one Saturday in a June long ago.

Kaylynne had gone to her sister Yvonne's on the Big Island to be with their father. The expensive, self-winding Seiko he always wore had stopped, a result of his prolonged inactivity. Although the family was able to joke about it, they took it as a serious omen. Candace and Ashley, little more than babies, had gone too. School wasn't out yet for nine-year-old Jared, who stayed home with me. They left on Monday.

On Saturday Big Tiny Zawoski barged into town. It was the summer of his Hawaiian commercial fishing debacle, his personal fast track to Madison and a drama MFA. We were at my homemade koa dining table, a full gallon of hearty burgundy between us.

Jared listened for a while to this gargle-voiced man with forearms as big as my thighs, then went to play with his Transformers. Earlier, I'd promised we'd go swimming. After Big Tiny's call I'd said we would definitely go swimming, but not yet. It was still morning. Plenty of time.

Then it was afternoon. Where had the time gone? "Dad, when are we going swimming?"

"Not yet. There's still plenty of time."

"That's what you said this morning."

"It's still true."

"But when?"

Sudden inspiration. "You know that rubber raft under your bed, the one we got at Penney's?"

"Yeah."

"How'd you like to take that with us?"

"What for?"

"We could go out in it. You could take your pole."

"I guess so. Sure." He'd only gone fishing once or twice, from shore.

"OK, we'll go as soon as you get everything ready. Get your pole and some extra hooks and sinkers. Look around in the back for some Pālolo jumping worms." During the rainy season, our backyard has the world's liveliest angleworms.

"Couldn't we use bread crusts?"

"I guess we could, but worms're better."

"It's dry in the back is why. There won't be any worms."

Big Tiny watched without comment. He'd already said Jared would break some hearts, but that was just one of those things between friends. Unlike me, Big Tiny always says the right thing.

"Bread's OK then. But you know the hard thing to get ready?"

"What?"

"The raft."

"Oh."

Jared still carried babyhood in his dimpled hands and elbows and in the roundness of his face. But it was not a surprised-looking man-in-the-moon oh. It was the inquisitive oh of precocious childhood. It meant if you show me, I'll do it. It meant proceed with instructions. It meant there would be no badgering. No tantrum. I was impressed. Big Tiny was too.

"You have to pump the raft up here."

"Why here?"

"So you don't waste time at the beach."

"Oh."

"Besides, what if it leaks? It's a lot better to find out here than wait till we get to the beach."

"Oh."

"So go get the raft and the pump and bring them out here by the table and I'll show you how to do it. And when you're done we'll go to the beach."

"OK."

Big Tiny and I nodded our approval. Jared knew he was being fooled, but he also knew he was being challenged. And he accepted in the spirit of one who takes challenges seriously and faces them with confidence.

I set the never-inflated raft in the hallway at the end of the table, connected the small hand pump, and made sure it worked. Why handicap him with faulty equipment? It wouldn't be an easy job. Let's not make it impossible.

Jared went to work as Big Tiny and I talked. And laughed. And finished the burgundy. And started on beer and a little blended whiskey I had left over from some time or other. There may have been an occasional backyard pot retreat. Maybe I still had a few of the magic mushrooms I'd gotten that time in Oregon and maybe we had a chew. Or two? We kept talking and laughing.

And Jared kept pumping.

Big Tiny and I looked over now and then to see how things were going. Each time the raft was plumper, and Jared kept squeezing that silly concertina hand pump.

"Looks like he's playing Cajun music," Big Tiny said.

"Jambalaya and a crawfish pieya," I said.

"Cawlijah was a wooden engine," Big Tiny said.

Too soon Jared had the raft full-sized and ready to go. It had been a good hour and a half, maybe more. It was time. We set the raft on the racks of my '68 Beetle. Shoehorned sideways into the back seat, Big Tiny was chuckling and whomping us both on the back for all he was worth, then chuckling some more. "By God, Carlsen, I've got to tell you one thing and I really mean this now, but I don't always like to be around kids and I'm not just saying it because he's *your* kid, but I really *like* your kid just like I like you, just a chip off the old Carlsen block, I guess, right Lars, God *dammer* what a day!"

We were headed for Kāhala. Big Tiny said he wouldn't need a suit. He'd just sit on the beach. The sky was bright and the air was warm—a perfect end to a hell of a day.

There are two alleyway beach accesses in Kāhala. One goes to a broad, sandy strand favored by sunbathers, sexual prowlers, and occasional swimmers. The other goes to a narrow band of jagged rocks bordering a shallow reef of dying coral and is favored by nobody. Except me. We went there.

Big Tiny had a bagful of Bud 16-ouncers. He sat on a rock with the beer in the shade at his feet. He'd have fun watching us have fun. "Catch me a fat ahi," he rumbled at Jared. "I'll take it back and show my skipper what we're here for."

I said, "How do you know your skipper's not here on vacation and just brought you along for entertainment?"

"Not the way he stuffs powder up his nose. He can't afford a day off, let alone a vacation." Big Tiny tipped his head back to finish his can of Bud. You could see the ragged trim line of his beard and his neck two feet thick on shoulders twelve feet wide. He was having a good time, but he'd rather be making money. He'd come to Hawai'i on a hunch instead of going to Alaska on another boat. In Alaska, boats were bringing in a year's wages in a week. A *good* year's wages. Bad hunch.

Jared and I pushed out over the shallow reef. The water was mildly agitated but clear enough to show bottom. I rowed while Jared sat at the stern fiddling with hooks and sinkers. We skimmed over the reef, back and forth, left to right when I alternated oars, rushing in quick surges when I pulled together. Even small gusts of wind altered our course.

"Wait till we get over a hole before you drop your line."

"OK."

"Otherwise you'll snag."

"OK. Dad?"

"What?"

"Do you think I'll really catch anything?"

"Never can tell, but I don't know why not."

"What if they don't like bread crusts?"

"Then you won't. But what if they do?"

"Then I will?"

"Why not? Get ready to drop your line. We're over a hole."

"OK."

I kept the oars busy trying to stay in one place, but the wind came up and the water got choppy. We bounced and whirled. Jared couldn't keep the bread on the hook. Too soft and wet.

"Try it without bait. Sometimes fish get confused in rough water and they'll bite a plain hook."

"Really?"

"I've known it to happen. Or sometimes they get so excited splashing around that they snag themselves by the tail."

"Are you sure?"

"I've known it to happen."

"Has it happened to you?"

"Um, I think so. I haven't been fishing for a long time, but I think when I was a kid I caught a bullhead on a bare hook and I think I snagged a sea-run cutthroat once."

"But you don't remember?"

"It was a long time ago, back in Bear Creek. Anyway, you can ask Big Tiny when we get back because he's a fisherman and I'm sure it must've happened to him. Besides, his memory's better than mine."

"OK."

"OK what?"

"OK, I'll try."

The first time Jared snagged the reef he thought he'd caught Big Tiny's ahi. A few of those and snagging the reef wasn't fun anymore. Before long he'd lost several hooks and yards of leader. He was out of bait, and the old man couldn't even keep the boat still. Fishing sucked. At least this fishing sure did. The surf got higher, rolling in slowly and evenly.

"Put your fishing stuff away," I said. "Let's catch waves."

It was easier to hold the raft's stern toward an oncoming wave than to sit geographically still. As the wave caught up to us and slid under, I had to row hard to keep us from flipping stern-over. We'd surf about thirty yards on each wave. It wasn't far, but it was fun.

Jared sat facing me flat on the bottom at the stern, grinning hard. When a wave picked us up and carried us, he rose up over my head. As it crested and we slid down its backside, I rose up over Jared's head. We teeter-tottered back and forth like that over every wave coming in, and then reversed, forth and back, as I rowed back out.

We were laughing non-stop and I was getting good enough on the oars to make it seem easy. In fact it *was* easy, so when Jared said, "Dad, could I try?" I thought, why not?

"Let's move over here where it's not breaking so much and get you used to the oars."

First he tried to push the oars. When I told him he was doing it bassackward he got so embarrassed that he missed the water on his first pull and fell over. We both laughed, he practiced, and soon he was ready to tackle the big surf. What better time for father-son bonding than facing eternity together in a rubber womb-raft on the amniotic sea? What better way than letting Jared take the oars?

A funny thing happened then. I stopped thinking about what we were doing and started remembering how I'd gotten there. From way back. I'd met Big Tiny and Kaylynne at almost the same time. I'd watched Monday Night Football and drunk free at The Attic in Waikīkī, courtesy of Big Tiny the bartender. I'd studied for my MA comps in a seminar with

Kaylynne. Then Big Tiny had gone to the Northwest to fish and write his book. And I had married Kaylynne.

I thought of the day we'd informed Kaylynne's father, a Big Island widower, of our intentions. He was visiting his sister in Kahaluʻu. We took him to a Chinese restaurant in Kāneʻohe for lunch. His strong, athletic appearance belied truth. Doctors said his youthful passion for spearfishing had contributed to his declining health, the heart condition that would lead to surgery before many years.

He was testy all the way to the restaurant, probably knowing something was up. Probably knowing *what* was up. Clearly he did not like riding in my shambling Volkswagen. Neither would he like his brightest, best-looking child marrying a divorced haole. But we hadn't told him yet, so he couldn't say anything. Yet.

It took a long time to order. Nothing looked good. We settled on egg flower soup, beef broccoli, chicken wings, fried rice. It came. Still nothing looked good. Nothing *was* good.

While Kaylynne ladled our second bowl of soup I broke the suspense by venturing the secret reason for our coming together on that occasion. "Kaylynne and I would like to get married," I said. The "I'm asking your permission" was left to inference. So was the "We're gonna do it even if you don't give your permission."

Masahiro Hirata stared down at his soup while I admired his thick, straight, still-black hair. Then, coldly intense, he glared at me. "You know why I don't like haoles?"

"No, sir."

"It's because haoles never keep their word. You can't trust haoles. That's why I don't like them."

"Yes sir. I'm sure there've been incidents both ways."

"Time after time I hear haoles say one thing and then go do something else. Time after *time.*"

"There's been enough misunderstanding on both sides to go around. I'm sure."

"Every time if a haole can do it he will cheat you. If you catch him at it he'll say it was a mistake or an accident. Words. That's all he's got."

This conversation went on for some time. He never said he did not want his daughter to marry a divorced man, a divorced *haole* man. And he never said we couldn't get married. But he never said we could. Finally it was over. We actually shook hands when we got back to Kahaluʻu. But we didn't shake hands after our modest church wedding, because he didn't attend.

After that he was always friendly, if not cordial. Whenever he came to Oʻahu, he ordered big, home-delivered Chinese meals from downtown, much better than our first one. (I think he assumed I had not acquired a taste for Japanese cuisine. *Could* not?) He told stories and gave me beer, though he drank none himself. Trying to loosen me up, to make me forget he hated haoles. A quiet haole was alien to his experience. He couldn't believe I was quiet by temperament. No doubt he distrusted my reticence. And me. Yet he showed few signs of it.

He loved his hapa-haole grandchildren, but after number three, Ashley, he said I should be castrated. It was one of those funny/unfunny things you might say about somebody you are trying to like and not succeeding. I became less reticent.

"You had *four* kids!"

"That was different. Times were different then."

"How?"

"Everybody had big families. Kids, everybody worked coffee."

"Did *your* kids work coffee?" They hadn't. Neither had he. Extremely un-Japanese, from my haole point of view.

"It's harder now," he said, and we dropped it.

After Kaylynne and I had scraped together the down payment for our small, Joe Pao house, he sent two mac nut trees from Kona. There was no snide note saying we could use them for income. He knew I liked trees; they were a gift. Years passed. The trees grew.

Then, only months before, at Christmas, he'd said I should get the Nobel Peace Prize for my work in making our modest house habitable. He was referring to Lech Walesa and my half-Polish ancestry. It meant he liked me. I had broken the stereotype by not breaking my word. And it wasn't because I hadn't given it—to Kaylynne, if not to him.

He and Kaylynne were sitting beside the fragrant Douglas fir, near the shoji doors I'd built. Stick-thin and frail, he'd long since had triple bypass surgery and valve implants. The valves were expected to last six years, at most. His were going on five and wouldn't be replaced. He'd recently had chemotherapy for cancer. It would be his last Christmas.

Half a year later, Masahiro Hirata's watch had stopped and he lay in his own bed in Captain Cook, my wife at his side. In Honolulu, his grandson sat across from me in a small rubber raft.

Jared had negotiated his first few waves, but the sky had darkened, the wind gusted, and the sea was rising. We were skidding sideways too fast on too big a wave. Then we were underwater. Suddenly I was afraid for Jared, who had never been in storm surf. A strong swimmer, he'd be all right if he hadn't hit his head and didn't panic. I grabbed the rope of the upside-down raft and reached for the coral bottom with my toes. We were in turbulent water over jagged reef. Relax and float shallow. Relax? Where was Jared? *Jared!* Oh. Over there, on the other side of the raft, calmly treading water.

"Hold on to the side of the raft."

"OK."

"Are the oars still in the oarlocks?"

"I've got one." He held it up.

"Then the other one should . . . ah, there it is." The second oar was floating just behind him. When I pointed, he grabbed it.

"Keep holding the raft. I'm gonna swim after the pillow."

The pillow was inflated plastic, about the size of the paper I'm writing on. Yellow on one side and black on the other, it bobbed like a decapitated duck only a few feet away. I took a couple of strokes and reached. Flip. Flip flip. A gust of wind blew it just out of touch. I took another stroke and reached again. Flip. Flip flip. Flip flip flip flip flip flip. Flip. There it rested, farther away than ever. I swam a couple strokes toward it, it flipped again, and I stopped. It was taking me farther away from Jared, whom I had considered in danger only moments before. Small and hard, the pillow was no aesthetic delight and had never served any function. Why had we even brought it? Let it go.

I turned and swam for the raft. Jared and I righted it, and I boosted him over the gunwale before climbing in myself. Then I got Jared back in the stern and set him to bailing with his hands while I took the oars. "Still got your pole?"

"It got tangled in the rope. I'm sitting on it."

"Wanna go in? It's getting kinda cold."

"OK." He looked ready to go.

We'd ride the waves toward shore, then aim at Big Tiny and slide in on the current. When I got ready to line up with the next wave, I noticed the pillow, still bobbing along in about the same place. What the hell—I'd just row over and grab it.

In two strokes the nose of the raft almost touched it. I reached out my sure-fingered right hand. Flip flip flip. Flip flip. Flip flip. Another gust. More strokes. I reached with the oar. Flip flip. More strokes. Another gust.

I got Jared in position to grab it. Another gust. Uncanny! The pillow lured us until we'd rowed and drifted a long way 'Ewa of Big Tiny toward Black Point. Then it just pulled away. Black yellow black yellow black. Yellow black yellow. Black yellow. Black. It flew higher now, kiting away on heavy gusts until we only glimpsed it, a small black dot, heading toward the cliffs. Then it was gone.

I'd turned the raft around to row back toward Big Tiny, but I made little headway against the wind and current. When I stopped rowing I quickly lost everything I'd gained. So I angled toward shore, trying to describe a reasonably straight line of slippage. Everything was bleak as twilight. The sky. The sea.

"I guess we'll never see that pillow again."

"Guess not," Jared hissed through clenched and chattering teeth.

"We'll get back pretty soon."

"Um hmm." Goosebumped and blue, he was stiffly huddled with his back to the wind.

Finally we beached so far down from Big Tiny that we carried the raft across lawns instead of beach rocks. We put the raft on top of the car, and Jared got inside with the windows rolled up. The sun was breaking through again.

Looking for Big Tiny among the rocks, I found nothing but a wet paper sack and some empty cans. "Over here, Lars!" he bellowed. "How about bringing me my clothes?"

He'd gone swimming in his underwear. He didn't want to come out because people were standing at a picture window watching the storm at sea. And him. ". . . almighty, Lars, I was yelling my lungs out at you. Thought you were a goner for the cliffs."

"Couldn't hear you over the wind. Chased that damn pillow."

"What pillow?"

"Ah, nothing. Just the little blowup job that came with the raft. Wasn't worth a shit, but it sure had me humping."

"How about throwing me that shirt?"

With his shirt on, Big Tiny erupted from the water in his skivvies. Still underdressed, to be sure, but Big Tiny thrives on informality. Once inside the alleyway, he quickly dropped his underwear and pulled on his cavernous Wranglers. He later dropped the rolled-up skivvies on the floor of my Volkswagen, but I didn't find them until after I'd taken him to Fisherman's Wharf and gone home. They looked like some feral afterbirth. I left them there.

Jared was still taking his shower—a long, hot one would be good, I'd told him—when the phone rang. It was Kaylynne: her father. She told me the time and how he had been slipping in and out of consciousness. "He knew it was coming," she said. "We could see him closing his eyes and going farther away. We could call him back for a while, just by the sound of our voices. He'd open his eyes and recognize us. But it was hard for him, you could tell. The last time, you could almost see him giving in to it. It was time to go . . . and he went."

Kaylynne talked quietly, in control. But the last three words produced a sob and silence. Hung over, numb with cold, my thoughts garbled and out of reach, I knew I should be sensitive and sympathetic. *Must* be. I'd known this was coming. Instead of memorizing a speech I'd been fooling around, not taking care of business. "Well, I hope you finally feel better," I blurted.

Sensitivity personified. It was exactly what I meant. I *did* hope she felt better. The long vigil was over now, and her father was peacefully at rest. I certainly hoped she felt better, but I knew I hadn't gotten it right. Quick, what could I add? Too late. I held a dead phone.

"Dad—could you get me a towel?"

As I hung up the receiver and went to the linen closet, I thought about what time Kaylynne had said her father died. It was precisely the time Jared and I were chasing the pillow.

During my several days' recovery from intemperance, I did a lot of things imperfectly. I got Jared and me on the correct Hawaiian Airlines flight to Kona, but when a long-time friend who worked the gate slyly tried to funnel us toward first-class I failed to understand until we were already seated in tourist. I was painfully awkward around my mourning, pissed-off wife, who was gorgeous in black even without makeup and would not allow me to speak to her, let alone caress and comfort her. At the wake I almost fought my brother-in-law's best friend for ridiculing my ethnic heritage while we were drinking Chivas. As one of the pall bearers (bottom left corner), the long-sleeved silky shirt I'd picked as aloha attire was conspicuously more formal than what the others wore.

After the ceremony, I was standing by myself at the gate of the cemetery and churchyard. We had put the coffin into the Cadillac hearse and taken off our white gloves. Under a nearby Singapore plumeria was Kaylynne's mother's grave of twenty years. I could see the fresh, crisply squared-off hole near its center. Hiro Hirata's urn of ashes would be placed there. Nobody had dug it. It had simply appeared a few days before.

My brother-in-law and a cousin had been pulling weeds when the grave fell in right before their eyes. Plunk. If the physical reality was easily explained in scientific terms, the symbolism was stark and real. And the timing was spooky. They went home and talked it over. Nobody had gone back until the day of the funeral. They hadn't dared. The hole over Sumio Hirata's bosom was still there, the size of a burial urn. Or a human heart.

That was the community's spiritual take on the death of Hiro Hirata and his long-awaited reunion with the mother of his children. I was happy to accept it and be astonished by it. But I was to have a modest spiritual revelation of my own, astonishing enough, if you are willing to accept certain debatable premises.

While staring at the hole in my mother-in-law's grave, absorbed in plumeria fragrance and who knows what eternal profundities, I heard the sweetest warbling this side of Hartz Mountain. It came from the direction of the old wooden church, where clusters of aloha-shirted men and tailored women stood and talked. At the very tip of the white cross on the square tower above the church entrance sat a bright red male cardinal, singing as loudly, clearly, and sweetly as I have ever heard. Directly behind and above the cardinal hung a perfect, brilliantly colored rainbow.

I looked around to see if anyone wanted to share the experience. Nobody else had noticed. They wouldn't appreciate my breaking into their conversation with my childish observation of a pretty bird. So I only watched and listened. Basking in the moment, you might say. It lasted a long time.

Something drew my attention to the grave. I don't know what. The warbling stopped. I looked up in time to see the cardinal fly behind a giant mango tree toward the mountains. The rainbow, now over the tree, faded to blue. So help me. Just. Like. That.

Most of us got into cars and went back to Yvonne's. What remained of my father-in-law took the Cadillac to the crematorium.

In her day, Sumi Hirata had been a guiding voice in the church choir. But I had never known Hiro or his family to be musical. If you study literature, you see what I'm driving at—the symbolism of the *male* cardinal as the spiritual representation of my father-in-law, blah, blah. But the fact that he had no musical talent, blah, blah. So the cardinal couldn't be *him*. Could it?

When Kaylynne and I got back on speaking terms I told her my story and how my interpretation all fit together except the music. "You always told me your father couldn't sing."

"He can sing now," she said. So.

After the funeral everybody went to Honolulu to relax, and I stayed in Captain Cook to housesit. I did some writing—quite a lot of writing on yellow tablets like this one—that I've still got somewhere but haven't read in years. I wrote about the funeral, of course, and about how on my first morning of housesitting a pair of cardinals perched and sang in a tropical peach tree outside the kitchen window while I ate breakfast. It was where Masahiro Hirata had always eaten breakfast. The warbling cardinals returned twice more while I was there, at exactly the same time on the following two mornings. I didn't see them again. After a week, I carried my tablets home, tourist class.

By the time I got around to taking Big Tiny's salt-encrusted skivvies out of my Volkswagen, they'd bonded hard to the floor. It took a wood chisel to get them loose. I washed, gift-wrapped, and sent what was left of them to Wisconsin for Christmas. The raft had long since been deflated and put back under Jared's bed, where it stayed for a lot of years.

Then came the Great Ground Termite Eradication of Autumn 1990. Everything that wasn't nailed down went outside. Later we took most of it back, but the raft is still here on the deck, like a giant wad of gum, as previously noted. I don't know why we left it out. Or why nobody has ever said, "Let's blow up the old raft and take her for a spin."

Another thing I don't know is why I have never told this story to Jared, who is now taller than me and craggy as a samurai. What are his memories of these events? Like me, and like Kaylynne, he keeps things hidden.

Like memory, creatures of the air flirt in and out of hiding. Doves coo from hillside Christmasberry trees. Bees work wildflowers. Mosquitoes work me. A pair of cardinals visits daily at a feeder in one of the mac nut trees. They are more raucous and demanding than sweetly melodic, but we love them. They didn't ask to be city birds.

BY JOHN HECKATHORN

HANALEI

Every time I get divorced I cry, big blubbery bursts of tears, usually at dinner time. My soon-to-be-ex-wife Diane finds these tears at the table suspicious. I'm not upset she's leaving me, she insists; I'm upset that I won't have anyone to cook my dinner. An unfair allegation if I've ever heard one, because Diane is a horrid cook and because, despite all good sense, I am going to miss her, her ramrod-straight posture, as if life were a military school, and her curly hair cut short like a helmet around her head, and her full lips set like a prune in disapproval, usually of me. I've lived so long with her disapproval, I'm afraid I'll collapse once it's gone, undone by the sudden lack of opposition.

Divorce is misery, all that loss coming at once, lost people, lost hopes, and that sense of loss which comes from knowing that you've screwed up once again. I don't want you thinking that I get divorced all the time—just twice, as many times as I've been married. I realize I'm risking reader sympathy here. *Who is this guy?* I can hear you thinking. *What's wrong with him that he can't stay married?* And you're proving exactly the point I'd like to make. Get divorced once and everyone's ready to cut you a little slack: You married too young, you picked the wrong person, anyone can make a mistake. But get divorced twice by the time you're 32 and everyone thinks you're a criminal.

I'm trying not to let it bother me. The purpose of life, as far as I can tell, is not to stay married; it's to be happy as much of the time as possible. Again, that's as far as I can tell: I've been known to be wrong about these things.

Actually, now that I reflect on it, the purpose of life is to stay alive. It's better, almost everyone agrees, to be alive than otherwise. If, of course, you're facing terminal cancer, or the certainty of torture, or the destruction of everything that makes your life worth living, then killing yourself might be a reasonable alternative. But you can't be expecting me, just to prove I'm a serious person, to start thinking about suicide. Which is why I say that the purpose of life is to be as happy as possible: The second you become persuaded otherwise, you begin entertaining gloomy thoughts.

Of course, lots of people lead long and satisfying lives immersed in deepest gloom, my soon-to-be-ex-wife Diane among them. These people do not commit suicide; they take deep pleasure in thinking the rest of us are shallow. What you need to be a successful suicide is not so much gloom as anger. Some months ago at the university where I work, someone's girlfriend went up to his room in the high-rise dorms and told him they were through. *We need to start seeing other people*, she probably said. *We're no good for each other anymore. I hope we can still be friends.* You've probably been through a similar scene; no matter which party you are, it's never pleasant. To show his displeasure, this particular broken-hearted lover plunged out his open window, ending up on a concrete courtyard 18 floors below with a squashy-sounding thump.

Nice, yeah? A nice way of telling your girlfriend *I hate you* and making sure she hears it, for years and years, even in her dreams. Nice also because our broken-hearted lover stepped out of life in front of a stunned audience. The courtyard was filled with students on their way to class. A good number of them screamed. A few, especially those who had been closest to where he landed, stepped into the bushes to blow lunch. Some began to rush around aimlessly, but most stood stock still, shocked at the way death had jumped out at them in public. One of them happened to be Lisa Tanabe, a tall, intelligent young Japanese woman with short black hair and an astonishingly beautiful face. With the fascination of someone glued to the television screen, she listened to the shrieks and astonished curses give way to rumors, saw the firemen roll up and wrap the ex-boyfriend in a green plastic tarp. When the firemen unrolled a hose and began unceremoniously to spray the concrete clean of blood, Lisa hurried away and, without thinking much about it, ended up where she'd been headed in the first place—my 1:30 writing class.

She was a little late. She slipped into her seat in the front row, took out her notebook, and sat staring into space. She was usually bright-eyed and eager, but I assumed her ongoing religious crisis had for the moment overwhelmed her. About a year earlier when her mother had suddenly died, Lisa had fallen into the hands of some evangelicals, who convinced her that the best way to escape her grief was to accept Jesus as her personal savior. They baptized her in the surf off Waikīkī and told her that the point of life was to do what they said Jesus said she ought to do, which was to throw herself into making more converts for the evangelicals. Her only problem was that she was a normal, healthy 21-year-old, who could hardly resist sleeping with her boyfriend, which the evangelicals assured her was exactly what Jesus didn't want her doing until she could marry.

So Lisa had some unhappy days, poised between the desires of the flesh and the prospect of eternal damnation. Thinking that she was no more damned than usual, I went about my business, explaining the rigors and joys of the English sentence, and everything was quiet until Charles produced the following example of a periodic sentence: "The cocktail glass, propelled off the lānai falling by a careless elbow, picking up speed according to Galileo's law of falling bodies, accelerating 32 feet per second, fell."

I didn't think it was a great sentence, but I liked the way it came down heavily on the verb *fell*. Janice put up her hand and said it would be a better sentence if Charles had left out Galileo's law of falling bodies, and several people agreed. Especially Lisa, who sat up very straight and said in a quiet, distinct voice, "He screamed all the way down."

It was like a poem: Nobody understood her, but it sounded like she knew what she was talking about. She said it once more, then broke down into quiet, decorous sobs. "They said he jumped on purpose. His girlfriend."

"Who?" I asked. I was still thinking about Galileo and the cocktail glass.

"I don't know!" said Lisa. "How should I know? He just jumped."

Then Carla spoke up. Carla, who up until that moment I had thought of as the girl with too much make-up who cut too many classes. She'd been inside the dorms when it happened, arriving in the courtyard in time to watch the ambulance drive off and the firemen hose down the concrete. Now she leaned forward and rubbed Lisa's shoulder, explaining to the rest of us what had happened. Lisa stopped crying a minute and gathered her books together. "I'm sorry, I'm sorry," she said.

Carla got up to walk her home. "It'll be all right," I said as they walked out the door—which convinced nobody, especially not Lisa. Halfway out the door, she turned, looking me straight in the eye, and said, "It bothers me he might be damned. They keep telling me suicides are damned."

"No," I said. But I lied. I think we're all damned. Consider what is going to happen to you even if you don't throw yourself out an 18th-story window in your early twenties. If you're lucky and don't catch some wasting disease at thirty; if the things and fools who run the world's countries don't shoot you or napalm you or unleash thermonuclear hell in your neighborhood; if your car doesn't blow a tire and send you spinning into a lane full of oncoming traffic; if no one throws you into prison for your political beliefs or into a concentration camp for perhaps no good reason at all; if none of the unimaginably awful things that happen to ordinary, perfectly nice human beings happen to you—what then?

You get inevitably older each day. You watch them bury your parents, your older friends, your contemporaries. Your dreams, being dreams, go mostly unfulfilled. Your children, if you're fortunate enough to have them in the first place, turn into people you never expected. You get old, get sick, and die.

And that's the best that can happen.

So I'd advise you to pause before condemning me as shallow when I say that the point of life is to be happy, to have a good time if at all possible. I don't want it to sound like I'm inviting you to a party. And I don't even want to sound like I'm telling you *how* to have a good time. Some people like their beef rare, some people like their fish raw. Some like girls, some like boys, and some like working themselves to death. Some like sleeping till noon, and some like getting up at dawn and running ten miles.

Do what you want. All I know is that my idea of a good time, at the moment, is to sit here on this beach chair, my clipboard propped against my knees, writing one sentence after another.

Not your idea of a good time? You have to consider the setting.

This is a story about Hawai'i, although you might be excused for not noticing that till now. It is a story about Hawai'i because that's where I live, in Honolulu, and because that's where I am at the moment, not Honolulu, but the long white-sand beach of Hanalei Bay, about 30 feet from the water. It is the last weekend of October, starting to cloud over late in the afternoon, but still warm. Hanalei, for anyone who doesn't know, is on the North Shore of Kaua'i, which is the northernmost of the Hawaiian Islands—or at least the most northern of the Islands anyone would want to go to, the rest being rocks and reefs now slipping slowly back into the ocean and being inched toward Siberia by the movement of the Pacific plate, having had their geological moment of glory as islands.

Hanalei has to be one of the great places on the earth. I haven't been to the Greek Isles, or to the South of France, or to Sri Lanka where the waves travel 6,000 miles from Antarctica without stop to crash onto the beach, but those places have to be great indeed to be better than right here: a nearly circular bay two miles across, with soft-sand beach sloping away gently into the bright blue water. The bay is at the end of a long, wet valley, still agricultural. It is peaceful, quiet, and nearly deserted at 3:30 on a Saturday afternoon. There are some houses dotted along the beach, small ones, but you can hardly see them. What you can see, starting about 60 or 70 feet from the shore and ascending the steep lava walls of the valley, are lawns and coconut palms and plumeria trees and flowering hibiscus bushes and ti plants and all manner of luxuriant vegetable life. I am surrounded by green, staring out at the blue sky and the blue water. I feel wonderful.

This is all, of course, too good to last. Not only is Kaua'i eroding an infinitesimal bit at a time, so that in a few million years it too will be a rock on its way to Siberia, but Hanalei itself doesn't have that long. Already the state Department of Transportation has plans for the narrow metal bridge which is the only way into the valley. They've let it go badly; now it's rusty and unsafe and due to be replaced by a multimillion-dollar multi-lane concrete monster, a bridge big enough to accommodate trucks and construction equipment. What then? Hotels, shopping center, golf courses. Condominiums with quarter-of-a-million-dollar one-bedroom apartments. Rich people from the Mainland and Canada and Japan. High-rises up and down the bay.

Oh well, it will last until Thursday when I have to fly back to Honolulu. It will probably last long enough for me to come back a few more times in my life. When there isn't any Hanalei, I won't be around to notice.

Why am I here? First, because my friend Randy, who used to copy my geometry homework in high school, has become a millionaire selling guitar amplifiers and can afford a house on Hanalei Bay. He's too busy to use it much, having to stick close to the amplifier factory in California. Most of the time he rents his house out, but he called me and said his rental for October had fallen through and I was welcome to the house; just pick up the key from the real estate agent.

Second, I'm here for a few days because my soon-to-be-ex-wife Diane needs the space—sorry, that's the way Diane talks—she needs the space to pack up all her stuff from our condo in Honolulu and ship it back to New Jersey. Why anyone in their right mind would want to move from Hawai'i to New Jersey is beyond me. But Diane is looking forward to it, having hated paradise from the moment she walked off United Airlines Flight 126 four years ago. She actually seems happy about having a one-way ticket to Newark Airport, but she needs the space to pack—and also, I'm guessing, to see her lover, whom I'm not supposed to know about. She hasn't been discreet. She haunts the mailbox. She says she's writing for jobs. But I doubt whether many firms write their prospective employees a handwritten letter each day. She was so anxious to get us off on time that I suspect her lover, whoever he is, flew in from New Jersey the same day the Beast and I flew over to Kaua'i.

The Beast, my two-year-old daughter Beatrice, is sound asleep now in a little tent improvised from an old blanket, a boogie board and a broken beach chair. On my other side, leaning against a back rest, sits my friend Willie, reading a book called *Blood and Money*. Willie frowns a little as she reads, concentrating, I guess. Every once in a while she gives a little chuckle of appreciation.

"You look like you're having a good time," she says, tipping her sunglasses down on her nose and looking over at me. "What's that you're writing? Another story?"

"So far it's seven pages on the purpose of life. I put in a section about that suicide Lisa saw last year, you know, the kid who threw himself out the dorm window."

"Don't remind me. I had to write a 10-page report for the chancellor on that one. He was in the College Opp program, and I had to explain why my advisers didn't prepare him better for college life. As if we could have known." She shakes her heavy head of curls. "This year I was tempted to put a little paragraph in the registration materials about always looking on the bright side."

"You can put my story in."

"Don't tell me you're giving people advice." She takes the clipboard from me and flips through the first few pages. "I like the voice," she says. "But when are you going to learn that the whole point of a story is desire, conflict, sex, violence?"

"What about happiness?" I asked.

"I don't think it's possible," says Willie. "It's almost impossible to write about a good character, and it's even more impossible to write about happiness. It'd be nice if you could do it. Wouldn't it be perfect if you could just capture a day at the beach like this, the sun rippling off the water, the trade winds against your skin, the smell of marijuana from the parking lot, the baby asleep, the sound of your pen scratching across your pad, then drinks, dinner, bed? But face it, Walt, happiness just isn't interesting."

She resumes reading her book about murder among the Texas millionaires. The Beast stirs, then falls asleep again. There are a couple of hours to cocktail time. Time enough for 20 or 30 sentences if I keep at it. Willie is an extraordinary-looking woman, and she has been my best friend for several years now. I wouldn't even put her in a story, not under her real name, anyway, if she hadn't been so superior about what to put in and what to leave out. Besides, anyone who has sat through all my ramblings on the purpose of life is good enough to be introduced to Willie.

Desire, conflict, sex, and violence. Willie sits next to me in her shiny purple one-piece bathing suit that shows off her large breasts. Diane, with her military posture, her chest flat except for her nipples standing at attention all day, was jealous of Willie's breasts, sure that I was waiting for the first opportunity to grab them. I have never been a devotee of huge breasts; they seem to me somehow uneconomical. On Willie, however, they look sort of generous and cheerful. She also has the world's most magnificent ass, which you can't see at the moment because she's sitting on it. What you can see of her is very nice, except for the five or six pounds around her middle which she could afford to lose.

The joy of writing these sentences—outside of their truth—is that Willie will be outraged when she reads them. This is adolescent, sexist, she'll say, concerned only with her outward physical appearance. Besides, she'll hasten to point out, I could afford to lose five or six pounds myself.

Still you'd want to see Willie, her huge head of curly dark hair, her unburnt face, peeling nose, and behind the sunglasses dark Scorpio eyes which sparkle with mischief, but reveal nothing, nothing at all.

For about two years I was in love with Willie, back when the two of us shared a tiny office and taught writing every semester. Since that time Willie and I have become assistant deans, she first, then me following her example, and we hardly see each other from week to week. Before we rose in the world, however, we fell in love. She was married, I was married, her husband was a bastard, my wife was pregnant. Finally, her huge, handsome husband left her. We saw each other every day; in fact, I do not think there was ever a period when I worked so hard, where I could hardly wait to get to the office every morning. We were hopelessly in love, we never said anything, not about that, anyway, although we spent hours and hours talking about everything else. Finally, one Friday afternoon when we were discussing how to teach the right-branching sentence, I threw my arms around Willie and started kissing her. "I think that was a mistake," said Willie. "Now we're really in the soup."

But nothing came of it, not really. Diane watched me like a hawk, and I was trying to be faithful. Only a creep, went my reasoning, would start up an affair while his wife was suffering through the Hawaiian heat carrying his child. Willie had some doubts about whether she ought to sleep with somebody married. And so, except for some fervent grapplings at odd moments, nothing happened. Once we took off all our clothes and got into bed—but it was the night after Beatrice was born. Diane was still in the hospital, and I couldn't, I just couldn't. So I got back up, put on my clothes, and left.

That was two-and-a-half years ago. Now the baby has grown into the Beast, the world's hungriest and most aggressive toddler. Now Diane is leaving me. "You can marry Willie now if you want," she says. Diane has a way of ignoring inconvenient facts. One of which is that Willie has already found a new husband, Emerson Chang, who is at this moment skimming the waves of Hanalei Bay on his flashy-looking windsurfer with its bright orange sail. Willie and Emerson have been married about a year, after living together for almost that long, and they seem very happy. I didn't marry Willie when I had the chance because I was trying hard to stay married to Diane, whom I couldn't make happy no matter what I did, and who couldn't stand living in the best city in the United States, Honolulu, and who, despite all her anti-racist rhetoric, never could adjust to living in this most Asian of American towns, where even the most militant and anti-authoritarian woman social worker was just one more loud haole. Damn Diane, anyway.

Willie hits me on the arm. "I just saw Emerson's board fly up in the air and I can't see him anywhere."

"Isn't that him?" About a quarter-mile out I see Emerson's board. Emerson isn't on it. By straining hard, I can pick out his dark head bobbing as he swims back to the board.

"I think he's in trouble. Why don't you swim out and see how he's doing?"

"He looks all right. It's calm out there, and he's a better swimmer than I am."

"Walter!" says Willie in a stern tone. I set down my clipboard and pen, pick up my goggles, glance apprehensively at the Beast, sleeping blonde and pink under the shade of the blanket. "I'll watch her. Just go."

I stand up and start stepping across the hot sand. "Don't rush out there like you're going to rescue him," says Willie. "Just pretend you want some exercise and happen to be swimming in his direction. But don't be all day about it."

I'm not a bad swimmer, but it was a solid 10-minute swim out to where Emerson was. My heart was pounding and my goggles were misted over by the time I found him. He'd gotten the windsurfer right-side up and was sitting on it, rubbing his eyes. "Hey, you all right?"

"Willie send you out to check on me?" asked Emerson. "I thought I was getting real radical. Then I leaned too far back and lost the board. I think it got me, or the sail got me, on its way back down, banged my head, and now I got something in my eye."

"Blood," I said. "That's blood. Looks like you've got a cut right there above your eyebrow."

"Shit. Willie's going to laugh at me."

"She's not going to laugh at you. She's worried."

"First she's going to make sure I'm OK, then she's going to laugh," said Emerson. "I went and brought this thing instead of my surfboard, thinking it was safer." He pulled himself up on the board and lifted the sail. I looked back toward shore; we were a long way out, and I wasn't looking forward to the swim in. "Hang on," said Emerson. I got a firm hold on the back of the board. Emerson set the sail, and suddenly I was yanked along the water like I'd been tied to a motorcycle.

When he first moved in with Willie, I used to hate Emerson Chang. Not only had he gone through Stanford Law sixth in his class, not only had he spurned the family firm until he'd proved himself on his own, not only did he run every morning and lift weights a couple nights a week, not only was he handsome, amiable, intelligent, modest, and good to Willlie and her daughter, not only, in other words, was he almost infuriatingly perfect, but he also wrote stories, good tight little stories in pidgin, that seemed to capture the life of these Islands in a way I never could. As I got to know him better, I realized that he had some faults: he drank a bit more than was good for him and argued with Willie all the time, although it is almost impossible not to argue with Willie.

The one thing Emerson was not, however, was talkative. Which led me to believe he'd been more shaken up by falling off the board than he was letting on. Because, despite the fact that it was terribly inconvenient, especially for me, to have a conversation while being towed in, Emerson wouldn't shut up.

"Willie's going to make fun, I just know it. Just like my mother, just like her. Chinese mothers are supposed to pamper their sons, but mine used to make fun of me whenever I didn't do what she wanted. She used to hate it when I surfed in high school. Good Chinese boys are not supposed to waste their time surfing; they're supposed to graduate top of their class from 'Iolani. So every time I got the smallest bit hurt, she'd start in making fun of me. I suppose now Willie's going to be on my case. You think you inevitably marry someone who's just like your mother?"

"Willie isn't like your mother," I said. But I swallowed a lot of water so it came out "Willie glug akkk spit mother."

"Yeah," said Emerson. "Just like my mother, except louder, of course. More merciless. They say if you get divorced you marry the same woman over and over. Is that true? You seem a lot happier now you're breaking up with Diane. But this is twice around for you, right? You must know a thing or two about the ways of the heart. How come you married your first wife?"

"Passion," I said.

"How come the second?"

"I thought I was being sensible."

"And neither worked," said Emerson. "Figures."

A gust of wind jerked the sail, the board lept forward. Rather than be dragged choking through the water, I let go. Emerson, leaning back on the board, holding on to the sail with two hands, shot toward shore. I swam quietly after him.

When I finally reach shore, Emerson is sitting on the beach, being comforted by Willie. The Beast is awake and crying. "She just woke up," says Willie.

"Hello, Beatrice," I say. "What's wrong?"

"Juice," she says and stretches up her arms to be carried into the house. I heft her up into my arms. "You're getting too heavy to carry," I say. "Juice," she says.

"You all right?" I ask Emerson, who is holding a towel to his wound. "Fine."

He looks a little pale, sitting on the sand, Willie's arms around him. I carry the Beast up to the house. Lisa, wearing a red bikini, looks up from the table where she is chopping vegetables for dinner and smiles, "Hello."

It is the same Lisa, Lisa Tanabe, who watched the suicide almost a year ago. Since then she's gotten out of school, broken up with her boyfriend, extricated herself from the clutches of the evangelicals, moved out of the house into her own apartment, and into my arms. We have been lovers for almost four weeks now, ever since I spotted her one evening at the McCully Zippy's, eating chili rice. I cannot look at her without feeling stunned. Her face is still astonishingly beautiful. The first time I ever took her out of one of the long, shoulderless, flowered sundresses she favors, I was shocked at how little there was of her, how nice what there was was. Her skin is honey-brown from the sun; she looks like a long, sweet strand of butterscotch toffee.

What is she doing here? Making dinner. It's her turn. As I set the Beast down on her own two feet, Lisa's knife flashes diagonal slices from a daikon. All around her are little saucers full of cut green onions, bamboo shoots, bean curd, garlic, watercress, peppers, ginger, eggplant.

"Looks like a ton of food," I say.

"We'll eat."

"Lisa, Lisa," says the Beast, stamping her legs up and down on the carpet. "Juice, juice."

"You want juice?" says Lisa. "Hang on a minute."

"I'll get it."

Both Lisa and I go for the refrigerator. "You look wonderful," I say.

"A little burnt from all that tennis this morning." She points out the red on her shoulders. "I wish we could stay here forever. I can't believe that in a few days I'll be back writing publicity brochures for HMSA."

I put my arms around her when I see the Beast climbing a chair to get at the table. I figure she, insatiable, is about to grab a handful of food, but—and by this time I'm already moving Lisa aside and moving toward the table—she goes straight for the knife Lisa left on the cutting board. "Don't!" I scream, and defiantly Beatrice picks it up by the blade and holds on tight, pulling it away from my grasp. She screams, but she won't let go of the knife, so fixed is her intention of keeping it away from me. I don't want to fight her for the knife, for fear she'll cut herself worse. "Daddy," she screams at me angrily. She's telling me to leave her alone. Finally, she seems to realize I am not causing the pain in her hand and flings away the knife, which clatters to the table. A drop of blood, then another spatters onto the white daikon. I grab her hand; she is still fighting me; there is a cut straight across her palm. She hits me with her free fist, then throws herself into my arms.

I carry her over to the sink and unfold her hand under a stream of running water. She starts to sob. The cut is deep, but not too deep. I try to hand her to Lisa, so that I can get the bandages and the antibiotic cream out of my suitcase, but now she screams and won't let me go. Lisa goes to find the bandages. In walk Willie and Emerson. The Beast starts screaming all over again.

"More blood," says Emerson. "Must be some punk rock fashion. She OK?"

"I turned my back for two seconds and she grabbed the knife." I am thinking of what Diane will say.

"Kids always grab exactly what you don't want them to," says Willie.

"Want to be blood brothers?" Emerson asks the Beast. He uncovers the cut in his right eyebrow. It is still bleeding heavily. The Beast screams.

"Maybe I should have said blood sisters," says Emerson. "Blood persons. I think I better lie down. I feel a little woozy."

Lisa reappears with the plastic bag full of first aid stuff. I put cream on the Beast's wound and, fighting her to keep her hand open, wrap it in a clean white bandage, taping it down with adhesive tape. "All better," I say. "Hurts," says the Beast and begins picking at the ends of tape, trying to get the bandage off. "She going to be OK?" asks Lisa.

"I think so." But by the time I get the kid into the shower to clean up the rest of her and get the sand and blood off me, I am sure that if I don't take Beatrice to the doctor, Diane will fix me with a stare so chilly that my heart will freeze. After our shower, Lisa reading the kid a story on the couch, I sit down with the skinny Kaua'i phone book and start calling doctors. It is Saturday afternoon and after a dozen phone calls, I have managed to contact a dozen answering services or, more probably, the same answering service a dozen times. At last I get a cheerful-sounding doctor named Honey, whose office is in Princeville. He takes checks and credit cards, he says, and will wait for us in his office. We shouldn't have any trouble finding it.

"We're going to take Beatrice to the doctor," I tell Willie.

"Wait a minute," says Willie. "We're coming with you."

Dr. Honey, when we found his office sandwiched between the gift shops and resort boutiques, was in his youthful fifties, slim, tanned, dressed for tennis. He had a vaguely British accent and a rapid, businesslike manner. He only glanced at Beatrice's cut hand, although unwrapping the bandage was enough to send the Beast, who was calm all the way here in the rental car, into hysterics once again. "Clean wound, not too deep. You scrubbed it up well, I suppose. No problem. Now, now, don't cry. You're a pretty little girl. Healthy lungs, though." He re-wrapped the bandage around her hand, then turned to Emerson, who was half-leaning against the wall, trying to look casual. "Let's get you on the table. You're going to need a few stitches along that eyebrow. Surfboard?"

"Windsurfer," said Emerson.

"Leaves the same kind of marks."

Emerson, pale, climbed onto the green vinyl examining table and lay down, crackling the paper cover underneath him. "I'm going to ask you all to leave," said the doctor to the rest of us. "Can't stitch with a steady hand if I'm worried about one of you fainting on me." He gestured at the door.

For the next half-hour I pace the tiny waiting room, my arms growing heavy as I carry Beatrice back and forth, trying to keep her calm. The moment I stop moving, she resumes her crying. Willie, too, is restless, sitting down, flipping through a magazine, jumping back up, pacing to the door through which I can hear Emerson's muffled voice. Lisa is busy cutting pictures out of a magazine with her nail scissors. "What are you doing?" I ask. When she hands the pictures to the Beast, the baby quiets immediately. I let her down to the floor and she arranges the photos in patterns on the carpet.

"Where's Pretoria?" Lisa asks, pointing to the doctor's framed medical diploma.

"South Africa."

Emerson emerges through the doorway, a neat square of tape over his shaved eyebrow. "Very stylish," says Willie.

"I need the checkbook." Willie hands it to him out of her purse. "How much do I owe you?" he asks the doctor.

"About 90 should do it," says Dr. Honey amiably.

Scowling, Emerson writes out the check. "Thank you," says the good doctor. "Always glad to help someone out. Remember: No alcohol, and if you have any of these symptoms, call my service right away." He hands Willie a mimeographed half-sheet of paper titled *Warning Signs of a Concussion*. "If he starts acting loony, bring him back, won't you?"

"Maybe we should just leave him," says Willie. "Otherwise we'll have to make a dozen trips."

Emerson glares at her. The doctor looks puzzled, then realizing it's a joke, laughs harshly, sending Beatrice back into tears.

"Why did you come here from South Africa?" Lisa asks the doctor as we are leaving.

"Had to get out before the bloodbath. Besides, it's paradise here." He smiles at Emerson. "Of course, no place is perfectly safe."

That night, the Beast asleep in her own room, Lisa's five-course Chinese dinner all consumed, we sat at the table talking story. Emerson was wearing sunglasses to hide the growing bruise around his eye. Willie started teasing him about going Hollywood. Emerson mentioned her weight. Willie countered with what a pig he'd been at his cousin Nalani's wedding. As long as they were talking about Nalani's wedding, Emerson said, they might discuss Willie's unpleasant remarks to his Auntie Ethel. "I think 'Stuff it, you old fool' was a bit harsh, don't you? I mean, she's a 60-year-old woman with four grandchildren. You could show a little respect."

"Haoles aren't filial," said Willie.

Lisa's small foot banged my shin under the table.

"We're not talking about ancestor worship here," said Emerson. "We're talking about common courtesy."

"Lisa and I are going to take a walk," I said.

"Have fun," said Willie, waving us away. She poured herself another glass of wine and turned to Emerson. "If you think I'm going to sit there and let her lecture me about how selfish I am for not having more children—I don't care if she is your aunt, Emerson."

I checked the Beast—sleeping soundly—and stepped outside with Lisa. The night was still, the beach empty, the only sound the soft susurrus of the surf. Overhead hung a plump yellow moon, nearly close enough to touch. As we crossed the beach, the moon seemed to hang more and more heavily above our heads.

"The moon is famous," said Lisa.

It struck me funny. Of course the moon was famous. It was the same moon everywhere, looming over Bayonne, New Jersey, lowering over

Wiesbaden, dominating the sky of Jakarta, Beijing, Osaka. The moon, goddess of all our lunacy, well known in all times and places.

"No," said Lisa. "The moon at Hanalei is famous." She began singing a song in Hawaiian: "Ku'u Ipo Ka He'e Pu'e One."

"Is that about the moon at Hanalei?" I asked.

Lisa smiled. "I forget the song about the moon. This one means, 'My love is an octopus on the sands of the beach.' Funny, yeah? My love is an octopus."

Tangled in each other's arms, we walk along the waterline under a moon as large and threatening as love. The water is warm, and finally I cannot resist stripping off my shorts and launching myself into the water. When I look back, Lisa starts to lift her dress, hesitates—there is no one more modest, in public, than Lisa—then with a quick scan round the deserted beach, pulling it over her head, dropping it on the sand, she runs for the water, arms crossed over her small breasts. As we swim, tiny microorganisms in the froth around us phosphoresce and our bodies are outlined with light.

When we return dripping to the house, Willie and Emerson have retired to their room, their voices still raised in a good-natured quarrel. Lisa and I shower, slip into bed. With two arms and two legs apiece we turn ourselves into love's eight-limbed octopus until, tired, we fall asleep.

Morning, bright and cheerful, I wake up before seven, without a trace of tiredness or a hangover. Lisa breathes softly on the pillow next to me. I listen to the sounds of early morning and realize that Beatrice is awake, playing in her bed. She is a good kid and has learned that adults are unpredictable when roused too early in the morning. She always amuses herself for a while before demanding everyone else wake up. I struggle out of bed and fetch her. "Daddy!" she screams and launches herself out of the bed into my arms.

I get both of us cleaned up and outside in our swimming suits before we wake anyone else. Once I set her down, the Beast runs toward the water, her little buns bouncing in her red Wonder Woman swimsuit. In the early morning light she looks cherubic, round and pink, and filled with joyous energy. But I am not one to confuse children, especially my own, with angels. Beatrice is as human a creature as I have ever encountered: vain, greedy for her own pleasure, impatient, ignorant. She doesn't understand that the waves to which she runs so eagerly can drown her. Or that knives will cut her, that falling off the porch will break her small bones, that cars will destroy her with a quick bump. She does not understand on this tender morning that love is an octopus ready at any moment to seize her heart and pull it under.

Nor does she understand that she is soon to be shuttled 5,000 miles every six months from one parent to the other. Diane is worried that living in Hawai'i will distort her picture of the world. Diane has a point. What do you tell a child who has run across the sands at Hanalei that will prepare her for New Jersey?

I run after her across the beach, one of my strides covering as much of the white sand as four of hers. Within moments I am beside her, scooping her up into my arms. "No," she cries and beats on me with her bandaged fist. "Got you," I say and tickle her stomach. She shrieks and throws her arms around my neck. "Leggo," she says and clings tighter. I carry her toward the gentle line of surf.

There is also much I do not understand. I do not understand why this small creature clinging to my neck loves me so uncritically, and why my love for her seems to transcend the pain of our circumstances. I do not understand why all of a sudden I have Lisa, the most tender and beautiful of lovers, lying sexy and asleep back in the house. I do not understand why there should be a place as perfect as Hanalei Bay, radiant in the still cool morning air. And I do not understand why I, of all the world's miserable hundred millions, should be standing here, my daughter around my neck, fresh croissants and coffee waiting for me back in the house, surf curling round my toes, happy.

WIZARD

1999, oil on illustration board

BY CRAIG HOWES

THE RESURRECTION MAN

Kona

saiah had been walking behind the bulldozer, checking for bones, so when it went over the ridge he didn't see the 'ohana members right away. They were sitting directly between the survey stakes marking the sides of the road corridor, and they certainly weren't going to move just yet. The dozer stopped, its blade rearing up, and Walter, the driver, told Isaiah to get Curtis from the workshed. It was a quarter-mile back, and Isaiah walked slowly, since he knew the boss would be mad. He also knew what was coming next, and that made him feel bad. About fifteen minutes later they walked back up the slope—Curtis, the construction foreman, in the lead, the police in the middle, and Isaiah well back. Walter was still sitting on his rig, smoking, looking anywhere but in front of the blade. Sitting quietly, their *ti* leaves and *lau hala* mats ranged about them, the 'ohana didn't even look up as the police moved toward them. This was the third time the police had removed the Hawaiians from this site, so there wasn't need to say much.

Then came the moment that always made Isaiah feel worst. Ben rose from the ground and lifted his arms slightly—not pleading, not threatening, simply gesturing. The police stopped. After what seemed an hour the sisters behind Ben got up and started walking down the ridge to the police vans below. Ben followed them down, eyes ahead, the police never touching him, and Arnold, the 'ohana lawyer, walked beside the police, talking about the road, about trespassing, about TV.

Standing to one side, not with the crew, not with the 'ohana, Isaiah watched everyone climb into the vans. Only Arnold didn't get in: he'd been standing outside the stakes so he could bail everyone out and talk to reporters. The vans headed off down to the paved shore road, and Curtis ordered Walter back to work. The front of the dozer dropped, then started scraping again, tumbling the mats and leaves over and over, mixing them with the powdery red soil that rose like a wave from the blade's edge.

Isaiah felt bad a lot with these days—mixed up. He felt bad every time the 'ohana climbed up to the ledge and sat down in front of Walter's bulldozer. He felt worse when he went into town and no one would talk to him. He even felt bad when he did his job. Isaiah didn't like walking up each morning, seeing the flat roadbed gouged across the slope, the line ending at the blade of the bulldozer that would draw the ledge farther on by late afternoon. He could quit, go back to laying net some, but $8.50 an hour was more than he'd made in a long time. He refocused his eyes on the red spray spilling from Walter's metal blade.

About 3:30, the first body came up. The dozer dropped into a shallow dip, with bigger rocks than usual strewn over the surface. Walter stopped in front of a large boulder, revved his rig, and surged ahead. Seconds later, Isaiah saw some brownish sticks spill from the blade. He walked over and picked up a piece of rotten branch, maybe an inch wide and five long. He threw it down. Only then did he notice the five teeth sticking out of another piece nearby.

"Waltah!"

Isaiah didn't pick this piece up, or the other pieces he saw, curved like shards from a bowl—or skull. Walter brought the rig to a halt and climbed down the side. He stopped abruptly when he saw what Isaiah had found.

"Shit! No more driving, maybe two days. The boss be real piss off; a dead Hawaiian more hassle than a live one on the road. Go tell Curtis."

Isaiah stumbled down the hill, thinking through every unsolved murder, every ghost story, every scrap of local history he knew. Was he in trouble? Walter hadn't seemed scared, though he'd stayed back when he saw those bones. God, he'd touched them! When he burst into the foreman's trailer, Isaiah was more confused than he'd been up top.

Curtis *was* pissed.

"Three days, maybe four, maybe a bunch, if it's anything like that time on Moloka'i," he said when they'd climbed back up to the job site and looked at the pieces of bone Walter's rig had scattered over the rocky surface.

"You've got good eyes, don't you? Walter didn't see the bones, did you Walter?"

"Not paid to look. Just drive."

"Stay here and watch the bones, Isaiah."

Curtis and Walter walked away, talking low. Isaiah looked at the fragment of jaw. He wiped a finger on his workpants, then put it in his mouth and felt along the sides of his own teeth. They were slippery, and felt hard. The teeth on the ground were brown and dry; one tooth was missing from the jaw. Isaiah moved his finger to where the dentist had pulled one of his molars. The hole felt small—this person must have been huge.

Curtis came back. He stared at Isaiah for a second.

"You're Hawaiian, aren't you?" he asked, and he didn't want to hear yes.

"My mother's side. My father Portagee, but my mother half through her mother, then Hawaiian back long time."

"Shit!" Curtis said this right to Isaiah, blue eyes staring into brown. "We'll have to phone those bastards who did the impact statement. Otherwise we'll have a Hawaiian convention up here." He walked down the hill, muttering.

Isaiah turned to Walter.

"What's Curtis talkin' about?"

"Archaeologists. They'll dig da buggahs up and move 'em, so we can grade. Maui one time, da guy told me, go ahead dig 'em up with one backhoe. Real fast . . . but no Hawaiians watching that time. Eh, next time, you stay blind, brah. We work faster."

When Isaiah arrived for work the next morning, someone else was there: a tall, thin *haole*. He wore a white straw hat; and he needed it, since without it his pale, freckled skin would have peeled like old paint. His boots were as beaten up as Isaiah's or Walter's, though more broken down at the back from squatting a lot. He didn't look like a worker—more like someone you'd see painting pictures of the bay—but he seemed at home on the site. His name was Hal, Curtis said.

Walter was pointing out the bones from the day before to him. "This was one big guy," the archeologist said, looking down at the jawbone. Isaiah was pleased; he guessed that yesterday. Then Curtis stuck his head in.

"So you're going to move him, and O.K. the grading?"

"Not yet. I want to find out if he's got company. Those big rocks on the surface aren't landfall, and if this guy was underneath one, they might be grave markers. I'll start looking now, and have some idea by tomorrow afternoon. Would you guys move that big boulder for me?"

Walter grumbled as he and Isaiah walked toward several large rocks. "They were under rocks on Maui. Plenny hard work now."

The two men put on their work gloves, to guard against centipedes and scorpions, then pried the boulder out of the ground, picking up shovels when their hands couldn't budge it any further. When it finally rolled out, Isaiah held his breath, scared he would see a skull staring back at him. There was nothing.

Hal squatted beside the hole. With a trowel, he carefully scraped about an inch of dirt from the sides. After examining the walls carefully, he scooped the dirt into a bucket.

"Have either of you guys ever screened?"

"One time on Maui," Walter said. He picked up the bucket and walked over to a wooden frame with wire mesh stretched over it that Hal had brought. After dumping the dirt in, he picked the frame up and shook it, as if panning for gold. The dust sifted through, turning Walter's pants red.

For the rest of the morning Isaiah carried the buckets from Hal to Walter. He wished he could be two places at once, to watch Hal slowly widen the hole, and to watch Walter screen until only bits of lava and shell were left in the frame. Soon Isaiah was almost running, since he found he could watch the screening and still make it back in time to get the next bucket full of dirt. Around 11:30 he was peering over Walter's shoulder, looking at all the tiny *pipipi* shells turning up, when he noticed one piece that was even smaller than the others. Walter tossed this stuff away, but Isaiah picked up the piece he'd noticed. A tooth. Half-afraid of causing more trouble, he walked over to Hal and held out his hand.

"Maybe da guy's tooth, yeh?"

Hal took the tooth from Isaiah. He removed an envelope and a roll of toilet paper from his pack. After wrapping up the tooth and placing it in the envelope, he wrote some numbers on the outside. "That's a baby tooth, so I don't think it's the big guy's. You've got good eyes. Why don't you screen for awhile?"

Walter was mad; he'd been able to smoke a cigarette between buckets. He didn't seem too happy about Isaiah's eyes either, muttering as he passed, "You better blind, brah."

Work now went more slowly, because Hal was using a brush instead of a trowel. After lunch, Isaiah screened out a shark's tooth, some fragments of volcanic glass, and his first false alarm: a small piece of bone that Hal said was probably dog. But he put both the tooth and the bone into envelopes. When Isaiah asked why, Hal said that archaeologists liked to know what people ate, "and that shark didn't walk up here." Isaiah was soon screening as fast as he could, then walking over to the hole. He felt something was going to happen.

About two, it did. Hal was smoothing down the sides of the pit when some lighter-colored dirt fell away. Carefully touching his brush to the place, with round swoops he slowly exposed a light-brown spot that within fifteen minutes bulged an inch from the wall. "I'll bet you a beer that's your *keiki*, Isaiah. Walter, go get Curtis."

Hal covered the baby's skull with a garbage bag, and whistled as Curtis came slowly up the hill.

By four the next day, Hal had put in five test pits, all under big rocks. He was only going to do three at first, but he found bodies in two of them so quickly that he tested a couple more. More things went into envelopes—shells, other animal bones, the white bone fishhook Isaiah found in the screen. With a tape measure and survey map, Hal marked out the pits with string. Isaiah caught onto the terms right away. The first hole was now C-4, and the one with the two *keiki* bones sticking out of the walls was C-12. The only pit with nothing in it was D-9, and that was funny, since the rig Walter drove was a D-9.

None of this made Curtis very happy.

"How many do you think are here?"

"I don't know, but it's going to take some time and more people to find out. I've got seven bodies exposed, and I've just been fishing. All I can guarantee is that any road going through here as it is now is going to have bodies under it."

"How long?"

"Can't say. I don't have X-ray vision like Isaiah here. I phoned back to Oʻahu last night and told them they'd better get a crew ready. You're just lucky your accountants had to budget for this."

Curtis was heading down the hill when Hal called to him.

"By the way, I want Isaiah and Walter working on this. They can help screen and move rocks. We're as worried about the locals as you are, and a couple on the crew are good public relations. Besides, Walter's got some experience, and Isaiah's a hard worker."

Curtis didn't say anything, but when the other archaeologists arrived, Isaiah was at the airport to help load the shovels, brushes, and boxes into the jeep.

That dig was the most exciting thing that had ever happened to Isaiah. Most of the crew were female, which set him back at first. He'd never thought he'd see a *haole* woman in work boots, the dust caked on her face. Isaiah was also amazed at how much these archaeologists talked. For the first couple of days he thought they were all Portagee: always gabbing, yelling back and forth about a bone, about a new layer in the earth—"stratigraphy," they called it—or teasing each other but never meaning it. They each knew one thing best. Lucy knew the bones; Eileen, the bottles, the fishhooks, what they called "artifacts"; Mort, the kinds of dirt. Isaiah soon knew who to call when something turned up in the screen. "Hey Eileen, I got one button!"

Isaiah liked the bones themselves best, or "the folks," as the archaeologists called them. The bones were brittle and often crumbled when moved, so each body was brushed clean, measured, and photographed before the archaeologists lifted the bones out of the earth, wrapped them in newspapers, and placed them in long cardboard boxes like the ones flower shops put anthuriums in. Isaiah thought he'd be scared but he wasn't, even when they removed the garbage bags covering the half-exposed bodies each morning, and he saw beetles running out of the eyeholes in the skulls, or when they found one body in a coffin with the backbones scattered and a rat skeleton lying next to the hips. Sometimes he wanted to cry when he looked at a completed *keiki* burial, the little skeleton all curled up sleeping on the dirt, or when he saw the little woman with the *keiki* lying below her ribs, and Lucy said she died when she was pregnant.

After awhile, Hal let Isaiah actually get into the hole and dig. Toothbrush and dental pick in hand, he soon found himself slowly uncovering a leg bone. Hal said, "The body you find is yours to finish." He watched for a bit, but after lunch he went back to his own work, and Isaiah was left alone. He was afraid of doing something wrong, but he soon stopped worrying, and concentrated on uncovering the body slowly. People who worked too fast were called "butchers."

Isaiah soon was digging all the time. He found he could slip his brush down between the ribs without breaking them, and he quickly learned how to work his way slowly around the body, brushing until it lay on its own little table of dirt. Sometimes the bodies were a mess, the bones scattered through the soil. Three bodies might be mixed up, and starting from the edges, Hal and Lucy and Isaiah would work slowly with their brushes, meeting over the knot of bones at the center.

The summer slowly passed, and Isaiah worked on. He was amazed that for three whole months now some very dead Hawaiians had been able to stop both Curtis and the road. Hal told Isaiah that by law any construction project had to pay for an "Environmental Impact Statement"— a report that described what the development was going to destroy—and if any signs of human bones or buildings turned up, then the contractors had to bring in archaeologists. Curtis once suggested that things might go faster if they just dug a big hole on the other side of the survey stakes and dumped everything into it. But the archaeologists kept brushing, screening, measuring, and photographing, slowly revealing Isaiah's past.

And with each day, Isaiah felt more strongly that it was his past, and not the archaeologists', that was being uncovered. The others treated the folks with respect—no dead body jokes, no fooling around with the bones—but Isaiah knew he was closer to these bodies than anyone else. As a child he'd heard stories about long-ago Hawai'i, and he'd thought sometimes about those ancient people fishing, or planting taro on the stone terraces still dotting the slopes. But the early Hawaiians had seemed unreal and flat to him—people painted on a wall or tapped into a rock, who would disappear when they turned their shoulders to the sun. Now he held their bodies in his hands.

Sometimes he thought about what he'd look like buried, and whether he'd want Hal digging him up. Isaiah decided that he wouldn't. If anyone brought him back to the surface, he'd want it to be someone like himself—another Hawaiian, or at least part, who had laid net off the reef, who might be family, who would be glad to know that he'd been there too. Isaiah started thinking that whenever someone builds a road, or a house, or a 7-11 store, everyone should have to stop for three months to think about the people—and not just the Hawaiians—uncovered and moved elsewhere.

On the last day, after Hal felt certain all the bodies had been found, Isaiah drove up to a church nearby for the reburial. He didn't have to go, but he wanted to see the end, since he'd been there for the beginning. Only a couple of the archaeologists attended; the rest had returned to Oʻahu. The little wooden boxes were lying side by side in a long trench Walter had dug with his backhoe in the corner of the cemetery. Though most contained the bones of people buried long before Cook came to Hawaiʻi, the minister said the bodies were "asleep in Christ," and he spoke about shepherds and pastures, although the church stood on a rocky slope looking out on the bay so far below. Walter turned on the backhoe, and with a roar it pushed the pile of dirt back down into the hole. Tears streamed down Isaiah's face, and he turned his head away for shame.

He was still wearing his work pants, and when the others turned to leave, he walked over to the new mound and turned his pockets inside out. Three months of dust drifted down, placing his people under the dirt they had been under so long.

On his way back to town Isaiah stopped at Ishikawa store and bought a shovel, a bucket, a whisk broom, and three toothbrushes.

East Maui

Hal was puzzled. He stood on a slope side, looking down at a body the backhoe had uncovered. Around him were boulders, grouped around the body almost like a miniature Stonehenge. This was the second time in a week he'd been here, the construction site of an office building for real-estate agents, dentists, and doctors. The similarities between this burial and the last one, some hundred feet away, were too striking to be merely accidental. Once again the bones seemed almost too clean. No clumps of dirt adhered to the shaft ends, no roots coiled around the long bones. And yet the bones were old—probably prehistoric. Hal guessed that the test pits he would dig under the surrounding rocks would turn up nothing, that this body was a single burial like the last one. He'd taken two days to test the area around the other burial, but with this one he'd just put in a couple of pits, and if nothing turned up he'd give the O.K. for construction to continue.

He squatted down to begin removing the body, glancing idly at the survey stake a few feet away marking the front corner of the construction site. Suddenly, he had a hunch he couldn't wait to test out. He borrowed a survey map from the foreman, and sure enough, the stake he'd noticed near the first burial marked the back corner of the site. He walked quickly to the other back corner. He found what he was looking for immediately: a few boulders scattered over the surface, circling a big one well set into the ground. He pushed the rock and almost fell over when, with no resistance whatever, it flipped out of the hole. With his brush, Hal moved easily down through the four inches of recently disturbed fill that covered the skull.

He stood up and stared seaward. Either the ancient Hawaiians had seen the corners of the construction site in a vision, or someone was using the survey markers to map out his own cemetery. Hal didn't even bother checking the fourth corner but headed immediately for the phone.

Leeward Oʻahu

It was a sunny day at Barber's Point—just a few clouds coasting down from the mountains. A fleet of limousines and military vehicles lined the sides of the dirt road, down near the shore. A hundred people were clustered together on the dead coral, some wearing three-piece suits, others decked out in full-dress military uniforms. After the endless introductions and expressions of thanks, the governor, a red carnation *lei* draped over his charcoal-gray suit, lifted the microphone from the portable P.A., and spoke.

"I think it's a wonderful thing that this project is now ready to go ahead. The people of Hawaiʻi join me in congratulating those who have worked so hard to make this project possible. It's good to see we can work together, but in Hawaiʻi, people have always worked together to make a special place. *Mahalo* to Colonel Frisbort and the many men who have worked so hard to make this a reality, and *mahalo* to those people, in government and in the business community, for their efforts. When the Hawaiʻi

Military Center for Business and Technology is completed, we will have something we can all be proud of."

There was a flurry of activity as reporters gathered around a piece of ground marked off with stakes and plastic streamers. The governor walked to his position between the colonel and the bank president. An aide presented each man with a silver spade, then they lifted their heads for the photographers, smiled, and drove their shovels into the earth.

The governor had never seen a skull before.

Hawai'i Nei

The next two months would be remembered as the summer of the dead bodies. They turned up everywhere: in condo developments on Maui; just under the sand that bulldozers pushed seaward to extend Waikīkī; even in the valleys, where city workers dug ditches to carry the runoff from upstream. Construction companies hired security guards to watch sites round the clock. The Carpenters' Union offered a reward of $10,000 for information leading to the arrest of "The Undertaker," as the media now called him. Composite drawings of any suspicious character seen buying a shovel appeared on the front page of the newspapers—almost all looked like Jimi Hendrix. Callers on phone-in shows could talk of nothing else; everyone from Martians to the former mayor was a suspect. People threw chicken bones into uncut lawns, hoping to teach lazy neighbors a lesson. Children buried each other under palm fronds, then played construction worker. Two fly-by-night mortuary companies offered to bury people in concrete, and crematoriums doubled their business. Honolulu went into a frenzy when police arrested a man burying his just-murdered wife in a playground sandbox. Within a month, over thirty bodies appeared—all in construction sites. Within six weeks, reporters from every major newspaper on the Mainland had filed stories.

As the first person to have figured out The Undertaker's ways, Hal found himself in the thick of things. Crackpot callers threatened him with death; others reported seeing armies of people marching past their front doors, carrying bodies and shovels. Many confessed to the crime—these calls usually came from asthmatic old men.

Despite these distractions, Hal had figured out some patterns. The "victims" had all been dead for at least fifty years, so The Undertaker was a grave robber, not a murderer. Nor were the bodies all Hawaiian; in fact, they seemed to represent every ethnic background—the long, robust bones of Polynesia; the slender bones of the East; the gold teeth and slightly curved long bones of Europe and white America.

The Undertaker was also very selective in his targets. Although Honolulu had the largest count, all the other islands had incidents—except Lāna'i, whose residents seemed almost disappointed. Most of the bodies were buried where they'd be uncovered immediately—the governor's experience was the most embarrassing example—but a couple had been stumbled upon only by accident. This promised new discoveries extending far into the future, each one stirring up again the complex feelings now pulsing through the islands.

What puzzled Hal most was where The Undertaker was getting his bodies from. Each one was clean and complete, with no evidence of the previous resting place other than the reddish color of the Hawaiian bones, buried without a coffin before or shortly after Cook. The bones were neatly placed in the earth, resembling the ancient Hawaiian bundle burials. Hal checked out the study collections at museums and at the medical school, but nothing was missing. These bones must be coming out of the ground, and someone was removing them carefully.

Hal also felt sure that The Undertaker had ended his campaign. Nothing suggested that any bodies had been buried after the first ones were discovered, and nothing was coming out of high-visibility locations any more. Hal felt frustrated at repeating "I don't know" to every question coming from the police, the press, the governor. But one thing he was sure of—The Undertaker had singlehandedly created the biggest flap about development Hawai'i had ever seen. At times Hal had to catch himself from admiring his opponent; he often wondered why no one had thought of this before.

Kona, toward Kohala

Some time later, Isaiah was driving along the highway, getting ready to make the turn up to his tin roof shack; up the slope he saw a jeep and three police cars parked out front. Hal was sitting on the hood of the jeep. Isaiah turned off his signal and kept driving. Miles up the coast, the sun drooped to his left, and the wind stopped blowing down from the mountain. At this time of day everything seemed sharper: he could make out every branch, every thorn on the *kiawe* trees.

He pulled off the main road, taking a dirt road upward, then turned up a side path almost hidden by brush. After bumping along for a few hundred feet, he came to an old metal gate held shut by a rusty orange chain. Isaiah had cut through the lock long before. He got out, opened the gate, and drove the car through. He picked up a rusty old padlock from off the dash, walked back to the gate, and locked it for good. He hadn't driven up here for about a month, and the path was once again almost hidden by weeds and tall grass. He drove up the path to where it ended, a few feet from the edge of a high ridge. He looked down at the canopy of trees hiding the valley floor from view. Putting the car in neutral, he reached in and let off the parking brake, then pushed. The car plunged out of sight; he stood there until he couldn't hear any more noise. No one would find him now.

He climbed upward past small terraces—some ancient house sites, some little farming plots, covered with lantana and *kiawe*. He carefully avoided a long open slope, burned out by a brush fire. You could see it from the road, now hundreds of feet below. When he reached the rocky overhang, Isaiah found his way to a sharp cleft, the only path through. As he came closer to his goal, the trees were larger, the undergrowth more tangled. He could hear the songs of those Hawaiian birds that now only lived high on the upper slopes. Up here the ground became dangerous. Cracks, sometimes only three feet across but hundreds of feet deep, lay hidden beneath the ferns and fallen leaves.

Although he had made this climb many, many times before, he was always surprised when he scrambled up the final rock face and stood on the terrace. Before him stretched the man-made plain, hidden from the road far below by the large trees growing on the seaward edge. But this time he felt relieved as well as surprised. He now understood what the old Hawaiians must have felt when they climbed here, this place of safety high on the mountainside. There were many such *puʻuhonua* in the islands: places where the breaker of a *kapu* could run to and find shelter, shielded by the power of the *aliʻi*. If Isaiah had heard the undergrowth below crackling, then seen someone stumbling and surging to the top, he could have urged him on—with laughs, with cries, with his hands, throwing rock after rock down at anyone pursuing the climber, gaining on the victim but too late to catch him.

The *heiau* and some house sites were grouped to his right, just in front of the place where the slope began rising again. Isaiah had cleared off most of the scrub, and the dark lava platforms stood out in the fading light. At the far end he'd replanted some of the farming terraces, even planting some fruit trees in a little grove. The water, clean and clear this high up, ran down the side of the platform. He wouldn't starve, even if he stayed here for years.

Isaiah now knew many places in the islands. Old graveyards, overgrown and abandoned, the wooden churches caved in or carried off in pieces for lumber. Many nights he'd spent among the headstones in the high grass, working with his tools and his flashlight, removing and bundling the bodies as Hal had taught him. All worksites by the ocean were familiar to him, and roads, moving along the sides of slopes—each one a new resting place for his people. He now knew airports very well, and how hard it was to get three or four long flower boxes onto interisland jets.

He'd hidden this, his masterpiece, most carefully, for he loved and feared for this place of safety most. He would be the last person to hide here; he knew that someday this place too would be found. First the helicopters would come, hovering. People from Isaiah's town, $8.50 an hour, would walk beside the bulldozers edging their way up from the road below, plowing toward this place, pushing the red dirt wave before them. Many Curtises, many Walters, paid by people with vacant or hidden faces, would cut down the big trees so the new owners and tourists could see the ocean. They'd leave the *heiau* standing out beside the pool, and waiters would tell the story of the Hawaiians and their "Cities of Refuge"—odd tales that books and time had turned into ancient history.

Isaiah looked at the plain once more. The entire surface was strewn with boulders. The Chinese he'd carried up and reburied here slept neatly in rows; his Hawaiians rested under rocks spreading out in circles. He'd put the *haoles* six feet under. The people he'd come upon by surprise when digging in churchyards he'd reburied the same way he'd found them—no marker, no surface sign. He'd replanted some small trees to mark out the areas, and the seeds had already taken hold, wrapping some of the boulders in vines.

He hadn't been able to figure out where they would start grading, so he'd made the best guess he could. He wanted to be the first silent figure to greet them—his people had taught him that watchmen needn't shout. All were ready. Chinese and Portuguese, Filipino and Japanese, even the *haoles*, brought here by Isaiah, not by sugar, pineapple, or God. And the Hawaiians. All would now silently resist, turning their faces to the light when the pursuers broke through, climbing in pieces onto the dozer blade, making each turn of the caterpillar track wrench a spirit out of the soil, demanding more time, laying true claim to this, their place. Isaiah's place. One hundred souls stripped to the essentials, waiting.

At one point near the edge of the plain, you can just see the bay if you look between the thick trunks of the *koa*. Isaiah had dug a hole for himself there and found roots. He liked to think of the roots slowly winding around him, inching onward to find water, passing between his ribs, through his eyes. Two plywood sheets piled high with dirt hung suspended, propped up by two-by-fours standing at attention in the hole. Someday, Isaiah would inch his body feet-first down between the supports. Then without hesitating, he would push the props away and embrace the red converging wave.

But not now. Not yet.

BY YOKANAAN KEARNS

CONFESSIONS OF A STUPID HAOLE

I'm trying NOT to be rude, trying not to act like a haole, but he's just NOT taking the hint.

He's haole. And not just haole, he's a mainland haole, with skin so white it could blind any shark it baits. So the more diplomatic I am, the less he gets the message that I wish he'd leave me alone. Polite discourse is a language as unintelligible to him as Pidgin is going to be the moment he leaves the linguistic safety of the airport and ventures onto the streets of Honolulu. Tomorrow or the next day or maybe next week before he goes back to New England, he'll be waiting for his snow cone at Waiola Shave Ice and the clerk will ask him, "What calah you like?"

His left eyebrow will creep up his forehead. He'll stare at the clerk from behind his wire-rimmed glasses, realizing only now, as the ice begins to melt, what a mistake he made by never signing up for my seminar on pidgins and creoles of the Pacific.

Of course, the only appropriate response in such a situation would be to smile nervously and nod, feigning comprehension, then run in the opposite direction. That's what I'd do. It's what any local would do, rather than risk making all the people lined up along the sidewalk wonder if she's *lōlō*.

But Greg's not a local, he's from Peabody, Massachusetts, so he won't even be aware he's keeping people from their shave ice. And in the unlikely event he IS aware, he won't care. He'll step back from the counter and ask the other patrons, "Does anybody here speak English?"

A few will answer this insult with stink eye, a few with wry smiles, all in silence, letting the stupid haole squirm. The clerk will point to the glass bottles of colored liquid next to the shave ice machine, each bottle capped with a metal spout. "You know, red, green, yellow . . ."

Relief will sweep over his face. "Oh, you mean what *flavor*?"

August 31, 1989 (Cambridge, Massachusetts)

It was Monday morning, a little before nine, and I'd just taught my very first class as a Harvard professor.

I explained the goals of the course, passed out the syllabus, described the exams and papers, and talked a little about myself, hoping the students would think of me as a real human and not merely their Linguistics professor. Among other things, I told them I was new on the faculty and I was originally from Hawaiʻi.

The class went fine. As the students filed out of the classroom, I heard one young woman say to another, "You think Professor Yap's really from Hawayee?"

"That's what she said. Don't you believe her?"

"I guess I didn't know anybody actually lived there, I thought people only went there on vacation."

*   *   *

I keep hoping he'll figure out that what I'm saying and what I mean are two different things. Otherwise, any second now, before we get off the plane, I'll have to say what I mean, which is something I don't want to do.

"And since you won't be working right away," he says to me while he fishes through the overhead compartment above our row, "maybe you can take me around the island in that car you're planning on renting." He finds what he's looking for and tosses it onto his seat, the one next to mine. I avert my eyes, like a vampire cringing at the unexpected sight of a crucifix. It's an officially licensed Harvard University backpack—crimson, sporting a crest with the Latin word for *truth*, VERITAS.

I grab my purse and squeeze ahead of him in the aisle. "I've got to start looking for a job, Greg," I remind him.

"Well, you still have to eat once in a while, Stephanie. Give me a call. My friends and I are staying at the Pacific Grand Hotel."

"I'm pretty low on cash right now," I remind him.

"Are you?"

"The house," I remind him.

"Oh, right, you mentioned the beating you took when you sold it."

The cabin door isn't even open yet and already he's violated three cardinal local rules:

RULE 1. DON'T RUB IT IN. I lost my down-payment and five years of equity in the sale of my house. I'm returning to Hawaiʻi without much cash and without a job. He didn't have to remind me I'll be mooching off my parents until I find work.

RULE 2. DON'T IMPOSE ON PEOPLE. He wants ME to take HIM sightseeing in the car I'll be spending my meager savings to rent so I won't be imposing on my parents when I want to go up and see Popo.

Rule 3. Don't shame people into doing something by making them feel obligated. He makes me look like an ungracious native for not offering to take him on an island tour.

That's all bad enough, but there's one more thing, not really a local thing, but a rule of my own: Never let a disgruntled former Harvard professor see your officially licensed backpack. She may become violently ill.

So why don't I just tell this jerk bluntly how I feel? I know he won't take it personally. In-your-face discourse is the only thing he understands.

It's because I'm afraid he might not even understand THAT. There are so many things haoles don't understand.

September 3, 1985 (New Haven, Connecticut)

Pam Zimmerman pulled me aside after the first seminar meeting of Advanced Methods for Language Reconstruction B: Preliterate Languages. I remembered her from Advanced Methods A: Literate Languages. She always wore white socks and Birkenstocks, even when it snowed, and in the spring she wore shorts, proudly displaying her unshaven legs.

"I hear you did pretty well last semester," Pam said.

"I did all right." (Rule 4: Don't flaunt your achievements because something may come along and humble you. Advanced Methods B had a reputation for weeding the Yale doctoral program of the "intellectually feeble.")

"Not ME," Pam admitted.

I agreed to get together with her every weekend at my apartment. Saturday morning, just past seven, Pam came up the walkway to my apartment, her arms full of books and photocopies.

I called from the front window. "Hey, Zimmerman, are you ready to posit the enclitic pronouns of Proto-Tikapakapian?" It was a joke. There's no such language.

"Only if you are, Steph."

"Well come on—" I started to say when I noticed her feet. The Birkenstocks were missing. Pam was in her socks. "Pam!" I yelled. "Where are your shoes?"

"I heard you make people take them off, so I left them in the car."

"But now your socks are filthy!"

She stopped just short of the doorway and looked down at the brown sole of one sock. "Is that a problem?"

Pam's a lawyer now.

* * *

Finally we're moving. The door at the front of the plane is open and we're filing down the aisle towards the line-up of flight attendants thanking us for choosing Hawaiian Airlines. Greg's right behind me, chattering away about how much fun it'd be to get together while he's in town. He taps me on the shoulder. "So what do you say?"

Why can't I bring myself to let loose with something unambiguous? *Frankly, Greg, you represent everything I detest about the mainland and I never want to see you or your backpack again because you remind me of the people who cost me my career. Besides, I came home to say goodbye to my grandmother, not to babysit a Harvard grad student on a goddamn Polynesian adventure tour.*

Why can't I? Because I spent twenty-two years as a local girl before I went to Yale. Eleven years in New Haven didn't turn me into a talk-too-much, talk-too-loud, no-mo-sense mainland haole, and even though the seven years I taught at Harvard gave me plenty of excuses to talk too much and talk too loud, still I resisted, frequently reminding myself who I am and where I come from.

Stephanie Keke'oke'omaiokanalu Yap, Kaimukī girl.

It's time to escape. As we emerge from the jetway into the crowded gate noisy with happy reunions, I drop back and quickly step aside, taking refuge with other passengers and their mothers and fathers and aunties and uncles. Greg disappears on the other side. If he looks for me in baggage claim, he won't find me there. I'm only traveling with my purse. Everything else I FedEx'd directly to my parents' house two days ago, along with what few belongings I didn't sell or else put in storage until I find a new job in a new city.

I'm floating in a sea of familiar-looking faces. Japanese, Chinese, Hawaiian, Filipino, Portuguese, and like me, blends of some of the above. I'm part of the majority again, Chinese-Hawaiian. And, yes, I confess, Irish too.

I'm hapa. Not what they called me on the mainland: mixed-race, bi-racial, half-breed. I'm back where people think it's strange when somebody calls herself an Asian.

"Come again? Wat you mean, *Asian*, sistah? You Chinee, o wat?"

July 7, 1990 (Boston, Massachusetts)

I looked up from the mortgage application I was filling out at Fleetship Bank. I'd gotten tired of living in an apartment, tired of big, ugly, dirty cities. I wanted a house where there were more trees and fewer cars. "Excuse me," I said to the loan officer, a young man in black and red suspenders who didn't look much older than some of my students. He'd introduced himself as Peter Tetreault.

"Yes?"

"I'm a bit confused by this section."

He took the application and gave it a cursory glance.

ETHNICITY (choose one)

__ Danish	__ Lithuanian	__ Black
__ Dutch	__ Norwegian	__ Hispanic
__ English	__ Polish	__ Asian
__ French	__ Russian	__ Other
__ German	__ Scottish	
__ Irish	__ Swedish	
__ Italian	__ Welsh	

"What seems to be the problem?" he asked.

"The ethnicities in the first two columns represent national origins."

"That's right. Different countries."

"Well, look at the third column. Asia's not a country."

"What's your point?"

"Denmark's a country, Italy's a country, Poland's a country. There's no such country as Asia."

"I don't see what the problem is. Your last name's Yap. That's an Asian name, isn't it?"

"Chinese."

"Isn't China in Asia, Ms. Yap?"

"Isn't France in Europe, Mr. Tetreault? Would you ever think of identifying yourself as a European?"

"There's no need to get upset, ma'am, it's only a formality."

"Where I come from, brah, you're a haole, and nobody cares if a haole is French or Swedish or Welsh." I snatched the form from his hand and put an X where it said OTHER and filled in the blank with *Chinese-Hawaiian-Irish*.

I got the loan anyway.

* * *

Now that I've experienced the joy of an airport family reunion vicariously (the Yaps don't do the lei-at-the-gate thing), I can rent a car—in spite of Mom's objection that she could send Dad to pick me up.

"Are you here on business?" the clerk at the rental car desk asks me. He's a young local who speaks without a trace of Pidgin, Hawaiian-

Portuguese I think, short even by local standards, though he fills out his red and white aloha shirt like a bodybuilder.

"Business? No, I'm coming home," I tell him while I rummage through my purse for some tissue paper. I've forgotten how humid May can be. I'm way overdressed in my tweed Ann Taylor coordinates and chilly-weather nylons from L. L. Bean. The skin beneath my bra straps is beginning to overheat and sweat is already beading in my armpits.

"Oh, you're a local girl?"

I pat my forehead dry. "My parents live on 10th Avenue. What'd you think I was, a businesswoman from Taiwan or something?"

"No, from the mainland."

God, is it that obvious? I haven't felt this foreign in six years.

October 2, 1990 (Sutton, Massachusetts)

Miss O'Mara, the town registrar, stared at me as though I'd been speaking Cantonese.

"Excuse me," I'd said (in English), "but could you please tell me where I can register to vote?"

Probably too polite. I should have said, *I want to register to vote*, or better yet, *Gimme a voter registration form*. But I'd just moved into Sutton, a farming town sixty miles west of Cambridge, and I didn't want to get a reputation as an obnoxious yuppy. My presence had already raised a few eyebrows at the post office and the grocery store. Being the only woman in town with slanted eyes and a funny name like Yap, no doubt I confirmed the townfolks' worst fears that Cambodians with drug money were moving out to the suburbs.

Miss O'Mara placed her palms on the desk, one wrinkled hand over the other. Like all the women who worked at Town Hall, she was well past seventy and single. "Perhaps you don't realize," she whispered, leaning forward, "you have to be an American citizen to vote in this country."

I'm sure my mouth must have dropped open. I did the staring this time, uncertain how to respond to a statement like that after twenty-nine years without anyone ever questioning my citizenship.

"Do you understand?" she asked.

I closed my mouth, placed my palms on the edge of her desk, one hand over the other, and leaned forward to look her in the eyes. "Miss O'Mara, I've voted in every election since 1980. My father, Stanford Yap, voted for the first time in 1952. His father, Koon Lee Yap, voted in the election of 1918, soon after he was granted citizenship in thanks for his service to our country in World War I. The first Yap came to America in 1887. That was my great-grandfather, Yap Ah Fat. My other great-grandfather was Bertram Kanahele, a man whose ancestors were the first people to reach the southern beaches of the Hawaiian islands. That means my family's been in this country at least fifteen hundred years. So, yes, Miss O'Mara, I realize you have to be an American citizen to vote—" I took a deep breath and smiled "—and could you PLEASE tell me where I can register?"

*　*　*

Popo used to say home is where you want to be buried when you're dead. For her, of course, that's Hawai'i, but even more specifically it's the Punti Chinese cemetery at the end of East Mānoa Road, just over the hill from her house in St. Louis Heights. She'll be with Yaps and Choys and Wongs.

I never felt that way about Sutton. I used to shudder, thinking about a tombstone with my name on it in the cemetery on Leland Hill, a single Yap next to Zebediah Dodge and Ezra Leland.

But the rental car clerk didn't see me as a fellow local, he saw an outsider. To be honest, I started wondering if I'm still a kama'āina soon after the plane left San Francisco on the last leg of my journey home. Just as I was getting over the shock and dismay at the idea of being stuck for five hours next to a student I know from Harvard, Greg started asking me questions about the 50th State.

"What's the size of the population?"

"I don't know," I said. "It was about a million the last I heard, but that was more than ten years ago."

"Was it in '58 or '59 that Congress granted statehood?"

"I don't remember."

"Who are your senators in Washington?"

"I think Dan Inouye's still there. I can't remember who replaced Spark Matsunaga."

"Never mind," Greg said, no doubt realizing he was asking the wrong person. He reached up and increased the flow of air coming out of the nozzle above him. Then he turned to me—or was it turned on me?—again. "I've been meaning to tell you how sorry I am you're leaving us. If it's any consolation to you, I taught with Amy Blackfelder before she left for the post-doc at Berkeley, and I think she's a first-rate historical linguist. Not to say your work on the influence of Polynesian languages on Pacific island creoles isn't top-notch, but that's simply not where Harvard Linguistics is headed anymore."

"Greg, do you know what my first book was called?"

"*Indigenous Tongues and Emerging Creoles?*"

"No, that was book number two."

"Number two?"

"*Indigenous Tongues* came out last year. My Yale dissertation, *Proto-Central Polynesian and the Indo-Pacific Controversy*, was published in 1990, a year after I came to Harvard."

Greg frowned. "But that sounds like the work of a historical linguist."

"It was. You see, I wasn't fired because I didn't do good work, or because I refused to do the kind of research the new regime demands. The simple fact is that your pal Amy Blackfelder wanted back in, so her dissertation advisor, Marty Thomason, made a space available."

"Thomason? The chair? He can do that?"

"Only with the blessing of his faction, now in the majority, which he had. Would I be coming home if he couldn't?"

Well, I admit I WOULD be coming home. To see Popo one last time.

March 23, 1995 (Sutton, Massachusetts)

I'd known for a month, but it took me that long to get up the courage to call Mom and break the news.

"What did you do?" she asked.

"Ma! I didn't do ANYTHING—anything wrong, that is—it's academic politics."

"Then you'd better start looking for a job, Stephanie."

"It's too late to apply for academic jobs that start in the fall."

"Then come home. Maybe you're not too old to do what you should have done as soon as you finished college."

"Ma, I'm a well-known scholar of Polynesian linguistics, I'm not coming home to get a job in a hotel."

"Dad plays tennis with the manager of the Pacific Grand Hotel. Maybe he can give you a job, but you better not tell him you have a Ph.D."

*   *   *

The clerk at the rental car desk asked me if I needed a map of Honolulu and I said no. Now I've gone all the way to Kāhala, running out of freeway. St. Louis Heights is back there somewhere. Where are those damn giant water tanks that look like golf balls? They were somewhere after the Bingham Street exit—big and white and round. That's how I used to remember what offramp to take. Did I miss them? Wasn't I paying attention?

I'd better slow down so I can see if I can make a U-turn just past Kāhala—

A guy in a white BMW is on my tail, honking his horn. I roll down the window and stick my hand out. The air is warm and damp, like I'm putting my hand in the shower. I wave him around me, but he doesn't notice because he's already pulling up beside me. He reminds me of a plumper version of my cousin Kelvin Coelho, Dad's sister's son, who sat next to me in sixth grade and liked to terrorize Timmy Franklin, the only haole in the class. Kelvin's an orthodontist now, with a Japanese wife and two kids who go to Punahou.

The Kelvin-lookalike flips me the middle finger and shouts something I can't hear. But I can read his lips.

"Stupid haole!"

Then he guns his engine and takes off towards ʻĀina Haina.

I pull to the side of Kalanianaʻole Highway. I'm trembling. Maybe I deserved to be called *stupid*. Maybe even *stupid shit*. But *stupid haole*?

I, Stephanie Kekeʻokeʻomaiokanalu Yap, am NOT haole.

September 6, 1971 (Honolulu, Hawaiʻi)

Timmy Franklin made the mistake of being the only kid in the sixth grade wearing plaid bell-bottoms the first day of school. He was new to Aliʻiolani Elementary, fresh-off-the-plane from the mainland.

At recess, Kelvin couldn't stop laughing. "Wat kine pants dat, haole boy?" he yelled to Timmy from the other side of the jungle gym. "You tink you Mick Jaggah?"

"Why do you talk like that?" Timmy asked.

"Like wat?" I said. I was hanging upside down from one of the top bars, right next to Kelvin.

"You talk funny."

Kelvin leapt from the jungle gym and stomped towards Timmy in his best Pākē moke swagger. I was right behind him. "Come hea," he ordered, "I like tell you someting."

By now Timmy must have sensed the danger. He shook his head.

Kelvin put his foot on the first horizontal bar, a final warning before he would go up and get him. Timmy climbed down. Kelvin puffed out his chest and used it to back Timmy up against the bars. "You know wat is today?"

Timmy was shaking.

"Today *Kill Haole Day*," Kelvin whispered.

Timmy looked at me. "You won't . . . kill me . . . will you?"

*   *   *

I found my way to Wai'alae Avenue and St. Louis Heights, with only a little confusion when I passed City Mill, which I thought was out near Aloha Tower and nowhere near Kaimukī.

The walkway up to the house is quiet, except for two voices coming from the other side of the overgrown mock orange bushes. It's Dad and Uncle Emory. They're hanging a new clothesline, repeating the same argument I remember from small kid time.

"No," Dad is telling Uncle, "loop um one time round da pole nough."

"Goin come loose, Stanford, you do um li dat!"

"Nah, nah! Good enough."

"You always like take da shot cut!"

"Eryting gotta be perfeck fo you!"

"Eh, perfeck mo bettah dan pretty soon da buggah come all hema-jang, you!"

For a second I think it's silly for these two men to be hanging a clothesline for a woman who's dying. But it's an act of defiance, isn't it? A way to deny that soon Popo won't be washing clothes anymore.

I leave them to their argument and go inside. Here's the threadbare green carpet the grandkids helped to wear out. Here's the jade carving of Kuan Yin I knocked over and decapitated one Christmas. And there's that smell. Vick's Vaporub, which Popo uses in place of the more traditional (and, more importantly, more expensive) Chinese tiger balm, slathering it on herself and anybody she can corner when the tradewinds pick up and she hears a sniffle. "Da wind open da pores, you see, and den you come sick!"

The entire family is crammed into the living room. There's only one explanation for such a large gathering. Popo's dying.

The Yap side gets the plastic-covered sofa. That includes the Coelho contingent minus Kelvin's father, who ran off to Las Vegas back when we were at Kaimukī Intermediate. Kelvin is telling his wife to tell the kids to be careful not to spill the passion orange juice on the carpet. I see now that the Kelvin-lookalike on H-1 looked nothing like the real Kelvin, who's got graying hair and a double chin.

The Changs get the uncomfortable chairs Goong-goong's father, Yap Ah Fat, imported from China. Popo's younger sister, Francine, the seamstress, and her son Bertrand, the hair stylist who never married, are all that's left on that side.

Some of the Kanahele 'ohana—mom's family—are here, too, in the dining room, sitting apart from the others. They never mingle with the Yaps and Changs on the rare occasions—usually funerals—when we all come together. Recently Mom admitted it's gotten worse ever since her brother Hiram joined the sovereignty movement, started calling himself Palani, and told Mom her in-laws are members of a settler population that helped the haoles displace Hawaiians from their rightful lands.

I take another step inside. They stare at me in silence. I smile. They don't. Auntie Francine points me in the direction of the kitchen, where I find Mom squatting in front of the refrigerator, transferring the ingredients for home-made Chinese medicines from plastic grocery bags to the refrigerator. I can remember watching Popo do the same thing, twenty years ago. Mom is looking old enough to be called Popo by the grandchildren she keeps telling me I'm supposed to produce.

"Ma," I say quietly.

She looks around the refrigerator door. She sighs. "You're late. You got lost?" She doesn't wait for an explanation before she takes me by the arm and leads me down the hall to Popo's room.

"Didn't the doctor give her at least another month?" I ask.

"She keeps telling us she's almost ready to go, but she has to say her goodbyes first."

"Why did everybody look so glum back there?"

Mom stops in front of the door at the end of the hallway. "Because what she's been waiting for has finally arrived."

"What's she been waiting for?"

"You, Stephie. And now that you're here, they know she'll give up and die."

She opens the door, nudges me forward, and closes it behind me. The Vaporub is strongest in here. My eyes begin to water and I can feel a sneeze coming on.

"Who dat?" Popo asks from her bed. Her voice is shallow and raspy. Her hair, which Mom told me had fallen out from the chemotherapy, is starting to grow back now that she's refusing to continue the treatments.

"It's . . . me," I answer, trying not to sneeze. If I sneeze, she'll insist on sharing her Vick's with me.

"Come close, I no can see too good nowadays."

I walk to the edge of the bed and sit down. I take her hand in mine. "Popo, it's me, Stephanie."

She squints at me. No, she's not squinting, it's a smile. "Oh, Stephie, I tought you was Mrs. Woolsey daughtah."

I smile back. "Are you teasing me, Popo?"

"No. How you figah?"

"Mrs. Woolsey's daughter is haole."

She coughs and reaches for the cup on the nightstand. I hand it to her. Chinese medicine, by the way it reeks. Reminds me of four-day-old fish. After she takes a small sip, Popo rests the cup on her chest. "Make sense now," she says, "why Tūtū Kanahele wen give you da name Keke'oke'omaiokanalu."

My forehead wrinkles into a frown. "I don't understand, Popo."

"You mean she nevah—" She's interrupted by a painful coughing fit. I take the cup from her so she can cough without knocking it over. She closes her eyes. Once her breathing quiets down, she drapes her hand over the side of the bed and points at the floor. "Try bring da tin can, baby."

I hand her what I assume is more Chinese medicine. "Popo, what IS this?"

"My tin can fo *tu* my gullahs," she explains, spitting out the phlegm she'd coughed up. She hands it back to me.

"Popo," I say, alarmed by the color of the liquid, "it's red!"

"Two days, now, I stay *tu*-ing blood. Every day, lillo bit mo. Good ting you come today." I give her back the cup of medicine. She takes a cautious sip. "Wat I was telling you? Oh, yeah, yeah, I remembah, da name. Wat Tūtū Kanahele tell you da name mean?"

"It means *the foam of the breaking waves*. She wanted my middle name to represent the power of life, like the life-giving power of the ocean."

"You wen study da Hawaiian language, you know wat *ke ke'oke'o* mean, eh?"

"Sure. Whiteness. It describes the foam."

"Maybe so, but dat not why she wen call you *ke ke'oke'o*. I was in da hospital, too, you know. She wen pick you up, no mo clothes on you, not even one diapah, and she say, 'No look like one Kanahele, dis *kaikamahine*, no look like one Yap. One hundred pahcent look like one Leahy. Jess like one haole.' But bumbye you came brown aftah you play at da beach long time, you no look so haole, you look like one hapa-haole girl. Maybe Tūtū tink she wen give you da wrong name. She tell you one fancy story about da foam. But now you come back from da mainland, you look like da foam on da wave, like one haole. *Ke ke'oke'o*. Da name not wrong."

"Popo, I'm not haole," I protest softly.

"Turn around, baby. You see da mirrah above my bureau? Wat you see?"

The reflection in the mirror is a woman in her mid-thirties, professionally dressed, with shoulder-length brown hair parted on one side and kept off her face with a dash of mousse and spritz. "I see me."

"Wat calah you skin?"

"Well, I lost my tan a long time ago."

"Wat calah? Like top soil?"

"No."

"Like Goong-goong's brown Impala?"

"No."

"Wat you see, den?"

I turn away from the mirror and stare into my lap. For the past eighteen years, people have looked at me, looked at my name, and seen a minority, an exception to the norm. Now that I'm home, people still see a minority, a different minority, a different exception to the norm. Not a local. "A haole, Popo, I've become a stupid haole."

She reaches up and strokes my cheek with a cold hand. "Stupid? Eh, sometime, someplace, everybody get one chance fo be stupid. Chinee, Japanee, Hawaiian, haole . . . anykine. You not stupid, *lei hou lek*, study hahd, get one Ph.D. When I look at you, wat you tink Popo see?"

"A haole."

"Nah! I see Doctah Stephanie Keke'oke'omaiokanalu Yap, my akamai granddaughtah who wen come home so her popo can see her face one mo time."

BY NORA OKJA KELLER

THE BRILLIANCE OF DIAMONDS

ith the birth of her only child, a daughter, my mother pulled jewels out of thin air, giving me a name that translates as "the brilliance of diamonds."

"I wanted to give you prosperity," she explained. "Something that my family couldn't give to me."

My mother's family is dead, her parents from tuberculosis, her brothers from disownment. She renounced both the older and the younger one when she "married" my American father. But they were the ones that broke into her room, shattering the bowls and cups their mother had given her and stealing the rice she had stored for the months that she would be too big with me to work at the American PX. They were the ones who wrote "dead" and "whore" in the dirt in front of her house.

"I thought a long time about your name," she told me. "A name can determine your life, who you will be. Each letter had a certain power, each person a special name, told in the stars. If you can find the secret of your name, you can unlock the universe."

In truth, though, I know my mother waited not because she was trying to decide on the best possible name, but because she couldn't get anyone to name me. In Korea, as she explained to me, the paternal grandfather is supposed to name his sons' babies. Since my mother didn't know the family of my absent father, and since her own father was dead, she had hoped a substitute grandfather, one of the *ahjishis* from the village, would volunteer. No one did; naming, I suppose, such a big responsibility.

She waited and hoped, however, long enough for several of the village gossips to start calling me *Moo Myun*: "Baby No Name." When my mother caught herself calling me that, she decided to read the stars and count letters herself, hoping to find—if not the right name—at least a name that wouldn't hurt me. Finally, she settled on Myung Ja, playing on the words for "name" and "sparkling."

Perhaps it was because of that pun, a confusing word trick, or perhaps it was because I was cursed with that two-month namelessness, a rootlessness of body and soul, that we wandered through South Korea and finally crossed the Pacific Ocean. Whatever the reason, my name, unable to find a place for me, got me lost.

When we first came to America in search of my father, I was only four, but I was lost even then. My mother says that I stopped answering when she called for me, choosing instead to hide in the dirty laundry basket, under the dirty clothes of the family my mother kept house for.

*   *   *

The lady was looking for smart, pretty Korean girls who knew how to speak English. "Sister," the woman said to my mother, "my sister-in-law in America is rich-rich now. Everyone who goes to America can be just like that!"

"Oh, really," my mother breathed, sitting forward, her back straight. She kept her eyes down, to show respect, but also to hide her eagerness. She watched her fingers stray to the edge of her dress and flirt with the rich tapestry of the couch, then willed them back to her lap.

"I can arrange for you to go there." The woman's voice was as soft, as insinuating and luxurious as the fabric and pattern of the couch. "And your baby, too, of course," she added. "Just think of what your girl can have if you work for my sister-in-law in America. My sister has her own business, a restaurant, a bar. She pulls in thousands, and in Hawai'i, no less."

"But Hawai'i is not America," my mother said.

"*Aigu*, Little Sister! Don't show everyone how uneducated you are! That's another thing about America, everyone is so so smart!" When she spoke, the woman's face pulled into a scowl as, rolling the vowels from the back of her throat, she spat out each word. "You just cannot believe. It's like a miracle: everyone is so so rich, everyone so so beautiful, everyone so so smart!"

My mother wanted to go so bad she could feel it in her stomach like a hunger. "But, older sister," she said, "how can I go when I am none of those things?"

The woman squinted at my mother, lips pursed, and pretended to consider. "I will help you pass the interview. Can you say," she said, switching to English, "'You look nice man. You like buy drink?'"

The woman's American sister-in-law sent her a paper-husband, a post office worker who lived in downtown Honolulu and was in love with the sister-in-law. After eighteen months of visiting the Arirang's happy hour and flirting with the sister-in-law who owned the bar, he had finally worked up enough courage to tell her, "I would do anything for you."

She had answered, "Marry my sister."

The man knew that my mother wasn't the owner's sister, but he came to get her anyway, because the owner had asked and because it was a free trip to Korea, his first time out of Hawai'i. He handed my mother a note from the bar owner. "Get married," it read. "And come in."

"After tonight," the man had said to my mother after they signed the papers, "you are American." After that night, with our new citizenship virtually guaranteed, we new saw him again.

*   *   *

During the time my mother worked for the American PX in Seoul, all she heard from everyone—including my father—was, "American Good, Best," so she was unprepared for the actual paradise America had to offer. When we got off the plane in Honolulu, my mother kept asking the bar owner, "This America? This America?" The wet wrap of heat, the smell of concrete and rain, and the smallness of the dilapidated apartments nestled between high-rise condominiums lining the streets reminded my mother of Korea during the war. Remembering the refugees from the North who lived in Seoul by hiding out in big wooden boxes, she said in English, "Look like *piramin*, look like broke house. No look American!"

The sister-in-law, whom we called *Ahjima* out of respect, laughed. "Just wait," she said.

My mother waited, all the time looking, as *Ahjima*'s navy blue Cadillac silently cut through downtown, then knifed along the coastline highway where, on the right, my mother caught glimpses of ocean between palm trees, and, on the left, confronted the solid brown and green walls of mountain that stood out stark and clear against the white and blue of sky. The brightness hurt her eyes.

When the highway ended, we turned up a hill lined with a series of black iron fences and rock walls that encircled big houses and private swimming pools. More than anything else, it was those bright sapphire pools overlooking the dark ocean that started my mother humming. "Hmmm," she said. "Now this is a little bit American."

"Yes, here, Hawai'i Kai, is where all the best people live." *Ahjima* signaled and turned into a driveway, into a garage which opened, as if by magic, like a large mouth. "You can stay with me until you find an apartment of your own. That way you can watch my kids until your 8 o'clock shift at the bar," she told my mother.

During the day my mother watched me and *Ahjima*'s two girls, whom I was taught to call sisters. They called me "dummy," telling my mother and me it meant "little cutie." When they played house, I was the pet, which I liked because I knew what was expected of me: barking and panting on all fours. "Dummy," they said to each other, "makes a good dog 'cause she can't talk right anyway." Once I tried to improvise, pretending to shi-shi on the floor. They rolled up a newspaper and hit me on the nose. The sisters liked that so much it became part of the script: "This bad puppy needs to be housebroken!"

I missed them when, after braiding their hair and packing their lunches, my mother drove them to school for the day. After dropping them off, my mother slept through the late mornings and early afternoons while I watched television. Whispering things like "please" and "thank you" and—more daringly—"Daddy," I pretended that Mr. Rogers was my father as I waited for the sisters to return home.

After their school and tennis lessons, having missed me all day, they would fly to pinch my arms and pull my hair. "Look!" Older Sister would say to Middle Sister, "She likes it! She doesn't even cry!" I learned to control pain, to look at it from outside of myself so that the sisters could admire my strength.

"Let me try!" Middle Sister reached for an arm. "Ugh, it feels weird," she said as a chunk of skin folded and lodged underneath her fingernails. "I feel sick."

"Wow," Older Sister said, not unimpressed, as the three of us stood looking at the white hole in my arm. "Dummy's tough." But when the blood started to ooze into the pinch-hole, she added, "If you tell on us, we'll beat you up and kick you out of our house!"

I slept with a butter knife under my pillow then, in case they jumped me while I slept, and became so tough that when visitors to the house knelt beside me to comment, "How sweet!" I spat in their faces and said, "I'll scratch your eyes out."

I never once told on the sisters, not only because I was afraid of them, but because they were my best friends. Though they weren't allowed to— because sweets were too expensive to give to non-family—they shared their after school Ding-dongs and Twinkies with me. Once we ate a whole box. Crouched in our bunk bed cave, blankets from the top bunk hanging over the sides, we sucked the frosting out of the cylindrical cupcakes as they told me what they learned in school.

"Willy Kealoha said the F-word today. Miss Jenkins got so mad she jerked his arm and left a big Indian burn." Middle Sister held out her arm, twisting her elbow towards me. "All around here, like that. He was supposed to sit outside class until he was ready to come back and apologize, but all he kept saying was 'F-word, F-word, F-word.' The whole class heard, but Miss Jenkins made like she never."

"What's F-word mean?" I asked.

"F-word," said Older Sister, "means your daddy is going to die. F-word stands for . . . fuck." She whispered the word and then turned to hit Middle Sister, whose mouth had dropped open, on the arm. "I'm just explaining it, okay? I'm not really saying it."

Older Sister then mouthed what looked like the words, "Fuck You." When Middle Sister and I sucked in our breaths, and Middle Sister started to yell, "I'm telling, I'm telling," Older Sister said, "I was only saying 'Vacuum,' you dopes." Middle Sister wasn't convinced. "Here," Older Sister said then, "have the rest of my Twinkies. I don't want them anyway."

As she watched us eat the last in the box, Older Sister added, "Besides, if I said it to Myung, it wouldn't matter anyway; she doesn't have a father."

"I do, too," I yelled, ready to jump on her.

"Liar," Older Sister said.

"Liar," Middle Sister echoed.

"Yes, I do!" The Twinkies and Ding-dongs made me feel sick.

"Where is he then?" asked Middle Sister, rolling her eyes at Older Sister who, not looking at her, scowled at me.

"I see him every day—" I felt like I was going to throw up and it was then that the sisters began to sing: "Liar liar pants on fire—"

"Every day. On TV, he's famous." At least the lower bunk was Middle Sister's.

"On a telephone wire—Liar—"

Then, just before I threw up, I made the biggest mistake of my young life: "My dad," I said, "is Mr. Rogers!" For how much I had eaten, nothing really came out: mostly a frothy white mess of bubbles. But it stank.

"Gross!" The sisters screamed as they jumped out of our cave, pulling the blanket walls with them.

"Dumb-ass," yelled Older Sister. "Stupid Dummy! Is that your name, huh? Dummy Rogers, huh? You're so dumb, you think TV is real. You think your name is Dummy Rogers."

"F-word, F-word, F-word," Middle Sister kept saying. "F-word, F-word, F-word." Then Older Sister had asked, "Well, Dummy Rogers, do you know what a 'hapa bastard' is?"

*   *   *

It seems I spent most of elementary school trying on different names, popular names that the cheerleaders and May Day princesses had. In class, instead of copying down what was written on the blackboard, I'd write—in script—"Kelli," "Barbi," "Suzi," "Staci," making sure to dot each "i" with a heart. I'd pair those names with the last names of the cutest boys in class. I practiced for the time when I could change my name into something less "weird," believing that a better name could transform—or at least mask—the abnormalities in my self.

Then in the summer before intermediate school, I met a boy who, though he wasn't the cutest boy in class, vaguely resembled Mr. Rogers. When I saw that his father looked even more like my role-model daddy, I decided that I had found the family I would marry into. My boyfriend belonged to a family, recently transplanted from Fort Pierce, Florida, that reminded me of The Brady Bunch, The Partridge Family, the type of family that I only pretended to belong to: the type of family that talked at mealtimes.

When I was invited to their house for dinner, his parents met me at the door, curious about the "new woman in their baby boy's life." "How nice! A Hawaiian girl," they said to me, and in whispers to each other, "Remember Honey?"

Before me, my boyfriend had "made friends" with another Korean girl named Hyun Yi. "My baby likes Oriental girls," Tommy's mother smiled. "I try not to take it personally."

"Now, Mother," the father said. "The Oriental people are a fine people. Very respectful." He looked at me. "Isn't that right, Honey?"

I wasn't sure if he was calling me "Honey" as a form of endearment, or if he had me confused with his son's previous girlfriend. This was cleared up when his wife jabbed him and said, not quietly, "That's Monk Cha."

The rest of the evening, through the baked ham and gravied potatoes, through the mushroom soup, canned green bean and Baco-bits casserole, through the apple pie with Cokes and Cool-Whip, my boyfriend's father continued to call me "Honey." Sometimes this was followed by a correction from his wife or an "excuse me," but for the most part it was as if no one noticed the mistake—not even my boyfriend. Each time I was called the wrong name, Tommy would look away, his face blank. I felt as numb as his face, unable to get up and announce, "My name is Myung Ja!"

I realized then that if I myself could not even say my name, that if when I whispered to myself, "My name is Myung Ja," my voice wavered, struggling in my throat as if with a lie, then my name was a lie. Myung Ja was not, could not be, my true name. My mother had made a mistake. I was not a diamond in America, just different.

After that visit with the parents of the boy I thought I would marry, I decided to find my real name, a name that matched the one he would give me, a name that would make me American.

*　　*　　*

"I tried my best," my mother said. "But, of course, I didn't know anything about stars and numbers and letters. If I had money then, maybe I would have given it to a fortuneteller, a professional name finder." My mother shrugged, then smiled. "I can give you some money now, but."

I wanted to tell her that I didn't blame her for the problems with my name, but because I did, I just said, "No, Mom, I think I have enough saved up myself."

She gave me the name and Kaimukī address of a "famous" Vietnamese numerologist, one that "all the stars go to." "Hundreds of people try to see her, that's how much in demand she is. Everyone lines up for her outside, for days, to speak with her. She charges five thousand dollars to find their true name. They pay because they know that, since they will make millions after they get the right name, what's five thousand now?"

"That's crazy!" I said. "We don't have that kind of money." I tried to calculate how long, how many years of birthday money it would take to afford a new name. "I won't go," I announced, but inside I was desperate, even more convinced of the pricelessness of a new name.

My mother patted my arm. "Don't worry," she said. "I already talked to her. Special price for me. And you. Fifty dollars. I told her we'll give her the rest when you make your fortune off it."

The house on Wilhelmina Rise was not packed with hundreds of people. In fact, as I opened the rusting wire gate to the weedy lot, it seemed no one—not even the fortuneteller—was there. I double checked the faded numbers on the house, then walked through the yard, past a sun-bleached and molding three-foot plastic replica of the Virgin Mary and Christ Nativity scene, and up the front steps.

"Excuse me," I called through the screen door. "Hello? I have an appointment with the fortuneteller . . . my mother sent me."

When I thought I heard a "Come in," I opened the door, slipped off my sandals and stepped barefoot onto the straw-mat floor of her living room. After my eyes adjusted to the dim room, I saw Christ. He was everywhere. Huge black velvet posters of Jesus—his sad, teary eyes framed in a halo of long blond hair and beard—were thumbtacked onto the walls. In the spaces between the posters the fortune teller had pasted various "Born Again" bumper stickers: "In God We Trust," "My Heart Belongs to Christ," "Honk If You Love Jesus."

She was on her hands and knees in the back of the room, wiping the mat floor with a dishrag. "Easier to clean than carpet," she muttered, then got up and shuffled into the kitchen. She was not what I expected, less...mystical. With her freckled scalp peeking through scanty grey hair, her fraying plaid shirt knotted over cotton draw-pants, and her bumpy, stockinged feet thrust into rubber slippers, she just looked like anybody's old grandma-san.

The fortuneteller seated herself in a metal chair at one end of a two-person, fold-out card table and lit a stick of incense. "Keeps the flies away," she said, waving at the smoke pooling in front of her face. Behind her, next to the only window of the room, was a large gold-painted cross, beginning to peel, adorned with a particularly gruesome Christ. Gouged by the Crown of Thorns, blood dripped into his face and down his body. His chest, ripped open, revealed a blue and red heart. I tried not to look at it.

"First," she said, pushing a pad and pencil towards me, "write your name." When I did, she took the top paper, folded it into the palm of her hand and said, "Now, tell me what you want."

I told her my story, beginning with before my birth, and explained why I needed a new name. "I want to be an American now," I told her. "So please find me an American name."

The fortuneteller closed her eyes and, lifting the pencil, began to draw numbers on the writing pad. Seven, three, eight, nine, one, over and over again, some of the numbers overlapping and canceling the others out. My eyes, blurry with incense smoke, wandered up to the Jesus above the window. The heart began to beat each time I blinked. I imagined blood pulsating out of the body, dripping drop by drop like rubies down a kitchen sink.

After a few minutes, the fortuneteller put down the pencil and opened her hand. "That'll be fifty dollars," she said, as she handed me the paper on which I had written "Myung Ja."

"But!" I said, then swallowed. "I don't understand."

"Cash," she said. "No checks." She laid the paper flat on the table, smoothing the crease with the flat of her palm. "This name is your shining, your brightness, your heart and treasure. I am saving you a lot of money and trouble to let you buy it back from me. . . . And tell your mama I said 'hi.' Good woman, her." The old lady laughed, cackling like a chicken.

I frowned at her and swallowed again as, unable to stare her down, my eyes focused on the table-top. "Old witch, old witch!" I thought to myself, over and over, like a mantra. As I continued my silent chant, willing myself not to blink, not to cry, a light from the window caught and reflected off the naming-paper she handed back to me. Its glare hurt my eyes, momentarily blinding me just like, it seemed to me then, like the brilliance of diamonds.

BY LAUREEN KWOCK

GAU

obin's mother always made the New Year's gau. One for each daughter's family and one for the neighbors on either side. There were five in all, sometimes six. Phyllis, Robin's oldest sister, with four sons in baseball leagues, always wanted two because the boys gobbled up the gau so fast.

Mama never got to eat much of her own gau—they were reserved for giving away or exchanging, but she ate someone else's gau, usually comparing it to her own.

"This one's too sweet," she'd say, or "They make it too soft."

What did other people think of Mama's gau, Robin wondered as she padded barefoot from her bedroom. Did they complain that it had "no taste," "not enough sugar," or was "so hard, I almost cracked a tooth." Did they let it grow moldy because they didn't know enough to cover it with a dish rag at night and take off the cloth during the day to let it air?

The grandchildren preferred the gau fried, not thinking of the sticky mess it made at the ends of chopsticks. Robin herself yearned for the smell of bubbling brown slabs of gau soaked in Wesson oil, but now that Roger was watching his cholesterol count—he would turn forty next month—she didn't fry anything. Everything was steamed, baked, broiled, or microwaved.

She drew open the living room drapes, peering out at the familiar Mōʻiliʻili mist. A rainy Saturday was perfect for making gau, her mother said. You couldn't go any place. Stuck at home. You might as well be stuck in the kitchen.

Roger was already out, headed for Kāneʻohe with Mike, their twelve-year-old son, for a round of golf. They'd be gone at least five hours, maybe more, depending on the traffic on the Pali and the number of Japanese tourists on the course. Robin might as well try Mama's recipe.

In the kitchen, she opened the cupboard, and lifted down the steaming pan and rack her mother had given her. Her fingers cakewalked through the recipe file until they reached a card marked "Gau."

Two months ago, Robin's mother had phoned her.

"Come to lunch, Sunday. Leave Roger and the kids at home."

"Why?" Robin had asked, hunched over the dining table doing paperwork from the bank. She couldn't understand why Mama didn't want Roger there; she usually fussed over her Chinese son-in-law.

"Never mind. Just come. I have something important to tell you."

Phyllis had also gotten a call, and so had Janet, the middle sister. Phyl drove them to Kaimukī in her new Buick, warning them that Mama must be dying and probably wanted to tell them.

Janet, switching stations on Phyl's car radio, thought Mama might be thinking of dividing up her jewelry. The last time Mama thought she was dying, she had given Janet a jade bracelet for her birthday. She had given Phyllis pearl earrings. By the time Robin's birthday had rolled around in November, Mama had finally gone to a doctor and realized she wasn't dying. Robin got a birthday card with twenty dollars.

Mama hadn't been dying, and she hadn't wanted to give them any jewelry. She simply wanted to tell them she was sick of cooking.

"Who isn't sick of cooking?" Phyllis asked, thinking of endless baseball pot lucks.

"We're all sick of cooking, Mama," Robin said, sitting in a saucer chair in the patio. Robin wasn't just sick of cooking—she was bad at it, which made the whole experience even worse.

"You don't cook that much," Janet told Mama, running a hose over Mama's potted plants.

Mama reached over and slapped her second daughter hard and fast on the wrist, then flicked away a dead mosquito with a crimson fingertip.

"I cooked for forty years!" she declared, glaring at them through her gold-rimmed glasses. "I'm tired. It's someone else's turn."

The announcement surprised Robin. Her mother didn't live with any of her daughters, preferring to live alone after their father's death five years ago. Mah jong, tai chi, and her lady friends kept Mama busy. So why the talk about cooking? She only cooked if she wanted to.

Hadn't they all chipped in last Christmas to buy Mama a microwave oven? Robin had shown her all the different brands of microwave dinners in the freezer section of the supermarket. Mama didn't have to cook.

"Here," her mother said, passing out recipe cards, one to each of them.

The *kung su pyung* cakes went to Janet. That was a very old family recipe, passed down from Maui Grandma. Even Mama very rarely made them.

"And now I know why," Janet had said when Robin asked if she had made any yet. "It's too hard."

David, Janet's husband, later confided to Roger that she had tried the recipe twice, throwing away dozens of rock hard or tasteless cakes. Enough to drive him to the poor house.

"Lye water. Do you even know what that is?" Janet had howled. Robin didn't know. She had trouble just saying *kung su pyung*. She was glad she hadn't gotten that recipe.

Phyl, who always had a crowd of people over to feed (baseball players, friends, in-laws), got the sweet sour pig's feet.

"Pig's feet are disgusting," Phyllis said. "I can't bear to look at them in the supermarket, all pink and whitish. Just imagine where those feet have been."

Robin wished she hadn't said that and wondered if she would ever eat sweet sour pig's feet again.

"I'm not cooking this," Phyllis declared.

And Mama gave Robin the recipe for gau. Robin had put the recipe in the card file and hadn't thought about it until a month before Chinese New Year, when Mama called to place her order.

"I'm not making any gau this year," Mama said.

"You're not?" Robin wound the telephone cord around her index finger.

"I told you. I'm not cooking anymore."

Everyone else wanted gau, too. Robin didn't plan on giving any to Mama's neighbors, since they weren't her neighbors, after all. But maybe one for Roger's mother and then her sisters. Phyllis, as usual, wanted two.

"Why did Mama give me this recipe?" Robin complained to her sisters. "It takes forever to cook. Five hours."

"Ever try making *kung su pyung*?" Janet asked.

"Pig's feet is no picnic," Phyllis retorted.

Mama had given other recipes to them over the years. There were the reliable jook and stuffed bittermelon. Jook came in handy during flu season or after Thanksgiving, a useful way to use the turkey carcass. None of them ate the bittermelon. All of them ate the gau.

Robin stood in her kitchen now, watching the valance curtains flap and wishing she could go outside. There was no way to avoid it. Today she was making gau. She picked up a square brown package of rice flour. Not mochi flour like the Japanese used, but glutinous rice powder which Mama had bought with her in Chinatown. The two of them had stepped into a grocery store, where Mama had shown her the *wong tong*, the sticks of brown sugar, and told Robin she must use them in the gau. That's all gau really was—brown sugar and flour.

Robin tore open a package of *wong tong*, and broke the sugar slabs in half. She added them to the water in her Revereware Dutch oven, then placed the pot on the burner and turned the heat on. When the melting sugar liquified, Robin took the pot off the burner to cool and checked the recipe card again. Line the steaming pan with ti leaves. Darn. She'd forgotten about the ti leaves.

Where would she find them?

Suddenly, Robin remembered her hairdresser Lonnie's shop just a block away. There were lots of ti plants in the front of the building. Of course, Robin might have to give her hairdresser a gau too. She yanked open a drawer and grabbed her shears, mentally adding Lonnie's name to her list.

By the time she got back to the apartment with the ti leaves from Lonnie, the sugar mixture in the pot had cooled. Robin was panting slightly, out of breath. She looked at the recipe. Line the pan with ti leaves. Oil first.

Oil the pan or oil the leaves? Robin took no chances—she oiled both. But how to line it? Did Mama mean put the ti leaves around the pan or lay them flat and let them overlap?

By the time she got the pan lined Robin swore she would never do this again. Ever. No matter what Mama or Phyllis said. They could buy their own gau.

Robin mixed the rice flour with the sugar by hand according to Mama's instructions, squeezing the lumps out with her fingers. It felt gooey, but it wasn't difficult. When the mixture was smooth, she poured the batter into the pan until it nearly reached the top. It resembled brown goop.

When the gau was finally steaming, Robin sat down at the kitchen table and ate a breakfast of Cheerios and milk. It was only eight o'clock. By noon, the gau would be done.

In the first half hour, Robin sponged down the Formica counters, paid her electric bill, watched cartoons, and made up a Longs list.

She had always been a fast worker. At the age of thirty-eight, she was in line for a vice-presidency at the bank. In banking circles, being Chinese helped. Everyone thought she knew a lot about money. Little did they know that she let Roger handle the checkbook.

The apartment grew warm from the gau steaming in the kitchen. Absently, Robin lifted the hair up and away from her neck. Time for a trim. She should have made an appointment with Lonnie while she was at the shop. Robin remembered how at her last visit Lonnie had mentioned the number of white hairs she was finding and how Robin might need coloring soon.

At nine, she checked the water level in the pot. It was down, so she added two extra cups.

Why had Mama given her the gau and not the pig's feet? She was tougher than Phyllis and could look at pig's feet in the market. Heck, she had even seen the pig's head hanging in Chinatown the day Mama had showed her where to buy the rice flour and *wong tong*.

Pig's feet took only two hours to cook. The *kung su pyung* took fifteen minutes, less if the oven was hot. So why had Mama given her the gau? Maybe to play a joke? Maybe to teach her patience?

Her mother had always been after her to slow down. As a child, Robin had always been in a hurry, wanting to do everything fast. As though life was a race, Mama clucked. A race until it was nearly over. Then you never want to finish.

Robin was the youngest. Hurrying was the only way she could keep up with her two older sisters. If she dawdled her sisters left her behind. If she couldn't do something well she'd just try to do it any way she could.

Was she still impatient?

From nine to ten Robin read half a detective novel and old copies of *People* magazine until her eyes began to burn. She finally tossed the book down. No sense fogging up her contact lenses. She needed an appointment to see her optometrist, and put that on her list of things to do next month. She was in no hurry. The next time she saw her eye doctor the verdict would probably be bifocals.

At ten-thirty, Robin began laying out a hand of solitaire on her kitchen table with a deck from the California Hotel. Mama's favorite Vegas hideaway.

She laid a red jack on a black queen, thinking of the last time her mother and father had flown to Vegas with their three daughters. Dad knew then that he was sick, but had gone on the trip anyway, giving his daughters money as though they were kids and not grown women making more than he ever had as a mailman.

Dad never gambled. He watched them gamble, got upset when they lost and told them to stop when they won. Robin flicked the ace of hearts over to the side of the table, thinking how much she missed her father.

Before Janet took Mama to Vegas last year, they visited Dad's grave and put a *poo look* on the headstone. They had won. This year, when Janet had gone by herself and put a *poo look*, she hadn't won. Dad was telling her to stop already.

Solitaire grew boring, so Robin decided to boil water and steam her face, a trick she learned from a women's magazine. It made her face feel softer.

Her face and the gau steamed together for fifteen minutes. At eleven o'clock, Robin opened the lid of the Revereware pot. The top of the gau looked drippy and was an odd two-shaded brown. The middle was sunken, like an old man's chest. Was this normal?

She telephoned her mother to find out. The phone rang and rang. Of course, Mama was out. This was Saturday. No one in her right mind was home on a Saturday morning. An hour more. Nothing to do but let it go. Robin left the gau alone and added more water to the bottom of the pot. For lunch, she ate a banana which was high in potassium, Roger said, and a good treatment for high blood pressure. She didn't have that yet. But it was probably waiting for her at the end of the finish line along with everything else: bifocals and age spots.

At noon, Robin poked the gau with a bamboo stick. It came away clean. Done. Finally. She stood back, feeling proud and relieved.

After three days, the gau was firm enough to cut. Robin put it in an empty Danish cookie can and drove to Kaimukī. It sat on her mother's kitchen table, looking lopsided. Some of the gau had seeped through the ti leaves.

"The next one will look better," her mother said, reaching into a cabinet and bringing out a Danish cookie can of her own. "For you."

"Mama, you made a gau!" Robin exclaimed when she looked inside.

Her mother grinned, her gold tooth flashing. "Just for you. Now you know it's not as hard as they think. Not as easy, either."

"I know."

Her mother sliced Robin's gau and her own carefully with a knife.

"It's good," Robin said, biting into her mother's gau. She savored the smooth firm texture and the not-too-sweet taste. This might be the last gau Mama might ever make.

Her mother sat down across from her and put two pieces on her golden wheat dinner plate.

"So's yours," Mama said, after trying Robin's.

"Truth?"

"Since when do I lie?" her mother demanded.

Robin finished the slice of her mother's gau, then tasted a piece of her own. She chewed it carefully. It was good. Not perfect in looks, but it tasted good.

"You're not dying, are you, Mama?" she asked as her mother put the teakettle on.

Her mother laughed. "No, just tired of cooking."

Robin drank a cup of tea and ate another slice of gau. "Why did you give the recipe for gau to me?" she asked.

Her mother glanced up, looking confused. Tendrils of white hair curled at the side of her neck. Steam from the tea fogged her glasses.

"What are you talking about?" she demanded.

"Why did you give the recipe for gau to me?" Robin repeated.

Mama shrugged. "I handed the recipes out one by one. You were the last. You got what was left."

Robin laughed. "So you had no special reason to give me the gau, Janet the *kung su pyung* cakes, and Phyl the pig's feet?"

Her mother shook her head. "You girls always think there's a reason for everything. Stop thinking so much. Eat your gau."

BY R. ZAMORA LINMARK

From the Stone The Virgin Mary Sees Everything: A Trilogy

I. Our Lady of Kalihi

irgin Mary lives at the top of Monte Street right below King Kamehameha School, but you don't have to be from Kalihi Valley to know that. You can be riding the skyslide in front of Gibson's department store, getting stung by a jellyfish at Bellow's, going on a buta hunt at Camp Erdman, or climbing the thirteen deadly steps near Morgan's Corner, but the millisecond you turn towards Kalihi Valley, or even think to, you see her: a woman walking out of a mountain carrying a baby in her left hand and a crystal ball in the other.

The first thing you notice is that she isn't like the other Virgins. She bears no fancy names like Regina Cleri or Medjugorje, for she was simply crowned Our Lady of the Mount. Not Our Lady of the Valley or Queen of Kalihi, but simply, Our Lady of the Mount.

She doesn't talk to children like Queen of Fatima because her mouth is veiled with asbestos. She can't dance when you blast the car stereo and shine your headlights on her, like Mary in Diamond Head Cemetery, because her feet are bound by a fat green snake with a pitchfork tongue. She isn't a jetsetting queen like La Naval, whose almond-shaped face, high cheekbones, slanty eyes, and flawless gown earned her a free trip around the world. And she won't heal the sick like Our Lady of Lourdes or perform miraculous feats like Our Lady of Mediatrix of All Grace, who showered the earth with roses, because on the day she was proclaimed Our Lady of the Mount, Hurricane 'Iwa stormed into the island and turned it into a garbage dump.

The buffeting winds jolted everyone and everything, including Our Lady of the Mount, whose tin-foil tiara and head were flung out into the Pacific Ocean. For months she stood decapitated at the top of the hill, waiting for Father Pacheco to collect enough donations to buy her a new head. When she was finally given the chance to think and see again, the parish of Our Lady of the Mount Church was a penny away from filing bankruptcy, for her disaster-proof head cost more than an arm and a leg. It was so expensive it came with a free crown and a makeover fit for a Halston runway. Sophisticated with the jaguar eyes of Bianca Jagger, pout of Sophia

Loren, cheekbones of Lauren Hutton, thick arched brows of Brooke Shields, and the attitude of a Studio 54 Disco Mama.

As you grapple your way up to Monte Street with a bouquet of roses in your hand, you wonder if this mascaraed diva ramping out of the mountain is the same one that spoke like a dream the first time you collapsed before her, in front of the green snake that grins at you from around her feet. You offer her the roses wilting in your hand and look up at her newly acquired face. She does not look at you sweetly or serenely as before, but points her catty eyes toward the ships anchored at Pearl Harbor, prowling to see which sailor will crown her Notre Dama de Noche. Or simply, Our Lady of the Night.

II. Bino and Rowena Make a Litany to Our Lady of the Mount

Hail Mary, Mother of Christ
Mother of Christ
Mother of the Cross
From the Cross Jesus gave you to us
The kindest, the most loving
Mother of all
We thank you Lord, our Holy Trinity
Father of heaven and earth
For giving us your own Mother
Mother of Perpetual Help
Mother of all sinners
Mother of all mothers
Who should be seen and not heard
Mother of all children,
Who should be seen and not heard
Have mercy on us
Give us strength for our daily bread
Most Immaculate Mother
Mother of weights and barbells
Holy Virgin of virgins
For it's you whom we plead
Mother of Divine Grace
For it's you who we need
To ask God to have mercy on us
Have mercy on us
Mother most pure
Queen of Camay

Mother most chaste
Queen of Lysol
Mother most flawless
Queen of Revlon
Mother undefiled
Queen of Generals
We pray for our country
The land of our birth
Have mercy on us
Mother of Chancellors
Queen of all queens
Have mercy on us
We pray for all nations
For peace to all nations
Have mercy on us
Mother of all ears
Mother of good counsel
Mother most admirable
Mother most honorable
Virgin of thy Father
Maker of heaven and earth
Virgin most kind
Virgin most powerful
Virgin most loving
Virgin most venerable
Virgin most asked-for
Virgin most merciful
Virgin most blessed
Mother of orphans
Mother of Annie
Pray for her
Mother of Madeline
Pray for her
Mother of Wonder Woman
Pray for her
Holy Sister of Mrs. Garrett
Pray for her
Holy Sister of Betty and Veronica
Pray for them
Holy Sister of Marcia, Jan, and Cindy Brady
Pray for them

Mother of Ambassador of Goodwill
Mother of Gary Coleman
Pray for him
Mother of Buck Rogers
Pray for him
Mother of Erik Estrada
Pray for him
Holy Sister of Fred and Barney
Pray for them
Holy Sister of the Jackson 5
Pray for them
Mirror of Justice
Queen of the Superfriends
Pray for them
Mother of all things
In heaven and earth
Queen of Longs Drugs
Pray for us
Queen of Castle Park
Pray for us
Queen of VISA, Mastercard & American Express
Pray for us
Queen of 5-star hotels
Pray for us
Mother of Ronald McDonald
Pray for us
Queen of the Vatican
Mother of Archie Bunker
Most High of all Highness
Queen of Eiffel Tower
Tower of David
Tower of Pisa
Tower of Babel
Queen of all Angels
Kelly Garrett
Sabrina Duncan
Kris Munroe
Queen of Slinky
We pray to you
Our spiritual vessel
Vessel of Salvation

Vessel of Devotion
Vessel of Martial Law
We pray to you
Lift up your hands
We lift them up
Most Glory of all that is glory
Open your mouths
We give you praise
Most Noble of all that is noble
Lead us to the gates of heaven
Queen of Pac Man
Queen of Space Invaders
Queen of Centipede
Carer of the sick
Shelterer from famine
Guardian of Luke Skywalker
Holy Mary, Mother of God
Pray for us
Queen of Martyrs
Queen of all wounds
Mother of my mother's bruises
Pray for her
Mother of my father's belt buckle
Pray for him
Mother of my mother's barbed-wire lips
Pray for her
Mother of my father's high kick
Pray for him
Mother of my mother's tetanus shots
Pray for her
Mother of my father's two-by-four
Pray for him
Holy Queen of all queens
Queen of Mercurochrome
Queen of bandages
Queen of a thousand excuses
Queen of sick calls
Queen of thirty-eight stitches
Queen of ICU
We come to you
Holy Mary, Mother of God

Mother of all mothers
Now and at the hour of our death
Amen.

III. Madeline and Pepito at Luneta Park, Honolulu

Manong Rocky is at it again, turning the living room upside down and inside out because he can't find the plastic bag that keeps him awake for days, and sometimes, weeks.

"And energetic, brah, no forget energetic," he says, though energy is the last thing to cross people's minds when they see his skinny body sprawled on the porch steps with his eyes staring out into space.

He enters the master bedroom fully made up like a honeymoon suite and goes straight for the closet. He slides the closet door open and begins searching for the Ziploc bag among the neatly pressed clothes. One by one he inspects each and every garment, feeling the pockets and digging his hand in. Halfway through the rack, he starts pulling the clothes off the plastic hangman and flinging them across the room, tearing the straps of dresses.

He reaches for the old boxes on top of the closet shelf and dumps their contents on the floor. He rummages through documents, family photo albums, and memorabilia, but comes up empty-handed. Frustrated, he yanks out the vanity drawers, frantically hunting for the glass pipe and crystals that he insists keep him going. And going.

"Where da hell she wen put 'em," he screams as he flips open the lid of the jewelry box, which, a few weeks ago, contained his wife's engagement ring, a pearl necklace, a diamond wedding ring, and a pair of sapphire earrings handed down to her from her great-grandmother. He trashes the entire vanity top, hurling perfume bottles, makeup kits, and a heart-shaped picture frame of their only daughter Rowena across the room.

He retreats to the living room and sits on the upholstered couch from Wigwam Furniture company. He pounds the coffee table, causing half-empty beer cans and a bowl of cereal to spill onto the stained carpet.

He gets up, walks into the kitchen, and starts tossing the canned goods onto the floor. He shoves his hand into an open box of Western Family baking soda, then sticks his forefinger into his mouth and sucks the powder until his teeth dig into skin. With blood trailing down his chin, he pitches the box across the room, hitting the bookshelf. "Fuckin' Pearly, you goin' get it," he screams.

*   *   *

The first—and only—time Manang Pearly hid the Ziploc bag from Manong Rocky, everyone in Hawai'i found out, courtesy of the morning and evening newspapers, the five local TV stations, a morning radio program, and COMAAH. Coalition of Mothers Against Abusive Husbands.

She was so badly beaten she needed forty-eight stitches and three surgeries to align her spine, remove a ruptured spleen, and extract shards of beer mug glass from her face. She coded three times, had five blood transfusions, and was tested for everything, including a toxic screen to see if she had been under the influence of alcohol or drugs.

She was seen by a dozen or so consultants, including a psychiatric intern who asked her if she or any members in her family had a history of mental illnesses. None. A hospital chaplain visited her room every three o' clock in the afternoon to recite the Angelus. Between the consultations and prayers, she was wheeled to the Rehabilitation Unit where she spent a half-hour learning how to move her upper and lower extremities, and another half-hour learning how to say wee-na, her daughter's nickname.

For weeks, readers found her making headlines in Section A of both *The Bulletin* and *Inquirer*. SPOUSE ABUSE HITS ISLAND AGAIN. HUS-BAND NEARLY BEATS WIFE TO DEATH. THIRD THIS YEAR BY FIL-IPINO. Listeners tuned in to Kimo & Kawika on P-39 AM to keep abreast of her condition, as well as to voice their own opinions and concerns regarding the issue. Viewers watched the local evening news, where each station devoted five-minute segments to her, Manong Rocky, and their only child Rowena. KRTV even treated Rowena to an all-you-can-eat ice cream at Farrell's after she spilled her guts in front of the camera.

Morning, noon, and night, Manang Pearly was the topic of current events pop quizzes, school papers, dissertations, and gossip. Diners, both young and old, talked of her victimization and passed it around the table as if it were salt-and-pepper shakers. Sympathizers throughout the island sent her gifts, food baskets, money, and toys for Rowena, along with letters which spelled out "sorry," "support," "hope," and "victim."

On the day of her discharge, local residents and tourists trekked to Monte Street in Kalihi Uka to catch a glimpse of the person who had so affected the lives of both Filipino and non-Filipino women. To them, she was a survivor and a victim, a saint and an idiot. Members of COMAAH had camped out the night before at the top of the street next to the grotto of the Virgin Mary. Manang Pearly was, as *The Bulletin* put it, the biggest news to hit the island since the bombing of Pearl Harbor.

As the Oldsmobile veered onto Monte Street, she peered out the window and saw a mob of people turning her front yard into a battlefield. Reporters, journalists, and militant members of COMAAH rushed to the car being driven by an off-duty officer, each of them dying to know if she had changed her mind and would press charges against her husband. "No," she said, "we have a daughter, and I cannot break a holy vow."

*   *   *

Rowena and Bino enter the house. Manong Rocky is sitting on the couch, brooding, a stripe of dry blood on his arm .

"Hi, Daddy," Rowena says, trying not to sound alarmed.

"Hi, Uncle Rocky," Bino says.

And the two run for Rowena's bedroom, crushing beer cans, cigarette butts, and soiled food.

"Bino, I'm scared," Rowena says.

"Let's get out of here, Wena."

She grabs her Paddington bear from the bed. Bino picks up the Madeline books strewn on the floor. And they whisk past Rocky, still malingering in his own world.

"Bye, Daddy."

"Bye, Uncle Rocky."

The screen door flings open. By the time it slams, Bino and Rowena are already at the Virgin Mary shrine right above Rowena's house.

"Oh, Bino, I'm scared," Rowena says, watching her father through the living room window.

"Don't be, Wena. We have Mama Mary to protect us."

"Will she protect my mommy too?"

"Of course, she will. And all we have to do is pray for her, okay?"

"Okay."

Upon kneeling, they raise their heads and gaze at the statue of a woman who watches the island from a stone.

"Hail Mary, we come to you"

"from sufferings of Almighty"

"endless pains on the Cross"

"please pray for my mommy"

"save her from dangers"

"ladders and snakes"

"pray too for Uncle Rocky"

"and other broken-down fathers"

"so that they may rise"

"and give love"

" and hope"

"and strength"

"to mothers"

"and children"

"forever and ever"

"Amen."

They make the sign of the cross then perform their own ritual of devotion to Our Lady of the Mount: picking flowers from the red tin-foiled pots encircling the shrine then kissing the toes of the statue before crowning her feet with poinsettias.

"Rowena, I got an idea," Bino says. "Why don't we play Madeline and Pepe today? We haven't done it in awhile."

"Okay, but I don't feel like running around Paris today. It's winter and we won't see anything even if we climb to the very top of the Eiffel Tower."

"Well, where would you like to go?"

"I dunno."

"How about Manila? Do you want to see the city where I used to live?"

"Yes, but how?"

"No problema, mi amiga. I am Pepe and mi padre es the Spanish Ambassador, remember?"

"Oh yeah, I keep forgetting."

"Okay, close your eyes and I'll take you to the most beautiful place in the world. Luneta Park."

As instructed, Rowena shuts her eyes and waits.

Bino begins mimicking the buzzing sound of a plane.

One minute passes

then two minutes

then: "Pepe how come I'm not seeing anything?" asks Rowena.

"That's because we're not there yet, Madeline. We're still flying over Guam. Just keep your eyes closed, and be patient. We should be landing just about . . . Welcome to Luneta Park, Madeline."

"Wow," Rowena says, "what pretty flowers. They look like earrings, Pepe."

"They're called santan, Madeline."

"And what's that huge ball over there?"

"Why, it's the globe fountain. Look where the water flows to, Madeline."

"A skating rink, Pepe! I see a skating rink but I forgot my skates."

"It's all right, Madeline. We can always come back. Want to walk around the park?"

Rowena nods. Bino takes her hand and they pretend to walk, the earth moving on imaginary treadmills.

"Pepe, I see a man made of stone."

"That's the statue of Dr. José Rizal, mi amiga."

"Who's he?"

"He's the national hero of the Philippines. He helped the Filipinos win their freedom against Spain many, many years ago."

Bino releases Rowena's hand.

"Don't leave me, Pepe," Rowena shouts, her eyes still closed.

"No, I won't," Bino says. "I'm only picking a flower for you to give to Dr. Rizal."

"But he's way up in the sky, Pepe."

Bino hands the poinsettia to Rowena. "Throw it to him, Madeline," he says. "Don't worry, he'll catch it."

Rowena throws the poinsettia in the air.

"Did he catch it?"

"Yes, Pepe."

"Now, he'll remember you forever."

Bino sees Manang Pearly unlatching the gate, dragging her body up the porch steps as if she is climbing the Himalayas. Bino waves at her but she doesn't see him.

Manang Pearly looks beat, having returned from her two jobs which began the night before and ended the following afternoon. From midnight to seven in the morning she's confined in a bullet-proofed cashier's booth at a 24-hour gas station on King and Kalihi, and then, from eight to three in the afternoon, she's scrubbing toilets and making the beds of tourists staying at the Sheraton.

With eyes closed and imagination wide open, Rowena points her finger at the Dole pineapple cannery. "Pepe, is that a palace?"

"That's the Manila Hotel owned by the First Lady," Bino says, his eyes guarding Manang Pearly who has surrendered herself to the rent-to-own couch from Wigwam.

"Do you know who she is, Madeline?"

"Isn't she the one with feet like Ms. Piggy's and—"

"And?"

"And the one who invited the whole world to her daughter's wedding?"

"That's right, Madeline. In fact, there's a party going on right now in the hotel garden. It's her son's birthday."

"Can we go, Pepe?"

"Siempre, Madeline. We are her special guests."

"This garden is so beautiful, Pepe. Japanese lanterns criss-crossing above a kidney-shaped pool. I wish I brought along my Strawberry Shortcake bathing suit, Pepe."

Bino keeps his eyes on Manang Pearly.

"I see a very beautiful woman," Rowena says.

"What does she look—" Bino's sentence is cut off by the appearance of Manong Rocky in the living room.

"Oh, she looks so peaceful, Pepe. Like Our Lady of the Mount. She moves so gracefully, as if she's made of water. I want her to be my friend, our friend, Pepe."

Bino doesn't say a word, holds his breath instead as Manong Rocky hovers over Manang Pearly. Bino squeezes Rowena's hand.

"Ouch, Pepe," Rowena yells, "your nails."

Manong Rocky smacks Manang Pearly to wakefulness.

"I'm sorry." Bino loosens his grip.

Manong Rocky hits Manang Pearly again, punching her so hard this time that her nose is in her face.

"Run. Get out of there," Bino shouts.

"What are you talking about, Pepe?" Rowena says.

"I mean, go to her, Madeline. Go and tell her how beautiful she is."

Rowena jogs in place.

"Excuse me, Ma'am," Rowena says, panting. "Excuse me, my name is Madeline and I think you're very, very beautiful. What's your name?"

Manang Pearly kicks Manong Rocky in the gut and scrambles for the door.

"Would you like to meet my friend Pepe, Señora Paz?"

Manong Rocky catches Manang Pearly's ankle. She trips and her face lands on the coffee table.

"Pepe, come and meet Señora Paz."

Blood paints Manang Pearly's face. She pushes herself up and struggles once more for the door.

"No," Bino shouts as Manong Rocky takes Manang Pearly by the shoulders and slams her against the entertainment center. One of the shelves gives in and buries Manang Pearly in Childcraft encyclopedia.

"Pepe, do you want to meet Señora Paz or what?" Rowena asks again.

"Huh?" Bino is stunned.

"Señora Paz, do you want to meet her or not?"

"Of course, Madeline. Of course I want to meet her," Bino says, trying to sound calm. Crossing the border back to the imaginary world, Pepe says, "I'd love to meet Señora Paz, Madeline. Where is she?"

"She's right over—" Rowena points her finger at her father dragging her mother out of the beaver dam of books. He then pulls her by the hair and bangs her face against his knees.

"She was just there a minute ago," Rowena says. "I told her I was coming back. Oh, we've lost her, Pepe. She's left, and I don't feel like playing this game anymore, Bino."

Rowena knuckle-rubs her eyes.

Manong Rocky swings Manang Pearly around and around, and as he lets go, Rowena opens her eyes and screams at the first sign of light: A woman, covered in slivers, flying with her arms out to embrace her daughter one last time.

BY MARY LOMBARD

THE SILVER PATH

Clifford had a routine. Every day he walked over to the park. Walking kept you young, that's why, so every day Clifford walked, only a few blocks. The same place every time, the back side of the park, the street side, the green pavilion. He liked meeting his friends over there, good guys, and passing the pupus and the time till Spark came. When Spark came, real stories poured. "Where you get all doze stories?" Clifford would say, and that was like one cue, eh? and everybody would laugh cause Spark's stories always started the same way. They always started with the silver path.

Ever since Spark quit his job bussing tables on the Lurline, it seemed like, he'd been hiding out from Matson Navigation, the reason being this silver path he went and laid down all the way from L.A. to Honolulu. Started with Spark leaning on the rail one night feeling like a pin-point in the dark universe and wondering who's steering the ship when all of a sudden he can't hear the engines, he can't even feel 'em under his feet. He's aware of something—something moving in the middle of this great silence. The way he told it, the moon woke him up. It came out, laid a path, raced the ship, hid again. Guy so shook he let go this knife he was fiddling with, he jus dropped it. And out of the dark it came bright—this flash, like a signal, a voice in his ear.

After that, night after night, the high moon showing where, Spark went ahead and dropped silverware overboard the side. More and more silverware, and anything resembling silverware. Knives, forks, even serving trays once in a while, Matson stuff, of course, and as the habit grew, he got more particular, so he started polishing it up first. He started scouting garage sales and thrift shops and bringing stuff from home, hiding it in his bunk till he figured he was over his path, the crew covering for him. Then one night a pot went clunk on the lower deck, and the boss noticed. Was not even a Matson pot that time but, the boss wouldn't listen.

So, the hiding. Years going by. Spark hiding while Matson waited. All the time Matson thinking the guy going back hang down one magnet for haul up all that silver. A fortune in silver. Clifford couldn't get over that.

Matson watching, Spark grinning, the path there. Winding and gleaming on the bottom of the Pacific Ocean, and pointing home.

"A silver path," Clifford would say. "As better den a movie any day."

Funny thing, though. This path began to lead Spark into real life, like it was showing him. One time it pointed into the city. They're docked in Honolulu at the time, after a big rain, and all of a sudden—the sun. He's squinting up this wet street, and he can't help but see its shininess, practically blinding. The ocean was dark that day but, he knew where his path was cause he seen it pointing, so he walked up the silver street straight to Lita's Bar and Grill and straight into the arms of his true wife. His third wife that time but, his only true one.

You'd think that would be the end of it, but no. The path kept on pointing the way, and his true wife was the one who cried when Spark left, who kept the juk and the noodles waiting on the stove for the returning Spark, who believed every single tale he ever told and who, later on, made him promise to go back and drop down her gold bracelet with both their names on it, and the shiny urn with her little bit of ashes in it. By this time Spark's not working the ships any more. He had to hire one fishing boat to get him in the shipping lane, off the east tip of the island, off Makapuʻu, in fact, where he could see the current marking the place below.

It seemed to Clifford like this path thing was catching or something cause it never really stopped. There was no real path out there, right? But it grabbed him, the story, eh? And it kept growing, it kept leading in and out of other stories and everywhere while they stay yakking in the green pavilion, every day talking story, everybody chipping in, telling new ones, improving old ones. Even the guy Take who was shell shock in Italy in the war cracking open his mouth, laughing so hard the tears running, running down, so before long, you felt like the whole world was wipe clean. Even talking the sex stuff or stealing candy bars from kidtime, you'd sit there feeling pure, like that, peaceful.

So, every day, the pavilion. Jus dropping by when they felt like it, someone saying, How bout the silver path. Jus kidding but, was enough to set 'em off. No hassle, no timetable, nothing like that, jus guys hanging out, spreading jokes, trying to top Spark, to sink Bones at cribbage. Ironwoods making plenty shade, the breeze lightly touching, the ocean keeping a steady beat on one side, cars humming on the other, people waving on their way to the beach. Nights the sausage off the hibachi so hot it burn the tongue. The bulb overhead dim but, plenty light for see their cards, the dark warm all around them.

So OK. One day Clifford saw a construction hut on the slope across the road from the pavilion. He said, "Eh, what's going on dere?" And Frank, who used to work in the transportation department, said too much cars parking over the road, li'dat, so they going make more places for park. Then Clifford got sick.

Was the stink virus going around, and the thing turned into pneumonia, and Clifford's daughter Charleen had to take him to the hospital. It was OK but, his legs came a little bit watery, so he had to take it easy for a while. He wanted to get back in his routine but, Charleen had a fit every time, so he fixed the disposal. That was one thing. He made Spam musubi for the kids' lunches for the week, too. But with everybody at work or school all day, it seemed like the house got more and more quiet, even with the TV turned up, and since Nathan, his son-in-law Nathan, had to use Clifford's Chevy to get to Pearl so Charleen could use the van to pick up the kids from A-Plus, he couldn't even drive over to the park for a card game. He called Spark a couple times, but the guy was out. Then Charlie came by.

Which was OK but, also tiring since Clifford had to do most of the talking. Not to mention walking in his weak state to the fridge to get the man a soda. That was Charlie, though. The long face, the big presence. "As OK," he'd say, "no bother, eh?" when you asked if he wanted a soda or something, like he never knew you all of a sudden, and then he'd turn around and glug it down in two swallows when you gave it to him. Plus, on top of that, the guy so manini with words he never even ask Clifford how he felt.

About the only thing Clifford got out of Charlie was, "You find pleny changes, don't be surprise. Dey patching da park," and he sounded more fed up than usual.

The next day Clifford decided if he could fix the disposal, he could walk a few blocks, so he set off. Then, by the construction hut, he saw idle machinery and a pile of lumber. A broad cut in the slope of the hill. A tractor in the middle of it and off to one side, bins of rubbish. And that was not all. Across the street, the ironwoods were trimmed, some cut to stumps, and next to them—nothing.

Clifford walked slowly to where the pavilion was suppose to be. Was jus the cement floor left now, cracked and covered with rubble. The caretaker's cottage. too, sliced in half, pipes hanging like guts. And no one in sight.

At first, he could not believe it. He turned away, blinked hard but— nothing. The ocean in front, cars going by like always but, no pavilion, and no one around for ask. The sight made the sweat come on his head. His shirt soaking. His legs not so good that day, so he went home.

He called Spark, and again, no answer. You could not expect the guy to stay home all the time, so he waited and after awhile, he called again and let the phone ring about fifteen times. He called around and finally Frank's wife answered. But Frank was over by Waipio-by-Gentry putting up a lanai roof for the new son-in-law. Finally, he got Charlie. At first he thought it was jus the Charlie mood. There was this long silence when Clifford mentioned Spark. A lotta breathing on the line. Then Charlie said Spark was ma-ke.

But Clifford was not about to take that crap. "You crazy?" he said. "He jogs, da guy! He not even fat! Whadaya mean ma-ke? You mean dead? Spark dead?"

"Ran a red light. Rammed his tin Toyota into one refuse truck. Head-on. Funeral was Buddhist. We cut you in da gift envelope."

"Charlie, how come you neva say nothing? You sitting right here drinking soda. How come you neva tell?"

"You still weak. I was gonna tell you Saturday when Charleen stay home. You owe Frank fifty bucks, eh?"

In his agitation, Clifford forgot about the pavilion for a while. Then Charleen came home, and the kids didn't even help her carry in the groceries. They began to bicker. They kept yelling, "You're dead, you're dead." Was jus the Nintendo, but. It didn't seem to Clifford like that game was so good for kids. He called Charleen, and she kept saying, "Just a sec, just a sec." And when the boys went to baseball, finally, the quiet was worse, like it came from inside the head or something.

In the kitchen, he forgot he wanted aspirin. "Funny thing, Charleen," he began.

"Oh! Wey-wey-weh-wait!" Charleen grabbed a pan from the stove and dabbed frantically at the burner with one of her good dishtowels. "OK, Dad, what?"

"Oh, nothing. Watch dat cloth, Charleen. OK, Spark maybe. I neva pay my last respects to Spark."

"You were in Queen's, Dad. We didn't want to upset you." Charleen was rooting around in the silverware drawer. "You need to respect yourself, if you ask me. You need to say, I'm OK and get well and plan something you can look forward to. Like going to Las Vegas." She brightened. "How's that sound?"

"I donne know bout Las Vegas."

"You always wanted to go to Las Vegas. So why not go with Bones like he's always asking you to? OK, where's that knife? The only knife in the whole house that cuts!"

"Da dishwasher."

"Honest, Dad! How many times do I have to say, Don't put the butcher knife in the dishwasher?"

"Wasn't me. As funny, though." He watched Charleen remove the skin from two white onions and begin slicing. "Was not long ago he went tell he seen da path, dis story Spark went tell. 'Da path,' he tell. So I ask 'Where,' an he tell, 'Da streak there, da long silver one, da water flat, as why.' I stay long time looking da ocean full of streaks, looking hard but, I neva seen no silver path. 'Where,' I asking. 'The line of current dere,' he tell, 'right dere.' I telling 'Where' an he telling 'There,' so finally. . . ."

"One sec. Rayleen! Turn that TV off and do your homework! Right now, Rayleen! Kay, Dad, I'm listening, go on."

"I cannot stay telling 'where' all da time, so I tell I seen it. The guy smiling, li'dat, telling how he went drop da silver, so I no can tell if he joking or not. Course, I know he went drop the silver. An da bracelet. Dat I know."

Charleen lifted an arm and ducked her head to blot her eyes on her sleeve. She lined up the slices and began chopping them in tiny squares. "Hand me that bowl, will you?" she said.

"Thing is, the guy acking like he knows, the way he looking, pointing at da ocean, smiling, like he really seen dis highway under da Pacific for take you home. For take you anywhere."

"What silver, Dad?" Charleen blinked and went on chopping.

"Spark . . . Spark went work on da Lurline, long time ago. He went drop da silverware tings overboard da side. For make da path."

"The path my eye! He dropped silverware over the side so he wouldn't have to wash it." Out of weepy eyes, Charleen glared at him. She blotted, and more tears welled up. He had to look away.

"I going see if Rayleen need help with da math."

"No Dad! Let Rayleen do her own work."

In the doorway, he paused. "Spark buss tables," he said. "He neva wash dishes or silverware." But Charleen was chopping, the knife loud in her hands. He decided not to tell her she went singe her cloth black.

That night he dreamed he fell in a hole and nobody would pull him out. He was stuck in there, seeing nothing. In the morning, he told Charleen about his dream but, she didn't think it meant anything, and maybe it didn't. But then, maybe it did. A couple days in the house and he realized that even though Spark was dead, he missed his routine. The dark hole, he realized, was the house. He needed to go out in the world to improve his vision. Clifford had one glass eye from fooling with firecrackers one time. The other eye was good but, was scary, the dream. He knew he had to go back and look, see who was around the park, see if his good eye fooled him, if maybe he'd made a mistake about the pavilion. He was pretty sick last time. He might even find 'em building one new pavilion.

But he saw no one he knew around. The parking lot was empty except for a few rusty surfers' vans and two yellow school buses. The kids fanning out behind their teachers, most of 'em wearing those big floppy shoes. A few mamas with their little ones the beach side. He stopped to watch a couple boys skimboarding in the wave wash. He skipped school plenty times to do the exact same thing but, he stood there like one grouch when they gave the teachers the finger. Which he for sure neva do. Course, as the way things going dese days. Da kids plenty mix up.

Shading his eyes, he thought about the day he and Spark stood by here staring out at the ocean full of streaks. You had to pay attention to the currents out there, you had to look past all the streaks that jus looked like paths to find the true path. Course, first you had to know the thing was there. Clifford knew but, the fake eye, eh? He never seen any path. Jus streaks. Spark called him 'Tosh' that day, too, the name they used to call him, instead of Toshio. Before they called him Clifford, or Cliff, then Dad most of the time, and now Bapa. He felt funny, though, like he owed Spark, like Spark pass him this favor and he had to pass 'em back. So he said he seen it.

Slowly, Clifford followed the shore line to the pavilion. From this side, too, the place still littered. A sign said, "DO NOT ENTER AREA CON-DEMNED." For warn off kids, probably. Though he was pretty sure it did the opposite. They never even start the new pavilion. He had to sit down.

How come dey went do dis? Cause it need paint? The council, or whatever, what dey went do? Everybody know da city low on funds, so how come dey went spend money on da new pavilion when da schools going slid-ing, li'dat? Cause as what da newspapers telling, dey telling da schools only getting da C grade, not even da C plus, dey neva tell nothing about tearing down pavilions everybody still using every day!

Clifford watched as across the street a tour bus pulled up next to the tractor. His gaze narrowed. From behind black slits, Clifford watched brightly clad tourists cluster about the bus and then walk to the edge of the cut, opening like one bouquet of flowers. Some stopped to snap pictures of the purple bougainvillea drooping. The other ones followed the driver. Clifford waited, motionless, while they crossed to his side of the road. J'like petals breaking off da bunch, he thought, more bright even den da bougainvillea behind 'em.

Clifford realized he was holding his side. He had one crick in his side, and his head felt cool all of a sudden in the breeze. He was sweating again. The sweat dripping.

"Eh, brah," the driver said.

Clifford lifted his hand.

The driver was looking. "You know when they gonna get this place finish?"

"Dey neva start yet." On his heels, Clifford sat still while the cameras aimed his way. He listened to the dull slap of waves on the sand. J'like one slow pulse trying for keep time.

The driver turned to his little group. "Next year we'll be parking here." He clumped around on the cement slab and kicked at the debris. "Grills over there, a playground, bathrooms, flowers, everything but a hot dog stand."

Clifford put his hand over his eyes and squinted up at the driver. He like stand but, da bones stiff, eh? He no like wobble, so he stayed put. "You get it wrong, man. Dey building one pavilion dis place. Da parking across da street."

"Zat right?" The driver squatted by Clifford. "You read the papers, old man? Cause, hey, bumbye this place going be one fancy park. They enlarging, you know." He gestured across the road and down to the cement slab under his feet.

"Not," Clifford said. He was trying to be polite but, the driver lean too close. Clifford felt invaded. Cold under the skull. "Da odder side maybe. Dis side for ones stay using da park, li'dat. Tables da beach side so da mamas can sit by da ocean for stay watching da kids, eh? Dis place for da odder ones. Sundays, da prayer service an da AA. Vets da odder days."

"OK if you say so, old man," the driver said. He stood up and stretched. "But maybe you better check it out." He led his group back across the road. Like a flower folding in on itself, the tourists drifted back into the bus. One with a bougainvillea branch. While Clifford sat rigid as the stump behind him, the bus turned in a swirl of dust and took off.

Clifford tasted dust. The sun bore down where he used to sit in the shade. Heating up his head, the sun. No more sweat running down, though. From behind his stillness, he thought about the situation till it began to make sense. Da pavilion coming gray, li'dat, old. More cars needing parking. Buses. Tourists.

Clifford had never felt hostile to tourists. Fact was he'd earned a decent living driving 'em all over the island, and he did OK for himself when he started his own business, Cliff's Taxi Service offering Specialized Tours. Now the island coming crowded. Everything different now. Was progress but. All the time, even though he seen it going on, he neva notice! He had to make one living, as all he knew.

Slowly, he stood, feeling dry and light in his anger. The guys on the council—what was they doing selling out the vets? He looked at the rubble. Up the road he saw one yellow bus drive out of the lot. The lot not even half full and already they building another one both sides of the road. They went broke down the pavilion and the ironwood trees. First Spark. Then the pavilion. Now flowers. They not planted yet but he could see 'em. J'like one funeral.

He had to laugh. Like the thing one big joke shaking him in the chest while he stay standing here, the foot one dead limb so he no can move, an he thinking for the first time of that damned path of Spark's going both ways!

He waited for the familiar sensation of jabbing pins to run up his leg. Then he stamped his foot and limped across the road. Ho, man! Dey already went set da boundaries with string. Da shape one flat square plenty big dis side. Dey ready for lay down blacktop already.

Following the string around the cut, Clifford kept going. He walked up the slope and on through the pili grass. The crick in his side hurt, and his shaking legs made him go slow, but he climbed partway up a rise, the one that looked like an old monk's head from the road, and stood there awhile, breathing, the grass rippling all around him, like it was alive, like it was breathing along with him.

When he got to the top of the rise, he was surprise to see it wasn't really the top. He was climbing the hump in the monk's back all this time and not the head. He kept climbing, though. Had no plan, the guy, he jus kept on gripping his side and climbing, stopping plenty times, panting, going steep places on all fours, topping the rise finally only to find the rise still rising. Or maybe it was another rise, he didn't know, he couldn't see the top, his good eye aching. Should of been cool up here but. Hard work climbing. Every step he went slide back in his rubber slippers. The place stay buzzing in his head. Too thin, the air up here.

Sinking to his knees he looked down at the park. Beyond, the ocean looking glassy in the late afternoon sun, and massive. On its surface, a ship, a dot. Above, a glint, a plane. Knowing better, he try yelling, "Go home, you bastards!" But the dry wind snatched his words, it filled his mouth, it reached down into all his breathing passages.

Breathing hard, he stay looking out to sea, looking way out, searching like he knew what for, knowing before he seen it what it was, and shouting, leaning into the wind and shouting, louder now, to his parents Masao and Betty Tanaka, to his brother Iwao, to his wife Marie and their son Robert Iwao Tanaka, to his sergeant Henry S.K. Watanabe, to his friend Spark Landoza and his true wife Nina, and to plenty others, too, before the clouds came thick, before the Koʻolaus threw down more shadow, while he could still see it, the silver path, wide and glittering. The silver path pointing in the sun.

BULLIES

1997, oil on illustration board

BY DARRELL H.Y. LUM

WHAT SCHOOL YOU WENT?

1. Kinnigarden

Mrs. Wagnah was our kinnigarden teacha. She was one old haole lady wit gray hair and her glasses was tied to one string so dat she no lose um. I donno how she could lose um cause she had big chi-chis and her glasses always stay dere j'like on top one shelf. And she had one nudda stuff, like one necklace dat clamp to her sweater, so da ting no fall off. She wear her sweater j'like one Supahman cape. And when she put on her art apron wit her glasses stuff and her sweater stuff, she get all tangled up and den somebody gotta help her figgah out how fo take um all off.

Mrs. Wagnah one pretty nice teacha. Only ting, she made you sleep during nap time. She was strick about dat. You had to put on your eyeshades and lie down on your sleeping mat and no talk and no move around. Even if you wasn't tired, you couldn't move around and you had to shut your eyes cause she said she going check. But how she going check unless she get x-ray vision? Most times she jes sit at her desk and close her eyes too, das when you can lift up your eyeshade and make funny faces at Fat Frances until she cry. Or you can play try-make-me-laugh wit John or Andrew. Mostly everybody was peeking and wearing their eyeshade on their forehead by da time naptime was pau.

Alfred was da only one who really sleep. Even when was pau nap time, he no get up. Yeah. Everybody put away their mats and he stay snoring in da middle of da floor and Mrs. Wagnah gotta drag him still yet on his mat, to da corner so dat had room fo storytime.

Alfred, he sweat da most of anybody and he use his gahlah-gahlah hankachief fo wipe his face cause every time he foget bring one clean one. Every morning Mrs. Wagnah tell us line up and she check if we went wash our hands and no mo dirt undahneat our fingahnails and you gotta show her dat you get one hankahchief and da juice money monitah and da lunch money monitah collect your money. Good when you one of da money monitahs cause den you can count da money and put um inside da Band-aid can and take um to da office.

Alfred, he always get da same old hankachief. I no tink he wash um. He use um for anykine: fo tie around his mout like one bandit, fo tie around his head like Zatoichi, fo tie around one eye like Zorro. Fo catch bugs in da dirt. Fo make parachute. And when he pau, he jes shove um back in his pocket. So every time, Mrs. Wagnah gotta tell him, "Time to bring a clean handkerchief, Alfred. We don't want to spread our germs around, do we?" And he use his hankachief fo his coin purse too. Mrs. Wagnah she use only two fingahs fo pick out Alfred's nickel and quartah from da middle of his hankachief so she no catch his gahlahs or his hanabuttahs.

Sometimes Mrs. Wagnah get two pencils and make uku check. Everybody gotta line up and she poke around your hair wit da eraser end of da pencils looking fo ukus. If you one girl and get long hair, she look long time. If you live Mayor Wright housing, she look long time. If you Alfred, she look extra long time. I always get nervous cause you donno when you going get ukus and if you get um, you gotta go to da health room and everybody call you "uku-boy." Alfred was "uku-boy" plenny times, but I wasn't, yet. Even if Bungy said I was. I wasn't, he lie.

One time, almost to summer vacation, when was real hot, Mrs. Wagnah said we had to quiet down and take a nap even though nobody could, was so hot. So we was suppose to be taking our nap and I was watching Alfred wipe his face with his gahlah-gahlah hankachief and den go sleep and I heard Mrs. Wagnah tell Shirley to be da room monitah cause she had to go to da office. I donno how come she always pick Shirley. She so sassy when she da monitah cause she no report da girls. But if any of da boys move around or talk, she report *every little ting*. Mrs. Wagnah nevah come back fo long time and everybody stay moving around and lifting up their eyeshades, peeking. Bungy went get up and look around da room and jes when Shirley was going say, "Ahunna-ko-ko-le-le, I going tell Mrs. Wagnah," Bungy went look out da door and tell, "Mrs. Wagnah went fall down! She stay lying on da ground!" We all went jump up and run to da door and Shirley was yelling at us, "You supposed to stay on your sleeping mat," and Fat Frances stay crying awready, "Mrs. Wagnah going ma-ke die dead!"

Bungy went open da uddah door cause couldn't see too good and Shirley still was trying to be da boss, "Not suppose to go outside," and he went tell her, "Aw shaddup, stupidhead" and she started fo cry real soft, "I going tell Mrs. Wagnah you went call me stupid. Not suppose to say 'stupid.'" I couldn't see anyting cause everybody was by da doors so I jes went stand on top da table awready fo see what was happening. Mrs. Ching from next door and Miss Greenwood, da principo, and da janitah, Mr. Rodrigues, all stay crowded around Mrs. Wagnah lying down. Mrs. Ching was holding one umbrella fo shade Mrs. Wagnah, and Mr. Rodrigues was fanning her wit one folder, and Miss Greenwood was holding and rubbing her hand. Shirley was going back and fort from one door to da uddah saying, "You guys bettah get back on your sleeping mat . . . Daniel, you bettah get off da table . . . I going count to tree. One. Two. Tree." Nutting went happen. She went tell, "I said one, two, tree!" Nobody went move, even her best goody-goody friends nevah move. So she went climb up on top da tables fo look outside, too. Miss Greenwood went look at us hanging out da doors and Mrs. Ching's class too and she went send Mrs. Ching back to take care of us.

By da time she went shoo her class back inside her room, we went back to our sleeping mats but we nevah even pretend we was sleeping cause we wanted to know what was happening. Mrs. Ching came into da room and told us Mrs. Wagnah had one accident, she went faint. She tink was heat exhaustion cause was so hot. Bungy went tell, "Das cause she always get da sweater on." And Shirley went raise her hand and tell her dat Bungy went get up from his sleeping bag and went outside da room. And Mrs. Ching went tell, "Okay, thank you, young lady." Bungy went smile big at her. Mrs. Ching wasn't going do nutting.

Shirley went try again, "But Mrs. Wagnah said not suppose to do dat!" Mrs. Ching said she would discuss it later with Mrs. Wagner. Shirley went look back at Bungy and stick tongue. Mrs. Ching said we could play quietly and she was going back and fort between da two rooms so we bettah behave or else she going get Miss Greenwood come watch us. Everybody said, "Whoa," and came quiet. Shirley went raise her hand again and say, "I can be da room monitah?"

And Bungy said, "No make her monitah!" and Fat Frances said, "Da ambulance went come!" and started crying again. Everybody went rush to da doors again fo watch dem put Mrs. Wagnah on da stretcher and slide her inside da ambulance. Da lights was flashing but nevah have siren. Bennett said, "How come dey no put on da siren?"

Fat Frances said, "Maybe she ma-ke awready!" and started fo cry again, "I no like Mrs. Wagnah ma-ke!" Some more girls started crying soft-kine and Mrs. Ching said, "No, no, Mrs. Wagner not ma-ke but she has to go to the doctor to see what's wrong so she might be absent for a little while."

We went watch until da ambulance went drive off da playground and jes when we heard da siren go, "Awwwrrrr," Alfred went wake up.

2. Firs Grade

Firs grade, we had Mrs. Perry. I was kinda scared of her cause she make you eat everyting on your lunch tray. When you in firs grade, you gotta go to da cafeteria fo get your lunch tray but you no can stay dere eat. You gotta carry um back to da classroom fo eat so Mrs. Perry can watch us, make sure we eat all our vegetables and we no can see da six graders making food fight. Me and Bennett always try walk *waay* behind Mrs. Perry so dat we can ditch da vegetables in da bushes before we reach da room. Couple times we went hide um in da milk carton but Mrs. Perry went check and she made us pour out all da peas and eat um. I almost went chrow up when I had to eat peas mix up wit milk. Once, we seen her make Shirley eat every lima bean even if she was crying "I no like, I no like" and she was crying so hard and eating lima beans dat she went chrow up all ovah da table. Yeah, you know. Ho, aftah dat, she nevah have to eat anyting she no like!

One time when had beets, Bennett went put um in his pants pocket and take um home. Only ting his muddah went call up Mrs. Perry and ask her how come Bennett went come home wit beets in his pocket. He fogot to ditch um, da stupidhead. One time Mrs. Perry went call my house fo talk to my fahdah. I figah da only time da teacha call up your house is if you went do someting bad, so I was scared, man.

My fahdah told me dat Mrs. Perry said I had to practice skipping so I no jam up da May Pole Dance.

"Hard you know," I told him. "She try teach us da dance only one way and I no can skip da way she teach us."

"But you gotta try."

I no like do da stupid dance. She tink I stupid like Alfred cause we both write left hand. She like me write like everybody else. Everytime she say raise your right hand, me and Alfred we raise our hand and she laugh and tell us, "Your uddah right." So quick we gotta change cause one time, she went tell everybody dat your *right* hand was your *writing* hand. Wasn't. She lie.

Daddy, he could write good wit his right hand. I wanted to write scrip like him. When he sign his name on papers la dat, he gotta get all ready: unscrew da fountain pen, wipe da tip wit Kleenex, and get out da blotter. Den he make his hand go in little circles. Circle, circle, circle. Den he sign real quick and blow and blot and come out perfeck. Sharp, his writing. I wish I could write scrip like him. He told me his teacha used to whack his hand wit da ruler if you use your left hand, das how he learned how fo write right hand but he still dribble da basketball and shoot left hand. He told me, "Lucky Mrs. Perry no whack your hand." I nevah feel lucky. Hard, you know. *You* try skip right hand way if you left hand.

But bumbye Mrs. Perry wanted to be my friend cause one time had one painting contest. Dey went bring one lamb, you know, one real one, like Mary-had-a-little-lamb-little-lamb-little-lamb, and da whole firs grade had to go in da yard wit their easels and paint da lamb. And one nice lady from da Art Academy went pick mine as da best of da whole firs grade. Yeah. Den Mrs. Perry wanted to be my friend cause j'like was cause of her dat my painting was da best. But wasn't. Most times she no even like da way I paint. She said everyting had to be correck: yellow sun, green tree wit red apples, white clouds, blue sky, green grass and flying birds dat look like one V.

I jes went paint da stupid lamb. Must be cause I went make da clouds and da lamb and da grass all look da same, all curly and fuzzy and funny-kine colors, cause Bungy went take da good colors and all I had left was purple, black, brown, and orange. Mines was mostly circles, cause I was tinking about da fluffy wool and clouds and Daddy writing scrip. So I went write scrip wit my brush. Circle, circle, circle. Even Alfred told me at recess time, "Nice, your painting."

Alfred no like do art. Everyting he paint look da same cause every time, aftah he pau, he tell, "Ugly" and he paint anykine all ovah his pickcha so end up all brown and ugly. And when he do schoolwork he use so much eraser he always make puka in da paper. No good lend him your eraser cause going come back all used up. Anyway, aftah da lady went pick my painting and put um up by da office fo little while, plenny guys was my friend. Even Throw Up Shirley nevah call me "Uku Boy" or "Alfred's Bruddah" too much.

Naptime, Shirley and Alfred and Kyle could sleep on top da desks cause dey had asthma and everybody else had to sleep on da floor. No fair. Was cold da floor. And everytime, aftah naptime pau, Alfred still stay snoring on top da desks except Mrs. Perry, she wake um up. Alfred he even sleep when we jes gotta put our heads down on da desks cause we too noisy or we gotta settle down aftah recess. I hate when Alfred do dat cause sometimes he come ovah to my side of da desk and he drool on top my work. Even if you draw one line on da desk wit your eraser and tell, "No can cross da line," he always stay on my side. Uji. And jes because I sit next to him, Throw Up Shirley say I going catch Alfred's uji germs. Not. Not going, yeah?

3. Fort Grade

Fat Frances Obata such a crybaby. When we get P.E. and gotta choose up fo kickball, her and Alfred always da last to get picked, so she cry. When Bungy tease her, she cry. When Throw Up Shirley fold one origami fortune teller out of one piece of paper and tell her fortune, "You going marry Alfred," she cry. Even if she only get one wrong in math, she cry. Sometimes I feel little bit sorry fo her cause she always stay by herself recess time cause if you like go on da jungle gym, da bull of da jungle gym, usually Bungy, make up one password like, "Fat Frances eat buta kaukau." And if you no say dat Frances eat pig slop, she still yet cry cause she feel sorry dat dey nevah let you on da jungle gym.

I hate it though when she bring one orchid fo Miss Von, our fort grade teacha. One cattleya wit foil wrapped around da stem, big and purple purple, almost black. No spots, no bugs. Perfeck. One real big one dat da teacha put in her hair or pin um on her dress or put um in her vase on her desk. And Fat Frances everytime massage Miss Von's back cause she da biggest girl in da class and probably mo strong den even Bungy, so Miss Von go ask her fo lomi-lomi her back. Wasn't fair man, cause Miss Von only like you if you bring her flowahs. We no mo nutting in our yard dat I could bring fo da teacha. Not unless you count da Christmas berries dat hang ovah da fence from da Witch Lady's tree next door. Dat I can get easy. But da teacha only like dat at Christmas time and den you gotta pick real plenny and dry um up and spray paint um gold or silvah. Supposed to look like holly but I donno what holly supposed to look like. Look fake when you spray paint um. Anyways, das not like bringing one giant orchid everytime.

Even Bungy always bring someting from his aquarium fo show and tell. One time, he went bring fighting fish in one long skinny aquarium divided up into sections wit pieces of plastic in between so dat da fish stay in their own part until he lift up one section and da two fish fight. Dey chase each uddah and bite each uddah's tail until you get da net and scoop one out or until one die. Bungy went put one mirror up to da glass, and da fish tink das one nuddah fish so he fight wit himself, da stupidhead. Da fish jes charge um. Fat Frances started fo cry fo da fish and Miss Von told Bungy he couldn't bring fighting fish anymore. So he started bringing crayfish. One time I went wit him to da river fo catch crayfishes so dat I could bring someting fo show at show and tell but he only made me do stuff like move da rocks and splash da water and chase um to him. Suckah. He nevah gimme any. I had to bring home my mayonnaise bottle empty. The only ting I could catch was grasshoppers, but anybody can catch grasshoppers, so das nutting dat. Sheesh, I couldn't even bring grasshoppers if I wanted to cause grasshoppers no last too long and dey only shet in da bottle. Even Bennett could tell about how his fahdah went talk on da ham radio to somebody in Australia and da teacha went show us where dat was on da map.

What I going tell? Dat my fahdah went sell six refrigerators in one day? Dat my muddah and me went pinch da tail off one whole bag of bean sprouts?

One time Alfred went bring one small peanut butter bottle to school and leave um in his desk and everytime he open um up and smell um and close um back real quick, secret kine. I went look at um but only had couple dead leaves inside. Nevah have insects or one cocoon so everybody tawt stupid Alfred went bring one bottle wit dead leaves inside.

When was his turn he told us he went wit his uncle up St. Louis Heights and went smell da eucalyptus trees and he brought some leaves fo us fo smell. And he went write "eucalyptus" on da board and told us dat koala bears, he went write "marsupials," eat eucalyptus leaves in Australia. We knew where dat was. Everybody went tell, "Whoa, Alfred," when he was pau.

Andrew went tell, "Eh Alfred, I nevah know you was smart."

Den Bungy went tell real loud, "Whoa, Alfred, we tawt you went save yo futs inside dere," and everybody went laugh and started calling Alfred "Fut-boy" until Miss Von had to shush da class wit da yardstick, wha-pak! She went bus um on her desk.

Aftah dat, I nevah see Alfred open up his bottle anymore.

4. Fit Grade

Da worse was Miss Greenwood, da principo. Nobody like get reported to da office cause fo sure Miss Greenwood going whack your okole wit da rubbah hose. She had um hanging up behind her desk. One time I had to deliver one note fo da teacha, Mrs. Tenn, Andrew call her Mrs. Ten, Eleven, Twelve. Funny guy. I had to wait inside Miss Greenwood's office and all I could look at was da black rubbah hose, looking mean and stiff, j'like Miss Greenwood. She was tall and skinny and always wear one white blouse and black skirt tight around her okole. I wondah if *her* okole evah got da rubbah hose. Doubt it. Sometimes right aftah recess when we all stay lined up by da classroom door, ready fo go back into da room, we can hear kids crying in her office. Big six grade kids stay crying and screaming, "Huh, huh, huh, ow-wee!" Some start crying even befo dey get to da office, dey know dey going get it. Dey got nabbed fo fighting or talking sassy or fo trying to scoop somebody's balls recess time. I nevah had da rubbah hose but Bungy went get um plenny times and Andrew almost as much as Bungy. Dey said you gotta sit on da chair while Miss Greenwood scold you and den she write someting down and when she stand up and close da door, dat means you gonna get it. You gotta bend ovah and hold da stool and she make sure you mo nutting in your back pockets and she swing da hose down first, den she whack you. Whoosh, pack! Whoosh, pack! Whoosh, pack! When Bungy go, he no cry anymore, he so used-to to it, I tink. He told me dat nowadays he fake cry cause if you no cry, Miss Greenwood whack you mo hard. So even if *sound* like he crying, he told me he only faking.

One time he went tell Alfred dat Louise like him and wanted to show him what color her panties was. Louise, if she like you, she count off her crinolines fo you and den she show you her panties last. But no ways she was going count her crinolines fo Alfred. Da girls all hated Louise cause she had bra awready in da fit grade so dey went dare Alfred fo lift up her dress and count her crinolines and see what color her panties was cause Louise like him. And all da boys went tell him, "Yeah, Alfred. She like you."

Dat time he got sent to da office right before recess and got real plenty whacks and we could hear him all da way down by da basketball court crying, "No tell my mah-huh-daaah! Huh, huh, huh. No tell my mah-huh-daah!"

When Alfred came back to da class, nobody wanted to look at him cause j'like he took da lickings fo us, cause we went dare him. He jes went put his head down and nevah look at nobody. He nevah cry, he nevah sleep. He jes put his head down and nevah say nutting to us, evah again.

BY GEORGIA K. McMILLEN

THE NAME

I was ten years old and still didn't have a name—and in a family loaded with names, each name with a story attached. Gramps was Kamakaʻiheʻoahi, The-Fire-Tipped-Spear—about a chief who bopped one of Cook's marines on the head with a paddle. Dad was Kakaʻe, The-Morning-Star—another chief, another fight. Aunty Harry was Kanoeonaona, The-Fragrant-Mist—after my great-grandmother who was a dancer in the chief's court. I dreamed of having a name like these that was long, pretty and special to my family. I dreamed of filling the hole between my first and last name with a name that would make me special too.

Why didn't I have a name?

I blamed Gramps. In our family my grandfather bestowed the Hawaiian middle name on each of his grandkids. That was rule number one. Rule number two was for us kids: Don't ask questions. Both those rules together meant, Shut my mouth. Shut my mouth even though they used Hawaiian name in hula class. Without one, my hula teacher gave me a "make-shift" name, Maipoinaʻoeiaʻu. Don't-Forget-Me. "Just until your grandpa gets around to it. He must have so much on his mind," she said.

The first time she called me using that name I refused to answer. She stood in front of me, hands on her hips, "Maipoina, didn't you hear me?"

I closed my eyes. Inside it was black and empty. That's what I thought of her stupid name. That's what I thought of her excuse for Gramps, retired more than ten years from the hotel and with all day to himself. He could have named me one hundred time times over.

I finally got my full name when they promoted my Dad to fire station captain. That Sunday there was going to be a ceremony with the mayor, the fire chief and even Miss Pearl City, Kalehualani Freitas—The-Heavenly-Lehua-Blossom. My grandparents had a party for Dad the day before, held at their house in Kalihi Valley where they had raised Dad and his nine brothers and sisters.

Dad and I didn't cook much, so we stopped and bought a bucket of chicken wings on the way to the party. By the time we drove into the valley, my grandparents' street was filled. We had to park down at the end and carry the chicken up to the noisy house. We walked past my teenage cousins standing around the cars. When they saw Dad they hid their cigarettes behind their backs. "Congrats, Uncle Bobby," the boys said.

The girls wore short dresses and stacked heels made of cork. They tittered to Dad, kissed him then wiped their purple lipstick off his cheek, "Sorry, Uncle Bobby."

They petted my head, "Howzit, Freddy-Girl."

"Freddy-Girl!" The cousins I played with called me. They lay on their stomachs in the grass in front of the house.

"Watch!"

A bed of ripe mangoes covered the street in front of the house. Mrs. Sasaki lived at the end of the road behind a high wooden fence and never looked at us. She approached, driving her blue Rambler. I ran to my cousins then dropped to my stomach. When Mrs. Sasaki drove over the mangoes, the ripe orange meat burst from the skin.

"Ho! Look how far my guy flew," one cousin said.

"My guy went BOOM across the road."

Dad stepped in front of us, blocking our view. "Get the hose and wash down the street."

"Oh!"

"Before the next car comes."

I jumped up and began running to faucet, but Dad said, "Not you, Freddy. You coming with me."

Hornets had built gray nests on the garage beams overhead. As we walked beneath them I studied the nests. I didn't see any, but knew they were there. Once, when I was little and my mother still lived with us, they had swarmed and stung me.

My aunties sat at a table near the kitchen screen door and next to the food table. I went from aunty to aunty kissing their cheeks. The heat and sweat had caused their eyebrows to run down to their cheeks. They held my waist and pecked at the air.

When Dad went to them they said, "There's our Bobby-Boy," and held his face by the chin. Dad was the youngest of ten. He had been in the newspaper on Friday: the youngest fire fighter to be promoted to captain.

But Vovo, my grandmother, said to him, "Since when does it take forever to drive from Pearl City? And look at this girl." That's how she always greeted me, Look at this girl. She held up my blonde hair for the aunties to see. "It's turning green."

Only recently. I had swim practice three times a week for an upcoming meet.

"It happens to a lot of the girls," Dad said.

"Not *our* girls," one aunty said.

"Rinse it with lemon juice," Aunty Harry said.

"No, that going make it worse. Use vinegar," Aunty Angel said.

"What you know about blonde hair, Angel?"

"I've known a blonde or two in my time."

My cousins ran through the garage to the back yard, the front of their clothes wet. I followed the girls, their long brown ponytails swaying behind them as they ran.

"Freddy." Dad pointed to Gramps and my uncles.

Their backs to the aunties, my uncles sat at their own table where they told hunting stories while drinking beer from the bottle, tilting their heads back to let it glide down their throats.

"Bobby-Boy," they called to Dad.

"Heard somebody getting to be a big shot."

"Heard somebody gonna shake hands with the mayor tomorrow."

I walked from uncle to uncle. Hello, kiss. Hello, kiss. They smelled like shaving cream and beer. I kissed Gramps. He smelled only like beer.

"Freddy-Girl, getting so tall," Gramps said, wrapping his arm around my waist.

"Like the mother was," an uncle said. Another bumped his elbow.

"I'm eleven next month," I told Gramps.

He tried to whistle.

"In two weeks," Dad said.

"So maybe this's a birthday party, too," Gramps said.

But no one knew. There would be no presents.

"What can your Gramps give you for your birthday?" he said.

I figured, Why not? "Well, how about my name?"

"Abe, you gotta be joking me," Uncle Joe said. "You never named her yet?" Uncle Joe was Gramps's only surviving brother, and my great-uncle.

"Pops," Dad said. "Just choose a name and finish already."

The uncles froze.

"Guess some people think they can tell me how to do my job," Gramps said. "Do this. Do that. Good boy, here's your tip." My grandfather was a bellman for thirty years in Waikīkī, carrying tourists' luggage to and from their rooms. The hotel forced him to retire after his second heart attack.

"Well, I had something in mind so I guess now's as good a time as ever." Gramps stood up from the bench and took a long draw on his beer. He cleared his voice and looked across the garage. "I get one announcement," he said.

The aunties kept talking.

"Everybody. . . ."

The teenager Thomas was at the food table. He heard Gramps and whistled through his fingers.

Vovo threw her hand to her chest.

Aunty Harry tried to swat Thomas's behind. "What's the matter with you?" she said.

Thomas pointed to Gramps.

His father, Uncle Eddie, told him, "Tell your other gangsters on the street to get in here."

Thomas whistled even louder to the teenagers.

The teenagers looked up, but wouldn't budge.

Uncle Eddie pointed his finger at them like a traffic cop: You—in here—right now.

They threw down their cigarettes and shuffled in. The girls crossed their arms over their chests and acted like they had somewhere else to go.

"Everybody knows that tomorrow they gonna make Bobby-Boy Captain Big Shot. I want to add to the occasion something for Freddy-Girl. It's time to name her—which I been thinking about for a long time, actually. Something to make up for the funny-kine name you folks gave her." Gramps eyed Dad. My first name was Winifred. I hated it too.

"The old fut finally got off his ass," Thomas said.

One of the girls punched him in the arm.

"Better not be Aunty Harry's name," my pregnant cousin Primrose said. "If I have a girl, I got dibs on that one."

"How come *you* got dibs on that one?"

"Ask. All's you gotta do is ask."

Gramps continued, "Guess that's what happens when you shack-up with these haole tourist girls." That's what Gramps called my mother, the Haole Tourist Girl.

Vovo stood up from the aunties' table. "Joe, take that beer away from him," she told Uncle Joe.

"Who we basically never had the chance to meet," Gramps said.

"Abraham, this isn't the time," Vovo said.

"Half-naked tourists, prancing around," Gramps said.

"Come on, Pops." It was Uncle Johnny, Dad's eldest brother. He and my other uncles had followed Gramps into hotel work. On the weekends they hunted pigs and goats.

"Cannot settle down with a nice local girl," Gramps said. "Think you too good for your own kine."

"Abraham, you making me mad," Vovo said.

"And who ever heard of naming a girl after Winnie-the-peg?"

"You making me really mad."

"It's Winifred, Pops. And she came from Winnipeg," Dad said. That's where my mother had returned when I was three. For a few years she sent birthday cards and letters. I kept them in an empty candy box.

Gramps told Dad, "Don't get smart with me, Bobby-Boy. I'll smack you, you get smart with me." Then he looked at Vovo, "And don't tell me what time it is. I going say what I want, when I want." He placed his hand on my head and said, "Not your fault, Freddy-Girl. Not your fault they name you for all their sins."

Vovo spoke through clenched teeth, her voice dropping to a growl, "Leave it alone."

Gramps' eyes bounced up to her. Mostly, he was all talk. But Vovo was for real. Gramps cleared his throat, "Here's something I been working on for a while." He touched his shirt pocket, "Oh, need my glasses."

The aunties hissed.

Uncle Eddie said to Dad, "Why didn't you just name her yourself?"

"Pops kept saying he would do it," Dad said.

The eldest, Uncle Johnny, said, "What Bobby-Boy? Sound like you still tiptoeing around Pops."

Uncle Eddie was the second eldest. "You think Bobby-Boy the one tiptoeing around Pops?"

"You going deaf now too, Eddie?"

"You the one on his tippy toes," Uncle Eddie told Uncle Johnny. "Cannot buy a lawn mower without Pops' two-cents."

"You the one, cannot finish painting your house," Uncle Johnny said, "how many years now?"

"You the one, drive that piece of junk I saw you parking down the street."

"You the one, three washing machines your house, poor Harriet still driving to the laundry mat."

"Shhh," Vovo hissed at them.

Gramps put on his glasses, then felt his back pocket and pulled out a slip of paper. There was a list of names, some crossed out. Some with a question mark. I tried to read it, but when Gramps saw he held the list to his chest. He started to say something, then took another draw on his beer.

"Ay Zezush! Hurry up," Vovo said. "I gotta go check my cakes."

"I been thinking of something that combines the old with the new," Gramps said. "Freddy's mother's family"—he glared at Dad—"who we never even met to this day, with our family here in Hawai'i. So"—he took off his glasses and held me by the shoulders—"Freddy-Girl, from now on your middle name gonna be, Freddy-lani. How you like that?"

I couldn't believe. Was he serious?

"Freddylani. Now, you got your haole side with your Hawaiian side. Side by side, kinda like."

A cousin whispered, "What did he say?"

"Freddy-lani," my cousin Lokelani said—Heavenly Rose. "I guess, Heavenly Freddy."

"Poor Freddy."

"First the green hair, and now this."

"S'what happens, your mom is haole."

I looked for Dad. He was walking to the back yard, his jaw clenching and unclenching. I looked at my uncles: Help me. But they fidgeted with the half-eaten plates of food in front of them. I looked at my aunties: Somebody, please. But they were throwing dagger stares at Gramps.

He didn't notice. He sat down again, took another draw on his beer and pulled me close.

"Freddylani," he said. "Now that's something different. I like it."

Vovo walked around the uncles' table and came at Gramps from behind, her long finger in the air.

"Uh oh," Primrose said, "look at this."

Vovo jabbed him in the back. I felt him jump.

"Abraham! What the hell kind of name is that?"

That was all the aunties needed: "Lazy bum!"

"Waits ten years then does this to the girl!"

"Hasn't she had enough hard times?"

"That damn haole girl."

"Bad news from the beginning."

"This all *her* fault."

"S'right. *Everything* her fault."

Gramps turned toward Vovo, his stiff back straining and me in his lap. Then he turned back to his brothers and sons: Help me boys!

But my uncles were playing deaf and dumb.

"Change it!" Vovo said.

The teenagers stepped closer, studying the lesson.

My aunties rumbled. Vovo eyed them, then said to Gramps, "Right now."

"Pops, there's plenty of nice names to chose from," Uncle Johnny said. "Like the ones you gave to the other girls."

Gramps pushed me aside and stood up. "You," he said to Uncle Johnny. "Who the hell do you think you are telling me what to do? My house? Boy—you get some goddamn nerve!"

Uncle Johnny tucked his head back into his shoulders.

"Easy Abe, " Uncle Joe said.

But Gramps said, "All of you, Go To Hell!"

My cousins threw their hands over their mouths. The aunties gasped. The teenagers raised their eyebrows.

Gramps sat back down. His voice went sloppy, "Besides, you like it, right darling? I guarantee nobody gonna have a name like that."

"That's for sure," one of the teenagers muttered.

It had gone so badly. I would return to school on Monday with less than I had before. I began crying.

"You see? You see what you did?" Vovo said.

"Freddy-Girl, don't sit with him anymore," Aunty Harry called to me.

"Don't cry, darling," Gramps said. "You got a real special name now."

"Unreal," a teenager said. "He's ready for the mental home."

"At least he didn't touch Aunty Harry's name," Primrose said. They walked back to the cars on the street.

My uncles said they had to check on the kids. The car. The beers and sodas. The ice.

In the last gold of the afternoon, my cousins drifted onto the grass. "Let's play Name the Baby."

"The baby's name is Lulu, so we calling her Lulu-lani."

"No. Booboo-lani!"

"No. Pupu-lani!"

They fell on the grass laughing.

I burst into tears again.

Gramps wiped the sweat from the beer bottle onto his napkin, lifted my face and wiped my eyes with the wet paper. "Don't pay attention those brats," he said.

Deep lines rutted his forehead. Others darted out from his eyes and down around his mouth.

"I got a secret," Gramps tried to whisper. "No tell nobody, but you always been my favorite."

I hate you.

"Feel better?" he said.

I nodded yes.

"Freddy-Girl, what did I tell you? Get *away* from him," Aunty Harry said.

My cousins were singing, "*Pu-pu, lani, lani . . .*"

"That's right honey, come over here and sit with us," one aunty said.

Aunty Harry put her arm around me, "Don't worry baby. You don't have to tell anyone what your name is. If they ask, just tell them—"

"None of their business," Aunty Angel said.

"Tell them you don't got one. Plenty folks no more Hawaiian name."

"Who Aunty?"

"People that ain't Hawaiian!" Aunty Angel said.

"Angel, why your mouth getting so fat each time I look at you?" Aunty Harry turned back to me, "Well, Mama don't got one."

"But Vovo is Portuguese," I said. Gramps was Hawaiian. My uncles, aunties and Dad were Hawaiian and Portuguese.

"OK, who else?" Aunty Harry looked to her sisters for help.

"Give it a rest, Harry," Aunty Angel said.

"Besides, you know Freddy-Girl," Aunty Harry said. "Freddy-lani is—ah—kinda interesting name. You don't have to worry about somebody else having that name."

"That's for sure." Aunty Angel again.

"Angel, you not helping."

"Angel-you-not-helping."

"Now you named after your mother's people." My mother's mother was Winifred.

"But everyone's already making fun of it," I said.

"And now you got a Hawaiian word in there."

"It's a stupid name," I said. "No one else has a name like that."

Silence.

"Just because everyone hates my mom."

Silence.

"Aunty, please ask Gramps to give me another name."

"You know I can't do that. You saw how he gets."

"But I hate it! I want a name like yours. Something pretty, like everyone else's name."

"Freddy-Girl, sometimes you gotta accept what's given to you," Aunty Angel said.

"But you didn't. After Uncle Davy left, Dad said you changed your name back."

"Listen to this girl—" Aunty Angel raised her hand like she was going to slap me.

"Shame on you for not being happy with what you've got!"

It was almost dark. The mountains lay on their back against the purple glow in the west. My cousins were running around the house now, "You're it! You're Pupulani!"

"*You're* Pupulani," Baby-girl said to Loke.

"If I'm Pupulani, then you're Freddy-lani!"

Baby-girl tried to hit Loke.

In the kitchen I found Vovo standing over a sheet cake covered with white icing. She held a plastic tube in her hand, her glasses resting on the tip of her nose. She had already written in green across the top, 'Congratulations.' While I watched she wrote 'Bobby', added a dash then tacked on a 'B', then an 'O', then a 'Y'.

"There," she told me. "Now, go tell Daddy time for cut his cake. He's in the boys' room." She pointed with her chin to the back of the house. "I hope Harry brought ice cream like I told her."

The lau hala mats crunched under my feet as I walked down the hallway to the room where my father and uncles used to sleep. Gramps sat in his Lazy-Boy in front of the TV. Wrestling was on, his favorite.

Outside the window my cousins' feet slapped against the concrete squares surrounding the house. Gramps laid them down so Vovo's feet would stay dry when she watered the plants in the early evening. One of the girls screamed, then the boys roared. Then all the girls screamed.

"Eh!" Gramps yelled through the dark window.

Dad sat on a sofa beneath the window, his eyes on the wrestlers. He said to Gramps, "Cut her some slack, Pops."

There was more screaming outside, then crying.

Dad stood and yelled out into the dark. "If I gotta go out there, you folks gonna be sorry."

More crying.

"Who's that?" Dad said. "Who's crying?"

I knew. I knew everyone's voice.

Loke called in to Dad, "Buddy-guys when knock down Baby-girl."

"Not! You the one," Buddy said.

"Not!"

Dad sat down again. "Pops, give her another name. Freddylani? Come on—that's just dumb."

"Mr. Big Shot. . . ."

"You were never willing to treat her the same."

"She's not the same," Gramps said. "Look at her. She got yellow hair going green. One nose like a sweet potato, everything covered in thick brown spots—"

"It's just freckles."

"Fat yellow teeth sticking out of her mouth—"

"I'm getting that fixed."

Then I realized, all my cousins' school pictures were framed and kept in the living room—except mine.

"We only got so many family names," Gramps said.

"So that's it."

"What the fuck else you thought it was?" Gramps sat up and turned to Dad. "You—You getting promoted tomorrow, but you got rocks in your head. I gotta spell it out for you? She's not one of us. She don't look like us. She don't act like us. All *your* fault. And one day she's going up there, find the mother, and that's it. You never gonna see her again. I not wasting our names on that."

Gramps fell back in the chair. The blonde wrestler with the long stringy hair lifted then dropped the another wrestler wearing a black face mask.

"Pops, I'm giving you a chance to change it."

"You threatening me?"

"You don't change it, I'll rename her myself."

"You? Bobby-Boy? The one I let the mother spoon-feed and spoil? Send to college on the mainland? I should've broken you, like the rest of them. You the one that needed it the most."

The matting crunched. Dad and Gramps turned to find me standing in the doorway.

"Ei nei," Gramps called to me, opening his arms.

I started to walk to him, but Dad said, "No Freddy, we're done here."

In the hall to the kitchen I told Dad, "Vovo said time for you to cut the cake."

But the kitchen was empty. From the screen door we saw Vovo in the garage. She cut the cake into squares, then slid the pieces onto paper plates. Aunty Harry scooped thick slabs of ice cream on the pieces. Loke and Buddy were first in line. They walked out to the grass holding the heavy paper plates in front of them like they were prizes.

Dad said to me, "Suppose we skip the cake?"

"But . . ."

"We'll get a treat on the way home, just you and me."

Why not? It wasn't a birthday party with presents after the cake. But still, "I thought the cake was for you."

"I don't know about that."

"Vovo will get mad."

"Vovo gonna be mad no matter what."

It was funny. It was true.

Then we heard Vovo say, "Where's that Bobby? Somebody go get him."

"Quick," Dad said. "The front door."

At the mouth of Kalihi Valley we stopped at the ice cream stand. I ate the chocolate shell off my cone, then made swirls in the soft-serve ice cream with my tongue.

Dad drank coffee. "Tomorrow morning I'll name you."

I stopped making swirls. "I don't have to keep Gramps' name?"

He pretended the name was paper, crushed it in his hand then threw it over his shoulder.

"What name will you give me?"

"I'll think about," Dad said.

I trusted none of it. "It'll be something stupid. You guys always name me something stupid."

"Come on, Freddy."

"Always." The ice cream needed more chocolate.

"Then what do you want?"

"I want a good name, but I want *you* to chose it. Why should I have to do all the work? It's your job." The ice cream dripped over my hand. "I don't want this anymore."

Dad took it, covered the cone with his whole mouth and swallowed the big lump on top.

Driving around Pearl Harbor, Dad said, "I'll find something nice."

"In one language."

"All in Hawaiian," Dad said.

"And, you know, pretty. Like the other girls' names."

"Pretty."

"Something nobody else has."

"Different."

"But not 'weird' different," I said.

"Not weird."

"Dad, you're making fun."

"Just getting it down: pretty, different but not weird. Tomorrow."

I couldn't see the harbor, but I knew it was there. "Dad, while you're at it, could you do something about my first name too?"

He tousled my green hair. "First things first, Freddy. Tomorrow, before we drive to the fire station for the ceremony . . . Tomorrow when you wake up, I'll have your middle name ready."

I believed him. And I believed that finally I would be complete.

Outside a young moon hovered over the sleeping mountains. "Dad?"

"I should have done it before," he said.

"Why didn't you, Dad?"

He started to say something, then stopped. We drove up our street. "I promise, Freddy. Your name will be the best name there ever was."

BY WENDY MIYAKE

MOON PEOPLE

ishermen are born in the full moon. Fat with light, drawing the sea toward them, cradling the water in their arms. The moon rocks them into a dream, gently letting them down to earth. They remember only the light. A clear line holds them to the moon as they emerge from the dark waters. They live a life here but they never die. They never die and so fishing stays in the blood. It is always a full moon.

On this night, the island lay blanketed in the darkness of the second world war. My grandmother rolled denim over the windows to join the collective darkness. She called the children inside before curfew. Time moved slowly within the plantation home. She watched my grandfather fixing a broken line on one of his fishing poles. He worked patiently—measuring the new *suji* line, attaching the right amount of lead and a new hook, then securing it neatly around the pole. My grandmother's face changed into a small smile. He would fish again tonight. The swells churning in the water failed to move him to fear. The patrol boats bobbing off the reef were just an inconvenience. At midnight, he grabbed his gear, two *musubi*s, and a pack of Camels and walked out the door.

My grandfather had come from Hiroshima, a fishing town in Japan. There he fished everyday. He came to Waialua to work in the sugar mill. In his free moments he would walk down to Puʻuiki Beach and stand like a monk on a rock and whip his line out a hundred feet. I never knew him alive. Instead we met in dreams. I fished with him in sleep.

The night was black. He set out down the dirt road that met up with Puʻuiki Road, leading to the beach. As he walked, he stayed near the cane fields. A shadow among the cane is the most someone would see of him. His rubber slippers disturbed the gravel and dirt as he reached the ironwood trees. They were giant monsters in the dark looming overhead. My grandfather loved the sound of the wind through the ironwoods. It was the sound of faraway tires on a smooth road. He walked quickly, letting the song of the ironwoods and the approaching sea harmonize in his ears like a lullaby. He neared the beach and walked to a secluded cove hidden by a forest of ironwoods. The waves rose and crashed with the near storm. They rocked the patrol boats beyond the reef.

He freed his line around his fishing pole and ran down to the water. He whipped the line and it sailed out a hundred feet or more. Sticking his pole in the sand between two rocks, he walked back to enjoy a *musubi* and a smoke. He fell onto his knees and began digging in the sand, using his hands like big shovels—scooping out the sand until he formed a hole deep enough for his body to fit inside. He sat in the hole and lit one of his Camels. A smile broke over his face spreading out a current of laugh lines. Peeking out of the hole he saw that the pole remained still, so he slid back, put out his cigarette and settled in to eat his *musubi*. He grew tired after the soothing feelings of the Camel and the food. His eyes fluttered closed.

He comes into my dreams. I fish only in sleep:

I am watching the dark tides rise higher in the early morning. I sit, quietly enjoying the white toes of foam lapping against my small feet. My black bangs, cut straight across my forehead, blow in the tradewinds and an old man I know only through pictures and stories stands beside me. His cheekbones are high and they tower above sunken cheeks. The hair is molded to the shape of his head and his thick glasses rest on a sharp nose. His features would be rather rigid if it were not for his eyes. They are soft brown, holding all the expressions his face cannot produce. "Grandpa! Grandpa!" I scream while tugging his old flannel shirt. His eyes twinkle at my excitement and we run down to the shoreline together. The fishing pole bends toward the water and the transparent line catches the first hairline glimmers of the sun. He reels the line in and the red fish glides on the water, all the way up his line. He lets the fish go. He throws out the line again, waiting for it to sail like a strand of hair to the far reef before he passes the pole to my small, waiting hands.

I look at my hands when I wake in the morning. They grow bigger and more lined and veined waiting for the feel of the smooth fishing pole in my hands. Fishing is passed down through the men of my family.

When my younger brother was born, he glowed in the darkness of the hospital room, making my father's eyes fill with water. My new brother's face was round and flat and he had a thick head of hair like a million short *suji* lines. My father would take him to the reef that jutted out with big boulders in Haleʻiwa. The waves rolled parallel to the rocks like a dark beast. They rolled smoothly, rhythmically and then they crashed. My father would take him to where the best fish hide.

*   *   *

My father has come home from Waimea Bay. It is late August, the season for *halalū*. It is only ten o'clock in the morning and he is standing by the kitchen sink cleaning out the bellies of the hundred forty-seven *halalū* he has caught today.

"I'm deah at five, yah, and dese people already choosing spots in da water," he tells me as I watch him clean. He does it joyfully taking the silvery *halalū* from his ice chest on the counter and cutting it open into a fleshy butterfly. The head and guts he throws into a plastic container. Soon there are so many heads staring accusingly at him. "Remembah dat old Filipino man dat used to fish wit me las summah?"

"The one who taught you how to transform a Vienna Sausage can into a bait holder necklace?"

"Yah. Dat's Mr. Domingo. Well, I wen talk to Ben today, and he said he wen *make*."

"He died? How?"

"He was at Haleʻiwa trying fo' get his pole outta da water. Da wave come, throw him against the rocks. *Make*." I look at the heads overflowing the container. I look at my father. I know what he is thinking. The ocean even in dreams is haunting.

*   *   *

Minutes later the sound of the line being pulled woke him. He jumped out of the hole and ran down to his fishing pole nodding toward the sea.

"Dis one big buggah. Bombye goin' be one *pāpio*. No, *ulua*. For real one *ulua*," he chanted to himself as his hand turned the gear quickly, then pulled the pole back. The pole bent under the weight of the catch. "Dat Haruo goin' be sorry he nevah like come tonight." His face grew slippery with sweat and his glasses slowly moved down his nose. His fingers were blooming red with the pressure of turning the gear. He kept at it. Turning and turning. Most of the line had been drawn in but he saw nothing silvery in the water. How strange. "Where's da *ulua*? Must be one *ulua*," he wondered. But nothing could be seen in the water. "Eh, someting's wrong."

He waded into the water. A body in a patrol suit rolled in with the waves. He pulled the body out into the ironwood forest. On the man's shirt his hook was attached. He removed it and gathered his gear. He hoisted the man on his shoulders and walked home, again staying near to the cane fields.

*   *   *

Two hours later he is still happily cleaning the fish. His world has gotten small and round since he quit work. There is only fishing and remembering left for him to do. When he began fishing in his retirement, he would only take one ice chest and go on days that were mild. Now he takes two ice chests and disbelieves the newscasters every night when they tell him the surf will be 3–5 feet. This is important, especially, at Waimea where the undercurrent is strong.

I told him just the other day that he should go into business designing unusual fishing gear for the seasonal *halalū* fisherman. His newest creation is a pair of all-purpose shorts. What he does is go to Salvation Army and purchase a used pair of shorts. Then he takes pockets off his old jeans and sews them in front. Finally, he attaches loops on the sides for his scissors and all the other equipment that he'd rather wear then carry. This project is as inventive as the Vienna Sausage can bait holder necklace.

My father has never taken me fishing. He refuses to. I want him to take me to the reef with the big rocks piled up from the sea. That place where you can get scared just peering into the ocean below—so dark, deep and unforgiving. But I am a daughter which sometimes is less than a son. I fish in dreams, I tell him. It's in the blood. The ocean is too haunting he says.

Today the beach wakes to a crowd. The fishermen line the shore waist deep in the water. They line up like a row of suspects staring down to see something below the dark surface. They dangle their long poles, some waving the ends to make the bait lively and more attractive. My father stands quietly near the rocks where kids jump off into the water. Ben is standing on one side of him and a young Japanese man is on the other side. The Japanese man watches my father pick a sliver of white *ika* from his Vienna Sausage can, secure it on his hook, then dangle the line out. A few seconds go by and the pole nods toward the water. As soon as my father feels the pull, he yanks the pole up. The hook is stabbed into the fish tight. He takes the hook off of the fish and places the fish in the net around his neck. Then he begins the process all over again. He pulls up one after another and the Japanese man looks at his own still pole and shakes his head.

"Eh. Wot kine bait you use?" My father answers without stopping his work, without turning from the ocean.

"*Ika*. Wot you get?"

"I get *ika* too, but not biting."

"Well, I tell you one secret. Since my friend Mr. Domingo wen teach me someting, I goin' pass down someting to you. You *gotta* buy 'um from dis certain store in Pearl City. No buy 'um any place else. Plus, yah, my bait old. I use 'um, put 'um back in da freezah, use 'um, put 'um back. Da buggah soo stink, I tell you. Maybe 'as why I catch more."

"Nah. You tink das why? Eh. Wot dat ting 'round your neck?"

"It's to hold my bait. Vienna Sausage can. Some guys dey use da Zippy's chili container but 'as too big for me."

I ask my father again to take me fishing by the reef with the large rocks. Where the best fish hide. Instead he shows me with his hands how to attach the hook to the *suji* line. All the while he tells me again my grandfather's story as if that would satisfy me:

When he got home with the navy man, I watched the commotion from my room. I was scared. I thought the way he hung on my father's shoulder meant that he was dead. He brought the navy man into the house and set him down on the sofa. The man gradually moved into a sitting position. I gasped, slapping a hand to my mouth hoping the man didn't hear me.

"Oi! Oi! Taka!" He called my mother loudly as he ran into their bedroom. My brother, Haruo, moaned something about the noise, then turned over and fell back to sleep. My father took the blanket off their bed and grabbed a work shirt and shorts.

"Anata?" She watched his commotion confused, the lines between her eyebrows deepened. She stood in the doorway of the kitchen, turning her attention to the navy man. He smiled. She looked away modestly. My father removed the man's clothes and dressed him in his own shirt and work shorts. The man was too big for the shorts so he sat there with the zipper and button undone. The shirt barely covered his wrists. My father wrapped the blanket around the man stepping back to assess his work. My mother came in with a plate of rice with slices of luncheon meat that were left over from dinner. The man ate the food thankfully. My father watched the man eat as my mother dried his uniform near the stove.

"Ah . . . you sleep." My father said when the man had finished. The man nodded and moved to the sofa and slept. I watched the man for the rest of the night. I watched as his large nose gargled the air and blew it out through his mouth. He was such a large man. His feet and legs hung over the arm of the sofa. My father also watched, drinking coffee to stay awake. He massaged the man's strained arm and weak legs.

Dawn seemed to burst out of the darkness when the neighbors came over. My father woke the man. "Dey take you back." The man sat up on the sofa. He had long legs with knees that came near his face when he was sitting down. My father helped him up. The neighbors grabbed his uniform.

They walked in a crowd to the truck. As the man slowly got in, my mother gave him a sandwich and some water. The man smiled at my father and shook his hand. No words, just an exchange of the eyes. The man waved, turning his head out of the window. My father waved until the truck could not be seen and the dust from the tires had settled back into Waialua.

Every weekend after that the man returned. He always brought a large tin box with red and white squares. It was filled with soda crackers. He came back every week for a long time.

"How many fish you goin' eat?" my father asks me as he pours shōyu and mirin over the butterflied bellies of the *halalū*. He is happy as if the ocean has returned something for what he has given.

"Two small ones."

"Only two?"

"There's too many bones."

"Oh yah. Remembah you wen get one tiny tiny bone stuck in your throat. Had to take you to Dr. Matsunaga. You stay deah gagging while he sticking da tweezers down your throat." He laughs at the memory. His memories of me are sweet he says. But there are other memories he can only mumble to the ocean.

We don't talk about my younger brother anymore unless it's a conversation with the ocean. My father still blames himself for not seeing, for knowing too late. For not being able to see in the black water for his son. For turning his back to the ocean. He is left with his memories and an abundance of fish. Offerings from the ocean. I am left with dreams and stories.

But the fisherman never really leaves. When my grandmother died, a year after my grandfather, my father decided to go out in the boat one day. He went alone. At least that's what people saw as he pulled away from the harbor. But deep in the water two dolphins sensed him. They followed him out, one on each side, like guardians. He fished for several hours in the evening. When it was time to come in, he saw the dolphins guide him back. The sea is fickle. It doesn't know what it wants exactly until it sees it. It takes and gives.

I still hear the cries of my brother. They are eerie lullabies that sometimes lull me into a sleep where I dream of him fishing, passing the pole into my hands. I fish in dreams. The moon is full. It's in the blood.

BY GARY PAK

HAE SOON'S SONG

hat you have to do," Suzy said matter-of-factly in Korean, "is let them feel your breasts." She sipped her soft drink through a thin plastic straw, then gazed across the empty dance floor, humming a few bars of Bruce Springsteen's "Dancing in the Dark." "But what they really like is when you fondle them."

Hae Soon, sitting across the table from Suzy, bowed her head in embarrassment.

"Let them touch you a little, just enough," Suzy continued, like a well-meaning older sister. "Otherwise, they'll order one drink and leave for another place. Or worse yet, they'll give their business to one of the *other* girls." She glared at the bar where the other hostesses were gathered.

With a tilt of her head, Suzy tossed ringlets of her lightened hair from one side of her face to the other. "And why don't you go to a hairdresser and have something done to your hair? You look like a little school girl." She waited for an answer. There was none. She shook her head. "I don't get it. I don't know why you want to work here. You've worked here for a week and all you're doing is wasting your time, your money. You haven't made enough even to tip the bar and housemother or to pay the taxi fare home. This really puzzles me."

"I'm managing," Hae Soon answered quickly, also in Korean. "And I don't have to—"

"And who are you calling cheap? Not me, I hope."

"I didn't say that."

"But that's what you were going to say. Just remember that I'm showing you all this because our families come from the same province. I don't have to do this, you know."

Hae Soon lowered her eyes. "No, I didn't mean it that way," she said.

Hanging from the ceiling, a rotating disco ball was showering the dance floor with spots of bright light.

Hae Soon turned towards the bar and regarded Jimmy Choi, the tired-eyed bartender, who was leaning against the cash register and watching the television set mounted from the ceiling. His baggy eyes, his sagging cheeks—*he looks like one of those fat-faced house dogs—what did they call them?—beagles?—the kind of dog that the American colonel's wife always brought into father's shop?* She read the time on the clock, then returned to Suzy, but only for a moment, afraid that Suzy might unleash her terrible temper again. Yes, she should be fortunate that Suzy had gotten her the job. Jobs were hard to find in Hawai'i, especially if one was an immigrant with very limited English.

But she never imagined that she would be a bargirl.

They were outcasts, treated like dirt, those women in the doorways.

On the way home from school to her father's modest tailor shop that was tucked in a narrow alley, downtown Seoul, she would pass the clubs with brassy music pouring out of the doorways. Those doorways that smelled of rice wine and perfume. On slow days, the girls would gather out front, their glossy tight skirts with slits on the sides showing their sleek white thighs, their cheeks powdered and lips painted red. And when they saw Hae Soon or any of her school girlfriends, they'd call out, "Pretty little girl! Ah! Pretty little girl!" Then, one day, one of the bargirls befriended Hae Soon—her name was Min Ja—and Min Ja gave Hae Soon a piece of wheat candy. The next day Min Ja called Hae Soon to an empty stool next to the doorway. Hae Soon sat, and they talked about Hae Soon's school, about Min Ja's home in Kwangju—they talked about Min Ja's picking of ripened persimmons and her grandmother making honeyed rice cakes—and they talked until the long shadows of passersby suggested the coming of darkness. And when Hae Soon arrived at her father's shop, she received a terrible scolding. But Hae Soon returned to that doorway and Min Ja who always had a stool and a candied treat for her. And then one time Min Ja quietly began braiding Hae Soon's hair, and after a while Hae Soon glanced back and saw that tears were in Min Ja's eyes, her eyes were blackening, dark streams of tears were dripping down her cheeks. *Why are Min Ja's tears black?*

They're bad women, her mother told her, don't even think of looking in there. And never walk past there again. Do you know what people will say if they see you there? Do you? Do you?! If you go past there again, I will tell your father.

So she stopped walking that route from school, for a long while. But one day she passed that doorway again. Every day she had thought about her friend Min Ja, and she missed her friend: the way Min Ja combed and braided her hair, her stories of her childhood, her soft pleasant voice. Hae Soon heard American rock 'n' roll music blaring out of the dark doorway.

She slowed her walk to a stop and stared into the establishment, which she had never entered, squinting her eyes at the loud and abusive music that made her ears ring. Before she could call for Min Ja, one of the other girls came out and greeted Hae Soon. *Are you looking for Min Ja? Lucky girl! She's gone off and gotten married to a rich man.*

Hae Soon ran from there, as fast as the flight of a newspaper down a gusty downtown street, as fast as the frolicking run of a mountain stream, running over slippery rocks, past crocks and carts of food, past the vendors' tables of bright goods, past the darting fish, past the scattering cats of smelly trash heaps. She didn't know why she was running. Was it because she was afraid to be caught dead in front of that house of the dark door-way? Was it because Min Ja had left without telling her? And when she was a good distance away, a block from her father's shop, she ran into a dirty, urine-smelling alley, leaned her head against the brick wall and cried.

"Look at her! Look at her, Hae Soon! Hae Soon? Hae Soon?! Look at her . . . there, at the bar. Last month she wasn't that big. Oh, my! No won-der I haven't seen her all this time. Where did she get the money to get those breasts? Her boyfriend, probably. She did it for him. Yes. He's an attorney. Hmph! So who cares?!"

Hae Soon surveyed the girl in the low-cut red evening dress. She sipped her Coke and brought her hands together on her lap, forming a fold-ed fan.

"You know," Suzy said, narrowing her eyes, "I introduced her to him. And she took him away from me. He was *my* boyfriend."

He was a poet. His name was Yong Gil. She met him at the universi-ty where he was student of literature and modern poetics. He was young and brilliant, handsome and brave. He wrote poetry that was powerful and beautiful, each word full with life meaning. One day, a month after they had been going together, he presented her with a book of poems, each poem a love ode to her. He explained to her that the book was two years in the making, the time he had endured a distant, feverish love for her.

And he of course wrote other poems, mainly poems of his great love for legendary Kumgansan—the Diamond Mountains—though he had never seen them since the mountains were part of the prohibited North. *The mountains are brave mountains,* Yong Gil told her. *Kumgansan are like the Korean people, standing strong and battling invaders and destroyers of everything Korean.*

It was romantic, being with Yong Gil. Romantic.

Her father did not like him. Yong Gil was too outspoken: he openly criticized the Chun Do Hwan government as being a fascist dictatorship and a puppet of American imperialism. He was a known subversive. He had been arrested once, maybe two or three times. But Hae Soon could not listen to her father: she was in love with Yong Gil and his vision of Kumgansan. At those secret student meetings, she watched Yong Gil speak, her eyes fixed on him, her face like a flower opening to a morning sun. And in the bitter, long, winter nights, their bodies as one melted the ice of the air.

"Let's go dancing tonight," Suzy said, her voice flat. She began humming the popular Korean song that was now playing on the jukebox, the song about the Man with the Yellow Shirt:

> *I don't know why, but I like him,*
> *That Man with the Yellow Shirt.*
> *I don't know why, but I like him,*
> *That Man with the Yellow Shirt.*

Hae Soon stared at Suzy, her thoughts of Yong Gil vanishing softly into the dark, empty atmosphere. "Yes? What is it?"

"There you go again," Suzy grumbled. "Always in your dream cloud. That's why the other girls outhustle you all the time. That, plus you don't put out. Do you really want to work here?"

Hae Soon straightened up. "Have some customers come in?"

"No—no—silly! How are we going to have customers on a dead night like tonight?" She looked away, shaking her head. "Look. Let's go dancing tonight. We could go down to Seoul Palace. I know the bartender there. He and I used to work at the Bluebird Lounge on Keʻeaumoku. He's really nice. And he has a cute brother working with him. Maybe I could introduce you. . . ."

Hae Soon shook her head.

"Oh! You're no fun!" Suzy folded her arms over her chest and sank as low as she could in her seat. "I don't know why you work here. All you do is sit around and sip your Coke. And dream. How do you expect to make a living in Hawaiʻi? And you with a child to support. You have to hustle. Work hard. Oh . . . I don't know why I talk to you."

Hae Soon's eyes moistened. Gently she dabbed her eyes with a paper napkin so as not to smear the mascara.

"Oh, I'm sorry," Suzy offered. "You know me. When it gets slow like tonight, I get this way. You're my friend. Our families come from the same province. It's like we know each other for a long time. Right?" She paused to check on an entering customer. Without looking around, the older local Asian man sat at the bar. "Look. I'm sorry I told you these things. All right? You forgive me?"

Hae Soon forced a smile and nodded her head. "It's all right. I know . . . I've . . . I've been stubborn."

"We're all like that. And we're all in this same disgusting boat. *Aiigoo*!"

"Maybe we can go dancing tonight?"

Suzy's eyes lit up. "All right . . . if you want to. And I'll introduce you to Tong Sul's cute brother."

Hae Soon waved off the match-making suggestion, shaking her head. "No—no arrangement. All right? Please?"

"You're still in love with him, aren't you?"

Hae Soon nodded, a shy smile rising to her face.

"Oh . . . come on," Suzy said, taking Hae Soon's hand. "You can be honest with me. I can understand. I was in love once, too." Suzy's eyes became distant. She let Hae Soon's hand go. "Sometimes . . . I wonder what is it like to be in love again. It's been such a long time." Suzy's eyes reached across the dance floor for the country love song playing on the jukebox. "What is his name again?"

"Yong Gil."

It was spring, and they had eloped. It was a beautiful time of the year. The air was warm and the earth fecund, and the blossoms on the apple and persimmon trees threw their ripe redolence into the air. And those wonderfully romantic and hectic days of love and lust and demonstrations against the ruling order lasted for all that spring and into an eruptive summer.

They had fallen asleep after a night of lovemaking when the police broke down their door. They beat a bewildered, naked, and struggling Yong Gil, then handcuffed him. They grabbed her womanparts and came near raping her with their batons in front of Yong Gil with his mouth of broken teeth when their professor friend, from whom they rented the small cottage, came storming out of the main house and demanded that the police leave immediately. They threw Hae Soon down on the floor, even with her showing five months, and started on the professor, slashing a baton across his face, then smashing his face into a whimpering mess. But they left without further touching her: maybe they were overdue at the station, perhaps they had to hustle up more radicals for their nightly quota. *Those dogs! They dragged Yong Gil clutching only a blanket for cover.*

"Yong Gil," Suzy mused. "That's a nice name. Of course, he must be very handsome. You say he is very smart, too?"

Yong Gil. I will love no one else but you. Forever.

> *Willow weeps like a thousand cranes*
> *With heads bowed*
> *And legs crossed:*
> *A hunger for fish they feel.*
> *We hide under its branches,*
> *Hear its weeping*
> *And feel our hunger*
> *Cursed from birth.*
>
> *But far away loom majestic mountains*
> *Of diamond spires and sides of jade*
> *And topped with emeralds.*
> *We may be careless,*
> *Wounded birds of love,*
> *Pushed to and fro by cold harsh winds,*
> *But when we reach the jeweled mountains,*
> *The ugly scars from hate*
> *Will disappear.*
> *We'll love again:*
> *Love seeds new love.*

"What did you say?" Suzy asked, her eyes wide with curiosity.

"Huh? Oh . . . Yong Gil. His name is Yong Gil."

"Yes, you told me that. But what was it you were saying after that?"

"Oh, I don't know." Hae Soon shook her head with embarrassment. "I don't remember."

Suzy frowned. "All right, you don't have to tell me. But tell me this. Why did you come to Hawai'i where there are no good jobs? The only thing a woman can do here is to work in a bar."

"I told you before."

"But I want to hear it again. Besides, what else is there to talk about? Is there any excitement in our lives?" Suzy spun a hard look over the crowdless room.

"I had to leave," Hae Soon said, biting her words.

"But you said you were a high school teacher. You had a good job in Seoul. You leave a good job to come here to make money hustling in a bar? You had a future in Korea. And anyway, what good is a teacher in America who can't speak English?"

"Let's go dancing tonight!"

Suzy threw her hands in the air. "All right. If you don't want to talk about it. You just get me all upset. You don't even confide in me. After all, I'm your only friend in Hawai'i."

Yes, a good friend in Hawai'i. But you wouldn't understand. You can't understand.

A customer staggered into the lounge, an old gray man, local Oriental. Immediately Suzy jumped up to greet him before the other girls could slide off their stools. Holding the old man's hand, she led him to a dim corner of the lounge and sat him down. Shortly after, she ordered at the bar, plunked a few quarters into the jukebox and made her selection of popular Japanese songs. Then she glided over to Hae Soon.

"The old man says that his friends are going to join him in a little while. When they come, join us. I've been with them before. They like to touch a lot, but they're big spenders."

Hae Soon watched Suzy's lean swaying hips as she sashayed to the bar to pick up the order.

Maybe I should walk like her. No. What am I saying?

She regarded the large digital clock behind the bar. Time was hardly passing tonight. And how long ago was it when she left Korea and Yong Gil? Seven months ago? A year? Ten years?

Why did she leave?

That ancient bronze bell used to resound over the university campus, signaling the end of the class period. She would wait for him down by the ancient royal fishponds, and there they'd walk hand in hand, something they couldn't do in public. And the nights they'd spend locked up in one of the stuffy study rooms in the library: alone, trusting, warm skin on warm skin.

Oh, Yong Gil! Why did they take you away? Do you think about our son? How we live our lives so—

"Hae Soon! Hae Soon!" Suzy shook Hae Soon on the shoulder. "What's the matter with you?"

Hae Soon straightened up and blinked, startled by Suzy's round, piercing eyes.

"Come on, Hae Soon. His friends are here. Quickly—before the others beat you to them!"

Hae Soon fumbled for her handbag—*oh, it's behind the bar, I forgot*—then sidled out of the booth. Straightening her dress borrowed from Suzy's copious and silky wardrobe, she followed her friend obediently, past empty booths to the carousing men. Suzy glanced over her shoulders, gave Hae Soon a look of warning, then wiggled and smiled and laughed as she joined the men, settling herself between two of them.

Hae Soon found herself smiling. And, mildly surprised that the effort was easier than she thought, she was copying Suzy's waltzing steps. The noticing men rejoiced with her arrival. One of them flashed his gold teeth, which shone dull and warm in the semi-darkness. Hae Soon sat down in the booth across Suzy. The table was covered with bottles of beer and platters of food. She poured beer into the glass of the strongly cologne-scented man sitting next to her.

"What's your name?" the man asked.

"My nam-ah? Oh—Hae Soon."

"No!" interrupted Suzy, emphatically shaking her head, then smiling. "Her name ez—her name ez—eh—Eva."

"How are you, Eva?" the man said with a smile. "How come you dunno yo' name?" The men laughed. "Eva, how 'bout you bring me and my friends one 'nother round?"

"Go to Jimmy and order three Budweisers," Suzy interpreted in Korean.

Hae Soon nodded her head and went to the bar. She gave the order to Jimmy Choi, then turned to the other hostesses and smiled. They were whispering among themselves, avoiding eye contact with her. Hae Soon paid Jimmy, then returned to the table with the order.

Suzy was in the arms of the grayish man, playfully diverting his hands from entering the openings of her dress.

Hae Soon looked away and served the beer. The strongly scented man patted the empty seat next to him. Reluctantly, she sat down, folding her arms across her chest.

"You pretty," the man said. "How long you stay here in Hawai'i?"

She shrugged her shoulders. Suzy tapped Hae Soon in the shin with the toe of her shoe, then translated into Korean the question for her.

"Oh—I t'ink so—fo' month-soo—already."

"You speak good English. My friends and me, all the time we come dis bar, but first time we see you. How long you been working here?"

She nodded, though not understanding what he had said.

He put his arm around her shoulders. Hae Soon shivered. "You have beautiful skin." He ran his hand up and down her arm.

Hae Soon looked at Suzy for help, but the grayish man's hand was all over Suzy's chest now, and Suzy's hand was lowered somewhere in his groin, out of Hae Soon's view. She closed her eyes, wishing she was imagining what she was seeing. Then the man next to her slipped his hand under her arms. She resisted, shaking off the advance. He grinned, snickered, and pursued more, his other hand gripping her outside shoulder, bringing her tighter into his snare. The man persisted, and she refused him, but finally, finally, she let him in, loosening the lock of her arms though not dropping them. The man found a breast and squeezed it. It hurt her. He kissed her on the cheek, his alcoholic breath burning her skin, that thick cologne smell rubbing off on her face. She trembled. She fought back a cry.

"You're very pretty."

"I—come back—hokay?"

"No," the man said, holding her down. "I like you here. You stay here and take care of me, and I take care of you." He pointed with his eyes to a small pile of money at the edge of the table.

Suzy was laughing. "Isn't this fun?" she said in Korean. "This old man is so small, but he's so funny."

The men finished their beers and asked for another round. Hae Soon leaped out of the booth, straightening her bra, and went to the bar before Suzy could unstrap the gray man's arms. She put in the order. The girls on the stools were giggling at her. Embarrassed, Hae Soon looked the other way, towards the open front door. It was raining outside. She thought of walking out.

They were walking in the rain the day she told him that she was pregnant. He was silent for a long while, his face furrowed with anxiety. Then, suddenly, he leaped ahead of her, jumping up and down while clapping his hands and shouting to the world, "I'm going to be a father! I'm going to be a father!" He dropped to his knees and begged her to marry him.

She could not answer. She was crying. She had never seen before Yong Gil so deliriously happy. It shook her. But she took his head and pressed it against her womb.

> Can you feel our baby breathe, my love?
> Can you feel our baby move?
> Can you hear the beating heart
> Like wings fluttering,

A thousand doves
Descending from the Heavens?

Hae Soon glanced back at the booth. Suzy was laughing with the men. Hae Soon didn't want to return. But the money. The money.

His face was battered, though his eyes were alert and filled with anger.

"Yong Gil!!"

"Shut up, whore! Hurry up! Get him out of here."

"And the other?" Pointing to the professor unconscious on the ground.

"Leave him. Hurry up! Let's go!"

His mouth opened, but his words were broken, unspeakable. He spat out a bloody tooth, then another. Coughed. In desperation he made weak gestures—his hands, arms, head—trying to convey the message to her: *Stomach?—Baby?—Are you all right?*

They handcuffed him and dragged him out the door on his bare ass.

Yong Gil, please understand. It's all for little Yong Gil, little one. So he can grow up big and strong, return home to find his father. And he'll get back at them, those bastards, sons of bastard pigs, for humiliating his father—

"Hae Soon?! What are you doing?" Suzy. "They're waiting and waiting for their drinks. Are you dreaming again?"

"I—I'm coming."

"And call yourself *Eva*. Don't you like that name?"

Jimmy Choi stared at her, then grinned at the other girls: What's wrong with this bitch?

"Oh—yes—"

"Come on. They're waiting." Suzy scurried back to the table.

Hae Soon paid the bartender, then hurried back to the booth.

"How come took you so long?" the cologne man asked.

Hae Soon forced a smile.

The man said something to his friend. They looked at her and grinned.

"Charlie says he like to date you," the man said. "But I tol' him fo' get lost. You mine tonight, eh, sweetheart?"

The man smiled broadly, showing his gold teeth. He corralled her with a large arm and kissed her on the cheek. He tried to touch her breast again, but Hae Soon pushed his thick calloused hands away. He forced his hand up her dress and grabbed her crotch. She shrieked, squirmed out of his grasp and jumped out of the booth. She grabbed an empty bottle from the table and broke it on his face.

"Hae Soon!!"

She grabbed the money and threw it at the men.

Suzy leaped out of her seat and tangled her arms with Hae Soon's. "Stop it!! Hae Soon!!"

The bottle had cut the man's cheek. Blood was streaming out of the wound. With anger and disbelief, the man stared at the blood dripping on his hand, then cautiously touched his face. He lunged out of the booth.

"You cunt!"

He grabbed Suzy, who was in the way, by the hair and tossed her to the side where she fell like a crumpled puppet.

"You cunt!"

A blow sent Hae Soon flying into another table. The man lifted her and beat her with an open hand until Jimmy Choi and the man's drinking partners could restrain him.

"You cunt!"

From the floor, numbed with pain, she watched the struggle, the commotion, the madness, as if she was an outsider looking in. Two girls from the bar began mothering her, trying to help her up. She pushed them away, then shakily pulled herself up. She grabbed her handbag from the back of the bar and started towards the door. But she stopped halfway across the dance floor. With the swirling spots of light covering her, she glared at the dogs, spat at them, then marched out of the lounge.

The rain had stopped. The air was cool. The boulevard was empty of cars. She gazed at the dark sky and took a deep breath before taking off her shoes and nylons. A block from the lounge a taxi slowed down beside her. She waved it away. She had no money for a cab, nothing for food and rent that was due in another week. How could she and little Yong Gil survive? On Yong Gil's thin volume of poetry? On sympathy from the dogs?

I don't know why but I like him,
That Man with the Yellow Shirt.
I don't know why but I like him,
That Man with the Yellow Shirt.

DAY'S WORK

he mill whistle blew far in the distance, and Rita looked across the rolling cane fields as the light rain from the mountains fell about her shoulders. When she heard the dull stamping of hooves around the bend behind her, she remembered that she had better hurry home. Tonight her uncles were coming over, and she'd have to be there to serve them.

She shoved one last handful of pig grass deep into her gunny sack, tied the bag off with a piece of fraying rope and slung the bag over her shoulder. As she walked homeward, a dirt-reddened wooden carriage squeaked and grumbled past, drawn by seven sweltering mules. The old wagon was filled with *hāpai kō* men, their thick protective clothing crusted and soiled from the chopping and loading of sugar cane. Since early morning, this crew had been carrying sticky bundles weighing a hundred pounds or more each on their backs and loading them onto railroad cars headed back to the mill. Now, after so many hours of unrelenting sun, the late afternoon drizzle mocked them with a faint arc of red, green and yellow against the mountainside, just past the banks of Waitā Reservoir. By the time the wagon pulled up beside Rita, the rain had ceased, the mirage of color fading. She looked up at the familiar faces and smiled. One of the Filipinos called down to the her as they passed, saying, "Hey, *inday,* you going like take our job someday, ah?"

Lately Rita didn't mind the long walks that took her to the fringes of Kōloa plantation. Twice a week she gathered food for her family's pigs, searching the ground for the dark green succulent vine that crept wild between the stalks of cane. She often found hidden among the rows ripe pumpkin, squash, and tomatoes, planted by field workers months or years before. Since her youngest brother had turned fourteen and gone to work in the sugar mill, she made these sojourns without him. Now, as she moved alone through the vast acreage, she found herself breathing in time to the pace of her own footsteps. Away from the constant clamor and activity at home, Rita found peace in the great expanse, losing herself in the fertile fields.

The grunting of pigs and scratching of chickens caged in the front yard greeted her when she arrived home. Effie was already pouring barley into the barrel, and Nando was splitting dried tree branches to kindle a fire that would cook the barley, pig grass and flour mixture before their father fed it to the hogs.

"Ah, so long you take," Rita's mother said through the kitchen window. "What, das all you bring?"

"No more grass near us anymore, Nanay. I have to go farther ef'ry time." She washed the soil from her hands at the white enamel basin as her mother rolled fried pastry dough in a plate of sugar on the kitchen table. A large steel pot of rice, chicken, and vegetables sat bubbling on the cast-iron stove.

"You hab to look harder. We cannot use too much da barley. 'As for da horses only."

"You only going sell 'um on Sunday anyway," Rita replied.

"Das why, two more days for make him fat. Da more fat, da more money I can get, ah? You know dese *pinoys*. When dey winning dey like to spend. Iss good luck to dem." Nanay wiped her brow with the hem of her tattered denim apron. "Unless you like us eat 'um ourself."

"I no like pork anyway," Rita said.

"Nobody tell you make friend wit' da pig."

Rita looked down at the table. There were already two dozen pastries wrapped in waxed paper. "Why you making so much tonight? Da cockfights not until Sunday."

"Dese *kaskaron* I make for you to take to da Caridad house tomorrow."

"What, I thought Tatay never like me babysit for them."

Nanay stopped rolling dough and turned away from her daughter to stir the simmering contents of the pot on the stove. "I wen talk to your father las' night. 'Sokay now."

Rita groaned. Not another job, she thought. Ever since she finished the eighth grade, Nanay seemed to load her down with more and more chores. "I wanted to see my friend Yuko tomorrow. She was going to lend me some of her books for next year." She watched her mother's face for a response, but none came. "You know, for school in da fall." The ribbons of dusk through the kitchen revealed creases above Nanay's eyes and around her cheeks that Rita had never noticed before.

"What for you need more school? You already can read and write, add and subtract, like dat. More smaht dan me." Her mother rubbed her growing belly. "Pretty soon I no can bake. Pretty soon one more mouth to feed. I need you to help me."

Rita fell silent. She had known how her mother felt all along. Neither of her older brothers went to high school, and she couldn't really expect to be any different.

"I tell you what. Da money you get from Mr. Caridad, we can use for make one new dress for you," Nanay said. "So you can start looking like one lady." Rita's mood brightened at this prospect. "Tomorrow, aftah you *pau* da babysit, you can go look at da material dey hab at Sueoka."

Rita went outside, around the back of the house, down the footpath that led to the stables. By now, all but the most stubborn animals were in their stalls, and she watched her brother and father try to corner the horse they called Boy. As her brother Perfecto raised his rope to whip the animal, Rita's father shouted, "No! No hit 'um. *Bumbai* he get mad." It was too late. After the rope cracked across the animal's shiny brown coat, Boy reared wildly, his hooves clawing the air in front of them. Tatay and Perfecto scattered out of his way. "Let 'um go," said Tatay as the horse galloped off down the road toward the grazing pasture. "He come back when he like eat."

When the family first moved into the house next to the stables, away from their friends in Filipino camp, it had seemed like a mansion, and Rita bragged to her Japanese and Chinese friends in school about their new home. But later, she overheard her parents speaking in Visayan about the previous stableman, who had to quit after being partially crippled by a bucking horse. Rita's father had been good with the mules when he plowed irrigation ditches in the fields, and his *luna*, Mr. Monroe, convinced him to be the new stableman when no one else would take the job. Now it was Tatay's job to watch over as many as three hundred horses and mules at a time, to pull them out of their stalls before sunrise and herd them back in by nightfall, to make sure that the same two animals were always paired together, that they were all fed and watered and that the stalls were cleaned.

As a child, Rita had taken secret pride in her father's diligence, his obedience to his boss. But watching Tatay struggle with this animal twice his size, she wondered how long it would be before her father was hurt as well.

The first of her father's friends arrived soon after dinner. During the past year, Rita had been allowed to linger in the makeshift wooden shack that Tatay built adjoining the kitchen, where his friends would come to visit and buy the homebrew that Rita's parents made. Since the Liberatos started making and selling beer, these Friday night visits had become a ritual for a few close friends of Tatay, and Rita enjoyed seeing these familiar faces in this otherwise isolated area of Kōloa. But tonight her mother had made sure that Rita bathed and put on a clean, if well-worn, dress to greet the men, and when they both heard the familiar four knocks, Rita was hurried out of the kitchen

"Go serve dem, Rita." Nanay stopped her first to comb her hair. She pulled three brown *shōyu* bottles full of beer from a bucket of ice and handed them to Rita. Then she pulled three more bottles out from under a loose floorboard and put them into the ice to chill. The beer was stored in these bottles as soon as it was brewed and was hidden under the floorboards in case Mr. Monroe or the sheriff came by uninvited.

Augie and Blas were already sitting at the overturned crate that served as their card table. Each man held a knotted denim bundle in his lap, a week's worth of clothes that they paid Nanay to wash. Augie had a broad, leathery face with a wide, thick mouth that always seemed to be smiling about something, and his stringy hair was threaded lightly with gray. He looked at Rita and grinned, revealing crooked, widely spaced teeth; pushed up from the tip of his flat nostrils were the wire spectacles that he'd lately taken to wearing.

"Ebry week she come more and more pretty, eh, Jose?" Augie said to Rita's father as Rita set his drink before him. His voice was low and full of jagged edges.

"You hush up," Blas said, pointing the neck of his beer bottle at Augie. "Rita iss still one baby. You one ole man awreddy." Blas was even darker than Augie, his face shiny brown, with a thin mouth that was often pursed tightly to contain the reedy tenor of his voice. His eyes were small, without much eyelid, more like Japanese or Chinese, Rita thought. But they were like a ricebird's, always alert, darting from one speaker to the next. He looked at Rita, curled his mouth upward and nodded, then quickly turned away.

Since her thirteenth birthday, Rita could feel a difference in the way her "uncles" deferred to her. It began to make her feel special, but a little uneasy as well.

"T'irty-six iss not so old yet. I am on-lee a few years older dan Jose, right? Ip I back in de Pilipines, I would hab one young beautiful wife, walking around *hāpai* like dis," Augie said, holding his hands out in front of him. "Like your wife, Jose."

"If she big like dat, would not be prom you. You would not eben know which end por plant de seed." Blas smiled conspiratorially to Jose. "Not like dribing one plow, you know."

"Ha. Listen to you. Your wife stay back in Luzon. I get same chance as you por make bebe, ah?"

"At least I get one daughter."

"How long ago dat? Twelb years? By now you por-get how you wen make 'um."

Rita watched Blas sit quietly now, wondering what it would be like to have a family far away for so many years. After the Chinese, Japanese and Korean waves of immigrant workers, the sugar company recruited only Filipino males to work in the fields, and many recruits expected to stay for only a few years before going home.

Augie took a quick gulp of beer, and wiped his mouth on his shirt sleeve. "Dis Jose da smaht one. He bring his wife wit' him."

"Good t'ing, ah?" Tatay said. "Who going wash your clothes, make you beer?" He stood up slowly, stretched and stifled a yawn with a fist. "I'm going to bed now, boys. Rita, take care of your uncles, eh?"

"Pretty soon I bring dem here, you watch," Blas said after Tatay had gone. "Ebry month I saving." He reached into his pocket and pulled out his wallet. "You see dis money?" Blas pulled out some neatly folded bills. "Ebry payday, like today, I put some money aside por da fare. I mark 'um, see?" Blas showed Augie and Rita a red-ink marking on the corner of a dollar bill. "Even ip I come here to drink, or gamble, I no spend dis money."

"Ahh, how long you been saving," Augie said. "By da time you get enough money, your daughter going be older den me."

"You wait and see," Blas replied, his fist lightly bouncing on the crate top. "I like see you talk when you see dem step off da locomoto."

"What you jokers arguing about now?" The voice at the doorway belonged to Nick, arriving late, with a guitar under his arm as usual. He wore a long-sleeved, printed shirt and pleated black slacks, a new, gray, broadbrimmed hat cocked at a precarious angle. Rita had begun to admire the way Nick dressed in fancy clothes, as if he wasn't really from Kōloa, but from Lihue or Honolulu even.

"Look dis guy," Augie said. "All dress up again. Who you dress up por?"

"I dress up for the lady, of course." He smiled at Rita, who studied Nick's fine, sharp features. Compared to the others, Nick was fairskinned, his cheekbones high under his almond shaped brown eyes. When he tipped his hat to her, Rita felt a pleasant, scary sensation.

"Neber mind, neber mind. You no can *koboy* her," Augie said. "I been go try awreddy."

Nick looked at Augie with mock disgust and said to Rita, "Don't listen to dis guy, *ading*. You know dese Ilocanos have no class."

Tatay would say that Visayans like Nick and her own family were more accustomed to city ways than Ilocanos, who were coarser, more down-to-earth farming people. Rita didn't see that it mattered much. In Kōloa, both Visayans and Ilocanos worked in the fields, and the *haole* bosses and other workers never knew the difference between them. Rita had met Ilocanos who were very refined, whose families had servants at home in the Philippines. And there were Visayans like her father, who had very little education and who had been a fisherman before coming to Hawai'i.

"You see dis Nick, hah, Rita?" Blas said. "Dis guy one *silk,* workin' da plantation store. No more family, das why can spend on da clothes."

"Say what you want. You're just jealous because I work with my mind. I don't carry the cane on my back like one *carabao.*"

"Hah," Augie said. "You work wit' your mout'. *Ho'omalimali* da store boss."

"I only tell him what he like to hear. I tell him how to do somet'ing, but mek him feel like he's da one wit' da idea. Maybe he give me raise, promote me, eh? One day maybe I have my own business, eh?" Nick fingered the neck of his beer bottle. "I'm not going to be like you Ilocanos. Only know how to dig da ground."

"So what," said Blas. "Iss honest work. Da only business you know iss to play poker and fight da chickens."

"At least I mek money," said Nick coolly, leaning back in the folding chair. He reached into his pocket and pulled out a small leather sheath. "Look at dis."

Augie reached over and opened the pouch, pulling out a shiny metal blade no longer than his forefinger. Surprised, Rita leaned in to look closer. She'd seen cockspurs on Sundays at the fights where she and her mother sold baked goods, but she'd never seen a knife like this up close, out of its element. Squinting, Augie ran a finger along the edge and passed it along to Blas. "Nice," he said. "How you get dat one?"

"Gonsalves, da blacksmith, he help me. I slip him one twenty-five-pound bag rice."

"Who dis for?"

"Da black one, you know, da one wit' da brown and red feathers around da neck."

"You going fight 'um awreddy?" Blas asked. "Kinda young still."

"No." Nick took the blade back from him. "Just right. He get da evil eye now. Hungry."

"You know wus da evil eye, Rita?" Augie asked. The other men laughed.

"You bettah put your money on dis one, my friends," Nick said. "He going be da big winnah."

"And what you going do wit' da money?" Blas asked. "Buy more clothes?"

"I don't know. Maybe I save 'um for da social box next month. I hear going have one pretty one entered dis time." Nick smiled at Rita.

Rita had only been to one social-box dance, a month and a half before. Parents of young Filipino girls on the plantation aged eleven to fifteen entered the girls in a kind of beauty pageant. The many Filipino bachelors would bid on the "social box" each girl held, a brightly wrapped package containing a roasted chicken or baked pie, or perhaps a shirt made by the girl or her family. The bachelor with the highest bid won the box and was invited to the girl's home for a visit chaperoned by her parents.

"What, Rita, you going be entered dis time?" Augie asked.

"I . . . I don't know. I guess so." Was that why Nanay wanted to make her a new dress?

The quiet in the room made Rita uneasy. Nick began shuffling a well-worn deck of cards. "You guys going try bid against me, bettah start winning tonight." He winked at Rita, and she felt the blood rush to her cheeks. "Enough talk already. Play cards."

Later, when the men had drunk a few bottles each, and when both Augie and Blas had gotten tired of losing to Nick, they entertained themselves by singing songs from their homeland. Rita had begun to learn these songs herself, and their coy melodies in 3/4 time would linger in her ear for the rest of the week. Now, before Nick had even gotten his left hand around the neck of his guitar, Augie was already singing "Puntung Biabol":

> Guava Jelly, Guava Jelly
> Tomorrow is Palm Sunday
> Put on your high-heeled slipper
> And wear your lace skirt!

And Blas, despite his quiet regret at losing again to Nick, started moving his lips as well. Soon all three men, and even Rita herself, were singing about guava jelly and coconut wine, Augie stomping his workboots on the floor, Blas drumming his fingers lightly on the tabletop and Nick beating the rusted strings of the old arch-top guitar. Rita found herself joining in, singing songs in celebration and remembrance of a homeland she'd never seen. "Here, *inday*," Nick said, after a short breather and another sip of homebrew. "I will sing you one you've never heard before." With a dramatic strum, he began:

Bright moon after an eclipse
which rose outside my window
I wish I never saw you
For my heart can't keep loving you.

When the *sampaguita* began to bloom
In the midst of my garden
My love for the moon was gone
If love is forced, my happiness is gone.

By the song's end, Blas was staring silently into the night, fingers clenched tightly around his brown bottle. Augie's eyes were half-closed, hands folded across his belly and his head nodding and jerking once in a while. Rita watched Nick cradle his guitar, fingering the strings with silent chords, and felt an uncommon heat flush through her. Suddenly, Nick slapped Augie hard on the shoulder.

"Come on, *pare*," said Nick. "Time to go." He took a quick look around the table, counted some change out of his winnings and pushed a pile of coins toward Rita. "For da drinks, eh?" He picked his hat up from the crate top and adjusted the brim over his forehead. The others mumbled their sodden farewells, and Rita watched the three bachelors shuffle through the crooked wooden doorway into the warm summer moonlight.

The next day Nanay didn't need to remind Rita about how to get to the Caridad home. The small, white, two-story house was located right in the middle of the town's single main thoroughfare. On her way there, she passed the Tanaka fishmarket, where fishermen sold their catch of 'ahi and *ulua* to plantation housewives. The heady scent of freshly baked bread wafted out into the street from Chang Fook Kee bakery, her mother's biggest rival when Nanay sold her own baked goods door to door. And a gang of children crowded the entrance to the Yamamoto Store, clamoring with excitement over the candies, crack seed, and dried abalone. Cradling the bundle of pastry that Nanay had made the day before, Rita could already imagine herself in a blue dress made from the cotton she'd seen in the window of Sueoka Store. The thought that Nick might bid on her at the next social-box dance made her smile and shudder slightly.

The Caridad house sat across the street from most of the stores, between the plantation's elementary school and the funeral parlor. A coat of fresh white paint lent the house an imposing air, an official look like that of the other buildings on Kōloa's main street. The building had been there for as long as she could remember, but Rita couldn't quite recall when it was that Mr. Caridad moved in. It was common knowledge that he had opened the first auto dealership In Kōloa, and he always displayed a number of new and used cars on the well-manicured front lawn. Rita's parents spoke of him fondly, and Mr. Caridad, a fellow Visayan who came over on the same ship with Tatay, was the godfather of Rita's oldest brother.

A sharply dressed Filipino man wearing a cream-colored, heavily embroidered Tagalog shirt and dark-gray, pleated slacks stood on the porch, puffing on a cigar. As Rita approached the steps, he smiled broadly, showing several gold-capped teeth. "Ah, sweetheart, you've grown so much." Mr. Caridad called into the house, "Eve."

"Oh, there you are." A pale, blonde woman in a thin lavender dress emerged from the darkened doorway. Rita had seen this woman with Mr. Caridad at the cockfights last Sunday, being introduced to many of the men there. Beside her stood a little boy, no more than two years old, hiding his face in the folds of his mother's skirt.

"Please," the woman said, shaking a blonde curl from her eyes. "Come this way. I'll show you what to do." She took the bundle of pastry from Rita and set it on a chair beside the door. Mr. Caridad reached into his pocket and pulled out a gold watch, blew a ring of smoke off the porch toward the five parked cars on the lawn and said, "Hurry now."

Rita followed the woman through the sparsely furnished living room hidden from the afternoon sun by heavy, olive-green drapes, into a smaller, adjoining room with a pūne‘e, a dresser, and a small, black trunk. Strewn about the floor were brightly-colored toys Rita had only seen in pictures—a yellow rubber ball, a blue and white jack-in-the-box with its clownface dangling out to one side and a bright-pink, plush toy pig.

"If he gets tired, you can make him sleep here," said Eve. Up close, the woman's face betrayed a haggard look, the crinkled lines around her eyes breaking through the crust of powder on her face. "This bottle is for when he gets thirsty." She turned to her son. "Rene, this is Rita. You must listen to her, OK?" Rene nodded wordlessly, rubbing his nose on the sleeve of his T-shirt. With his golden brown skin, almond-shaped eyes and light-brown curls, Rene was the most beautiful little boy she'd ever seen.

The sound of men talking came from the porch, Mr. Caridad welcoming some friends. "Have to go," said the pale woman, adjusting the sash around her waist and opening the front of her dress slightly below her neck. "Just keep him entertained."

Rita thought she recognized the voices. She cracked the door open, and saw Augie smiling and shaking Mr. Caridad's hand. Blas stood beside him and in front of Eve, looking nervously around the room. She watched the woman offer the kaskaron to the men, and was about to wave a greeting to her uncles when she noticed Rene climbing on top of the black trunk next to the dresser, trying to reach for something. Rita picked up the boy and set him on the *pūne'e,* then reached around him to open the drapes. Sunlight poured into the room, and she could see Mr. Caridad standing in front of a car in his yard, talking to a few other Filipino men who had arrived.

Eve opened the door quickly, a wad of dollar bills in one hand. She crossed the room to the black trunk, lifted the lid and shoved in the money. She lowered the lid quietly, almost reverently.

"Ma," Rene cried out suddenly, pointing through the window. "Sun. Outside."

"Try to keep him quiet," Eve whispered to Rita.

As Rene sat and scribbled shapes onto a note pad, Rita could hear footsteps ascend the stairway until they were right above her. She heard a woman's voice, Eve's, and a man's, their low murmuring like the bland recitations of church patrons. Very soon she heard the soft squeaking of bedsprings, then five or six violent shakes that rattled the floor above until she heard the hoarse, catarrhal sigh she knew belonged to Augie. In the relative calm that followed, Rene dropped his pencil and began to declare his boredom in rapid, syllabic nonsense.

She watched the child climb atop the trunk again and pull down the small, painted enamel basin that rested on the dresser. He perched the basin on his head, his beaming cherub's face the reddish hue of a ripe mango. Rita picked up the boy and set him in front of the full-length mirror mounted on the bathroom door.

"You see?" she whispered, as she adjusted the basin on his head. "You look just like a little sailor." She was kissing Rene hard on the cheek in a sudden gust of affection when his mother rushed back into the room.

"Sorry, sweetheart," said Eve, crouching beside them. She lifted the basin deftly from Rene's head before stepping quickly into the bathroom. The boy started to whimper. His mother emerged from the bathroom, threw the basin's liquid contents out the window and slid the basin back onto the bathroom floor before rushing back into the parlor. She slammed the door shut on Rene, who began to cry out loud.

Rita tried to remember what she had done to stop her own younger brothers and sisters from crying, but this beautiful toddler's contorted face and noisy wailing filled her with an unexplainable terror. She picked the white basin up from the bathroom floor, but was struck by its newly acquired antiseptic smell, like the smell of the detergent that Tatay used sometimes to wash out the stables. Rene snatched the basin from her and, gripping the helmet in his tiny fists, grew quiet.

After the eighth pair of footsteps had descended the stairs, Rita lost count. Some stayed upstairs for as long as fifteen minutes, but most, like Augie, came down almost as soon as they went up. Each time, Eve came into the room to perform her ritual with the trunk and the basin. After the last man came down the stairs, Eve opened the guest-room door and whispered, "You can come out here now." Rene was fast asleep on the *pūne'e* facing the open window.

"Dat kid make so much noise," Mr. Caridad complained in the parlor, as he chewed on one of Nanay's pastries.

"Well, at least she was able to keep him out of sight. If she keeps babysitting him, she'll learn how to keep him quiet. After all, it is her first day."

The woman gave Rita a whole dollar, and patted her cheek. "Thanks, sweetheart. Come back next Saturday, OK? I'll be here for a month."

Rita unfolded the bill. Its upper-right corner was marked with red ink. Sueoka's store would close soon, but she didn't feel like shopping for material anymore.

And when she opened the screen door to the late afternoon light, Rita found Nick standing at the bottom of the porch steps, looking across the dusty street as if across a vast ocean, oblivious to the cursing and laughter of the boys outside the pool hall and the bustle of the last-minute shoppers hurrying home. Buttoning the cuffs of his long-sleeved, striped shirt, he turned, chewing on something, and saw Rita looking down on him. He swallowed quickly, wiping the grains of sugar from his mouth. He looked up at her with his penetrating brown eyes, weakly turning up the corners of his mouth as he said, "Good afternoon, young lady." Rita felt something drop inside of her, her breath leaving her as a spirit leaves a corpse, and with moist eyes watched Nick walk slowly and deliberately down the now barren road, as if tracing footprints laid there long before he was born. With the waning sun at his back, he stopped just once, to look at his own shadow in the street while he adjusted the brim of his new gray hat.

BY GRAHAM SALISBURY

WHY WE HAVE RAIN

I t was the biggest laugh I'd had in a long time, my cousin Keo coming down from old man Alejandro's Barber Shop as a balahead. "Might as well do it now and get it right," Keo had decided. If he'd have asked me I'd have told him there was no way a sleepy Big Island barber like Alejandro could do balahead any better than the Army. But Keo thought so, and that's all that mattered.

His new look had us all rolling, especially Uncle Raz, who told Keo he looked like a torpedo. Aunty Pearl and Uncle Harley just smiled and leaned up against their son, proud as peacocks.

I rubbed my hand over the stubble on his head and told him it felt like pig's hair. He laughed, and punched me in the arm. "At least I no get pig's breath, eh?"

He looked ridiculous—tall, somewhat thin, but with muscle, deep red-brown skin, and bald as a mango. Ridiculous, but strong, dignified, and only six weeks out of high school.

"What are you two boys going to do without each other to get into trouble with," Aunty Pearl asked the day Keo was to leave for the Army.

"I don't know about this pantie," Keo said, "but I'm going to see some action."

"Sheese! The only action you're going to see is push-ups for being so ugly." I reached to shake Keo s hand. He squeezed as hard as he could, but couldn't make me flinch. "Not bad for a high school boy. Maybe the Coast Guard will take you after all."

I'd never heard of Vietnam before the war started. Then strange new words started popping up every week, on TV and in the papers—Viet Cong, Saigon, Haiphong, the Mekong Delta. Though I could hardly imagine any of it, a wave of heat rolled through my stomach whenever someone spoke of "Southeast Asia." Like Keo, *Vietnam* was something I would soon have to face.

Keo wrote to Uncle Harley and Aunty Pearl several times from boot camp, and a couple of times from the war zone, usually with a short note to me at the end of each letter. But the last one anyone got from him arrived in my mailbox.

He started out telling me about an operation in the Province of Tan Yuen, then seemed to wander off into whatever was passing through his mind.

...A friend of mine died last week, a couple of bullets in his lungs. He stared up at me and said, "Please. . . ." Then he died. This is a cruel country. There are scorpions here, and cobras as bad as the Cong. I'd like to napalm them all, hit them with Sky Raiders and Phantom jets. I'm not on earth, I'm in Hell. It's 120 degrees and everything sticks. This is a pitiful place. I can't even laugh anymore. Who cares, anyway?

The letter was wrinkled, as if he'd stuffed it in his pocket a time or two, and he'd written with a blunt pencil, the words smudging into each other toward the end. I sat out on the rocks by the ocean for a long time after reading it, and never showed it to anyone.

Not long after that a man drove up Uncle Harley and Aunty Pearl's rocky driveway in a white, four-door Plymouth. It had been raining for two days straight and mud caked around the tires of his car.

Uncle Harley had just left for Hilo to sell fish. Dad was in Honolulu buying boat parts, and Aunty Pearl had insisted that I come stay up at their house until he got back.

The man waited in the car while Aunty Pearl shushed the dogs, then hurried through the heel-sucking mud to the porch with his hat crooked under his elbow. Raindrops freckled his khaki uniform, spreading into dark splotches as he stepped up out of the rain.

"Good morning, Ma'am," he said to Aunty Pearl, then nodded to me and said, "son." He hesitated a moment, glancing over his shoulder at the clods of mud he'd tracked up onto the porch, then he turned back to Aunty Pearl. "Is this the home of Harley Mendoza?"

Aunty Pearl dipped her chin once in answer, and told him she was Mrs. Mendoza. The rain pushed into the trees around the house with a constant *shhhhhh* sound. When the man identified himself as Sergeant Decker, U.S. Army, I could feel Aunty Pearl tighten up next to me.

"I'm sorry to have to tell you this, Ma'am. Your son has sustained a serious casualty." Aunty Pearl gasped, and he quickly added, "He's okay, he's alive and doing well."

I put my hand on her back. Heat bled into my fingers through the thin material of her sweeping mu'umu'u. Her eyes, pinched by high, fleshy cheeks and brooding forehead, watered instantly.

Sergeant Decker waited a moment before continuing. Aunty Pearl sat down in her chair, next to Uncle Harley's, where they'd lived a thousand sunsets together. She closed her eyes, but Sergeant Decker went on.

"He was with his platoon near Da Nang, crossing a rice paddy. The boy in front of him stepped on a trap and was killed. Shrapnel hit Private Mendoza's leg, just below the knee, and he lost the small finger on his left hand. But the leg . . . the leg was shattered it had to come off from the knee down."

Sergeant Decker spoke softly, with a warm, comforting accent. When Aunty Pearl started to cry he took his hat from under his elbow and held it in his hands. Rain drummed on the metal roof of the house and splattered down to muddy puddles in thin waterfalls. Sergeant Decker glanced toward Uncle Harley's pig pen, but caught himself and apologized. He said he was from Georgia and it reminded him of home.

He put his hat back under his elbow. "Your son is doing fine, Mrs. Mendoza. He's at the 249th General Hospital in Tokyo. He'll be coming home as soon as he's well enough to travel." Then after a pause, he added, "If there's one thing I believe, it's that there's no adversity a soldier can't overcome if he's lucky enough to have people who care about him. Some don't, you know."

Before he left, Aunty Pearl took his hand and praised him for having the courage to do a job as difficult as his.

"Yes, Ma'am, it's a hard thing to do, all right. But when I see that a boy has something to come home to, it makes it a lot easier." Sergeant Decker tipped his head and said he'd be in touch.

After he'd gone, we sat on the porch for a long time without saying anything. Then, through her tears, Aunty Pearl brought up every foolish thing Keo had ever done in his life.

On a hot, blue-sky day more than six weeks later Keo came home. Aunty Pearl started crying when he first appeared, leaning on a pair of crutches. Uncle Harley hurried out to the plane and helped him down the stairs. Keo hooked his left arm over Uncle Harley's neck and held the crutches in his free hand. The left pant leg on his uniform was folded up and pinned short.

We were all there—me, Dad, Grampa Lynn and Tutu Max, Uncle Raz, and a bus load of other people. Keo didn't say much when he saw us, just smiled and glanced around quickly through watery eyes. His face was thinner, with cheeks that curved inward. His hair had grown back, but was cut short and trimmed close around his ears.

When he saw me pushing in, his eyes brushed by like a passing Jeep, as if embarrassed. I put three strands of *maile* that I'd gotten from the rainforest around his neck and gave him a quick hug.

I tapped the side of his arm. "Some people will do anything to get out of the Army."

Keo ducked his chin. "Yeah."

When we'd given him all the leis we'd made for him you could hardly see his face.

It wasn't until after sunset that evening that I finally got a chance to be alone with him. I caught him slipping away from the house and all the people who'd come to see him. He hobbled down to the pig pen and leaned into the fence on his crutches.

I came up from the side and spoke softly so I wouldn't startle him. "Six of them, now. Uncle Harley just got that black and white one a couple of weeks ago."

Keo made a low, scoffing sound. "Where I was, these things walk around the place like dogs."

We both stared at the shadowy pigs sleeping in a clump. The coolness of the night air made the smell from the pen crisper, stronger.

"How about I cut school tomorrow," I said. "We can go fishing out past the airport—take a cooler and spend a few hours."

"Fishing?" The way he said it was almost as if he hadn't heard me.

"Yeah, let's go out by the airport."

I thought he was thinking it over. A couple of pigs shifted, then settled down again. They looked a little green in the glow of the yard light. When someone in the house laughed, Keo stepped back.

"Fishing?!" he said, louder, as if swearing it. He took one of his crutches and slammed it against the fence. One of the pigs grunted awake. Keo hit the fence again, and then threw the crutch at the pigs. They wailed awake and lumbered around squealing.

Keo raised the other crutch, but I caught his arm as he was about to throw it at the pigs too. "Keo! Slow down. That's not going to help anything."

"What do you know about it, cousin. What the hell do you know about it?"

Uncle Harley came jogging up behind me. "What's wrong with the pigs?" Keo yanked his arm out of my grip. Uncle Harley looked into the pen, then back at us. The crutch lay in the mud, in clear view, but he didn't say anything.

Keo turned away, hopping on one foot. Then with the remaining crutch he made his way back to the house. The pigs grunted and shifted nervously when I climbed through the fence to get Keo's other crutch.

Uncle Harley's face looked as pained as I'd ever seen it, even more than when Aunty Pearl had told him about Sergeant Decker, and Keo's leg. "Its got to be hard for him, Sonny. Jesus, I wish there was something I could do."

I handed him the crutch. "I know what you mean. All I did was ask him if he wanted to go fishing. I guess I better let him get used to being home a while."

Uncle Harley put his arm on my shoulder as we walked back up to the house. "It's not your fault," he said. "He knows that. He's just . . . hell, I don't know. God damn war."

Keo had gone into his room and closed the door, so I waited outside until Dad was ready to leave. I sat on the porch with my feet on the top step, bent forward, leaning into my knees with my arms crossed.

On the way home Dad and I talked about old man Nakamura, who'd lost every finger on his right hand when some monster of a fish took the small tuna he'd had on his handline and ran like hell with it. But when his hand had healed, he'd gone right on fishing, just had to figure out a new way to get the line up. Dad said Keo would do the same.

"He'll figure something out, Sonny."

I sat on my hands as the cool night air whirled around in the open Jeep. "I still can't believe he lost a leg. . . ."

Dad drove in silence a while, then said, "I don't suppose he can either."

I stopped by to see Keo everyday after school, but soon cut down to once a week because he didn't seem to want me around. I usually found him sitting on the porch with his pellet rifle. Once, during the first week, he shot and wounded a dove. It flopped around in the dirt down near Uncle Harley's ice house. He never bothered birds before, neither of us did. Keo shot at it five or six times before it stopped flapping.

"What did you do that for?" I asked.

"Do what, cousin?"

"Shoot the bird."

"Why not?"

It irritated me, the way he called me "cousin," saying it with his eyes glazed off toward the trees. I may as well have been some *haole* guy from Hawaii Prep. "You've never shot birds in your life," I said.

"Got lots of time now. I can shoot them all day long if I like." Keo finally faced me. His eyes—I can't say just what it was, but they weren't Keo's eyes. The smile in them was gone. With the rifle in one hand, he reached out and pointed it at me. "Take a shot. See if you can hit the dead bird."

I stepped down to the yard. "I don't shoot birds, dead or alive. Hey listen, I'll come back another day."

Keo rested the nose of the barrel on the porch and turned his head toward the ice house. Then, still with one hand, lifted the pellet rifle, aimed slowly, and shot at the dead bird. A puff of dust exploded a few feet away from it.

Three weeks later Uncle Raz's charter boat, the *Flying Fish,* rose and fell alongside the pier, riding slow, wide swells that moved into the harbor and thumped up against the sea wall. The sky was clear and the water light turquoise green under the afternoon sun.

I sat on the pier with my spinner and gazed across the harbor to the island—a coast lined with palm trees, the old royal palace guarding its small, sandy cove, just below the steeple of the first missionary church; Kona Inn with its long, iron-red roof poking through the coconut trees; a lazy town peeking over the sea wall, one- and two-story buildings facing the ocean like a line of old men in wicker chairs. I would never have told a soul other than Keo himself, but I was thanking God in those moments that I hadn't seen what Keo had seen, and feeling so scared that I soon would, that I refused to believe there was any other world than the one that existed right there in front of me.

"Sonny." Dad stood on the stern deck of the *Flying Fish* with one hand on the cabin roof. "Come on the boat for a minute."

Uncle Raz and Uncle Harley sat at the table in the cabin. "Get a Coke, in the ice box," Uncle Raz said, pointing his chin to the cooler. I dug one out of the crushed ice and pried the cap off with a can opener. No one said anything until I was sitting on the bunk across from them.

Uncle Harley spoke first. "We've been talking about Keo. He's getting worse every day, sitting around the house doing nothing, growing his beard, shooting his pellet rifle at everything that moves. Even his mother can't break through to him."

I nodded as he spoke. "I know," I said. "Whenever I go up there we never have anything to say. I try to bring up things to do, but he either doesn't listen or tells me it's all kid stuff and that it isn't like it used to be anymore. He's just not the same person."

Uncle Harley leaned on the table with the fingers of his hands laced together. "Sonny," he paused, then went on slowly, "do you think you can get him to come down here. If he gets out on a boat it might bring him around. Maybe not, I don't know. But he can't just sit around doing nothing."

The cold Coke bottle hurt in my fingers and I switched hands. I shrugged my shoulders.

Uncle Raz shuffled a deck of cards, first with his thumbs, and then under his palms. The ocean lapped and plopped against the side of the boat. Uncle Harley went on. "Raz says he'll take the two of you marlin fishing, full day. You think Keo would go for that?"

"I don't know. But if he doesn't he's too far gone for anyone. Before he left to the Army, he'd have sold me to a tourist for a quarter to get to do that."

"How about Sunday?" Uncle Raz said.

"Sounds good to me."

The dogs knew the sound of the Jeep and didn't bother to bark when I drove up with the news about marlin fishing with Uncle Raz.

I found Aunty Pearl sitting in the kitchen peeling mangoes, and slicing them into a bowl.

"Where's Keo?" I asked, flopping into a chair on the other side of the table.

"In his room."

I started to push myself up, but Aunty Pearl said, "Wait, he's sleeping."

"Sleeping? It's three o'clock."

"He sat on the porch by himself all night." Aunty Pearl handed me a slice of mango on the knife blade.

"I'll come back later," I said.

"No, no. It's time he got up. Go see him—he may not show it, but he's always glad to see you."

I nodded and pushed myself up. "I don't believe it, but I'll go see him anyway."

Keo's room was dark and smelled like stale sweat. He'd cut up an old cardboard box and taped it over the one window in the room. He lay on his back wearing only a pair of Army-green boxers, the crook of his right arm covering his eyes, and the pellet rifle resting beside him. The skin on his left knee, where the leg ended, was dark and gnarled, like the twisted root of a banyan tree.

Keo's beard was thick around the jaw and mustache, but splotchy in the cheeks. He didn't look like Keo at all.

"What do you want, pig's breath?" he said without moving his arm.

"So what are you doing sleeping in the middle of the day?"

"Day, night, what's the difference?"

Keo may have looked a mess, but his room was immaculate. His shell collection was symmetrically regimented on two long shelves, from his large spiral conch down to the miniature pearl-colored auger he'd found off White Sands Beach. The surface of his desk was bare and the chair snugly centered under it, clean and precise. The room was as sharp as a steel fish hook.

"Uncle Raz doesn't have a charter this Sunday," I said. "He wants to know if you and I would like to catch a couple of marlin. He says the fishing's pretty good."

Keo took his arm off his face, sat up, and rubbed his eyes. "How the hell am I going to catch any damn marlin with one foot?"

"What," I said. "Since when do you reel in the line with your feet?" I folded my arms over my chest and looked around the room, then added, "Balance. Put your foot in the middle of the foot rest and pump with one instead of two."

"Sheese." Keo shook his head. "You have no idea, man."

"What if I make something to fit between your leg and the foot rest, so you can use both legs?"

Keo pushed himself up and hopped over to the wall where his crutches stood, then went back for his pellet rifle. "Come," he said.

I followed him out to the porch. Keo squinted against the white sky, then crutched himself down past the end of the pig pens to Uncle Harley's ice house. "Birds don't come near the house anymore," he said.

On the far side, where he couldn't be seen from the house, Keo leaned his crutches up against the wall and settled down onto a wooden box. He took the rifle and pointed into the mango tree at the edge of Silva's pasture. "See that mynah bird on the right? The lower branch?

"What are you shooting all the birds for?"

Keo held still, then shot the bird. Five or six other birds flew out of the tree. He handed me the rifle. "You shoot one."

"I told you before, I don't shoot birds."

He put the butt of the rifle on the ground and his hand around the barrel. "You don't know nothing, man."

In our silence the birds came back and settled into the tree. "What about Sunday?" I asked.

Keo jerked the rifle off the ground and threw it to me. "You and Raz feel sorry for me, so you want to take me fishing. Okay, I'll go. But first you shoot a goddamn bird."

Keo glared at me through eyes that held nothing but anger. I turned and raised the rifle. It was well oiled and the pellet pumped easily into the chamber. The bird was just minding its own business when I hit it. "Okay, you son of a bitch. I'll be here to get you at seven o'clock Sunday morning. Be ready."

Keo smiled and reached for the rifle. Before I gave it back, I pumped pellets into it, one after the other, and blasted them into the ground around the tree, chasing the birds away for the rest of the afternoon.

"Pretty good trick, cousin," he said. I threw him his rifle and left him sitting alone behind the ice house.

Aunty Pearl came out on the porch and asked what all the shooting was about. I strode by without looking up and said, "Ask whoever-the-hell-he-is out behind the ice house."

By eight o'clock Sunday morning I was sitting on the roof of the *Flying Fish* with gallons of clean ocean air pouring into my face. Keo lay on the padded, bed-sized fish box on the stern deck having said more to the fishing rods than to me or Uncle Raz. His pellet rifle stood nearby, wedged between the bunk and the cooler.

Behind us four resin lures skipped and twirled in the wake, two mid-range 50-pound-test lines, and two 130-pounders pullied high by the outriggers on the sides of the boat. The day was clear, and the island grew bluer as we trolled away from it.

Uncle Raz sat sideways behind the wheel talking with Dad on the radio. "The island looks pretty green down here," Dad said. "I guess that's why we have rain," which meant there was a ton of birds on the southern fishing grounds due east of the long, green, rectangular pasture high on the rising face of the mountain. "Rain" meant active, very active—fish were biting. Dad and Uncle Raz changed their codes every week to keep radio eavesdroppers confused. Uncle Raz slowly headed the boat south so as not to draw too much attention if anyone was watching him.

After Keo had agreed to go fishing, Dad and I worked the last few nights of the week in Uncle Raz's garage on a contraption that Keo could stick on the end of his leg so that he could have the support of both legs in fighting a big fish, if we got lucky. We made it from a two-by-two we got at McWayne's. Dad set it in a lathe and carved out a stick-leg the way Uncle Raz carved out his lures. I cut up an old rubber glove for a skid-pad, and tied it onto the bottom with fishing line. Dad made a cushion on top with leather and foam rubber, and made a strap with a belt that Keo could tighten around his thigh to hold the thing in place. I bent my leg at the knee and gave it a try. It was wobbly, but it worked.

When I gave it to Keo on the boat, he studied it a minute, then threw it onto the bunk, and hopped out to the fish box. Uncle Raz made a face and shrugged his shoulders. I decided to go up on the roof and breathe some fresh air.

At about ten o'clock the boat rolled suddenly into a starboard turn, not too sharp, but enough to tell me something was up. It took only a few seconds to find what Uncle Raz had seen.

Noio. Sea birds. Hundreds of them. Agitated terns working about three acres of ocean, rising against the thin, blue outline of Maui, then falling and slapping the water to lure the fish up. I wondered if Keo would shoot at them. If he did, he wouldn't be shooting long with Uncle Raz around. I scrambled down from the roof.

Uncle Raz edged the frothing ocean where zillions of flying fish skimmed the water trying to escape larger fish below and birds above. I grabbed one of the big reels and started pulling in the lure.

"Never mind that," Uncle Raz called. "Keo and I will get them. Get a small rig ready for catching a bait fish."

He throttled down to neutral and ran back to the reels. "Keo, get the line on the starboard outrigger."

Uncle Raz saw me plowing through a box of lures and pointed to a drawer under the bunk. "Get a pink one, they'll strike pink before anything else. Pink with a pearl head."

He turned to Keo. "Come on, the lines."

Keo didn't move.

I fumbled around in the drawer while Uncle Raz preached to me, pulling in all four lines himself. "Live bait has to stay *live*," he shouted back to me. "It's like playing chess with your Grampa Lynn—you got to out smart 'um, you got to cheat."

I attached the small, quarter-ounce lure directly to a fifteen-pound-test nylon line, skipping the more visible wire leader. Uncle Raz made a big deal out of telling me that fish had brains, and good ones, and could spot a fake quicker than I could.

As he finished reeling in the big rigs, he carried them into the cabin and laid them on the bunk, ignoring Keo as he passed. I could almost hear his thinking: *If Keo is going to be a cock-a-roach, then he can damn well be one.*

Uncle Raz brought the *Flying Fish* up to trolling speed. I set the bait rig in a rod socket and dropped the pink lure into the wake, letting out about seventy-five yards of line. "Set the drag loose so it won't beat up the fish," Uncle Raz yelled from the cabin.

He put the boat on auto pilot and came aft to study the lure working in the wake. He pressed his knees up against the stern transom. "It's going to come fast. I can feel it."

Keo looked off toward the horizon as Uncle Raz walked past him to the wheel.

We wove in and out of the feed, dragging the single pearl-headed lure into the action, moving in the same direction as the running fish.

If this had been a couple of years ago, Keo would have been pacing the deck and throwing his own ideas out to Uncle Raz, who would have shouted back, "Yessir, cop'm sir, so solly, cop'm, so solly," and Keo would have scoffed back with something like, "Lōlō old geezer."

The boat droned back and forth through the birds, muffling their cries. Behind us, in the wake, a *noio* and skimmed the surface just above the lure, then peeled away. The sun turned hotter on the ball of my shoulder.

A bait fish hit the pink lure in less than ten minutes. When the reel started clicking, Uncle Raz brought the boat down to neutral. I reeled the fish in, easily, so I wouldn't damage it.

Uncle Raz came back with a heavy trolling rig and a threaded twelve-inch bait needle. He put the rod into one of the holders on the gunwale, then bent over the transom and lifted the silvery-blue, striped fish aboard. He held it away from the boat, keeping its flapping body from banging against the hull. A small *kawakawa,* maybe eight pounds. Uncle Raz put the fish into the crook of his arm and turned it upside down, covering its eyes with his hands to calm it.

I felt like a tourist seeing some amazing trick for the first time. When the fish was still, Uncle Raz held it belly up in the palm of his hand. It didn't twitch a muscle. It was the strangest thing I'd seen in years, as if it had been hypnotized.

Keo watched Uncle Raz with the fish, as captivated as I was, though when our eyes met he snickered and turned away.

Uncle Raz removed the lure and threaded the bait needle through the *kawakawa's* eye sockets, just above the eyeballs, right eye to left, and made a loop. Then, he ran a hand-sized live bait hook through the loop and twisted it into place. When he was finished the hook stood point up on the head of the fish like the comb on the head of a rooster.

The instant he had finished, Uncle Raz leaned out over the transom and put the fish back into the ocean. It swam off, a little sluggish at first, then seemed to regain its spirit and burst down into the depths.

The whole operation took less than fifteen seconds.

I peered over the gunwale and watched the fish dive. Flickering silver flashes of sunlight glinted off its flanks and shot back up at me from rich, blue-black water.

"Let him run a bit," Uncle Raz said. "It's got to look natural."

He left the reel on free spool and let the *kawakawa* run. The ocean was still calm, but the wind was rising. Exhaust sputtered out from under the hull whenever the stern rose out of the water. I dug into the cooler for a Coke, and tossed one over to Keo. He must have been pretty hot wearing jeans the way he did to cover up his leg. He put the bottle up against his forehead.

Uncle Raz held the line and let it run through his fingers. "I can feel every move the bugger makes through my fingertips," he said. "Stupid fish, though. Must be down about seventy-five fathoms. Not going to live long down there."

When the bait fish stopped its dive, Uncle Raz told me to bring the boat up a notch. I went forward and inched the throttle to a crawl. Looking back through the cabin, Keo's head was outlined in shadow, and beyond, Uncle Raz worked the fish in brilliant open-deck sunlight.

Still holding the line in his hand, he glanced over his shoulder at Keo. "With as much bird action as this," he said, "something could strike anytime. You ready for some fishing?"

"You catch 'um," Keo said.

"Can't. Got to gaff it, and bring it aboard."

"Then Sonny."

Uncle Raz shook his head. "You better wake up, boy. Plenty guys have problems worse than yours. Bombye you no good for nothing."

Keo turned away, toward the port sea.

The boat inched forward, rocking slowly in the swells.

I wondered what Keo was thinking. Did he still dream about islands beyond the horizon, down in the deep Pacific, of sailing to Fiji, or flying Pan Am to San Francisco? Or had he really given up on everything like he wanted us to think? Damn Keo.

The deep color of morning sea faded under a climbing sun. It would turn silver later in the day when clouds rolled out from the island. The bow rose and fell hypnotically as we trolled through the birds. I nearly fell asleep at the wheel listening to the slow drone of the engine.

"He's running," said Uncle Raz. "Sonny, come." I put the boat on auto pilot and ran aft to the stern deck. The line tightened in Uncle Raz's hand and moved off to the port side of the boat.

"He's spooked about something. . . I can feel it."

Just then something hit the bait. Uncle Raz let go of the line. "Take it in, take it in," he whispered.

The reel clicked, then stopped, and clicked again. Uncle Raz ran into the cabin to the controls, but before he got there the reel started screaming.

Line raced off, bending the rod nearly to the water, looking as if it would snap.

Uncle Raz jammed the boat to full throttle and would have sent me overboard if I hadn't grabbed the fighting chair. Black smoke poured from the stack as we lurched forward.

I was near the reel, but let the boat strike the hook deeper into the jaws of whatever had hit the bait fish. Then Uncle Raz shut the boat down. The stern rose in the rushing wake. I unhooked the safety line that was attached to the reel, but left the rod in place.

"Keo," yelled Uncle Raz. "Take it, this one's yours."

Keo almost spit when he answered. "I told you I'm out of it, leave me the hell alone about this fishing crap!" He grabbed his rifle and pumped a pellet into the chamber, then fired out to sea.

Uncle Raz glared at him, looking as if he were ready to punch him. "Take it, Sonny," Uncle Raz said, staring at Keo.

I hesitated a moment, then pulled the rod from the socket and jerked back on it twice, striking the fish one last time. Line burned off the reel as I bent against the pull, trying to release the drag and ease the pressure. Uncle Raz wrapped a kidney harness around my lower back and hooked it to the eyes on the reel. I placed the butt of the rod into the silvery socket in the fighting chair and put my feet on the foot brace. Line whipped back and forth off the spool, tearing out into the ocean as if it were tied to the back of a Jeep racing down hill at fifty or sixty miles an hour.

"Shee," Uncle Raz said, now ignoring Keo. "This is one bugger of a fish! Let 'um run! When he slows, tighten up on the drag and hold him."

I bent forward in the chair with both hands on the reel and the pressure of the rod tugging at my back through the harness. I'd get to the drag when the dang thing stopped running.

The line emptied off the reel so fast I thought there'd be nothing left but a clean spool in a matter of minutes. The fish managed to rip off five or six hundred yards before I could slowly tighten the drag and choke off the run. Usually a marlin would jump and show itself. But this one sounded. The point where the line hit the water off the back of the boat raced toward me. The fish was taking it straight down. Maybe it wasn't a marlin at all.

Uncle Raz ran back to the wheel and pushed the throttle forward, pulling the boat away from the approaching line in an attempt to vector the fish out of its dive. But it was too late. It had already gone deeper than either of us cared to think about. The pressure alone at that depth would make the line feel as heavy as a block of concrete the size of Kona Inn's saltwater swimming pool.

Uncle Raz put the boat in neutral and waited at the controls.

When the fish ran left, Uncle Raz pulled right so the line stayed directly off the stern. Some fishermen preferred to keep it off the corner of the transom, but Uncle Raz liked it centered.

"Gotta be a tuna, boy," he called from the wheel. "You're gonna pay for this one."

With the stern of the boat facing the island, I began to work the fish, pulling back, using the harness to carry the weight, then bending forward and reeling in whatever amount of line I could steal.

The birds moved off a hundred yards or so, now scattered. The pressure on the line was so relentless that I had to hold my breath when I pulled back, eyes shut and teeth jammed together, my face swelling up like a balloon fish.

For the moment I'd forgotten about Keo, thinking only of the fish on the end of the line. But he startled me when I opened my eyes after one long, neck-popping pull. He was at the transom dipping a bucket into the ocean. One crutch lay against the gunwale. He scooped some sea water into the bucket and set it on the deck near the fighting chair.

With the crutch, he pulled himself up and hobbled into the cabin. "You think you can handle this thing, little man?" he said as he passed.

"With room to spare, cock-a-roach."

He was gone for a minute, then returned with a fat, natural sponge that he soaked in the bucket. With a hand on the fighting chair, Keo dripped water over the reel to cool it down, then squeezed a sponge-full over my head. It chilled at first, but ran luxuriously down my neck and soaked into my T-shirt. "Use your legs, cousin. It's all in the legs."

Johnny Honl's boat, the *Kakina,* appeared off the starboard stern. A man in a red shirt was watching us through a pair of binoculars. The boat kept its distance and trolled toward the birds, now feeding farther west.

Keo limped with his crutch to the transom and studied the water. The fish wasn't running, but was pulling away from me with more muscle than I could return. The rod rainbowed out over the stern as I waited for the fish to give.

"If he dies on you, you're never going to get him up," Keo said.

"I wish he *was* dead, then I could make some progress."

Keo grunted, like Uncle Raz would grunt at a stupid remark. "You ain't got that kind of muscle, cousin. Maybe you better cut the line and save us all a lot of time."

I pulled back on the rod until the tendons in my neck ached. "I'm not letting this thing go until it's sleeping on the deck."

A mongoose had more patience than Keo Kalani Mendoza. He was antsy, like when he'd decided to join the Army. "They're going to draft me anyway," he had said. "Might as well get it over with."

We'd driven over to Hilo to check out the possibilities. He wanted to talk to the Navy and the Coast Guard, as well as the Army, but brushed the Marines aside with a wave of his hand. "Forget those guys, too much work."

We spent a couple of hours going back and forth between the recruiting offices, asking every question we could think of. The recruiters looked pretty snappy in their flawless uniforms and black spit-shined shoes. Almost got me signing up right along with Keo, except that I had another year of high school to get through.

He ended up going with the Army because it was the shortest tour of duty. I pushed for the Coast Guard, but he wanted in and out as fast as possible. Once his mind was made up that was pretty much it, even after the recruiter told him that with the war going on in Vietnam, the Army wasn't going to be a piece of cake. It wasn't a yacht club like the Navy. The Army needed men, not pretty boys in white shorts.

Keo had guts, I have to admit, even though I sometimes wondered how many candles burned in his brain at any one time.

An hour passed. The sun drenched me in sweat and burned the skin on my arms. Every now and then Keo dragged himself off the fish box and hopped over to drip a sponge of water down my neck, then another on the reel. When I thanked him and told him the fish was as strong as a cow, he said, "Running out of gas, little man?"

"Never," I said.

"Two bucks says the thing beats you."

"Make it five and you're on."

Keo patted me on the back, like he would a child. "It's a deal, dreamer. Just don't pop a gut trying to do something bigger than you are."

Once, the fish made a run, and Uncle Raz backed the boat down after it. I reeled in the slack, a few inches. Then the fish stopped and held.

I'd been struggling with it since noon when the sun was high and the water reflected the cloudless, blue sky. By four-thirty everything had turned grey, and the surface chop had grown restless. And so had Uncle Raz.

"Cut the line already," he finally called from the cabin. I couldn't see him, but I imagined him sitting at the table with a beer, playing solitaire and shaking his head every time a card stumped him.

"No," I said. "I can handle it."

Keo made a snickering sound from the fish box.

Uncle Raz came out on the deck and stood beside me. "Probably dead. Could be sharks have gotten at it, too."

My forearms hurt the most, especially my right from turning the handle on the reel. I almost couldn't turn it anymore. And what if Uncle Raz was right about the sharks charging in and whacking out sections of the fish, ripping the flesh, and slinking off with meat hanging out of their mouths? As much as I hated to admit it, even to myself, I knew I didn't have enough left in me to muscle up a dead fish a hundred fathoms straight down.

Five o'clock came and went. Then six. My back, legs, shoulders and arms had sunk into the numbness you feel when you go beyond pain, and I was beginning to wonder how sensible I was being about the whole thing.

Uncle Raz came out and opened up his pocket knife. "Come on, Sonny. We don't have the time and you don't have the juice to bring that thing all the way up from China."

He reached for the line.

"Don't cut it! I can do it!"

"This is stupid, give up already. That damn thing's beat you."

"Look at the reel, I'm gaining line. Get away with that knife!"

"Sorry, Sonny," Uncle Raz said, bringing the knife up.

Keo's crutch suddenly poked out between the knife and the line. "Time to let a real man do the work."

Still holding the knife near the tip of the rod, Uncle Raz made a puzzled face and cocked his head. "Sonny, did you hear something? I thought there were only two fishermen aboard this boat." He turned toward Keo, and mocked surprise when he faced him.

Keo leaned on one crutch. "Back off, gramps." Then he turned to me. "Let me show you how it's done, son."

"Shit," I said. "I've almost got it."

Keo snickered. "You got nothing left, is what you got."

I closed my eyes and took a deep breath, then leaned forward and unhitched the harness from the reel. "I guess it won't hurt to let you clean up."

Keo threw his crutches on the fish box and hopped into the fighting chair. Uncle Raz and I hooked the harness around him. For all our joking, reeling in a dead fish, if it was dead, was nothing but hard work, and could sometimes even be impossible. The pressure was just too great.

Keo started to pull, but had a difficult time balancing his weight on one foot. He cussed out ten or fifteen new words he'd picked up in the Army, then gave in. "Sonny, get that stupid stick you made and strap the damn thing on."

Uncle Raz made a face at me that said, "well, well." I went into the cabin and got the stick-leg off the bunk. The strapping part was kind of awkward, but it held the stick-leg in place well enough. Keo lifted it and tapped the rubber end on the foot brace. "Too long," he said.

By seven o'clock the sky had lost its glow, and all of us were almost certain we were dealing with a dead fish. Keo bit into the job like a dog on a pig hunt, pulling in a good hundred yards of line before admitting that the only chance we had of landing the thing was to vector it up by moving the boat forward, then reeling in line as we backed down again.

It took us another hour, but it worked. When the spool was finally full, Uncle Raz left the boat in neutral and came back with a flashlight to peer into the dark water for the first glimpse of whatever-the-damn-thing was. But even he was excited about finally getting to see it.

He gave Keo a pat on the back. "Keep her steady, Long John Silver. You've almost got it."

The wire leader came inching out of the water. Keo reeled it all the way to the eye on the tip of the rod. Uncle Raz gave me the flashlight and reached out over the transom. Hand over hand, he pulled the mysterious fish the last few feet to the boat.

I got the gaff and stood next to him. Keo unhitched the harness and let it fall to the deck, but stayed in the fighting chair with the rod still in the socket. He took off the stick-leg and threw it on the deck by the fish box.

The fish was barely visible in the black water, even with the flash-light. Uncle Raz took the gaff and hooked it under the body. There was no explosion of flapping and splashing as there would have been with a fish with any life left in it. He pulled it over the transom and let it thud to the deck.

"Shee," said Uncle Raz, bending over it.

It seemed odd not to have it flopping around splattering blood every-where. It just lay there like a block of ice.

"Sonabadingding," he said. "This one was a big bugger."

I went into the cabin and turned on the light. A warm yellow glow illuminated the stern deck, and defined the huge, bullet-shaped head of the fish. *Ahi,* a half-eaten monster yellowfin tuna. The dark, blue-black ridge of its back, and striking golden fin above shiny silver sides, spread back from a huge round eye and pained mouth, thickening out into a fat body that cut violently off just to the rear of the dorsal fin, the rest ripped away by deep-sea sharks.

Uncle Raz squatted down for a closer look. "Must have been pretty near to two-fifty." He shook his head. "Poor bugger."

He removed the hook and lifted the fish. "Still around a hundred-thirty, with only half. Damn lōlō sharks." He looked up at Keo and laughed. Despite all his boasting, Keo wore the face of a man dead beat into the ground. "What you want to do with this baby," Uncle Raz asked.

Keo raised his chin to the sea. "Give 'um back to the sharks and call it your taxes for the year."

"Hah! I'll take it."

Bent and bow-legged under its awkwardness, Uncle Raz lifted the tuna and dropped it over the transom. I splashed a bucket of water over the deck where the fish had been. Keo put a hand on my shoulder and hopped back to the fish box.

Uncle Raz dug us both a Coke out of the cooler and threw over a bag of Saloon Pilot crackers. "Let's get out of here," he said.

I stowed the fishing rods in the rack above the bunk and sat on the floor beside the table to rewind the leaders on the lures. Uncle Raz turned out the cabin light so he could see the lights on shore.

The muscles in my forearms were as tight as mooring rope. I wanted to ask Keo how his knee felt, where it had pressed up against the padding on the stick-leg. But I didn't. He'd probably already gotten more involved than he'd planned.

He sat on the edge of the fish box, a lone silhouette rising and falling against a faint horizon. It occurred to me that Keo had only shot his pellet rifle once all day. He reached down to the deck for the stick-leg. I turned to Uncle Raz, but he was dozing at the wheel. When I looked back Keo was trying to make the damn thing stay on the stump of his leg, silently strapping it on, and pushing himself up to test it. I watched him for a while, then went out and sat on the gunwale.

Keo lifted his leg and pointed the stick-leg at me. "Maybe you could make me a fake foot so I could put a fin on it and be a frogman in the Coast Guard."

I shook my head. "Maybe I could, cousin."

He lay down on the fish box and said, "You pantie."

BY GRAHAM SALISBURY

THE YEAR OF THE BLACK WIDOWS

(1959)

ack Christensen, the new boy from California, had convinced Keo, and the rest of the sixth grade boys, that they'd be in a barge load of trouble when they went to the big school up in the highland jungles, and had to deal with the seventh and eighth graders. Keo, being a year ahead of me, was the first to have to face the unknown—seventh grade, and the shadowy school ten miles up the mountain, a place that suddenly loomed before us like a long, grey squall moving in from the sea.

Dark as it all seemed, though, it existed only in our minds. None of us knew for sure what lay ahead. There were rumors and distorted facts passed down from older brothers and sisters, but no one really knew. Except Jack. He'd never been to the school, and hadn't known anyone who'd gone there, but still, he knew, because he'd seen it all in Los Angeles. They smoke and drink, and fight, he said. They join gangs and carry knives.

No one wanted to believe him, but there wasn't one of us who could ignore him. We'd form our own gang, he told us, and call it the Black Widows. Any sixth grader who wanted protection could have it. All he had to do was swear to help any other Black Widow who got into trouble—and, Jack added, to do whatever he said.

One morning a couple of months before summer, I walked into the school yard and found Mrs. Carvalho, the principal, lowering a dead mongoose down the flagpole. Almost all eighty-seven kids in the school were standing around watching her. The mongoose was tied to the halyards by its tail.

Keo, Jack and four other boys sat watching the whole thing on the steps leading up to the veranda that fronted our L-shaped, four-room schoolhouse. Bobby Otani, a fifth grader, sat next to Keo, trying to keep from laughing. But the others, all sixth grade Black Widows, were stone-faced. I went over to join them.

"What's going on?" I asked. Keo ignored me. Bobby Otani snickered and Keo elbowed him. I sat on the lower step, below Keo. Mrs. Carvalho untied the mongoose and marched toward us holding it by its tail, pinched in her handkerchief. The mass of kids stepped aside as she moved through them. "Which one of you did this?" she asked.

Immediately, the boys behind me said, one after the other, "Not me, Mrs. Carvalho; we didn't do it; not us."

Mrs. Carvalho searched our faces with suspicious eyes. "I want *all* of you in my office after school." She walked up the stairs past us, still holding the mongoose, the entire school following her. Some of the fifth and sixth grade girls smirked as they went by.

When Mrs. Carvalho was out of sight, Bobby Otani burst out laughing. Keo stood, and moved away from him with a disgusted look on his face. Bobby, like me, wanted to be in the Black Widows, but Jack wouldn't let any fifth graders join unless they proved to him that they wanted it bad enough. Jack had told us a week ago that he would be thinking of a test, make us do something we didn't want to do, something that proved our loyalty.

Now, Jack came down the stairs and grabbed Bobby by the shoulder of his shirt. "If you want to die before the sun goes down, just keep it up."

Bobby Otani sobered, and said, "Okay, okay." Jack's eyes sliced through him, then threatened the rest of us, almost wild with anger. Bobby pushed at Jack's hand, still gripping the shirt, but Jack stopped him with another glare. No one said a word. Then Jack went up and crossed the veranda to the classroom, with the rest of us following in silence.

Keo put his hand out and stopped me. "Jack says the mongoose was a warning. Someone from the high school put it there to remind us who's boss." Then Keo sniggered. "Bobby thinks Jack put it there himself."

"Did he?"

"Who knows?"

Mrs. Lee, the fifth and sixth grade teacher, shook her head as we walked in, then started class as if nothing had happened.

Jack Christensen wasn't like the rest of us. He knew more, lots more. He came from the mainland, a place the rest of us could barely even imagine. The one thing about him, though, was that you could never outdo him. No matter what you told him, he'd seen or done it one better. He'd moved to the islands from California just before the school year started. Dad said his mother and stepfather were like a lot of people—they come to the islands thinking life will be easy, then find out that it's just as full of problems as anywhere else.

We gave Jack the nickname of Jack da Lōlō, meaning Jack the Crazy, because he was crazy—not *Crazy* crazy, but peculiar crazy, a real odd duck, as Uncle Raz liked to call him. But Uncle Harley thought Jack was lonely. Keo and I argued against that opinion until we ran out of words, but Uncle Harley just told us we were too young and too caught up in the boy to see it.

Keo and I liked Jack because he was always surprising us, and we hung around with him just to see what he'd do or say next. He had the power to hold us speechless with the things he told us, like all the stuff about the seventh and eighth graders. And he had the advantage of being taller than anyone else in school, at least two inches taller than me, and one taller than Keo He never went barefoot to school, like the rest of us, but always wore black tennis shoes and jeans, and a T-shirt with the sleeves rolled up. His hair was usually greased back, with a clump hanging down over his forehead. He was Keo's age, but *seemed* a couple of years older because of his size, and because he knew so much more about the world than we did.

"Just wait till next year," he told Keo. "You'd better learn to protect yourself because you're going to get into a lot of fights in the seventh grade." As a fifth grader, I hadn't thought much about it, but Keo had, and all that Jack was telling him pulled him under, like a whirlpool. You could see it on his face, and in his eyes, and in the two vertical scowl lines between his eyebrows.

When school let out, Mrs. Carvalho made all seven of us sit along one wall of her office. Everyone had gone home except the teachers. She glared across her desk at us for several minutes before saying anything, looking as if she were trying to determine which one of us had the nerve to run the mongoose up the flagpole.

"I know one of you boys put that mongoose up there," she finally said. "And I know that you *all* know who it was, because you have that guilty look on your faces."

We sat there staring at the floor, silent as the picture of her two grown sons leaning over the back of a lazy cow, framed on the wall behind her.

"Bobby Otani," she said. "What do you know about this?" Mrs. Carvalho was pretty smart, going straight to the one most likely to tell her what she wanted to know. But Bobby just shrugged his shoulders.

She asked each of us the same question and got nothing but shrugs, and silence, or a whispered, *I don't know.* Then she made us sit for about twenty minutes while she worked at her desk, as if we weren't there at all.

Just as I was about to doze off, Mrs. Carvalho stood up. "Okay, boys," she said. "You can go, but I want you to remember that I'll be keeping my eyes on you." As we started to leave, she tipped her head toward Jack and added, "You boys should be setting a better example for our new student."

A few weeks later, just after midnight on a Saturday night, Jack stole his stepfather's car and drove up the hill for Keo, then Bobby Otani, then back down for me. When Jack had learned that none of us ever *snuck out* at night, he couldn't believe it. In California, *everyone* sneaks out, he said, then told us to be on the road in front of our houses at midnight.

With the dogs all standing around watching me, I climbed out of my bedroom window, just as Jack had told me to do. Dad was asleep in the living room, where he always slept. I could hear his breathing through the wall. I wore shorts and a sweatshirt, though the night air at sea level was still warm. The yard was silver-grey in the weak glow from the yard light.

Jack's stepfather's car was a brand new green Oldsmobile four-door that reflected moonlight off its shiny hood as it approached, lights flashing off and on as a signal. My house was set back into the trees, down closer to the ocean, and when Jack pulled up and turned off the headlights, the road went black.

Keo sat in front with Uncle Harley's twenty-two. Bobby was in the back. He stuck his head out the open window. "Come on, get in," he said, almost whispering. Keo and Jack kept quiet. I slid in next to Bobby, and Jack turned the car around in our driveway. I wondered what Dad would say if he found out what I was doing.

"Where we going?" I asked.

"Shoot rats," Jack said. "At the dump."

"You don't want to be up at the dump at night without a gun," Bobby said. "I heard there's a crazy man living there, but no one has ever seen him. He hides in the day and only roams the dump at night, looking for food. Isn't that right, Keo?"

"That's what I heard," Keo said. If Keo had heard it, I would have heard it, too, and I hadn't. Still, it could be true. Who knew what went on up there? The dump was a strange enough place in full daylight. Something was always moving around—birds, rats, wild cats, starved dogs, and mongoose. Why not a crazy man?

"Where'd you learn to drive?" I asked Jack.

"It's easy. The car's automatic, they're always automatic. That's what my stepfather likes. Anyone can drive this thing."

"He knows you drive it?"

"Sure."

"Does he know you have it now?"

"Of course not."

"It's more fun to steal it," Keo said, sounding as if he'd known Jack for years.

"It's not stealing," Jack said. "I just borrowed it for a while."

Keo sat like an Army guard, holding the twenty-two straight up, butt on the floor, like a flagpole. He glanced out the window on his side of the car as if driving around in the middle of the night were something he did all the time.

I leaned forward with my arms on the back of Keo's seat, peering into the beams of light exposing the old road up to the dump. We were like a small band of outlaws heading for a crime, the four of us riding silently. Getting caught wasn't even a passing concern. I felt, in those moments, invincible.

Jack drove slowly into the dump, a huge, sloping, rectangular area carved out of the jungle of trees on the side of the mountain, far enough away from the village so you couldn't smell it. Carefully, he snaked his father's spotless car around broken glass and watery mud holes. The smell was different in the cool night air, not sickly like it was in the heat of the day, but sharp and biting.

Just above the dump itself was a flat area wide enough to turn a truck around. The dump flowed downhill in heaps and rolls. Jack parked the car on the edge of the turnaround, facing the downward slope, and turned off the headlights, then the engine. We waited a moment, listening to night noises coming up from the moonlight-grey field of garbage below.

"You got the flashlight," Jack asked.

Keo flicked it on and sent a beam down to an old refrigerator lying on its side. Then he turned it off, and with a length of fishing line, strapped it to the barrel of the twenty-two.

"What are you doing that for?" Bobby asked, as excited about being at the dump as a dog in a Jeep.

"So we can see what we're shooting at, what do you think?"

We got out of the car and stood on the edge, looking down into the ghostly mounds, black trees all around, a bright ring of illuminated mist around the moon. Jack took the rifle from Keo and turned on the flashlight. The beam followed the path of his aim, first lighting up a bottle, then a tire. "Pow!" he said, then shut the light off. "Listen."

Things were alive and moving around below us, noises from the far corners, tin cans tipping over somewhere in the middle. Jack turned the light back on and aimed around the dump until the beam reflected the glassy eyes of a mongoose, frozen between steps, low to the ground and rat-like. Jack shot. The bullet winged it, and it squealed, and flipped around a couple of times, then disappeared into the garbage.

We had to stay up on the dirt part because we were barefoot. Jack wore his black tennis shoes, but didn't want to go down into the dump alone. He put his hand on my shoulder. "Find a cat. This place is loaded with them." The beam flopped around in the trees as he handed me the rifle. Keo said he thought he'd seen one over to the left when Jack was running the light around.

"How about a bottle," I said.

"Don't be a sissy," Jack said. "Go on, shine the light around."

I moved the beam slowly over the mounds just below us, maybe the length of eight cars away, and found a mongoose.

"Go ahead," Jack said. "Take a practice shot."

It was an easy target, like the coffee cans Keo and I set up in the pastures around his house. The mongoose didn't squeal when I hit it, just fell into a small hump and didn't move.

"Good shot!" Keo said.

Jack didn't say anything. I kept the beam on the dead mongoose, its brown body looking like a pile of mud. I'd never killed an animal before. I felt sick to my stomach. In Kona everyone shot mongooses. They were pests, they got into your garbage, into your garage, into your cooled trash fires, and made a racket under your house. Even Dad shot them. Still, I felt sick, like there was a hole in me and all the excitement of the night was quickly draining away.

"Now find a cat," Jack said. "You want to be in the Black Widows, don't you?"

"Sure," I said.

"Then your test is to shoot a cat."

"But. . . ."

"A cat. Shoot one or forget about the Widows."

We spent an hour or so looking around for cats, but only found more mongooses. Even the crazy man wasn't there, but that didn't stop Jack from trying to scare us with sudden moves, whispering things like, "What was *that*?"

Jack drove fast going back down to sea level, jabbering the whole way with Keo. I sat in the back seat hanging onto a grip on the door. Jack bet Keo he could drive through the village without getting caught, and slowed when we dropped down toward the pier from Palani Road.

"I've got an idea," Jack said, half turning toward the back seat. "You two want to be Black Widows, right? Well, Sonny can go back up to the dump and shoot the cat. That should prove he wants to be in bad enough. And you, Bobby, can put it in a bag, and hide it in Mrs. Carvalho's office."

"What?" Bobby said. "I could get kicked out of school for that."

"Take it or leave it," Jack said. Keo kept quiet, as if it didn't matter to him one way or the other whether Bobby or I became Black Widows.

I thought the whole thing was stupid. "Why do we have to prove ourselves, and not you?" I asked.

"Because I'm the leader."

I sat back in the seat trying to figure out how everything had gotten so confusing since Jack had come to the island. With just me and Keo, everything had been simple. We didn't shoot mongooses, or sneak around at night in *borrowed* cars, and we never worried about the school in the highlands. But now Keo was a Black Widow, and almost a stranger.

We made it through town without getting caught, because there was no one around to catch us. The street was empty and pale under the few lights along the road. Bobby talked the whole way down to my house about what Mrs. Carvalho would do when she found the cat in her office.

Just before we got to my driveway, Jack pulled over to the side of the road and turned off the headlights. I got out and peered back into the car. Jack leaned forward, a shadowy silhouette staring past Keo at me. "Get the cat," he said.

Keo looked away when I caught his eye, and said, "See you."

Thick trees on either side of our rocky driveway reached out toward me, their night shadows swallowing up the moonlight like bug-eyed bottom fish in a great oceanic abyss. Our small, wooden house glowed in the clearing under the yard light, and beyond, the trail of the moon lay like a ribbon of silk on a quiet sea.

The dogs heard me and came trotting out. I crept into the house, past Dad, sleeping in the living room, and gently closed the door to my room. Except for the quiet hiss of the surf, the night was as still as the street had been after Jack, Bobby, and Keo had driven away, leaving only the faint echo of Jack's command—get the cat.

A week later, Grampa Joe drove down and picked up Keo, and then me, and took us back to his place to help out with his coffee orchard, a small, five-acre farm with about 2,500 trees. He paid us fifty cents an hour when he needed help.

In the morning, we spread rat poison around the edges of the orchard, then sprayed diesel oil in among the trees where weeds had started poking through. Later, Grampa Joe wanted us to help him gather up and haul off some old boards and tires that had cluttered his yard for as long as I could remember. Tutu Max must have gotten after him.

At noon, the three of us sat out in the yard, in a small grassy area, one of several flat terraces that stumbled down from the road above.

Grampa Joe's whole place was on a hill, as was all of Kona, except down along the coast where I lived. The island itself was just the top of a deep undersea mountain rising out of the Pacific Ocean.

All morning I'd been thinking about how Keo had become so quiet and moody. Jack seemed to consume him, to consume all of us with his stories about high school, and with the fear and doubt that settled in behind them. *Forget that junk that Jack says,* I finally told Keo, but he just said I didn't know my brains from a dead jellyfish.

"So what are you boys up to at school?" Grampa Joe asked.

Keo shrugged, eating one of the tuna sandwiches Tutu Max had made for us. Grampa Joe turned to me, and I shrugged too. He kept looking at me, waiting. "Keo's a Black Widow," I finally said. "It's a gang."

Keo held the sandwich in one hand while he ate, staring off into the trees.

Grampa Joe took a drink out of an old, dented silver thermos, then peeked over at Keo. "What do Black Widows do?" he asked.

Keo shrugged again. "Nothing . . . just hang around."

Grampa Joe picked at the grass, then shook his head and laughed, once, like a *humph.* "Black Widows," he said to himself.

"I'm going to be one, too," I said.

"What do you mean, *going* to be?"

"I have to shoot a cat first, to prove I'm worthy."

"Sheese, are you kidding? Really? Shoot a cat? Whose stupid idea was that?" He glanced at Keo, but Keo just kept on eating his sandwich.

"A boy named Jack," I said. "He's the leader. It was his idea to make the Black Widows."

Grampa Joe watched me, waiting for more. He seemed interested. "Shoot a cat?" he asked again.

Keo glared over at me.

I looked down at the grass, remembering killing the mongoose, and thinking I'd better not say too much more and give our night trip to the dump away. "A cat," I said, almost in a whisper.

"You want cats? We'll see lots of them when we take this junk to the dump," Grampa Joe said. "No loss if you shoot one, but what a stupid idea. What does that prove? Nothing. Only that you can shoot." He turned to Keo. "Did you have to shoot one, too?"

"No."

"He's a sixth grader," I said. "So is Jack."

Grampa Joe nodded, then shook his head and continued eating his lunch in silence, curling his blackened, diesel-oil-covered fingers around the stark white bread of his sandwich, as if they were as clean as the inside of a mango.

On the way to the dump, Grampa Joe stopped by Keo's house so we could get the twenty-two. Boards stuck out of the back of the old car, the trunk wide open. Grampa Joe didn't even bother to tie it down. We'd have to make two trips; there was so much stuff.

The dump was quiet when we got there, no other people around. But the dogs were out, bone-sided, emaciated creatures poking around down near the lower end. Mongooses were everywhere, scurrying from cover to cover, long and sleek, with ratty tails the length of their bodies. After we emptied out Grampa Joe's trunk, Keo took some shots at them, hitting nothing. The noise scared the dogs off, but they slunk back when the shooting stopped.

"Sonny," Grampa Joe said, pointing off to the right at a spot half way down, away from the dogs and mongooses. "A cat. Hard to see right now. Wait a minute," he said. "She'll move."

I squinted into the sun, then shielded my eyes with my hand. The cat moved, a spotted one, mostly orange and black, looking like it was stalking something. It picked its paws up slowly, one at a time, and held them in the air before each step.

Keo handed me the twenty-two. I climbed down off the edge and picked my way through the debris, this time with a pair of thongs on my feet. Grampa Joe and Keo squatted low to the ground behind me, watching.

Like the mongoose, the cat was an easy target. I followed it in the notch, the bead on its shoulder. The wooden stock against my cheek was sun-warm and the casing smelled of clean oil, even through the stench of the dump. I could have shot and joined the Black Widows immediately. But I moved the barrel a fraction of an inch to the left and fired, missing by a foot. The cat jumped, then disappeared into the field of decaying camouflage.

"You pantie," Keo said, standing up.

Grampa Joe stayed down on his heels, laughing silently and shaking his head, as if he'd known all along that I'd never shoot the cat.

I shrugged, and said, "Missed."

"No kidding," Keo said, crossing his arms and turning his head to the side to spit.

Grampa Joe picked up a stick and creaked himself up, then stepped down off the edge. He poked around in the garbage and came up with a rancid-smelling ribbon of something that looked like squid. "Use this," he said, holding it out to me on the end of the stick. "Set a trap. Bombye she come back—and Keo and I come back, too. Next load. You wait here, she come back."

After they bounced out to the main road in Grampa's old car, I picked my way down to where the cat had been. The sky had turned white, high clouds having set in. Humidity seemed to rise from the stillness of the dump itself, leaving a sticky film over my arms that made me want to jump into the ocean the minute I got home.

I found the cat in a small cave formed in the folds of a pile of cardboard boxes. Its eyes flashed out at me, like coins wrapped in cellophane. It wasn't alone. Four multicolored kittens shrunk back next to it as I peeked in. The mother hissed at me, and tolerated my being there as long as I didn't move around. I squatted down and watched them, holding as still as the old refrigerator.

After a while, the kittens began to get restless, creeping slowly out of the shadows into the sun. Though wary of me, they got braver, jumping over each other and spreading out around the mouth of the cave. The mother stayed where she was, her front feet tucked up under her.

I laid the squid an arm's length away, moving as slowly as I could. Three of the kittens came over to sniff at it, one by one. The fourth wouldn't get anywhere near it. But one of the three brave ones inched its way around the squid, coming within reach, as if it had forgotten I was there, a dirty white one, with a splatter of black and orange spots on it.

The kitten sniffed at the squid, then licked it enough to see that it wasn't fit to eat, and turned its head away. Very slowly, I reached out and pinched it at the back of its neck. The other kittens ran back into the cave.

Curled up and hanging from my fingers, it was as light as a plumeria lei. It struggled a little, but mostly just stayed curled up, its eyes stretched back, probably scared spitless.

I pulled my T-shirt over my head with my free hand and slipped it down my arm, then pulled the cat's head through the sleeve. I wrapped the rest of the shirt around its body, a wad of T-shirt with a scrubby cat's head poking out. It hissed when I let go of its neck.

When Keo and Grampa Joe returned, I was sitting on a wooden chair that I'd found, one with a broken back. The kitten had gotten used to me by then, and had stopped hissing. I stroked its head constantly, but kept it wrapped in my T-shirt. Keo's twenty-two lay on the ground next to the chair.

Grampa Joe laughed when he saw the kitten. "The cat shrunk," he said.

"There are three more of these down where the big cat was," I said.

Grampa Joe shook his head and started taking the junk out of his trunk. Keo came over and bent down to scratch the kitten's ears and got a hiss for it. "It's got to get to know you first," I said.

"What are you going to do with it?" he asked.

"I don't know. Keep it."

"What for?"

I shrugged.

"What about Jack?"

"He said to get a cat."

"He said to shoot a cat," Keo said.

"I know, but maybe he'll change his mind."

Keo stood up. "Jack? He won't. Only your shooting the cat will prove anything to him. You have to do it just like he says."

"Do you do everything he says?"

Keo shrugged and picked up his rifle. "He hasn't told me to do anything yet."

"But if he did, would you? If he told you to shoot a cat, would you?"

"Easy."

"Okay, then. How about a dog? Would you shoot one of those?" I said, pointing to the dogs nosing around in the bottom of the dump. Keo loved dogs. If he said yes, he'd be lying.

"Stupid question, I'm already a Black Widow," he said. "I don't have to do anything." Keo took his rifle to the car.

By the time Grampa Joe dropped me off at my house the kitten was getting pretty antsy about getting out of the T-shirt. Grampa Joe told me I'd better soak the shirt in alcohol after carrying a mangy, flea-infested dump cat around in it. His arm hung down the side of the car door, the engine idling. "Listen," he said. "I've known lots of guys like this Jack, who like to talk big and make you scared. Sometimes they were mean pachooks, that's for sure. But most of the time they were all smoke and no fire. Don't let him make you do something you don't want to do." Then he scratched the kitten's head and backed out to the main road.

When Dad came home from fishing, he found me sitting on the stairs leading up to the porch, introducing the kitten to his four dogs. I'd tied a length of nylon line around its neck, like a leash, so it wouldn't run off and get killed by a mongoose. The dogs were curious, inching up to sniff at it, but holding off when the kitten hissed at them.

Dad asked where I'd gotten it, and I told him the whole story, including the part about Jack and the Black Widows. His eyes narrowed when I told him Jack wanted me to shoot a cat to prove I was worthy to join the gang.

"Is Keo going along with all this?" he asked.

I nodded. "He's already a Black Widow."

Dad stood in the yard looking up at me with his hands on his hips, wearing only shorts, with shiny dried fish slime by the pockets from wiping his hands on them. "So, you were going to shoot a cat because you wanted to be a member of Jack's gang?"

I nodded.

"Did Keo shoot one?"

"He didn't have to. He's a sixth grader."

"What about Jack?"

I shook my head, then told him that Jack had shot a mongoose.

"Everyone shoots mongoose," he said. "But cats?" He paused a moment, then asked me why I wanted to be a member of Jack's gang.

"For protection. Jack says we're going to get into a lot of fights with the eighth and ninth graders. He says they carry knives."

"You believe that?"

I shrugged, and said I guessed so.

Dad put his hand on the back of his neck and looked off into the trees. "Do you think your Uncle Harley and I would let you and Keo go to a school where the kids carried knives?"

I thought about that a moment, then shrugged and said, "I don't know." I hadn't considered it before. It never entered my mind that Dad or Uncle Harley ever even thought about what we did at school, except ask us how our grades were once in a while.

Dad shook his head and stared down at the ground. One of his dogs licked his hand, and Dad stroked the back of its neck. All four of them were hanging around waiting to be fed. Just beyond the end of the yard, waves thumped against the rocky shore, under the red clouds of sunset, blazing through the trees.

Dad started up the stairs, and put his hand on my shoulder as he passed. "If Sonny Mendoza can shoot this cat, or any cat, then I don't know a thing about my own son." He nudged my head with his hand, then added, "Take that scrubby rat and soak it in the ocean until all the fleas float off, then you can bring it inside the house."

On Monday, I left home later than usual, and walked slowly so I'd arrive at school just as it was starting and wouldn't have to talk to Jack until recess.

I'd made a small dome-shaped pen out of chicken wire and staked it into the yard, a place for the cat to stay while it was getting used to its new home. I figured out that it was a female, and decided to call her *Pōpoki*, cat. When I left, the dogs were lying on the grass nearby, watching her with droopy tongues, panting.

At recess, Keo came up to me before going outside and asked how the cat was, then told me Jack was expecting to see it. Keo said he hadn't told Jack it was alive.

I stayed in the classroom after Keo went out to join the Black Widows under *their* tree, a billowing monkeypod that Jack had commandeered as their meeting place. Only Black Widows and invited guests could sit under it.

Mrs. Lee asked me if I was feeling all right, and I told her that I was. She sat on a desk and studied me. "After as many years as I've taught fifth grade boys, Mr. Mendoza, you can't tell me that nothing is bothering you. A boy *never* stays inside at recess unless he's sick, it's raining, or he has a problem."

I told her a lie and a truth. Everything was okay at school, but I was worried about my new cat. I told her I didn't want a mongoose to get it, then went outside before she could ask too many questions.

Keo, Bobby Otani, Jack, and four sixth grade Black Widows sat under the *Tree of Webs*, as Jack had started calling their meeting place, building more into his Black Widow idea everyday. Three sixth grade girls sat with them.

"Hey," Jack called when I came out into the yard. "Where is it?" The girls and the Black Widows turned and looked over at me. Seeing Keo among the band of taunting eyes made me feel lost, as if I were in a strange school, and he was just boy I'd never seen before, not my cousin.

"I have it," I said.

"Good!" Jack said. "So show us?"

"It's at home."

Bobby Otani pinched his nose. "Must be getting ripe," he said.

Jack stood and puffed up his chest, then strolled over to me, the group following him as if he were the greatest entertainment to hit the islands in years, which for most of us, he was. "Black Widows!" he called, waving to the girls as well. "Come in close."

A low round of sniggering ran through them as they surrounded me. Keo held back a step, and mostly kept his eyes on the ground.

Jack went on. "Sonny wants to be a Black Widow, and we want him to be one, too. So I gave him a test. Anyone who's not a sixth grader has to take a test." Jack peered into the eyes of everyone in the group, masterfully capturing their full attention. "If he passes," he went on, "he's in. If he fails he's out."

The Black Widows and the girls were dead silent. Jack had a way of doing that, spellbinding everyone into statues.

"His test was to shoot a cat at the dump and bring it to me in a box."

I think that startled the girls. All three of them moved closer. One opened her mouth to say something, but kept quiet, squinting her eyes as if Jack's order to kill a cat was so appalling she couldn't find the words.

"Tomorrow," Jack said, staring at me with penetrating eyes, "bring it to school."

Keo shook his head when I glanced over at him. He must have been picturing Jack's reaction when he learned about the kitten.

The next morning I took *Pōpoki* to school in a small box, leaving late again, and walking into the classroom with everyone sitting at their desks watching me. Word had spread in whispers that I was bringing a dead cat to school. But within ten minutes the whole fifth and sixth grade knew there was nothing dead in the box at all, by all the noise the kitten made.

Even Mrs. Lee heard it, and came over to take a look. "It's so cute," she said, picking it up and showing the class. "I can see why you were so worried about it."

Jack refused to look at me the whole morning, acting as if I didn't exist. Keo kept to himself too, and so did the rest of the Black Widows.

At recess, I took the box outside and was immediately surrounded by a horde of girls wanting to see her. Jack and the Black Widows went over to the Tree of Webs, but within a few minutes, came over and broke through the girls. I stood holding the box with the kitten's head peeking through the slightly opened top.

"I said a *dead* cat, stupid." Jack glared down at me, looking as if I'd made a fool of him. "Kill it."

A hush fell over everyone. No one moved, or even dared to breathe. Keo, standing behind Jack, seemed surprised, and his face looked as serious as if he'd been told his dogs had run off. Jack reached for the box, and I jerked it away. "You little punk," he said. He slapped the box out of my hands. When it hit the ground, *Pōpoki* stumbled out and rolled into a forest of feet, then sprinted away. I started after her, but Jack tripped me, and fell on me, sitting on my stomach, slapping at my face. "Sissy little punk," he said.

I turned from side to side, trying to dodge his hands, my arms pinned under his knees. I heaved up with my stomach, but he was too heavy. The stinging slaps turned into blows. One of them hit my nose and sent a pain through my head like I'd never felt before. I squirmed and twisted, but the blows kept coming, harder and more painful.

Then suddenly Keo slammed into Jack, knocking him off me. The ground shook when they hit. The Black Widows spread away, some of them saying, "Get him, Keo, get him."

I got up on my hands and knees, blood from my nose dripping down into the dirt. Keo and Jack rolled back and forth, their faces contorted, making spiking sounds. Jack pushed Keo away, and scrambled to his feet. Before Keo could get up, Jack kicked him. Keo fell and tried to slide away, but Jack kept going after him. I staggered over and hit Jack from behind and knocked him to the ground again.

"Boys! Stop it, *now!*" Mrs. Carvalho yelled, suddenly appearing, swatting at us with a yard stick. I let go of Jack. He jumped up with his fists clenched, glaring at me with demon eyes.

"Sonny! Keo!" she said. "Go to my office! You should be ashamed of yourselves ganging up on Jack." Then she turned to Jack and told him to follow her. When I told her I had to find my cat, she said, "Not another word!" But as Keo and I made our way through the crowd of kids, I saw Bobby Otani with the cat, handing her to Mrs. Lee.

Dad was disappointed in me when he heard about the fighting, especially since Mrs. Carvalho called him and asked that I stay out of school for three days. He took me out fishing with him until I could go back, making me scrub the deck after every fish he caught. Keo just stayed home and shot at tin cans with the twenty-two. Jack had to stay away from school, too, but we didn't see him around and didn't know what he did during that time.

Mrs. Lee seemed genuinely pleased to see me when I returned, and even asked about my cat. I told her she'd gotten to like the dogs, and hung around with them all day, and that no mongoose would even think of bothering her with them around. She patted me on the back and told me to try to stay out of trouble.

Jack now sat under the Tree of Webs alone. The Black Widows had drifted apart. Only Mrs. Carvalho couldn't see Jack's mean streak. The rest of us stayed away from him, watching him from the opposite corner of the school yard. He usually spent the entire recess throwing a pocket knife into the ground, trying to get it to land blade down.

Around two weeks after the fight, Mrs. Carvalho came into our classroom and asked Keo and me to please follow her outside, she had something for us to do. Everyone in the room watched us leave, as if we'd been condemned to a beating in her office.

When we got out on the wide veranda, she searched our eyes, never changing the expression on her face. "You are excused from school for two hours," she said. Keo and I just stood there staring at her, having no idea what was going on. Then she broke down and smiled, and tipped her head toward the school yard. "Go with him."

Grampa Joe leaned up against the hood of his car with his arms crossed. "What's going on?" Keo asked as we approached him.

"Nothing," he said. "I'm just taking you to lunch."

Keo and I looked at each other, then got into the car. Grampa Joe fired it up and drove us up the hill into the highlands, saying only that he had something he wanted us to see.

The parking lot was full of cars when Grampa Joe drove into the high school. "We're having lunch here," he said. "You know the guy, Herman Fukuoka? The guy with the coffee trees next to my place? His wife runs the kitchen."

"But why eat here?" Keo asked.

Grampa Joe tapped Keo's shoulder and said, flicking his eyebrows, "Good food."

The cafeteria was buzzing with students, many of whom we knew from last year at the elementary school. A couple of them waved and came over to eat with us. The lunch room was loud. Everyone seemed excited, but the guys who sat with us said it was like that every day.

The whole time we were there Grampa Joe kept quiet, just ate his lunch and listened to us talk with our friends. When lunch was over, he drove us back down to the elementary school, talking about his coffee trees all the way. When we got out of the car, Keo asked again why he'd taken us up to the high school for lunch, but Grampa Joe just said, "Good food," then asked me how my flea-bag cat was doing. I said it was doing fine, and he left. We didn't see him again for three weeks.

After a while, Jack, Keo, and I were talking again, but we never brought up the cat, or the Black Widows, or the fight we'd gotten into. We didn't even talk about high school. But Jack did confess that it was he who had tied the mongoose to the flagpole. He thought it would be funny.

As the school year ended, Keo's worry changed into boldness. He was going to the big school next year, you could see it in the way he walked, and the way he started holding himself more erect, pushing out his chest. He went to work for Uncle Harley that summer, weighing and buying fish from the charter boats, and from the small commercial boats, like Dad's, then selling them in Hilo. And I worked with Uncle Raz as his deck hand.

Jack met us on the pier one afternoon, to say goodbye. He told us his parents were moving back to California. Keo and I had finished work and were sitting in Dad's Jeep, waiting for a ride home. Jack stood on Keo's side, still wearing jeans and T-shirt with sleeves rolled up, and greased-back hair. Our conversation was full of long silences, where each of us paused and looked off somewhere.

"Hey," Jack said after one particularly long quiet spell. "Maybe you could start up the Black Widows again."

Keo nodded, staring straight ahead at the steering wheel with a blank look on his face. "Maybe," he said. Beyond Jack, the ocean was turning slightly pink. Waves thumped easily into the rocks on the other side of the small boat landing.

Jack pulled a pack of cigarettes out of his back pocket, something we'd never seen him with before. He tapped one out and stuck it in his mouth, then pulled a wooden stick-match from his front pocket. There was no breeze on the pier, but still Jack cupped his hands after striking the match on the side of Dad's Jeep. His cheeks sank inward as he lit the cigarette and sucked in. A cloud of smoke surrounded his face and squinting eyes. Jack shook the flame out. His eyes watered, and he coughed.

"Nasty things," he said, taking the cigarette and hiding it in the palm of his hand, pinching it between his thumb and first finger. Then he pointed the pack of cigarettes at us and shook a few of them half way out of the pack. Keo and I each took one. "Nasty, but not bad," he went on. "Hey, look me up if you ever get to Los Angeles." Jack backed away, then turned and strutted off toward the seawall

"Hey lōlō," Keo called, then waved.

Jack turned, walking away from us backwards. He smiled, and flipped us off, then went on.

Keo smiled, then we both laughed. There was something about Jack that you just had to like. I started to throw the cigarette away, but Keo said, "Wait! If you don't want that thing, give it to me. It's good for cleaning face masks, better than seaweed."

We both sat in the Jeep watching Jack make his way along the seawall toward the trees on the other end. Just before he jumped off the wall, he flicked what was left of his cigarette out into the ocean. Even from where we sat on the pier, you could see it twirl out in a graceful arc, spinning flawlessly into the water, as if he'd been smoking and flicking the butts away every day of his life.

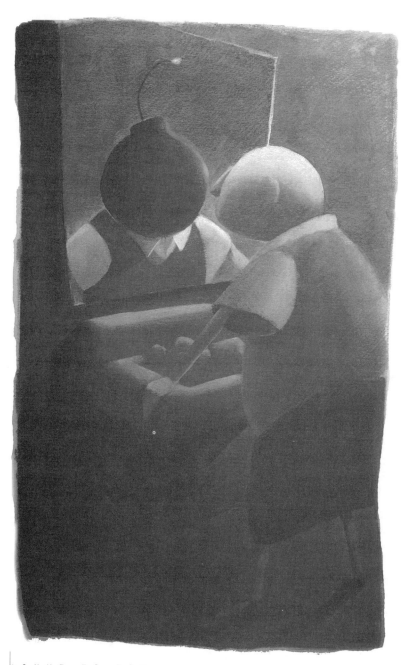

COUNT TO TEN

1997, oil on illustration board

BY WILLIAM D. STEINHOFF

HONOLULU HAND GRENADE R AND R

We were so young, ignorant, and violent then. Now my anger has faded and I can see some bizarre justice in Clark giving Barbara Jean a hand grenade for a wedding present. We were in Honolulu on R and R from the Vietnam War, and more specifically, he gave her an anti-personnel concussion grenade. You see, Clark thought he was going to marry Barbara Jean in Honolulu, and I was going to be best man.

Originally, Clark was going to send the grenade back home with Barbara Jean, so she could give it to his brother. But Clark changed his mind about the hand grenade after Barbara Jean told him she was pregnant and was going to marry Harley Featherstone, who had an upholstery shop for cars in Flint, Michigan, called Harley's Cool Seats.

Getting back to the hand grenade, nobody knew Clark had it but me, and I thought he was going to send it to his brother Charleton. (Clark's mother named all of her eight kids after movie stars.) Clark said Charleton was going to throw it into a gravel pit and see if it would blow up some fish.

Clark still wanted to marry Barbara Jean even after Madame Magyar told him not to, the night before Barbara Jean arrived in Honolulu. But he never married Barbara Jean, then or later. And I forgot all about the hand grenade until after Clark sort of killed himself. Actually, he didn't kill himself, the Viet Cong did that. But he let them.

Anyway, the night before Barbara Jean arrived, we were walking around Waikīkī and we saw this little cubbyhole next to the restaurant where we had decided to eat outside. There was a sign with big red letters written in some kind of European-style writing. It said, "Madame Magyar, Vaticinator. Fortunes Told and Readings." Clark pointed at it, and I knew he would want to go there after we finished eating. He believed in all that mumbo jumbo stuff because his mother didn't operate on all eight cylinders. Like if a bat flew through the yard it meant someone was going to die, or garlic would keep girls from getting pregnant. I never did find out what girls were supposed to do with the garlic.

After dinner we went to Madame Magyar's and sat at a little table outside of her cubbyhole office and Clark paid her twenty bucks. Madame

Magyar was real slick-looking. She had pitch black hair and she wore dark clothing that made her pale white skin look even paler. Before I said anything she looked at me and said, "You don't believe in my powers, but you will someday."

I just shrugged and smiled, because I had downed several beers and didn't feel like arguing with her. Besides, it was Clark's idea, and I went along because I always knew I could count on him to back me up, too.

So Madame Magyar started swishing these tea leaves around in a big cup and talking while she looked at the tea. She told Clark that she sensed a lot of confusion and doubt, that he should think long and hard before making some big decision or he would regret it. But most of all, he should not marry the person he planned on marrying. He should forget about her and not marry until the right combination of sevens came up. She didn't explain that, but said Clark would know when it happened. He would figure out the right combination because it would be obvious to him and not others.

Clark nodded in agreement, but I could see it really shook him because he was real quiet afterwards. I knew it would be useless for me to say anything against Madame Magyar. Clark believed her and he was between a rock and a hard place. I asked him if he wanted to get some more beer, but he said no and went back to the hotel room.

Clark really wanted to marry Barbara Jean because the months in Vietnam had turned her into some ideal woman in his mind. He never saw her the way she was. I realize now that what Clark hoped to gain from marrying Barbara Jean was a sense of security that he did not have within himself.

Our views of marriage were quite the opposite. After having listened to my parents fight over such stupid things as signing an income tax refund check, and having seen some of my fifteen brothers and sisters go crazy, I thought that anyone who got married was nuts, and having babies was totally insane. Clark's oldest brother was queer and Clark was ashamed of it, but in other things our backgrounds were very similar. Both of our mothers were very neurotic and our fathers very ignorant. My father worked as a core maker in the Buick foundry. Clark's father worked as a machinist at a Chevrolet plant. We both quit high school in the eleventh grade, and we joined the army together one year later. We'd been in Nam about six months when the Tet offensive came.

Sometimes now when I think about Clark, I feel the hand grenade was really my wedding present, too. I probably would have stopped Clark if I had known about it at the time. If I had stopped him, I probably would not be living in Honolulu now with Sandra Sachiko Mizukami, and working at the Pearl Harbor shipyard. I might have died, or gone back to Flint and spent my life heat-treating transmission shafts at Buick Motor Division, because that's what I did before I went to Vietnam. But it wasn't so clear then, and I only came to understand it fully when I went with my eight-year-old son Tommy to a replica of the Vietnam Memorial that some veterans' group brought to Honolulu.

Tommy asked if all of them were dead and I said yes, and he looked sad and said it must have hurt. And I said it only hurts when it happens, and when you think about it later. Beside Clark's name, Tommy taped a flower he had picked from our yard. Next to Tommy's flower was a page from a 1965 year book from Punahou School, which Tommy goes to now. Written on the page was, "We miss you. Love, Mom." On impulse, I snapped to attention and saluted with tears in my eyes, both for Clark and for the mother who left the yearbook page.

Tommy asked if he could salute and I said yes. When Tommy saw me crying silently, he cried silently too, and we walked away hand in hand. I told him someday we would see the real thing in Washington, D.C., and Tommy asked if we could take a live orchid from our yard and leave it in front of the wall by Clark's name. And I said that Clark would like that.

But getting back to where all this started, it was May, 1968, after the Tet offensive was over and we had helped kill over four thousand V.C. outside Bien Hoa, which is near Saigon. Clark and I and some others got a special ten-day R and R because the colonel said we had done a good job stopping the Viet Cong. We were the division recon, and all of us had walked point for units of the 101st Airborne during the clearing of the Bien Hoa area after the V.C. had shot their wad.

The colonel didn't know it, but we killed all the Vietnamese in our area. Maybe he did know and didn't care. Maybe he was playing a role, as Dr. Bahlman, my second psychiatrist, used to say about people when they were doing one thing but their emotions were telling them something else.

Dr. Bahlman said his name was very Freudian, but I didn't know what that meant at the time. He said he shot himself in the foot so he could get out of the Korean War, but I never believed him, though he did limp a little. Later when I was getting better, when he said it again I told him he didn't have the balls to shoot himself in the foot. He said I had made a pun on his name, and we all laughed in our therapy group. He said he had even considered turning queer and becoming a homosexual. He asked me if I would consider doing that if I had to face war again. I thought about it and laughed and said that I might, because it probably was less painful than being a hero. Everybody laughed at that, and Dr. Bahlman said I was growing emotionally.

But getting back to the colonel, he's now a big shit in the army because I see him on TV sometimes talking about the contras in Nicaragua. The only thing he did in Vietnam was stop the APC drivers from running over the piles of dead bodies when we heaped them along the roads that went through the rubber plantation. He didn't really stop them, because the APC drivers only stopped when he was around. When he wasn't, pieces of body were flying off the treads like gobs of brown, slushy snow from cars in Michigan. And there are lots of piles when you have over four thousand dead bodies.

The colonel didn't see it when one of the APC drivers ran over some live prisoners that had been taken to a collection point. I didn't see it either, but Clark did, and it bothered him. It was the only thing I can remember him saying about the war that bothered him. He said the Viet Cong had their hands tied and some airborne guys just threw them in front of an APC driver who wanted to run over them. When they tried to crawl away, they were picked up and thrown back in front of the APC as it turned around. Clark didn't throw anybody in front of the APC, but he said he didn't try to stop them. Nobody else did, either. Later he wished he had tried to stop them.

Anyway, Clark and I both got Bronze Stars and I came to Honolulu to be Clark's best man. Otherwise I would have gone to Bangkok with all the other guys, because the girls were easier to find and they were a lot cheaper. When we left Saigon, both of us looked in the "no questions" box, which was a wooden box on a pole by the gate where you walked out to the R and R plane. You could drop in the box any illegal stuff that you had been thinking about taking on R and R with you, and there would be no questions asked. There was a kilo of marijuana in there, Thai sticks, all kinds of ammunition, lots of drug stuff, and a .45 caliber automatic pistol.

I picked up the kilo of grass and the pistol and thought about sticking them in my AWOL bag I was carrying on the plane. I would have kept the pistol and sold the marijuana in Honolulu. But I decided not to, because I didn't want to take a chance on messing up Clark's wedding, even if he was marrying Barbara Jean with her Cadillac body and her ten-cent mind. Clark looked in the box and glanced at me, but he had his grenade well hidden and didn't hesitate at all. The customs guy in Honolulu didn't even look in our bags. He jokingly asked us if we had any M-60 machine guns. We jokingly replied that we never went on R and R without them.

The day after Barbara Jean arrived, I was sitting in the bar of our hotel when Clark came in and motioned for me to come to an isolated booth. Clark was all pale-looking like he hadn't slept at all. He slumped down in the seat and in an almost pleading tone said, "She's pregnant.

Harley Featherstone. She's going to marry Harley. She wanted to tell me in person, and she wanted me to have a good time on R and R."

I knew Barbara Jean. I even screwed her once, but I never told Clark that. I could just see Barbara Jean gossiping with her girlfriends about having to go to Hawai'i, and thinking how noble she would look to others for doing her duty. But I knew Barbara Jean really didn't want to miss out on a free trip to Hawai'i paid for by Clark, because all she would get from Harley was a weekend trip to Traverse City, or maybe a couple of nights at the Hawaiian Gardens Motel in Holly, down the road from Flint.

When Clark had recovered somewhat from the shock of Barbara Jean being pregnant, and he finally realized he couldn't change her mind to marry him, the thing that was really bothering him was having sex with a pregnant woman. Being very ignorant myself, I couldn't really give him any good advice. I tried to tell him just to let her sit in the hotel room and get home on her own. But I knew he wouldn't, because Barbara Jean was emotionally stronger than Clark and Harley put together. They were both smarter than she was, but no question about it, she was stronger. Barbara Jean would go after security and fight to control her nest with all the energy and the narrowness of her small mind.

I realize now that Barbara Jean was a good survivor, and that she used what little brains she had to the maximum, which is more than most of us can say. She knew what she wanted, and saw how to get there. Years later when I told my psychiatrist Dr. Bahlman about Barbara Jean, he said his first wife was like that. He said she wanted to marry a doctor, and she nailed him in his senior year of college with sex. He said she was much more experienced than he was.

Barbara Jean and Madame Magyar were a lot alike, too. They let others be emotional while they survived. I went down to the state courtroom recently and watched a trial where Madame Magyar was charged with swindling a Canadian woman tourist from British Columbia out of $25,000. It seems this woman believed she had an old Indian curse put on her by some medicine man, and came to Madame Magyar because she had heard about her helping another woman who was sexually inhibited and now had a good sex life, even though it cost her $10,000. After a week of private sessions the woman felt cured and went back to Canada, but the curse came back in Kamloops, British Columbia. So she wanted a refund. When the story hit the TV and newspapers, it turned out Madame Magyar had clipped several people for a total of $85,000 and was working on a few others when the shit hit the fan.

I can't be too hard on Madame Magyar because my father-in-law Takeshi, who is a descendant of a class of untouchables in Japan called

Burakumin, is an exorcist in Honolulu. We have had a lot of friendly arguments about this. But he says since his ancestors had the untouchable jobs of dealing with dead bodies and slaughtering cattle, it was natural for him to deal with evil spirits, which, according to him, come in varying shades of evil. He says he lets the people tell him how evil the spirit is, and then God sets the price. Before I started living in Hawai'i I would not have believed all of this, and I still don't, but I have a more tolerant attitude toward evil spirits now.

When I first got out of the army I worked as an apprentice welder on the new football stadium. And when some of the supports started moving, most of the workers were convinced it was evil spirits. There were two schools of thought on this. One school thought there were really evil spirits, or the ghosts of old Hawaiians were getting pissed off at us for disturbing their graves. The second school was not so sure about the evil spirits and ghosts, but felt it would not be polite to show disrespect for old traditions. So all work stopped until a Hawaiian kahuna, or priest, was called in to bless and purify the grounds. The engineers said to themselves it was underground springs, but when they poured more concrete they made sure the kahuna splashed water on it.

You see, it's kind of hard to pin anyone down on evil spirits, ghosts, or religion in Honolulu because there are so many beliefs mixed together and existing side by side. Take this: a Filipino Catholic guy I know at the shipyard consults with a real live witch doctor, whom he refuses to name. But he never tells his priest at confession, because he would not want to hurt the priest's feelings. So he is quite willing to be tolerant even of me, an atheist. Like he says, maybe I just haven't found the right spirits yet. He just tells me to be patient, because there are lots of them out there, and sometimes they are busy for years.

He told me he was arguing with his daughter, who wanted to marry a guy he didn't like. He knew the guy had bad spirits, because the witch doctor told him so. One day he very confidently handed me a newspaper story about how the guy was killed after he had downed a couple of six-packs and his car hit a big monkeypod tree. My friend went by and patted the tree afterwards and poured some fruit punch mixed with gin on the ground to say thanks. As he said to me, "Da kine monkeypod say geevum, brah. He can take it. Ford junk. Da buggah dead." I bought him a plate lunch that day to show him respect.

As the shipyard bookie, Philip Wong, says, "Hey, brah, you gotta go along because you nevah know what somebody got goin' for dem." I guess he should know, because he never seems to lose at the cockfights, even though he's lousy on picking football winners. As Wong says, if you were sure of winning all the time, there wouldn't be any fun in gambling.

One time we went to the cockfights and he won $5,000, but then the cops raided the place and we had to run. While we're running, he turns to me and says, "Hey, you take this. You can run faster and maybe you won't get caught. Besides, the cops won't believe a haole was at a cockfight." He never doubted for a minute that I would give the money back to him the next day. I had thoughts about keeping the money as I was running flat out through the kiawe brush, but the good spirits prevailed and proved Wong right.

So, even though I don't really believe in spirits myself, I do get the feeling sometimes that some unknown force in the spring of 1968 propelled Clark and Barbara Jean in one direction, and me in another. Like I said, I forgot all about the hand grenade, but Clark decided to give it to Barbara Jean for a wedding present. She didn't know it until she opened it after she married Harley Featherstone. I didn't know it until an agent from the Army Criminal Investigation Department came to see me at Tripler Army Hospital and asked me about the grenade and Barbara Jean.

By that time, Clark was already dead, and it was all mixed up in my mind who was responsible for killing him: Barbara Jean, the V.C., or Clark himself. I hated her for it just as much as I hated the V.C. But when you get right down to it, Clark just gave up on life and killed himself. If he hadn't wanted the V.C. to kill him, they probably never would have, because Clark was even better than I was at crawling around in the dark outside the perimeter and wasting V.C. That was what we did every night, and we were damn good at it.

To be more specific (specific is a word I learned from Dr. Deborah Bacon, my first psychiatrist at the VA clinic in Honolulu), Clark hit them with a ball-peen hammer that had a piece of guy wire attached to a hole in the handle. He would wrap the other end of the wire around his wrist so he would not drop the hammer and lose it in the dark. I usually stabbed them, but I sometimes used a hatchet rigged like Clark's ball-peen hammer. I kept experimenting with various things to find the perfect weapon for killing people in the dark, but I never did find it.

Sometimes we killed women and kids, too, but they were all V.C. because they all ran around in the dark after we told them to stay in the village. They would help the hard core V.C. plant mines and booby traps. Once I killed a grandfather. I knew what he was because I felt his beard afterwards. And once Clark killed a grandmother and a little girl. You could usually tell the ages of the V.C. by feeling their faces, but sometimes people there got old very quickly.

Clark had been real quiet ever since he said goodbye to Barbara Jean in Honolulu. On the plane back to Vietnam he didn't say anything, but then nobody felt much like talking. The first night back we were out all night crawling around, but I went back inside the perimeter by myself before dawn. Just after daylight, two guys from our squad came running into the mess hall and said they had seen Clark walking toward the V.C. village by himself, without any weapon in his hands. They said he just kept walking with his hands up until he disappeared into the jungle brush. They yelled at him, but no one was going after him until the area had been checked for booby traps.

With a sense of dread, I went out with the search party. I kept saying to myself, "Goddam that bitch Barbara Jean." We checked the village and threatened everyone, but since the captain was with us, we couldn't really get tough with them.

The next morning the V.C. left what had been Clark outside our perimeter. When I saw it, I burst into tears and felt my body going into convulsions. Before I fainted I heard the lieutenant say to make sure it wasn't booby trapped. Someone later told me that it wasn't.

The only thing I remember after that was getting on a plane with some wounded guys and flying back to Hawai'i. Some nurse asked me if I would help her change I.V. bottles. I remember that I held them up with my eyes closed. After I got to Tripler Army Hospital in Honolulu, I just remember sleeping and eating. I knew some people were asking me questions, but I don't know what I said.

The first thing I really remember was an older woman who came with a nurse, asking if she could have lunch with me. She had silver grey hair, she chain-smoked cigarettes, and she talked like a machine gun. Her name was Karen Sexton, and she was a volunteer. She just started asking me questions about where I came from, what I did before I joined the army, did I have a girlfriend. After a couple of questions and answers she said, "You can tell me to shut up if you want. I'm a compulsive hysterical type, but I don't bite."

When she said she didn't bite, I started to laugh and I didn't know why. I laughed and tears rolled down my face. Then she got up and said, "Wow, I'm on a roll. You know I tell jokes and I can dance, too. I once toured with the USO in World War II." She kept coming back every day, and the nurses kept giving me pills. Finally one day, she asked if I wanted to see her house. She lived near Diamond Head crater, right on the ocean. She even had a swimming pool and a bunch of guard dogs, but they only licked my hands.

She laughed and said, "For $2,000 I get hand kissers. Maybe I should have hired a bodyguard. No telling what he might kiss." Her husband traveled a lot for a pineapple company, and her daughters were away at college on the mainland. She said she was in charge of keeping the cockroaches and termites from taking over the place. We walked on the beach and I played with the dogs by throwing sticks into the ocean and they swam after them. She cooked all kinds of strange things I had never eaten before, like chicken paprikash and stuffed grape leaves. She went to cooking school to become a gourmet chef and wanted to open a restaurant, but her husband said he needed her to keep the roaches and termites in their place. So she cooked for herself and the dogs. She said the dogs refused to eat sauerbraten. She threw up her arms dramatically and said, "Can you imagine a dog refusing to eat sauerbraten? Next time I'll get German dogs." I thought that was very funny, even though I didn't even know what sauerbraten was.

We talked mostly about sex, or rather she talked and asked me questions about it. I didn't know much about any of this, but Karen went into great detail about everything. When I looked blank as she talked about diaphragms and spermicide, she even brought out a portable blackboard and drew pictures. She laughed and said that at heart she was a dirty old lady and really liked to perform for an audience.

The most important thing Karen did for me was to show me plants and flowers. She knew every damn plant and flower in Honolulu. Sometimes I helped her move big potted plants around, or trimmed the bougainvillea for her. She took me to meetings at Foster Gardens, and to the university arboretum. I even helped Karen make flower leis of plumeria blossoms and carnations for some of the guys at Tripler.

Before I met Karen I only ate things if they were sweet or not too sour, and in the tropical fruit area I only ate bananas and pineapple. Karen was always handing me a guava, passion fruit, lychees, and the thing that became my favorite, an avocado sandwich on homemade bread. I still see Karen sometimes. I think she drinks too much, and even she admits she is addicted to cigarettes. As she says, she is a compulsive personality type, and if she gave up cigarettes, she would become addicted to something worse. She is developing new types of orchids, and I see her at all the orchid shows. I always smile when I see her or think about her.

I wish I had been able to give her something in exchange for all that she did for me. Later, when I talked to Dr. Bahlman, he said she was very lonely and probably wanted to make love. At the time I couldn't imagine anyone with money being lonely. I was so overwhelmed with my own pain and confusion that I couldn't see other people's problems or give much to them.

Slowly I began to learn trust and let go of the anger. It may sound simple, but it wasn't. That was when I was still seeing my first psychiatrist, Dr. Deborah Bacon. I learned later that she didn't like men much, and Dr. Bahlman said she couldn't maintain objectivity with her patients. The VA sort of decided that she needed to find another job. She did two things for me, besides scaring the shit out of me most of the time.

There was this girl I met, and she was really putting the pressure on me to get married. Once she even claimed she was pregnant. When Dr. Bacon heard that, she said to take her to a gynecologist, and gave me the name of a woman doctor. But when the girl heard where I was going to take her, she said she wasn't pregnant after all. Also, Dr. Bacon told me to tell her that I was too immature and had too many problems even to think about getting married. Dr. Bacon said she would tell me when I was ready to get married, and then I could tell the girl. After that, the girl gave up and the next month she married someone else. So for a long time, I had this insurance policy against marriage. I would just tell girls that my psychiatrist said I was too immature to get married.

The other thing I learned from Dr. Bacon was that women were stronger than men. She said we are not living in a caveman society where we had to beat the shit out of animals, so muscles did not count for much. Dr. Bacon said it was mental and emotional strength that counted in our modern day society, and that women were superior to men in this. She recited all kinds of studies to prove her statements. The one that convinced me was her own statement that women live longer than men, therefore they are stronger. After I heard that, I started taking better care of myself and not working as hard. I also stopped feeling sorry for women.

Dr. Bahlman laughed when I told him all of this, but he did agree that women lived longer. He thought it was because men had more stress on them from their jobs. After hearing this, I decided not to marry any woman who did not want to work full time. If it came to one of us staying home, I was going to be that one and only. But that has never been a problem with Sandra.

The only problem with Sandra is her mother. She is a cold stone racist. As Dr. Bahlman said, she wants to deny my humanity because of my color. She didn't want her daughter's pure Japanese blood corrupted by marrying a Caucasian, or haole, but Sandra's father Takeshi told me the Japanese were originally half Korean anyway. When I went to the house, Sandra's mother would go downstairs and not talk to me. Even after we got married, she wouldn't talk to me.

Sandra thought she would change after we had Tommy, but she didn't. So I refused to go to Sandra's parents' house on New Year's, or to let her take Tommy there. To Japanese, New Year's is the big holiday and everyone has lots of food and lots of relatives come over. There is plenty of sushi and beer. The men drink and watch football games. Sandra and I had a lot of arguments because I wouldn't let her take Tommy there, but I didn't back down. I said if she denies my humanity because of my color, then she must be denying half of Tommy's humanity, too. I said a half of a racist is still a racist, and I didn't want my kid associating with a racist.

I finally got even with Hazel Mizukami. She is a public school teacher and is always pushing education, both for money and status. She is what Dr. Bahlman calls hard core new middle class. She came from a poor family, and Sandra's father worked at the shipyard while Hazel went to the University of Hawai'i. Now she is a high school math teacher, and is embarrassed that Takeshi still exorcises bad spirits. But hell, he sometimes makes more in a week from that than Hazel does from teaching. Besides, Takeshi came from the Burakumin class and that bothers Hazel. She tries to cover it up, but everyone knows.

I finally fixed Hazel when Tommy turned five. Without telling anybody, early one morning I went down to Punahou School to turn in Tommy's application. Punahou is a very famous private school in Honolulu. There I was with all these pushy middle class mothers in line behind me. I had on my shipyard working clothes, because I had to go to work later. The women talked to each other, but not to me. Anyway, I handed in my application and it was number fourteen. Tommy could already read when he was three and a half, so Dr. Bahlman, whose two daughters went there, encouraged me to give it a shot. Dr. Bahlman said they might even give Tommy financial aid.

Well, Tommy aced the test and the interview. The woman who did the oral interview commented that Tommy was a very secure and mature child. I smiled and said his mother is very secure and his father is working at it. She sort of smiled, but also looked a little puzzled at that.

Anyway, when the letter came that Tommy had been admitted, they asked me to come down to the financial office and this very nice Chinese lady, Mrs. Lum, asked me questions about my finances. I said I was working at the shipyard and that Sandra was going to the University of Hawai'i studying to be a bacteriologist, but that she was an R.N. and worked at Queen's Hospital on the weekends. So Mrs. Lum did a little calculating on her calculator, smiled, and said they would offer us a half tuition scholarship, and I would have to pay the other half. She said when Sandra started working full time, then we would have to pay the full shot. I had no argument with that, and asked where I paid. She said all I would have to pay now was the deposit that would guarantee Tommy a place in the class of 1999.

I still hadn't told Sandra about any of this Punahou business until it was all double locked up. When I showed her the letter of acceptance and the paid deposit slip, she started crying, not because she was sad, but because she was happy. I asked her to make a reservation and invite all her family to come to the Pearl City Tavern, which is a pretty classy restaurant even if they do have live monkeys running around behind the bar in a glass cage. She started laughing and said, "You've done it! You've really done it! My mother can't say no to a Punahou grandchild. She will want to brag about that too much not to come to the Pearl City Tavern."

And sure enough, Hazel came. I waited at the bar with Tommy while Sandra sat at the table waiting for everyone to show up. Tommy was drinking a Shirley Temple, and I was drinking a double Singapore Sling. I looked at Tommy and told him he was a great kid and that I was proud of him and loved him very much. He wanted to play with the monkeys and feed them the fruit from his drink. When I saw that everybody had arrived, I picked up Tommy and carried him to the table. Everyone stood up and clapped, and Tommy asked if it was his birthday. I looked right at Hazel and said, "It's better than a birthday because you will have more of those, but today you're a member of the Punahou class of 1999, and you will be that forever."

Tommy didn't think it was a very big deal, and asked if he could have a cake. He was very happy when I told him we were going to have his favorite cake, chocolate, for dessert. I sat him down next to Hazel and said, "I don't know which half got him into Punahou, and it didn't say on the letter of acceptance. The lady in the admissions office told me he got a perfect score on the admissions tests."

Then I handed Hazel the acceptance letter and sat down at the far end of the table, next to Takeshi. He handed me an envelope under the table and when I started to raise it up, he motioned for me to put it in my pocket. Then he smiled and said softly, "You done a good thing. Sandra's done all right marrying you, and I just hope I live long enough to see Tommy playing football or baseball at Punahou."

He raised his drink and I picked up my Singapore Sling and he said, "Kampai!" When I got home, I found five one-hundred dollar bills in the envelope. I bought a thousand dollar U.S. savings bond for Tommy with it.

But it wasn't easy getting this far, and lots of times before I married Sandra I thought about going back in the army. In the army, you can avoid getting involved with people emotionally. All you have to do is do your job, and stay out of trouble. Nobody pokes into your personal life, and nobody asks where you go on the weekends. And after Clark got himself killed, I knew I never wanted to go back to Flint and the Buick Motor Division.

A couple of years after Sandra and I got married, we went to Flint to pick up a car that one of my brothers had gotten for us at a discount from GM. Sandra said at first she felt strange being around so many haoles, but later she learned that it was her problem. When she realized that no one was going to look at her funny, she relaxed and enjoyed herself. Sandra was always better than I was at adapting to new situations. She just took everything in like she was visiting a living museum. We went on a tour of the Buick assembly plant and when she saw how the people worked, she looked at me and said softly, "Now I know why you don't want to do this anymore." I told her it was even worse in the wintertime because you never saw the sun.

We went by ourselves to see Clark's grave. I poured a bottle of Clark's favorite Jim Beam whiskey on the grave after taking the first swallow. I gave Clark a casual salute and walked away.

I drove by Harley's Cool Seats and we saw Harley fixing somebody's upholstery. He was bent over, hard at work. I thought about stopping and giving him my Bronze Star for having set in motion all the things that changed my life. But we just drove by.

Clark's brother Charleton told me about Barbara Jean and the hand grenade. Clark had rigged it so it would not go off until the box was opened. Fortunately she was alone in the bedroom where she put the wedding presents. I was glad that she hadn't opened the present at the wedding reception. The explosion blew her through a sliding glass door, but it did not harm the cat that was sleeping on the bed. I didn't ask if it was a black cat.

Afterwards I thought that there isn't any justice in the world but what we make for ourselves. But this thought, like much of my life, is constantly being revised.

BY CATHERINE BRIDGES TARLETON

THE FISHING CLUB

Kalani cupped his hand around the Zippo, blocking the sharp breath of the wind—ka makani, his grandmother had taught them—whipping down the hill like it does on this part of the island. He had parked his wife's old Dodge at Kishimoto Store so nobody would recognize him right away, leaving the pickup in the driveway at home. With his cigarette lit and pointing up at the dark sky, he surveyed the stars and congratulated Hiro for picking a good night for it. The moon three-quarters full was just beginning to lift off the shoulders of the mountain and it would hang bright and blue overhead for long enough to light their way down and back. The wind was good too. If anybody did happen to be close enough to hear them, the sounds would be drowned out by the moans and groans of wind.

He took a long drag on the cigarette, exhaling downwind. The smoke vanished seaward. There were no boats, as usual, and that was good too. Kalani was glad for these things; they seemed to give favorable signs for the job, and made him feel a little better. He had reservations about this, that was for sure, but they had convinced him it was not only the right thing to do, but that it might work. He leaned back against the warm hood of the Dodge trying to smoke peacefully, waiting for the rest to get there, knowing he was early, like always, and watching for shooting stars.

In a little while the phone in the phone booth rang. It was Ronald, just leaving home, and he had the stuff. A little shudder of chicken skin crawled up Kalani's forearm, but it was too late to be nervous now. Ronald would pick up Hiro, his neighbor, and they would be there in ten minutes. Kalani hung up the phone and took another look around. The old Kishimoto Store was right on the main road to the resorts on the coast. It had sat here on its own as long as Kalani could remember, in the middle of acres of kiawe scrub brush, with the one public phone that always worked and the little parking lot for watching the sunset and listening to the radio, before cruising up the hill to town, sometimes with a girl, or meeting the boys for a few beers. Traffic passed up and down the road, like a diamond bracelet coming towards him and a ruby bracelet going away, stretched and ready to break apart. "Too many damn cars," he said to his cigarette. "It used to be dark here at night. "

A flock of single headlights, the motorcycle club, growled toward him in their staggered single file. "And quiet," he said. One of the headlights peeled off as Dwayne and Ellen Hicks pulled into the parking lot. They're too old for ride the bike, Kalani thought, but they were haoles so they didn't care, and he didn't expect them to listen. They were fun to have around and even at 60 they liked to suck 'em up and talk story with the rest of the fishing club. Dwayne had adapted the bike a couple years ago after Ellen's hip surgery, when she couldn't straddle the big Harley anymore. So now she had an ingenious sidecar, lovingly crafted out of a canoe.

"Hey, howsit Kalani? I thought you quit smoking." Ellen rushed up to him for a kiss on the cheek and he obediently crushed the Camel out on the gravel.

"My grandchildren, they give me hell about it," he said, shuffling his feet, "But I tell them if they live long enough to do anything for 57 years they deserve to keep doing it, too."

"You still make love to your wife, don't you?" laughed Dwayne as he settled the bike. He waved at the passing fleet of motorcycles and signed off on his radio, replacing it in the caddy.

"Well, I still make love, but never mind with who." He chuckled and affectionately rubbed the fender of the old brown Dodge. "Hey, what did you bring that motorcycle for? Anybody's gonna know it's you folks."

"Kalani, you worry too much. I told you, anybody asks, we tell them we went fishing, just like always," said Ellen.

"Yeah, but we never met here and parked here before."

"Yeah, well this time we did," said Dwayne, ending the argument. He pulled his knapsack off the bike and produced a folding shovel, flashlights, a canteen. "Here, take a little shot of courage. Where's everybody else?"

Kalani took a pull on the canteen and passed it to Ellen. "Jimmy's wife is sick and she won't let him out. Ronald and Hiro are on the way. Stanley got called into work."

Dwayne spat on the ground. "When's that man going to retire? What's he been there, thirty years? Does he think the place will blow up if he leaves it? That hotel will have to drag him out of there kicking and screaming or else bury him right there in the boiler room floor."

"Well, you know him, yeah?" said Kalani, refusing a second turn at the canteen, "He talks to the machines. He started doing it right after you and I left. He has names for the boilers, and my son says he talks to them just like they was people."

"He always was crazy," Dwayne laughed. "Remember that time the boiler room flooded and he wouldn't let Housekeeping in until he took down all the nudie pictures?" They laughed. Kalani felt better. He usually did around these two. They had a way of doing that.

More headlights came into the lot, but it was a young man they didn't know, stopping to use the phone. They recognized the bellman's uniform from one of the hotels and nodded hello.

"So where's your fishing things?" Kalani asked loudly.

"Here, here," said Ellen, pulling rods and nets out of the canoe, and a small cooler. Kalani made Dwayne stow the shovel back in his knapsack and lit another cigarette.

"So as soon as the rest gets here we can go *fishing*!" Kalani announced.

"Yeah," said Dwayne, "Where's your stuff?"

Kalani, very businesslike, walked to the back of the car and stared blankly at the spot where, had this been his truck, the tackle box would be. The bellman finished his call and drove away, with Kalani still staring and Dwayne and Ellen roaring in laughter. Finally, Ronald's truck pulled in with no headlights on and he and Hiro and Hiro's grandson James piled out calling hello to everyone like always.

"Shh, shh!" Kalani cried, "No names, remember? Don't say anybody's names!"

Ronald patted him on the head. "There's nobody around, *Kalani*. Who's gonna hear us, *Kalani*?" (Kalani muttered under his breath.) "What did you say, *Kalani*?"

"I said no names, and no kids. What did you bring him for? This is dangerous what we're doing!"

"That's why I brought him," said Hiro calmly, "If there's watchdogs over there, James can run for help while they're eating *you*, and the rest of us might have a chance." Everybody laughed except Kalani.

"Watchdogs?" he asked, nervous again. "Ellen, do you have any meat at your house? Run home and—"

"There's no dogs," said Ronald officially. "Hiro been over there plenty, days and nights, and there's nothing except one gate."

"Yes," said Hiro. "James and I been fishing there almost every day— just like we said—and there's nothing over there. No fish either. His mom thinks we're crazy but I keep telling her *you* caught the biggest menpachi of your life over there, and I'm gonna beat you!"

"Me?" Kalani was tired of being teased and the moon was up and ready; so was he.

"Where's your fishing things, Kalani?" asked Ronald, throwing knapsack and poles into the back of his truck.

"Shut up," said Kalani. "Here's ti leaves." He took a KTA package from the back seat and passed it around, instructing them to each take one and keep it with them tonight. James asked why and they told him it was for good luck.

Ronald unfolded a greasy piece of paper from his pocket. "OK," he said, "let's look at the list."

If there were bears in Hawai'i or Portugal, these were Ronald's ancestors. His size gave him instant authority in their group, and had for maybe twenty years. Never married, he lived alone near the beach and still worked at the hotel where they all had, keeping an eye on crazy Stanley and his boilers and bringing all the fresh gossip to his retired friends in the fishing club.

"Shovel, flashlight, fishing things. Boltcutters?" Kalani had them. "You got your locksmith tools, Dwayne?"

"Yep."

Dwayne would cut the padlock off the chain link fence and switch cylinders with a brand new Master padlock while the rest were digging.

"Beer?"

Ellen patted the cooler. "And more back at our house when we're pau."

"OK, anything else?"

"Where's the *stuff*?" asked Kalani.

"In the truck," Ronald said, re-folding the list.

"I want to see it." Kalani said and everyone paused and looked at Ronald. This had more or less been his idea from the beginning, and no one had really wanted to know where "the stuff" was going to come from. Ronald said he knew, and that was good enough for them. The fun had been the planning—sitting around the park drinking icy beers and watching the turtles pop their heads out of the water like little submarines. They had spent many evenings pleasantly arguing over the plan, the place, the time. "The stuff" had just been what Ronald was bringing, like the boltcutters and the beer.

Now here it was, real. Ronald looked at their faces, especially James's, whose 11-year-old eyes were wide as the moon. He only knew he was helping his idolized Grampa with some secret plan, and seeing grownups get so quiet all of a sudden about whatever this stuff was (which he had sat beside in the back of the truck) was getting pretty scary.

"You sure?" Ronald asked, and paused ominously. They nodded.

Kalani spoke up bravely. "Yeah, for all we know you dug up your old dog and brought his bones."

"Dog bones don't look like human bones," said Ellen. "That wouldn't work."

"Well maybe he dug up his mother-in-law."

Ronald snickered. He had loved the dog. "OK," he said. "Come here."

They walked over to the truck and stood around it looking into the bed. Among the usual clutter of gear was an old burlap bag. "Get the flashlight, James." He found it at once. Ronald's massive fingers untied the knot and pushed the sides of the bag down. On cue, the wind howled and the moon hid behind a small cloud. James's hand made the flashlight beam tremble as it scanned the pile of long, curved and knobby objects that could easily have been rocks or coral, except for the perfect human skull in the center of the pile with a perfect bullet hole through the middle of his grinning face.

Kalani hung onto the side of the truck with one hand and crossed himself with the other, saying a fast prayer to Jesus, Mary, and Joseph, and any of the Saints who might be available. James hid under the truck, and the rest were transfixed, except Dwayne, who patted the skull and started off, "Alas poor Horatio. I knew him well. . . ." until Ronald smacked his hand away and Ellen said, "Yorick."

Again, headlights turned into the parking lot, and this time it was a police car. Ronald covered the bones back up, and sensing his band was near panic said, "Everybody get in the truck, nice and calm. James, come on out now and help them. Kalani, you get up front."

The policeman pulled right up behind them and got out of the car with his big flashlight panning the area. "You folks need any help?" Everybody froze. Kalani was ready to faint. He gave up on the saints and called on the family 'aumakua, asking just for strength enough to lift his leg up into the cab. "Oh hi, Uncle." The cop put down the light and walked over to shake hands with Ronald.

"Walter!" called Ronald. "How's that car running since we rebuilt the carburetor?"

"Some fast, Uncle Ronald. Thanks again."

"What time you get off, Walter? You like go fishing with us?" The truck began to quiver on its tires.

Walter laughed. "Oh, I'm off now. I just stopped here to take the light off." The crew in the truck, who had started breathing again when they heard the word "Uncle," now gripped the sides of the truck and looked heavenward, as if they could somehow levitate it and blow away with the wind. Walter and Ronald went over to the Trooper and unbolted the police light from on top, then stowed it in the back. It was a blessing that Kalani, who had finally managed to get himself into the front seat, couldn't hear the conversation. James stared at the burlap bag. Finally Ronald and Walter shook hands again and Walter drove away.

"Don't worry so much! Walter's family hates to go fishing," Ronald said, slapping Hiro on the shoulders. "Ready to go?" He hoisted up behind the wheel and started down the road.

It was a ways to the entrance of the construction site, a bumpy windy ride for the folks in back. They pulled off onto the shoulder and waited till there was no traffic in either direction, then the big Ford maneuvered fairly easily around the chain, and down the gravel road to the place where the new hotel was being built. Ronald turned off the headlights when the moon came back out and in a couple of minutes, they could see the flashing safety lights of the cranes like red-eyed dinosaurs reaching their long necks out of the pit.

When they were close enough, Ronald turned the truck around, facing mauka for a quick getaway, and stopped the engine. The dust was swept away by the wind.

Kalani spoke for the first time since the cop had come. "This is crazy," he said. "We have to go back."

"No," said Ronald, getting down out of the truck.

"We're gonna get caught," Kalani insisted. "We're gonna get caught for trespassing and go to jail!" He began the process of lowering his feet, then legs, then torso to the road, unable to remember when Ronald had lifted his truck up so high.

"Shut up," said Ronald, slamming the tailgate open.

"James, help them with their things," said Hiro, again unperturbed. "Kalani, we all agreed that it was time to do something besides talk, so here we are. Have you changed your mind? Do you want them to build this hotel?"

Kalani searched for his Zippo. "No, but I don't want to go to jail either. Besides, this isn't going to really stop them. It's their land now; they paid for it and they don't care about bones. They'll just move them if they *do* find them, or plow right over like the other hotels did."

"That's true," said Hiro, producing a match to light his friend's cigarette. "It probably won't do any good."

"Yeah, Kalani," said Dwayne as he helped Ellen climb down off the tailgate. They probably won't even find them, like you said. It won't make any difference."

"There's already too many godddam hotels anyway," said Ronald. "Too many goddam golf courses, too many cars, too many people."

"That's right." Kalani nodded vigorously. "It's already too late!" Hiro nodded too, and handed him the boltcutters.

"That's right," said Ronald. "Three years ago they didn't have enough people for the jobs in the hotels, and now they're building more of them at the same time they're laying us off."

Dwayne shouldered the knapsack and Ellen carried the cooler. Everyone was almost agreeing with each other that this was a futile waste of time as they began walking toward the pit.

"Ronald?" asked Ellen quietly, "Did you lose your job?"

"What job?" said Ronald.

They walked up to the chain link fence and Dwayne took the boltcutters ceremoniously from Kalani, and snapped off the padlock. Holding the cut lock in the tool's jaws, he kicked the big gate open for his wife and his friends. He gave them a militant nod, slipped out of the knapsack and unrolled the pouch of locksmithing tools. "I'll be down in a minute," he said to Ellen as she gave him a little good luck pat on the back and picked up the knapsack.

They sneaked around the pit, to the north wall, the place Hiro and James had reconnoitered on their way to the fishing spot. The construction work, apparently, exposed a lava tube, causing the dig to stop, so they could collapse the tube and re-pack it. Hiro knew this could have been a natural mausoleum for Hawaiians anyway, and he knew this was the perfect place and time to do their planting. Hiro had been thinking about planting while they made their way. How many bushes had he planted at the hotel in twenty-one and a half years? How many times had he shared a strawberry guava or sweet tangerine with the guests' children or their children, or hacked open a coconut for them? How much of himself was left there growing in those gardens, and would the boys that came after him remember how much to water, how much to fertilize, how much to prune? His life work was growing things, and now he would try to stop a whole hotel from growing. He thought to himself and shook his head, "Weeds."

They gathered at the designated corner and Hiro looked down in. They were too late.

"Oh no," he said. They must have blasted out the whole tube. Or else it was a lot smaller than it looked. Let me have the flashlight, James." The beam showed a straight vertical wall dropping into blackness. Hiro looked woeful.

"I told you," said Kalani.

"Shut up," said Ronald.

"It's OK, Grampa," said James.

"There must be another spot we can bury them," said Ellen, always pragmatic.

"Where?" demanded Kalani. "This is as far as they're gonna dig! Where can we put them *now* so somebody will find them?"

"Shut up and let me think," said Ronald, and they did. Dwayne came up, his job finished and the lock ready to replace.

"What's the problem?" He evaluated the situation, half-listening to their explanation, and looked around the site slowly. "Are you sure they're not gonna dig anymore?" he asked Kalani.

"Yes. Absolutely. My cousin drives the cement truck and they're coming in for the first big pour next week," he answered.

"Ronald," said Dwayne, "Didn't you tell me they're gonna tear down all these rock walls?"

"That's what I hear," said Ronald. "That professor from UH and a bunch of archaeologists from the mainland came out here for their survey years ago before any of this, and decided that all these walls," he waved both hands in the wind, "were just something farmers put up for their gardens, and they weren't important to save. So the contractor, Mr. Johnson, is gonna tear them all down. They're not very good Hawaiian walls anyway. You can tell because the rocks don't fit together right, see? My grandfather worked on the walls down in—"

"OK!" said Dwayne. "Let's put the stuff under one of these walls, and when they knock the wall down, they'll find Mr. Bones."

Kalani shook his head. "Hawaiian people would never build a wall on top of a grave, and they would never dig a grave under a wall."

Dwayne was undeterred. "No, they wouldn't, but this guy has a bullet through his head, and besides we don't know if he's Hawaiian or what."

"He's Hawaiian," said Ronald.

"OK, OK," said Dwayne, "So somebody shot him, and hid him under this wall. OK? How old are the bones?"

"Old," said Ronald.

"And how old are the walls?" Ronald shrugged.

"OK, we're here. We got everything together. Let's just do it. What have we got to lose? What do you think Hiro?"

"I think," he said, calm again, "That we ought to go over to that wall and drink a beer." That was an acceptable suggestion, the best part of which was that they could go outside the fence, put Dwayne's padlock in place and breathe easier. Sitting on a wall, beers or no beers, bones or no bones, was a lot less scary than trespassing on the foundation of the new hotel. James was particularly relieved, and—the first one out the gate—he found a suitable kiawe tree to pee behind. The wind had calmed down too, and the bright moon seemed to agree with their decision as Dwayne clicked the lock neatly in place, then as an afterthought wiped it and the chain with the edge of his T-shirt.

They selected one of the closer, more dilapidated stone structures, V-shaped. There were six beers in the little cooler so Ellen gave one to James too, and Hiro didn't say anything. They drank together under the stars as they had done for so many years.

"So, Ronald," she finally asked, "Tell us where you found the bones."

Ronald sat on the flattest available stone and sipped on his beer. "I won't tell you where," he said, "But they're real, and they're Hawaiian. My grandfather used to tell me about this secret graveyard up in the hills where our family was buried. And one night, when I was about James' age, he took me up there to the caves. It was dark, not like this, and no wind. Everything was still, and cool and very quiet—no birds, no lizards chirping, no cars. We had to hike off the road in this pasture, and the grass was wet, and to me it was deep. It rubbed on my legs like fingers or something." He rubbed James's leg with one big hand, damp from the cold beer can. "And in the middle of the field was a rise and a crack in the ground where there was one lava tube. It was dark as hell, and Grampa said to go inside there, but I wouldn't go first, so he crawled in with the flashlight and I held onto his belt with my eyes closed and never let go. We crawled for a long ways and then he turned the light out and started to chant in Hawaiian, but I didn't understand what he was saying so I got really scared and started to cry. He told me to open my eyes, but I couldn't because I was too scared, so he got all piss off with me and said 'Go' so I backed out of there as fast as I could and just sat there in the grass outside for a long time until he came out. And you know what he had in his hand? This guy right here."

Ronald reached into the sack and pulled out the skull. His audience gasped. "He said, 'This is your great-great-great-grandfather, and he's shame that you're such a coward. But he says one day you're gonna need him, and when you do, he'll be waiting for you right here.' And he took the head and he rolled it back into the lava tube and there was—Poof!—this big flash of light, like lightning inside there. And he would never take me back again, no matter how much I begged."

Ronald handed the skull to James who held it, awed, in both hands, peering into the bullet hole. "Who shot him? he asked.

"Who knows?" was Ronald's reply. He finished his beer and crushed the can. "Let's get to work."

They moved a small section of the wall at its V and tried to dig out underneath, but the camp shovel, intended to work in the soft dirt at the site, was practically useless in the thin hard soil. They managed to make a depression big enough for the skull and had to settle for covering up the remaining bones with rocks and some sandy dirt they scraped up. It looked realistic enough in the dark and it was getting very late.

As they turned to go back to Ronald's truck, somebody suggested that a prayer would be a good idea. Ronald didn't feel like it so they asked Kalani to pray since he had the most Hawaiian blood anyway.

"Heavenly Father," he began, "We brought these old bones down here from their rightful place up mauka, and we didn't mean any disrespect by it. We ask your forgiveness and we ask their forgiveness, and we hope that we didn't do anything too bad to upset the other spirits here by the ocean, and the ones up there in the cave. We are sorry for interfering, but we did it for try and stop them from building this hotel, because we think our island has enough, and people have to speak up about that because we're the ones here on earth right now. We don't think that Ronald's great-great-great-grandfather would have minded helping us. Thank you. Mahalo. Aloha. Amen."

And so they loaded up the truck and went back to their cars. The moon was way low on the horizon over the ocean now and nobody really felt like drinking anymore, so they shook hands and Ellen kissed cheeks all around. Kalani took out one smoke for the drive home, then remembered his wife didn't allow smoking in her car. He put the cigarette back in the pack and back in his shirt pocket and noticed the lighter wasn't there, but didn't think anything of it. He was tired. They all went home and so did the moon.

Nothing happened for three days. Then Kalani heard from his cousin that the big concrete pour had been postponed, and the fishing club called a meeting to exchange information. Nobody had much and the general consensus was to wait some more. Nobody had Kalani's lighter either, which was bothering him, and he had already been by the Kishimoto Store to look for it. Hiro and James had gone fishing by the site as usual. They took turns spying and fishing one whole afternoon from after school till dark. Unfortunately that day they were really biting and the two spies returned home with a full bucket of fish and not much information.

By the end of the week, the pour was scheduled again, and Kalani's cousin revealed that the delay was only due to some equipment being delivered from the mainland. Ronald went down and applied for a job with one of the contractors. He managed to nose around and find out that while they were waiting for the concrete, they had started work on the stone walls. They were methodically bulldozing them and putting the rocks aside to rebuild around some of the landscaping. Especially with the concrete's delay, Mr. Johnson was anxious for the crews to be occupied, so he directed his foremen to clear the entire area of rock walls, starting with the walls closest to the road and working their way makai. Although he had met with some resistance from the more traditional members of his crews, progress was being made.

A few more days passed, and then Stanley from the boiler room heard from the fuel oil man that all work had stopped, that the men assigned to the walls had walked off the site, refusing to come back to work.

It didn't take long for the news to get around the island, and with the news, hundreds of arguments over the ancestry and authenticity of the bones. A team of archaeologists, hired by the developer at great expense, descended on the area. They cordoned off the whole site with yellow tape and attacked the ground with whiskbrooms and teaspoons. Native Hawaiian groups came with ti leaf-wrapped offerings and leis and chants and ceremonies, and immediately several different groups of demonstrators claimed some relationship. They camped out nearby and made picket lines up and down the highway. Of course reporters and TV crews made a camp of their own, and swarms of curious tourists and locals alike came and parked cars on the shoulder, climbing the lava to peer over the yellow tape, hoisting children on their backs for a glimpse of something which might turn out to be historic or important, or worth talking about.

The police rather quietly began an investigation of their own, persuaded by the developers. They insisted, despite claims of the protestors, that a full archaeological survey had been completed prior to any construction. They weren't sure what they suspected, but they were suspicious. Questions were asked, through some of the same channels that the fishing club had used—the cement truck driver, the fuel oil man, Mr. Kishimoto at the store, fishermen, cousins, aunties, co-workers. All had opinions; all had theories, but the appearance of the bones was conspicuously mysterious.

An old kahuna came down to see for himself one morning. He passed through the layers of observers undisturbed, and approached the V-wall deliberately, slowly, almost unnoticed, until he cast his bent and aged shadow onto the back of one archaeologist, who was crawling along the wall's base with a paintbrush, sweeping grains of sand and searching. The shadow froze him, instinctively made him cover his head and lay in the dust unmoving. The kahuna was not looking at the worker or the wall. He stood like a kiawe tree, and watched the ocean as if waiting for a ship, silently. In a moment he laid a wrinkled hand on the wall, feeling, then stopped and picked up a handful of earth and let it sift through his fingers. He shook his head. The prostrate archaeologist righted himself and showed the kahuna the table where the bones had been placed for cataloguing, photographs and study. The kahuna held up the skull and looked through its empty eyes at the blue sky. He smiled and replaced it, and walked away.

Kishimoto Store was booming. He could hardly stock enough sodas to keep up with the demand and his wife had started a brisk plate lunch business in the back. He had even rented half a dozen port-a-luas and got around the pay toilet law by selling Charmin by the yard. There was no place to park. The phone had been used so much that vandals finally thought it was worth their time to break in and steal the coin box. So the pay phone at Kishimoto's was out of order for the first time anybody could remember.

The fishing club was relegated to meeting at the Hicks' house. They drank cold beers and cooked meat on the grill. Ellen put out a pot of rice and they listened to Kalani complain.

"It's more worse now!" he whined. "More people, more cars; you can't go fishing down there anymore; picket lines on the road; somebody broke the phone. We didn't fix anything. We made it worse."

"Kalani, you sound like an old lady," said Ellen, flipping the top and passing him another beer. "This will all settle down soon and people can get on with their lives."

"I don't think so," said Ronald, emphasizing the 'so' by swatting a mosquito on his arm. "My sister-in-law works for the construction company and she says if the developer has to pay for much more delays, they're gonna fold up and go back to the mainland, and if *that* happens, her company might go out of business."

"A lot of folks are gonna lose their jobs," Hiro added, alternately shaking his head and nodding.

"That's right," said Kalani, "we messed with something we should have left alone. We messed up, that's what we did!"

"So what you like do, Kalani?" Ronald said, "Take them back?"

For a minute the fishing club looked at each other in silence. If this was a solution worth considering, the wheels of their collective reason were slowly beginning to turn. In the pause, a few drops of rain made polka dots on the picnic table, then stopped.

Hiro looked at the sky. "I'm going home," he said. "Don't ask me what I think anymore. You folks do whatever. I'm not saying it was a mistake, but—I'm going to stay home for a while."

Dwayne turned from the grill, plopping another plate of steak on the table. "No way," he said, waving goodbye to Hiro, "The deed is done. It was easy to go in before. It's damn near impossible to even go over there now."

"We made somebody angry and we have to make it right," Kalani said, wiping a stray raindrop off the back of his neck.

"If you really want to make it right," said Ellen, "Let's go forward and tell the truth."

"What truth?" Ronald growled. "That we broke into somebody's property and planted some bones in the ground? But really they lease it from the state, and the state stole it from the family that lived there before, that the king gave it to, and that king stole it from the chiefs before him. So whose land did we go trespass on? And what truth did you want to tell? That land doesn't belong to anybody except whoever happens to be there at the moment and right now that land belongs to those bones. So I say we let them stay right there and have their fun."

It began to rain in earnest and they scrambled inside with plates and pots and steaks and beers, leaving the grill to steam and sizzle on its own.

Ronald drove home in the rain, grumbling to the windshield wipers. He had not told his friends about the conversation with his nephew, the cop. Walter had called up and asked him about the night he ran into the fishing club at Kishimoto Store. He had asked about the skull with the bullet hole, which he remembered from other campfires and other stories as a boy. Walter had also let him know that the experts were almost pau. They had not found anything except the one series of bones, which they determined not only to be younger than the wall, but definitely brought there from someplace else. Dirt stuck in the crevices did not match the dry dust near the site. Police were now thinking more in terms of foul play than history, and there was talk of the FBI coming in. The archaeologists were giving up and turning the whole site over to the legal authorities. The picture was becoming very crowded, and he had almost decided, no he *had* decided, to let Walter take him in to the station.

It rained for two days and nights, one of those once-in-twenty-years Kona storms that beat down on the islands like some insane car wash. The archaeologists and demonstrators, the tourists and news people all took a couple days off and calmness returned while all plans, including Ronald's, were on hold.

Early in the morning of the third day, Kalani drove down to Kishimoto Store for coffee and gossip. The island looked freshly painted, still damp in the new light of pre-dawn. He took note of some small damage along the way: a tree down by the church, the flooded out garage of a house on the makai side. The road was washed out near Kishimoto Store, and most of the construction boys had been called in to help clear it.

Dwayne was there too, already sipping coffee from a Styrofoam cup and watching the bulldozers slowly push the rocks, listening to the operators talk to each other on the CB. They shook hands and watched a while together. Kalani smoked a cigarette. They leaned on the motorcycle, and remembered driving the big machines; they remembered other times, other storms. They were interrupted by a squawk from the bike's radio. It broke through the usual radio patter as if some hand had snatched the mike from another.

"This is Johnson up at the site. I want everybody back here right now—and get the water truck with at least 100 feet of water hose. And keep the heavy equipment on the road—do not go off the gravel until you talk to me. Got it? The Old Man is gonna be over here on the next flight, and he is not gonna believe this. Let's get moving people."

"Let's go," Kalani said. "Your bike can get through."

"You sure?" Dwayne's eyes twinkled. Kalani had never even remotely considered the motorcycle real transportation. Kalani stamped out the cigarette and Dwayne kicked the engine awake. Kalani allowed his curiosity to overcome his fear of the bike, and climbed into its outrigger. They easily rode past the roadworkers and down to the construction area, no traffic. Not much was left of the V-shaped wall where they sat and drank a beer that night. It felt like a long long time ago. A few people were there on the ground, crawling around in the mud like a demolition derby for babies. Shouts of "Look over here!" and whoops and swearing in amazement cut through the air and the distant rumbling of the earthmovers. Dwayne drove right through the yellow tape and nobody even looked up.

A single upright figure stood by the wall, watching the sparkling ocean. It was the old kahuna. He seemed very happy to see them and smiling, gestured them over. "Come," he called, "look." As they walked towards him, one of Kalani's rubber slippers came off in the mud. When he peeled it up, the figure of a warrior, his spear raised, winked up at him from the rock beneath, then disappeared back into the oozing mud. Kalani knelt and wiped his hand over the lava rock, and a second warrior stood beside the first. Petroglyphs! That's what they were doing!

The ground was literally crawling with crawling people, frantically wiping the rock, uncovering a whole panorama of the carvings. There were acres of warriors, families, animals and plants, and new strange symbols and shapes they had never seen before—thousands. In some places the bare rock revealed much more, and hints of structures, clues to foundations. The more expert an archaeologist was, the more excited and the more muddy he got as the pages of this very ancient book began to turn for them.

Soon a parade of vehicles rolled back into the site with a fanfare of rumbles. Mr. Johnson looked around in amazement as the archaeologist in charge of the moment animatedly explained.

"The walls, remember? They were for agriculture. The farmers on this side of the island terraced the land to keep the soil from washing away during the worst storms, and when we moved the *walls*, and it *rained*— Look! Just look!"

The rainstorm had scoured more than two feet of topsoil off the lava in some places, revealing messages from a settlement much older than the gardens planted above it, much older than anything found on this island. It was inarguably the widest expanse of petroglyphs any of the University people had ever seen, and the symbols were so unusual, so many new ones to study, completely different from anything previously found anywhere in the island chain. This was a legend uncovered, an unimagined chapter of history predating history, buried long ago and forgotten by other Hawaiians in other times.

By the end of the day, the circus had come back to town, bigger and better than ever. The developer himself, Mr. Johnson's boss, came down to the site in person and even he took off his shoes to walk out and touch the carvings in the rock. As he passed by he looked down into the foundation of his hotel and saw a tiny reflection of himself in the water at the bottom. Maybe he thought about how fleeting the reflection in the water was, compared to the one in stone.

The TV cameras showed him speaking to an interviewer about working together with the community towards whatever end was most beneficial to the citizens of yesterday, today and tomorrow. The news analysts said that meant he had great plans for a museum, a cultural park and a study center, and they showed the whole site on TV, with all the muddy people and the mysterious civilization under their feet like ancient newspapers. The fishing club, happily at home watching TV together, cheered.

The cameras did not show a moment later, when the developer took a cigar out of his pocket and walked over to a remnant of rock wall to put his shoes back on, where sat an old bent man, poking into the ground with an oʻo stick. The developer was feeling very historical, very proud and male, as if he himself alone was responsible for this incredible discovery. When he sat on the wall, the old man asked, "What have you found here today?"

The developer pointed with his cigar and crowed, "This is the most significant archaeological find on this island, ever." He waved one hand in the sun, and searched his pockets with the other. "I found the opportunity of a lifetime—a place in Hawaiian history!" He watched the old kahuna scratch the o'o on the ground. "And what have *you* found here?" he said.

"Zippo," he said. He snapped it open, and gave the man a light.

HAʻINA KA PUANA

Haʻina ʻia mai ana ka puana: "Tell the summary
refrain" [the introduction to the final stanza of
the hula chant, a way of saying "Now is the end
of my song"]
— Pukui and Elbert, *Hawaiian Dictionary*

We were three thousand miles from Hawaiʻi that summer I first
heard Hawaiian music. We had never been there, had barely even
heard of it. This was, after all, not even seven years after
statehood. But there were Hawaiian records stacked on the floor in a
corner of our living room, and two plastic ti-leaf skirts in a clump on our
back porch. Whenever my brother Tim and I played catch in the yard, my
sister played cheerleader and used them for pompons. The California air
was hot and dry, and bougainvillea grew wild on the steep hillside behind
our house. My mother practiced arranging hibiscus in her hair. It was my
father's first summer in Vietnam.

Every Saturday Mom piled us four children into the Buick station
wagon with an efficiency and urgency that rivaled our Sunday morning
trips to Mass and clearly identified her as a military wife. At 8:45 sharp
we were off to the base Recreation Center, enrolled in all sorts of activities
with what seemed like every other military kid in the North County. In
the parking lot the kids tumbled out of cars driven by mothers with
determined faces. They were keeping us *busy,* keeping our young hands
and minds going, distracting us—they hoped—from any thought of our
fathers' absences. Swimming, archery, tennis: there were lots of things to
keep us busy. My youngest sister Catherine wailed away in the Kiddie
Room; she was just three and that's all she knew how to do. Andrea
floundered with ten other future ballerinas in the big room on the main
floor. My brother and I sprawled in the dust across the field, firing rifles.
Tim told me he pretended the targets were VC soldiers sneaking up on our
father. "You know," he'd say, his face squinting as he sighted his gun, "these
targets are just about the same size as a head." He became a good shot.

The wives' program was just as organized and just as tacitly
desperate. Throughout the sewing, painting, cooking, and dancing classes,

you could hear music, the clanking of pots and pans, and the continual rise and fall of women's voices in conversation.

My mother was in a hula class taught by a woman from Hawai'i. All the courses were taught by the wives themselves. They looked out for one another, as the wives of soldiers have always done. The hula teacher was Mrs. Inaba. "That's *koo-moo-hoo-la*," Mom corrected us once when we asked if she liked her teacher. "It means 'hula teacher.'"

"What kinda words is that?" I asked.

"Hawaiian words," she told me.

Tim said, "She don't talk American words?" He was suspicious; he told me later that he thought she looked like a VC.

Mrs. Inaba was a plump Japanese woman. I learned this the first time I spoke to her; she corrected me when I asked if she was Hawaiian. "Actually," she added, "I'm Okinawan." I suppose she was young. She looked much younger than my Mom, but I can't say for sure now. Back then all adults looked pretty much the same age—old—to me. She had longer hair than I'd ever seen on an adult lady, though. Usually it was tied up in a bun, but when she danced, she let it down. It fell almost to her waist. I tried to imagine my mother with hair that long.

I loved listening to Mrs. Inaba's voice; it was higher than any other mother's I knew, and I thought she talked funny—not just those Hawaiian words, either. I couldn't quite tell what it was that made her sound so different. The way her voice rose and fell, maybe, or the way she said "yeah" so often when she was talking, like she was asking a question even when she wasn't.

Mrs. Inaba's husband, like my father, was a Marine. They were both in Vietnam. I wondered if they knew each other. I hoped they did, because I was a little worried about this Sgt. Inaba. What if he looked like Mrs. Inaba? In Vietnam someone might think *he* was VC. Anything could happen over there. I didn't want to ever see Mrs. Inaba cry like I'd seen some of the kids at my school cry.

I never really thought of my mother as just another adult in a world of adults until I began to watch her in her hula lessons. Upstairs at the rec hall she was not in charge like at our house, but just one of fifteen women stumbling through "Sophisticated Hula" or "Lovely Hula Hands." Left arms up, right arms sweeping in an arc in front of them, palms open. Hips swaying like waves in a pool when a lot of kids are playing: no order, just continuous choppy movement. "Ladies, smile, yeah?" Mrs. Inaba would call over the music. And the ladies would smile, my mother too, hyper-real smiles, wide and bright. The air was filled with pretty music, the whishing of plastic grass, and feet slapping on the floor (they danced barefoot—I loved that). And if the women were lucky, they could forget for a while not where they were, but where their husbands were.

My mother borrowed a half dozen records from Mrs. Inaba, and my brother and I listened while she practiced at home alone. I loved to look at the pictures on the record covers of the women in flowery swimsuits or red grass skirts. They held the tiniest guitars I'd ever seen. The blurred background of a *Hawai'i Calls* record cover hinted at greener grass and trees than anything in California. I looked at the names of the songs, couldn't pronounce any of them, and tried instead the singers' names: "Kwee Lee . . . Koo-Eye Lee. . . ." I twisted the funny-looking names out of my mouth for my brother. "Well, at least I can say the names."

I sort of enjoyed watching Mom dance alone. She tried to sing along with the records, as Mrs. Inaba did. Her voice wasn't as high, and she sort of mumbled the words she didn't really know. Even so, without the rest of the mothers around her, I found myself not comparing her to the others. I just watched her; she seemed to me to move better, and her smile was more real.

On top of the TV set was a photo of my father. He'd sent it from Vietnam. Tipped back on his head was a big green helmet, and his hands rested on his hips. He wore a holster and a gun. He seemed to be grinning at my mother whenever she danced in our living room.

*　　*　　*

Mrs. Inaba came over to our house fairly often. She never wore her shoes inside; I could always tell she was there because her sneakers sat together neatly right beside our front door. I came into the living room one afternoon and found her talking on the sofa with my mother. Two cups sat on the coffee table alongside some strange-looking squares of food—I didn't know what—on dishes with Japanese designs. I said, "Hello . . . uh, I mean, 'aloha,'" and Mrs. Inaba smiled back at me.

"Mrs. Inaba and I are going to practice my hula," Mom told me. "And we don't want any interruptions." A recital was coming in a few weeks, and my mother wanted to do a good job.

"Can I watch? I won't make any trouble."

She said okay, and I sat cross-legged on the floor against the wall. Mrs. Inaba slid a record out of its cover and gave it to my mother. "This is a pretty song," Mom said. "I like to dance the part about the birds."

"I'll tell you how it was written," said Mrs. Inaba as she stood and moved to the center of the room. "Queen Kapi'olani wrote it as a love song for her husband, King Kalākaua, while he was on a trip to San Francisco. She wrote it to say how much she missed him." She was silent for a moment, looking at the photo of my father. "But he never heard the song," she finally continued. "He died in San Francisco before he could come home."

I'm sure that Mrs. Inaba and my mother were silent for only a few seconds; perhaps they weren't even thinking particularly about anything. My mother put the needle down on the record, and came to Mrs. Inaba's side: four hands, birds lifting themselves gently into the sky. The singer began. Then a brief glint of reflected light flitted like a shot across our living room: a car turning into our driveway. I rose to my knees, looked out the window. Olive green sedan, the Marine Corps emblem on the side. *For government use only*, it said in stark white letters beneath the anchor and globe. Two men in uniform were in the front seat. The passenger got out and squinted at the address beside our door.

"Mom."

My mother heard the pitch of my voice. She stopped dancing and looked through the window. "Oh, my God," she said as softly as the music in the background. Mrs. Inaba came beside her, saw the Marine in his crisp khaki uniform walking hesitantly to the door. She took my mother's hand and they did not move, even when the doorbell rang. My mother stood still for a moment longer, barefoot in pedal pushers and a flowery yellow blouse, then straightened her shoulders and squeezed Mrs. Inaba's hand. As she walked to the door I thought how graceful she looked, at last like a real dancer. She opened the door slowly, her face calm and her eyes strong: "Yes?"

The man had a boy's voice. "Sorry to bother you, ma'am." I could see the yellow paper he held in his right hand, and I knew what it was. "I'm looking for Bobolink Drive, but I can't seem to find it. Could you tell me where it is?"

My mother's bearing didn't change, but I could hear the breath escape from Mrs. Inaba. It reminded me that I, like her, had not been breathing. My mother said, "It's half a block down to your right." Her hand flowed smoothly, a slow-moving bird, as she pointed over his shoulder. "There's no street sign; that's why you missed it."

"Thank you, ma'am. Sorry to have bothered you. Good afternoon." The young Marine turned to go, the official telegram flapping a bit in the light breeze.

My mother closed the door. I had never seen her cry before. The music continued in the background. I couldn't understand the words, but the music soothed.

My mother came back to Mrs. Inaba and took her hand. Her voice was very shaky. She said, "Can we start over again?"

BY LEE A. TONOUCHI

WHERE TO PUT YOUR HANDS

Everytime I went my Grandma's house she always gave me da same lecture. Wuz Valentine's Day so I went fo' visit her drop off candy li'dat. Plus I had fo' drop off da orchid my Ma guys bought cuz her and Pa wuz going Pearl City Tavern fo' dinner. Usually my faddah no let me drive all way town side, but so long as I came back befo' dahk he sed can. Naturally Grandma wuz all happy fo' see me. I walked down da driveway waved both hands in da air and yelled "Grandma!" so she knew dat I wuz coming. She looked through da kitchen jalousies and she sed, "Is dat you, Aaron?" She opened da screen door and I dunno why but wen I handed her da stuffs her hands wuz acking all shakey ah. At first I tot maybe wuz cold, but actually wen I walked into da house wuz kinda hot. Ever since dey wen cut down da mango tree da house always come hot now. Today da house wuz supah stuffy too so I toll her I wuz going open some windows li'dat, but she sed, "No. Mo' bettah leave 'em close, bumbye people can see inside." I tot dat wuz strange cuz she always grumble wen we go my oddah Grandma's house dat their house no mo' air, but I nevah say noting. And da house wuz kinda quiet too today. Usually the TV stay on or my Grandpa stay listening to his Japanese radio station. Strange dat my Grandpa nevah say noting today too. Usually wen I come I yell "Hi Grandpa," too, but I tink he wuz sleeping cuz I nevah hear him yell "Eh, who dat come!?"

My Grandma tanked me fo' da candy and she toll me tell my Ma guys tanks too. She wanted me fo' hug her ah, but I nevah like. Embarrassing. I nevah hug her since small keed time. Feel weird hugging people. I dunno muss be a teenage guy ting I guess. Gotta be macho ah. So I jus did da fass kine pat pat on da shoulder. My Grandma axed me if I wanted to stay fo' dinner. I toll her "Okay, but I gotta eat early." I wuz kinda hoping she would offer cuz oddahwise I would have to go home cook myself one Tyson Turkey TV Dinner. Last time I wen cook dat my friend wen call and I forgot about 'em and came all ko-ge.

Anyway, soon as I came my Grandma wuz giving me da lecture about how I gotta fine one good kine wife who going take care me. Wife? I tot. Gee

Grandma, I gotta kinda get girlfriend first try like. She wuz all "Hakum you no mo' date tonight." "Cuz Grandma, I gotta fine da right girl. I no like choose any kine girl you know." Das wot I sed, but da troot wuz, I wuz too sked most of da time fo' talk to girls.

Since Intermediate School time I wuz sked fo' talk to Joy. She wuz like my ideal. Since Intermediate I always had her in at least one class. I wuzn't sure wot she wuz really. Maybe little bit Japanese, Hawaiian, Filipino, and maybe little bit Haole too. Woteveah she wuz she looked full on Local. So Local dat fo' da second straight year she wuz May Day Queen. I dunno why but everytime I wanted fo' talk to her I got all nerjous. And I came all sweaty too. So I figured da bes way not fo' get all anxiety attack is jus not fo' talk to her. Joy wuz pretty smart. She always scored high on tests and stuff, but I wouldn't say she wuz a nerd or nothing. Cuz one pretty nerd is like one contradiction in terms ah. So mentally she wuz up there. And ho physically she wuz pretty uh . . . developed fo' one Sophomore. But you know wot wuz da one ting dat impressed me da most—she wuz always supah friendly. Even though me and her, we nevah had one conversation dat lasted mo' than couple minutes and not like we evah did anyting out-side of class, but she still always sed hi to me wen we passed by in between classes. And not jus "Hi" and pau, but da kine "Hi" and da wave. And not one quick wave too, but da kine wave within da wave where all her fingers stay up den slowly starting from da pinky dey go down until at last the index finger goes down and den she do 'em one mo' time. Take like tree times as long as one regular wave, her patented five-finger linger wave. Ees like she wanted fo' make sure dat everybody saw dat SHE wuz waving at ME.

My Grandma always sed, "Anykine girl you choose, me no like. Make sure you no marry popolo girl now. Grandpa no like blacks. And no can be Filipino. My friend son from Lanikila go marry Filipino; now they divorce. Only two months you know. And no can be Chinee. Remembah your Uncle Richard, look he marry Chinee and look she take all his money and go leave him fo' marry Haole man. Japanee maybe, but depen on da family."

My Grandma so choosy. Going be one miracle if I evah do fine da right girl. Usally wen my Grandma give me da lecture I jus zone li'dat until she pau. Sometimes I tink in my head—but not like everybody pure someting li'dat. Take Joy fo' example. She all kapakahi. Jus by looking you dunno wot she is. And not jus her ah, I mean plenny people hapa ah. So sometimes I felt like saying "Oh but Grandma, wot if she half Japanese, half Haole, and half Hawaiian?" I nevah like get into all the wot-if scenarios so wen my

Grandma wuz pau and went into da kitchen I decided fo' cruise in da living room watch little bit WWF wrestling. Sometimes my Grandpa watch WWF wit me cuz almost like his sumo. I wuz going ax him if he wanted fo' watch, but ah I figgah he sleeping ah. Plus, I wuz kinda zoning ah, not really into da matches. Usually my Grandma's girl lecture no boddah me, but today wuz Valentine's and I wuz hoping I wuz going get one in da mailbox wen I went home. I wuz kinda worried.

Cuz wuz jus dis pass week I went to da Leo Club dance in da school cafeteria and I wen dance mostly wit da girls who wen ax me. Eh, I not ugly k if das wot you tinking. Had some girls wen ax me. I remembah I wanted so bad fo' dance wit Joy. I nevah like ax her cuz I admit, I wuz too chicken. I remembah da cafe wuz so crowded. I wuz getting so hot. I couldn't figgah out how fo' stand so I jus stuck my hands in my pocket. Wuz getting mo' sweaty in there, but at least could wipe 'em off small kine.

I had my eye on Joy da whole night. I saw all da different guys she danced wit. I kept track of who she axed and who axed her. Not like I toll anybody I liked her ah, but cuz dey wuz invading my turf I had fo' put some of my friends on my doo doo list. I made da kine mental comparison fo' see wot all da guys she axed had in common fo' see if I had chance. Had chance. Everytime one song came on I sed K dis goin' be da one, but everytime had one fass song and me I like take tings slow ah so I jus waited. I missed some opportunities wen da slow songs came on and befo' I could make my move some oddah girl came up to me. Befo' I could even make my move. Das my cool way of saying I nevah get any moves fo' make. But I wuz learning, making 'em up as I went along. I learned wea da bess place fo' stand wuz. Not by da wall cuz in case get one chic you like avoid. Need room fo' maneuver ah. Not by da punch bowl, cuz mo' chance you might spill on top you li'-dat. Get all nerjous da hand start shakin' ah. Mo' worse you might spill on top her. In fack, James did dat and like da gentleman he wuz he offered fo' wipe 'em off her chess. Da stupid pervert. Da best place fo' stand wuz by all da Math club people cuz you can look good ah. Hey I pretty smaht you know. Some girls I could ax. I wuzn't dat chicken like some of my friends who made ME go ax fo' dem. "Oh, Carrie, James like you dance wit him. Nah c'mon, he really like you, you know. I promise he not going spill again. Aw c'mon. C'mon. C'mon. Pleeeeeeeeease. Shoots you going chance 'em den." See easy fo' beg wen you not axing fo' yourself. See I know all da secrets.

I no tink my Grandma would give her vote of approval for a lotta girls at dis dance. K, my Grandma would probably say dat Leslie is too fat. I mean I not da kine superficial kine guy dat I only judge by looks. Wot I saying is dat da girl gotta be healthy looking. Eh, I like my potential wife live long time ah. And take Charisse. She too skinny my Grandma would say. I can dig dat. I like curves. I tink my Grandma would like hips cuz gotta have plenny grandkids ah. My Grandma would probably like breasts too cuz mo' healthy ah fo' my kid if he get breast milk. Da mo' plenny he get da mo' bettah ah. I no dig doze artificial kine formulas. Gotta tink all natural. Noting beats da real deals dude. Joy would be perfeck if wuzn't fo' dat ethnicity ting. I mean mo' bettah ah if she all mix up anykine. Cuz like dogs fo' example, those pure bred kine, dey die young. But da kine poi dog, dey live long time ah. Ho, conflict now dis kine rules.

Maybe wuz only to my eyes ah cuz dey say beauty is in da eye of da beholder, but to me Joy wuz definitely a beauty to behold. Wuz almost twelve o'clock and wuz da lass dance of da night and had da Kool And The Gang song, "Cherish." Ho, of all da songs fo' pick, dat wuz my favorite song. Wuz kinda ol' already, but still I liked dat song. I could hear da sea gulls gulling. And my body started swaying side to side. I wuz all in la la land tinking of how perfeck would be jus me and her on da dance floor. Dis night would be da firs of many nights as tonight would be da night dat we would fall in love. As da chorus started playing I looked all ovah the room, looking, looking fo' Joy. She wuz gone. No tell me she went shi shi break. Not now. Wuz the lass song. No mo' songs aftah dis. No mo' songs tonight. No mo' songs evah. As I wuz getting all frantick, I started sweatin'. I could feel myself getting all hot. And wuzn't da kine good kine hot, but da kine nervous kine hot. Da kine hot dat dis going be one vital crossroads in my life kine hot. Da kine if I screw up tonight den I going be one geek fo' da ress of my life kine hot. Ass why I wen go jump outta my faddah's shoes wen somebody wen bump butts wit me from behind. Literally I wen jump ah cuz my faddah's shoes wuz big. I nevah get dress shoes li'dat. I wen go bend down fo' fix my shoes and as I wuz tying da laces somebody wen go bang into me. Wen I looked up, staring right at me, wuz Joy. She sed "Oh excuse me." And wen I stood up again, she smiled and sed "Hi." I couldn't tink of anyting fo' say back, so I just sed "Hi." But wuzn't da kine simple kine "Hi," but one extended, gradually fading "Hiiiiiiiii" extending da "i's" hopefully long enough fo' me to add on someting at da end but unfortunately befo' I could come up wit anyting witty or clever to say, I ran out of breath.

I remembah my Grandma sed dat wen she and Grandpa got together she wuz only nineteen. At first Grandpa's dad nevah like her, but aftah awhile he came to like her. Wen Grandpa's dad died Grandma wuz by his bed. She had fo' clean up his shi shi pan and stuff. He toll her tanks li'dat.

She sed "Remembah, befo' time you no like me remembah Otoosan?" He nodded weakly and sed "Befo' time me no likey, but now me likey" and he put his hand on her hand. The next day he jus nevah woke up. So I dunno why dey nevah like my Grandma. I tink someting about dey from different village back home or someting. I dunno, these ol'fashion people not so smaht I tink. Cuz c'mon, you gotta figgah if you only can marry people in your village den pretty soon everybody going be all related and you going get all mutant kine babies.

My Grandma called me over to eat. She axed me wea my mom guys went. I toll her dey went PCT. My mom liked da monkeys. Usually my Grandma's food wuz pretty good, but today fo' some reason nevah get taste, but I nevah say noting. Fo' long time wuz quiet. Den she wen ax me one weird question. She sed "Aftah you marry, wea you going buy house?" I toll her "Uh, Kahala Grandma. No worry I going fine one big mansion." Den she wuz silent. I dunno, my Grandma wuz acking all weird. She toll me dat wen I buy house, she no like me stay townside cuz too much crime. She sed she no like me stay country side cuz too abunai. So finally I toll her "Den wea you like me live Grandma? No mo' no place else fo' go. Mainland? Ass worse." Den all of a sudden I wuz confuse wen she toll me SHE wanted fo' move. But she cannot move, I tot. Dis house get memories. Wen I wuz a lee-dle boy, every weekend I used to go my Grandma's house cuz she used to babysit me. Until I wuz like twelve around. Her house wuz always pretty cool cuz had da big mango tree outside. I used to love dat mango tree. My Grandpa used to pick 'em wit his stick ting and pass 'em down to my Grandma who wen stick 'em in bucket. Every mango season we used to give all da neighbors. Sometimes people jus used to come by and ax for mangoes and my Grandma used to always give even if we nevah get dat much. Usually had plenny though. But da lass few years hardly had any and da few dat had people used to come and jus steal 'em li'dat. Had fo' pick 'em wen green cuz if we waited till wuz ripe would be gone. Lass year da tree had termite so dey wen chop 'em. Now she wanted fo' move. "Olaloa," she sed. She explained dat Olaloa stay Mililani side. Da suburbs? Olaloa supposed to be one gated community fo' old people or someting. There everybody look out fo' each oddah. More secure she sed. Mo' safe.

Wen Joy sed "Hi" to me wuz like major danger cuz dis wuz like new uncharted ground. Tings wuz easy wen me and Joy kept our distance. "Hi" from afar, never up close. Now we wuz talking in one social context. I cannot ax "Oh, you wen do your homework?" "You wen study fo' da test or wot?" "Wot's da chemical symbol for Krypton?" Somehow I knew we had a certain chemistry though. Could she possibly like me too? I mean I not da most good looking guy in da world ah. Maybe by relative comparison to da dorky Math guys around me, but definitely not da most good looking in da room. I mean I not da smahtest, well maybe top ten percent. But maybe cuz I funny. Plenny people say I funny.

"Huh?" I sed as I realized dat she wuz talking to me and I wuz tinking too much to myself again. "I was asking you if you wanted to dance?" Wow, so wuz like she wuz saving dis last dance fo' me? Das so sweet yeah. I mean who could turn down one line like dat? She wuz saving da lass dance fo' me. Meaning dat all da oddah guys she danced wit da whole evening befo' nevah really mattah. Michael Furoyama, Rommel Ofalsa, Ashley St. John, Langford Logan, Kyung Taek Kang, Brian Chong, Tyrell Gospodarec, Chad Maialoha, Matt Takamine, Eric Young two times, and Mr. Hirata all nevah mattah cuz while she wuz dancing wit all dem she wuz really only tinking about me. I dunno how long I took fo' answer but seemed like wuz, wuz, wuz one really long time. Dat whole night I dreamed of dancing wit Joy. But now I wuz having second tots. My hands wuz getting mo' sweaty now dat she wuz actually here. Pretty soon my pockets going get so wet going look like shi shi stain. Dis wuz like too fass fo' me. Me and her nevah even fass dance befo' and now I gotta make physical contact. Hands on hips? Hands on da arch of her back? Or would we go all da way, hands completely around? I had no idea wea fo' put my hands wit her. Wot if I danced too close? Wot if my sweaty palms got her dress all wet? Wot if I stepped on her feet? Wot if I screwed up so bad dat everybody wuz going talk about me. Da entire Sophomore class would probably gossip and make fun li'dat and razz me fo' da rest of my high school career. Wuz I ready, wuz I prepared to take such a big risk? Finally aftah much contemplation I toll Joy, "Uh, I no feel like dancin' . . . Uh, but you like talk? Maybe too noisy in here ah, uh . . . you like go outside talk story leedle while?"

Outside wuz kinda quiet. Maybe too quiet. I jus leaned against da wall and formed a smile wit my lips as I looked at her. She apologized for banging into me. I explained wuz cuz da shoes. Den had plenny silent moments and I nevah know wot fo' say so I jus started bobbing my head and smiling wit my lips hoping she would say someting. Soon. Da silence wuz broken wen all of a sudden, fo' no reason, she just started giggling. Mus be my shoes I tot? I toll my dad wuz too big fo' my feet and dis only wuz going be one cafe dance. I gave her my puzzled face and I axed why she wuz laughing. She sed she wuz tinking of da way I sed "hi" before. My "hi" sounded like a deflating balloon.

"Well das cause you knocked all da wind outta me," I sed.

"That's because I didn't see you."

"Why wuz you looking fo' me?"

"I almost didn't recognize you in your nice clothes."

"Why, you saying I usually dress all bummy?!"

"No, I like that Aloha shirt."

"Ah ees okay. Wuz on sale. Did you see James's Aloha shirt? His one is cool."

"Was it a blue shirt?"

"No, purple."

"Oh, I didn't look good."

"But . . . you always look good."

"Hah?"

"But you always *look good.*"

And she looked puzzled fo' like two seconds befo' she finally caught on. Den she laughed so hard dat she made one piggy noise. Wit dat she had me all laughing too and she covered her mouth and tings settled down fo' awhile and den we jus started full-on laughing togethers. Finally she calmed down and she offered me one compliment back, "And you're not so bad yourself."

"Why tanks, I've been saying my prayers and taking my vitamins."

"You mean like Hulk Hogan?"

"How you knew dat? You watch wrestling?"

"Yeah, why? Is there someting wrong?"

"Oh no, you're weeeeeeeird."

And we jus talked and talked fo' hours. About wrestling. About how funny I wuz. About how weird she wuz. About if she could make any other animal noises wen she wuz laughing. About all kines of stuffs. We jus talked and talked aftah dat and befo' I knew it we talked fo' like almost an hour already. My Ma and Pa wen buss me wen I got home. My first time taking out da car by myself and I break curfew. Pretty stupid ah. But wuz worth. She gave me her number dat night and I called her the next day and we talked fo' almost da whole day.

I dunno how I could have so much fo' say den, but noting fo' say now. My Grandma wuz showing me her brochure for Olaloa and all of a sudden she jus started crying. I started fo' put my arm around her, but nevah feel like wuz da right ting fo' do. I mean she should be telling my mom dis, not me. Not my place fo' say anyting. But I knew I needed fo' say someting so I sed, "No need go Olaloa Grandma. I come take care you." I dunno why I sed dat cuz not like I wuz ready fo' transfer school. What about Joy? And not like I can take care my Grandma. Not like I can cook. Not like I know how do laundry. I wen try one time and my fluorescent green T&C jacket came all Hypercolor. Not like I know how fo' do anyting. I jus got my license and

I no tink I can take my Grandma anyplace cuz townside I dunno da roads so good.

Aftah awhile my Grandma calmed down leedle bit. She toll me dat Grandpa wuz moving to a nursing home. Ho, I wen look in fass kine wen I came in, but he looked da same. I jus assumed he wuz sleeping as usual. My Grandpa had hod time walking ever since his stroke. My Grandma sed dat fo' da pass couple weeks he wuz having problems eating so dey might have to feed him from one tube so he probably gotta go Maunalani nursing home up Wilhelmina Rise.

Wuz quiet fo' kinda long den she sed "Tell your mom call me wen you get home k." I nodded. She looked like she felt kinda awkward and I guess I did too. Cuz not like I evah saw my Grandma cry befo'. Only once wen I wuz shmall and she wen go give me spankings den I wen go pass by her room and I saw her crying on da bed. Now I felt like crying too, but Grandpa wuz kinda sick fo' long time already so we all kinda knew dat he wusn't going get any bettah.

I jus sat there wit my hands closed together between my legs. Finally she sed, "You would come stay wit Grandma?" I nodded and she laughed. "You cannot take care Grandma. You still boy yet, you still going school." I wuz gonna argue dat I could transfer, but I knew she wuz right. She den changed da subject and axed me if I sent anyone a Valentine's. I toll her I jus sent out to one girl. She axed wot her name wuz. I toll her Joy. She den axed, "Wot her last name?" Den she gave me da lecture again. But midway thru she looked at me and stopped and she sed, "I guess nowdays cannot tell from lass name no?" I nodded and she continued "Maybe no make difference. So long as you fine good kine girl, naugh. So long she take care you, Grandma happy." Den she axed me how my dance wuz. I toll her how long I talked to Joy on da phone. Approximate kine. Around eight hours. Forty-tree minutes. And twenny two seconds. And I toll her how da firs ting I wuz going do wen I went home wuz check my mailbox. My Grandma sed "No rush go drive wen you go home now." Den she sed "Good you find girl. No fun wen you alone." Den it struck me. Wot if I wuz at da dance and no one axed me to dance. Wot if all da oddah guys in da Leo Club had da bubonic plague and I wuz da only guy in da room and Joy and all da oddah girls went lesbo and only danced wit each odder? Wot if no one cared for me den? Wot if no one cared for me ever? Wot a frightening tot it wuz fo' be all alone. I wanted say someting fo' stop my Grandma's watery eyes, but I came all teary eyed too as I wrapped my arms around her, hands clasped tightly.

BY PETER VAN DYKE

WORDSWORTH AND DR. WANG

he apartment block was one of those old two-story places you still see here and there in Waikīkī, with just 22 units altogether. The land it was built on must have been worth a fortune. All around were big, gleaming towers, and the Japanese were cruising the streets looking for real estate.

Dr. Wang owned the whole complex. He lived in No. 4, where he could watch out over the parking lot, the mailboxes, and the laundromat. The sign on the apartment door announced:

Herbert K. Wang
Doctor of Herbal Medicine, Ret.
No Soliciting

You could see him every day at the mailboxes just as the carrier finished delivering the mail. The mail carrier was a woman named Karen. Dr. Wang was more outgoing around her than around any of his tenants, even those of us who had been there for years.

"What did you bring me today?" he'd say, "not more bills, I hope."

"Looks like a lot of love letters," she'd reply. Karen got her job done, but she was willing to exchange pleasantries too.

Dr. Wang was a short old man, almost completely bald, with large liver spots on his head and a dark, fleshy mole just over his left eyebrow. He avoided eye contact. Even if he was right in the laundromat with somebody he'd known for years, he wouldn't say anything. He just pretended he was alone. He'd nod back if you forced him to, and he'd say a few things like "No change" or "Machine broken," but he kept the conversation to a minimum.

He was a man of letters. He communicated through the written word.

There were signs plastered all over the apartment building, all the usual ones: "Parking for Tenants Only," "No Soliciting," "Visitors Park

Outside"; and a few weird ones too: "No Loitering," "No Firearms," "Post No Bills," and "Beware of Dog."

This last one was unusual because dogs were forbidden by the lease agreement signed by all the tenants. Dr. Wang wasn't the kind to use a standard lease form, either. He wrote his own, and the rule against animals was especially stringent:

> Tenants shall neither keep nor allow on the premises any pet, animal, bird, reptile, amphibian, or insect. Nor shall tenants encourage wild birds or other wild or feral animals on the premises, including pigeons, cats, mongooses, or stray dogs. Violation shall be cause for immediate eviction, with tenant held responsible for treatment for fleas, mites, or other pests resultant thereof. Said animals shall immediately be surrendered to humane authorities and destroyed.

The lease was full of all sorts of unreasonable rules and regulations: No radios after 10 p.m., no overnight guests, no slippers left outside doors, no nails in the walls. We all broke those rules all the time, of course.

He wouldn't tell you to your face when he thought you were breaking the rules. He'd write notices and put them on the bulletin board in the laundry room:

> Residents were extremely disturbed last night by the raucous gathering at a second floor apartment between the hours of 9 p.m. and midnight.
>
> Remember that our sleep restores us, and makes us bright, active, and productive. You may be able to sleep during the morning hours, but duty calls the rest of us to be up and about with the sun.
>
> Rule No. 8 in the Rental Agreement clearly states that all noisemaking is to cease at 10 p.m.
>
> Repeated violations are grounds for eviction.
> > Respectfully,
> > Dr. Herbert K. Wang

Under the signature, someone wrote: "Wang Wanks His Weenie."

The parties went on for about five months before Dr. Wang had the tenants evicted. They were university students and they loved their reggae. Just before the eviction, Dr. Wang had one of his frequent letters to the editor printed in the local paper. Those of us who made a hobby of poring over his works—we called ourselves "Wangologists"—could tell that he was planning a move. This was the letter:

LOUD MUSIC MAKES POOR STUDENTS

What passes for study among modern youths looks more like moral dissipation to a member of the older generation. The brain is nurtured in quiet and harmonious peace. No Einstein can develop under the influence of the screeching, nerve-wracking "music" of the day, yet our modern students seem to spend most of the time with the stereo turned too loud.

We must take care of our bodies in every respect, in order to succeed in our studies. The ears must be protected from loudness. Regular hours of sleep must be maintained. When the body is healthy, the spirit is strong, and education can proceed.

Today's students seem to be insensitive to their community. The student's job is to study. It falls on the rest of us to work.

The university should take responsibility for its unruly members. Is discipline no longer practiced? Sometimes a harsh action is the best lesson.

Dr. Herbert K. Wang

There was little doubt among the Wangologists as to what the letter meant, and sure enough, just two weeks later, the reggae beat was stilled.

Those students were not the only ones to rate a mention in one of Dr. Wang's letters to the editor. Many of us had our turn. Marsha Yost inspired a letter. Newly divorced from a military man, she had moved from base housing to the Waikiki Sea Villa apartments, as our place was called.

YOUNG LOVE NEED THOUGHT

We are all swept away by young love at some juncture in our lives. Who has not looked at a starry-eyed lover and wanted to say, "Yes! I will!"

But when it comes to love, we would do better to look before we leap. Too many young marriages break asunder these days. Too many happy couples flounder on the rocks of dismay.

The real tragedy visits the little ones, the fruits of the ill-begotten love. I have seen many examples in my life of children of a broken home. There is no strong man about the house to call "Daddy." There is nothing to counterbalance the kindly, forgiving love of the mother. The child may take advantage of this situation and grow up without a proper sense of respect for his elders.

Young people of Hawaii, think before you say "I do." Our children are our most precious heritage, and let's give them a good start in life!

Dr. Herbert K. Wang

Marsha told us that the boy had started calling Dr. Wang "Dr. Doo-Doo-Head" in the last few weeks, in spite of the "good licking" she administered every time he said it.

Marsha got into more trouble with Dr. Wang over her boyfriend, Roy. Like everyone, Roy had trouble finding a parking place, and when he stopped in for a quick visit, sometimes he took a chance and parked in an empty space in the parking lot. After all, Marsha's place was on the ground floor, so they could just jump up and move the car if the person who had the stall came back. He was parking in Chong Be's place anyway, and Chong Be worked all day for Duty Free at the airport.

One day we heard Roy shouting and cursing in the parking lot, and we knew Dr. Wang had done it again. There was a notice pasted on the tinted window on the driver's side of Roy's El Camino. It read:

WARNING: This car is parked illegally. The parking lot reserved for tenants only. Visitors must park on the street. If you park here again, you will be towed immediately.

The Management

Roy was angry and he let everybody know it, but that was the last time he parked in the parking lot. You needed a razor blade to get those notices of Dr. Wang's off your car window.

Dr. Wang always seemed to get his way, in spite of his curious methods of enforcing the regulations. After all, he was the landlord.

Then one day in January, a crumpled notice in an unknown hand appeared tacked to the laundromat bulletin board. It certainly wasn't the work of any of the tenants, and Roy would never resort to the written word. The whole note was in capital letters, and there were stray ink marks here and there. The paper had been wadded and unfolded and pressed by hand before it was tacked to the board. It read:

> GODDAM YOU AGENTS OF THE RED CHINESE GOVERNMENT ARE TAKING OVER THIS CITY THEY ARE CAPTURING THE MINDS OF THE PEOPLE BY THEIR INSIDIOUS PROPAGANDA. YOU CAN HEAR IT IS BROADCAST LATE AT NIGHT WHEN YOU ARE ASLEEP. THEY ARE AGENTS OF SATAN AND ENEMIES OF DEMOCRACY. IT IS TOO WARM HERE SO YOU CAN'T WAKE UP AND CATCH THEM ONLY THE PEOPLE WHO SLEEP OUTSIDE ARE FREE.

It didn't take an expert to figure out that whoever wrote this probably did sleep outside. Waikīkī has its share of street people.

The note stayed on the board for three days amidst the lists of rules related to the laundromat, homilies, clippings of Dr. Wang's letters to the editor, and a few desultory want ads put up by the tenants.

When Dr. Wang saw the note, he read it carefully, and then removed it and carried it between his thumb and forefinger to the trash can by the Coke machine. He washed his hands in the laundry sink before he left.

That afternoon, the author of the note showed up. He came through the parking lot pushing an empty shopping cart. He parked the cart by the laundromat door, went in, and used the sink. He washed his hands and ran the water all over his head. When he was finished, he pushed his tangled gray hair back and ran his fingers through it a few times, and then shook his head so violently that drops of water flew over the folding table halfway across the room.

He walked to the bulletin board and stared. He muttered, closed his eyes, and wagged his head back and forth, and then looked again. He cursed. For the next few minutes he stared intently at Dr. Wang's notices and letters.

As he read them, he erupted in scornful laughter from time to time. When he was finished, he walked away, and as he left, he stopped at the trash for a routine inspection. After digging down a bit, he uncovered his note, and he immediately lost interest in the remaining contents of the trash can. He walked out of the room reading his note. He folded it carefully and put it in his pocket before he pushed off with the shopping cart.

We called him Wordsworth, after the poet. It was just a name somebody came up with, but it stuck. He was a big Caucasian man. One eye looked off to the left and half his teeth were missing. He never wore shoes and his bare feet were encrusted with grime.

The next day, he was back. He posted another note. This note was a little fresher looking.

> I HAVE TALKED TO GOD DIRECTLY ON THE RADIO AT KAPIOLANI PARK. HE IS VERY ANGRY, HE SAID HE WAS GOING TO SEND THE PEOPLE TO HELL, TO BURN THERE BECAUSE THEY REFUSED HIM AND THEY WOULD NOT ACCEPT HIS WARNING. HE IS GOING TO LET THE DEVIL HAVE HIS WAY WITH THEM. THERE IS A MAN IN PUYALLUP WASHINGTON WHO WILL TELL YOU ABOUT THE RADIO WAVES THAT ARE FILLING THE AIR RIGHT NOW WITH COMMUNIST MESSAGES. THEY ARE GOING TO UNDO EVERYTHING AMERICA STANDS FOR. I KNOW BECAUSE WE TRAVELED TOGETHER FOR 6 MOS.

This letter was posted for no more than an hour when Dr. Wang appeared to empty the change machine. He treated this note with the same contempt he had shown the earlier one. This time, however, immediately after disposing the message, he went to his apartment and hammered out a reply, which he stapled neatly on the board in the laundromat.

TO WHOM IT MAY CONCERN:

> This board is to be used for approved notices only. A person or persons wanting to post notices must obtain permission of the apartment manager before posting them. This is not a public forum. Go to the "Free Speech" areas of the university if that's what you want.
>
> These facilities are for the use of persons doing their laundry only. Other individuals are asked to leave the premises immediately.
>
> Dr. Herbert K. Wang

Wordsworth was back the next afternoon for a wash-up. He went to the board and studied Dr. Wang's latest pronouncement. After a few derisory snorting noises, he addressed the notice board with an emphatic, shaking, raised middle finger. He held his posture for several minutes; at the same time, he clenched his teeth and uttered a strained growl. He seemed ready to explode into violence, but before he did, small Jack Wray, the only witness to this display, slipped out the side door and retreated to his apartment.

The next morning was remembered in the annals of the conflict as "The Morning of the 'Fuck You' Notes." To compare the litter of notes in the parking lot with snow would be an exaggeration, but nevertheless, the comparison was made more than once. What seemed to be flakes were torn-up deposit envelopes from the automatic tellers of several banks in Waikīkī. On every bit of paper, in angry capitals:

FUCK YOU!

It was a work of prodigious madness. Dr. Wang was out sweeping up for hours, and for days afterward we found the odd notes here and there in the corners: FUCK YOU!

Dr. Wang responded carefully. He strengthened his basic sign collection with the strategic addition of a dozen or so "No Trespassing" and "Tenants Only" signs. We waited for the next move.

Wordsworth was around the parking lot more and more. He found a shady spot to slump against the laundromat wall for an afternoon nap. When he wanted sun, he took to sitting on the chain that separated one side of the lot from the street, humming an odd, mad tune so that the pedestrians on the sidewalk skirted wide around his spot.

The police showed up frequently. Usually when they pulled in and conferred with Dr. Wang, Wordsworth was nowhere to be seen. Once or twice they talked to him, but he paid no attention to their threats.

Four days after The Morning of the "Fuck You" Notes, Dr. Wang posted a new letter in the laundromat:

TO WHOM IT MAY CONCERN:

A certain unpleasant man has taken up residence in our common area. At first, I did not force him to leave, for I believe that charity and kindness of one human being to another is dear to the human spirit. I tried to walk in the footsteps of Lao-Tse and Jesus, who advise us to love one another.

But this man does not deserve our love and charity, for he has shown his true character through acts of vandalism and violence. He has shown that he has no respect for the principles of private property which are guaranteed in our Constitution. His "letters" talk of God and American values, but his actions speak otherwise. Love is not returned upon the man who would take your charity and spit in your face.

So, a word to the wise is sufficient. If you see this man, tell him to leave immediately. If he will not obey, please call the police (911).

Dr. Herbert K. Wang

For several days, an uneasy peace prevailed. Wordsworth was somewhat less in evidence, and Dr. Wang's letter remained unmolested on the notice board until some third party added, just below the signature:

Wang's brain needs liposuction.

A little later, in another hand, this was added:

What about Wang's butt?

It was difficult to see the justice in this last remark as Dr. Wang was a skinny old gentleman who had no backside at all apparent within his trousers.

Then one early morning we awoke to the sound of hammering. Wordsworth was tacking his rebuttal to the laundromat door.

The rebuttal was in the form of a list. There were gouge marks in the door from the chunk of concrete Wordsworth had used as a hammer.

1. WHAT IS THE MATTER WITH YOU? AREN'T YOU AWAKE? THIS MAN IS THE ENEMY!
2. GOD HAS SAID THAT HE WILL STRIKE DOWN THE RICH SINNERS. WHEN ARE YOU GOING TO WISE UP?
3. I PAID MY TAXES EVERY YEAR THROUGH 1971.
4. THE RADIO WAVES HURT MY HEAD.
5. I HATE IT HERE.
6. HOW CAN HE TALK ABOUT CHARITY? WHAT DOES THAT COMMUNIST KNOW ABOUT CHARITY?
7. I THOUGHT THE PEOPLE IN HAWAII WERE SUPPOSED TO HAVE SOME ALOHA.

8. WATER IS FREE. AIR IS FREE. HOW CAN I STAY CLEAN IF HE WON'T LET ME USE THE WATER?
9. THERE ARE A LOT OF EVIL PEOPLE IN THIS WORLD.
10. WHY DO THEY LET THOSE PIGEONS FLY AROUND AND SHIT ON EVERYTHING? WE COULD EAT PIGEONS.
11. I AM A PERSONAL FRIEND OF THE GOVERNOR OF THIS STATE. HE IS GOING TO DECLARE THIS APARTMENT BUILDING CONDEMNED AND MAKE IT INTO A SHELTER FOR THE HOMELESS.

The police came a couple of hours later and Dr. Wang showed them the list and the marks on the door. In the evening, he posted a triumphant notice:

VANDAL ARRESTED

The police arrested the vandal who harmed our laundromat door. He is the same man who has been disturbing the peace here for the last few days. We owe a sincere debt of gratitude to the officers of the law.

Dr. Herbert K. Wang

However, Dr. Wang's triumph was short-lived. Two days later, Wordsworth was back in the parking lot.

There began a running battle. Every day one side or the other posted some new diatribe. Dr. Wang's, of course, were neatly typed and tacked up in the corner of the bulletin board that he reserved for his regular pronouncements. Wordsworth's, on the other hand, were scrawled everywhere: on the walls, over Dr. Wang's notices, on scraps of paper strewn here and there, stuck under windshield wipers, and stuffed into mailboxes.

It was like a battle between two well-matched boxers. Each delivered damaging blows, but neither flagged. Dr. Wang fought with precision and artistry, Wordsworth with zeal and energy. Their respective themes never changed: Dr. Wang insisted on the rule of law and the rights of property; Wordsworth reiterated his mystical revelations of God and the Communists.

Then after two weeks, Dr. Wang had another letter published in the newspaper:

HOMELESS PROBLEM AND THE LAW

There is a scourge upon the land. It is called the "homeless problem." Perhaps you have seen them on your street.

The police are powerless to act. Government cannot put its foot down. Property owners must stand by and see their constitutional rights trampled by this vocal minority.

Why are we supporting these freeloaders when there are "Help Wanted" signs in every store window? Perhaps in our compassion we have gone too far, for is it not more compassionate to teach a man to fish than to give him a fish dinner?

Are certain people above the law? There is a law on the books in every community that states very clearly that you cannot sleep outdoors. If I were to rob a bank, I would be arrested. Why aren't these people recognized for what they are, common criminals?

I hope that our leaders will come to their senses before it is too late. We must act swiftly and sternly, with gentle wisdom, to end this "scourge upon the land."

Dr. Herbert K. Wang

With the publication of this letter, the conflict entered its final phase.

Two days after the letter was published, Dr. Wang posted it in the laundromat. Wordsworth spent that afternoon sulking under the corner folding table.

By 4:30, Marsha's wash was done, and she went to the corner table to sort and fold. She set to work methodically, without ever having noticed Wordsworth right at her feet.

Wordsworth moaned, but Marsha took it for the sound of an out-of-balance washer in the row right behind her. Then Wordsworth flailed his arms about mindlessly. He was probably as unaware of Marsha as she was of him.

One of his hands came to rest against Marsha's ankle. A rough, wrinkled, battered hand against an ankle smooth and slightly plump. Marsha screamed.

She backed up in horror and shouted, "What the fuck are you doing down there?"

Wordsworth stared at her, but did not reply.

"I'm getting Wang, you creepy old bum." Marsha rushed out of the laundromat.

Minutes later, she came back. Dr. Wang followed her to the corner table. He was shaking. "Get out. Out, Goddamn you. This is for tenants only," he said.

Wordsworth struggled to get out from under the table, knocking it hard with his head and elbows several times in the process. As he emerged, Dr. Wang backed away. "I'm warning you. I'll call the police."

Marsha retreated behind the Coke machine. Wordsworth moved toward Dr. Wang with his fists clenched. Jack Wray's afternoon paper was on a chair between them, and when Wordsworth saw it, he picked it up and threatened to beat Dr. Wang with it like a dog.

Dr. Wang stood his ground for a few seconds, and then broke and ran, with Wordsworth close behind. "I'll get you," Wordsworth shouted as they ran across the parking lot. "I'll get you, old man."

Dr. Wang barely made his apartment in time, but when the door was shut, Wordsworth gave up the chase, tossed down the paper, and walked away laughing.

An hour later, Dr. Wang left the apartment complex in his car. When he returned, he was not alone. In the car with him was a German shepherd.

It was hard to sleep that night. Just after midnight, somebody's car alarm went off on the Ala Wai across from the apartments, and wouldn't shut down for an hour. Then Roy and Marsha had an argument that didn't quiet down until Roy finally slammed the front door and stomped off into the night.

The next morning there were no clouds anywhere, not even over the mountains, and there wasn't enough breeze to move the coconut leaves. Sensible people were getting ready to go to the beach. The Wangologists, however, were gathering in the laundromat, one by one, each drawn independently by a sense of impending crisis.

The morning hours ticked by and there was no sign of either Dr. Wang or Wordsworth. By 11:30 we were tired of waiting. Jack Wray said he was going to give up and go to the bank. His laundry was long since dried and folded.

We heard a rattling noise, like the sound of Wordsworth's shopping cart. Marsha looked out. "It's just Karen with the mail," she said.

There was more rattling, and Marsha looked again. "It's him," she said. Wordsworth was cutting across the lot, right in front of Dr. Wang's apartment. He leaned heavily on his cart and stared at his feet as he walked.

Dr. Wang's door cracked open and the brown shape of the dog emerged. He stopped and stared at Wordsworth and his cart, then flew out after him, barking furiously.

Wordsworth was slow to react. At first he tried to push his cart before him as he ran; then he abandoned the cart and started for the laundromat. The dog was all over him, barking and snarling, jumping as high as his shoulders. Wordsworth seemed to see us staring at him from the laundromat, and he swerved away. He went back to the hall where the mailboxes were, disappearing from our view behind the mock orange bushes between the parking lot and the walkway.

We were all afraid of the dog except for Jack. He was the one who went out and saw what happened.

When Jack got around the hedges to the mailboxes, he saw Dr. Wang struggling to get a leash clipped onto the dog's collar. The dog meanwhile had his jaws locked around one of Karen's muscular calves. Wordsworth had escaped.

Karen needed thirty stitches in her leg. Mail service to the apartments was suspended for a week until Dr. Wang finally took the dog back to the pound. We all had to go to the branch office to pick up our mail.

Wordsworth never showed up at the apartments again, although from time to time, people saw him around Waikīkī.

Karen was taken off our route, and the new mailman was old and taciturn, and predisposed to dislike Dr. Wang. It must have taken some of the pleasure out of Dr. Wang's life; he stopped posting notices in the laundromat all the time, and it was a full five months before he had another letter to the editor published:

MAIL CARRIERS DESERVE OUR PRAISE

The mail must get through. We owe a real debt of gratitude to the people who carry out this solemn oath, for our whole democratic system relies on the U.S. Mails. These men and women serve us without thanks or recognition for a job well done. They face real dangers, even in Hawaii, where our gentle climate spares us of the sleet and snow that plague the Mainland states.

The dangers here are of a human variety, in the person of the common street criminal. Their motive may be robbery, or merely vicious assault, or the mail carrier may be innocently caught in a crime in progress. The result is just as deadly.

These troubling times call for tough measures. Maybe our postal workers should be armed. Wouldn't we all sleep a little better knowing our friends were well protected on their daily rounds? I know I would.

Dr. Herbert K. Wang

HELPER

1998, oil on illustration board

BY JOHN WYTHE WHITE

UNSTILL LIFE WITH MANGOS

I

One morning, reading the paper, she hears a mango fall. An abrupt snap of release, a rustling descent through thick leaves, a thud that sounds too heavy, a bounce, a settling in the underbrush. She walks outside to fetch it. The sun on her face feels strong for so early in the day. The ground is already warm.

Yellow and orange fruit, bright as flame. Before now, she has seen them only in Mexico, much smaller. This one's as big as a softball but oddly shaped, a roundness radiating from a flattened axis, "oblong" too ordinary a word for such an eccentric variation. Spheroid? Ellipsoid? Ovoid? It looks like a swollen comma.

A thick drop of sap oozes from the broken stem, leaving a shiny trail on the skin, sticky on her fingertips. Up in the tree is a spectacle of mass ripening, mangos in every phase of change, like maple leaves in autumn, turning from dark green to crimson to orange to bananaskin yellow. She remembers a maple tree a few blocks away from her childhood home. Whenever she mentions it, nobody believes her. No one can conceive of a maple tree in Los Angeles, an autumn in Southern California.

Mosquitoes attack her ankles, sending her back inside. Fortunately Hawaiian mosquitoes are small, leaving minor bites that stop itching after a few minutes. Their California counterparts raised lumps she would scratch for hours.

In the kitchen she rinses off the dirt, peels the skin and eats the orange fruit down to the seed like corn off a cob, rotating it while chewing, leaning over the sink, juice dripping from her chin and fingers. It is the most accommodating fruit she has ever eaten, with no major obstacles on the path to gratification. Easy to peel, no fibers to pull off, no pulp or seeds to spit out, nothing to pick from between her teeth, only juicy, creamy fruit, sweeter than the ripest peach or plum.

She closes her hand over the flat-sided seed, template for the fully mature shape, the maximum swelling of flesh. This is the seed of the fruit from the tree in the yard of the cottage she lucked into, a complete but tiny house, further dwarfed by the mango tree, its branches partially covering one side of the roof. A bonsai house, well-kept, where she will remain in her recently-reduced circumstances as long as the landlord allows. Forty-two, divorced, childless, adjusting to solitude, her old life has been cut away, all the people and places, and a new one grows from what's left. She knows it will not be the same, but she doesn't know how it's going to be different.

Her first mango, and one is all it takes. The rash appears within twenty-four hours, on the soft undersides of her wrists. Lumpy, unbearably itchy, it reminds her of poison oak—a curse she thought she'd left behind. Scratching makes it worse, possibly even spreads it, but not scratching is unthinkable. When it comes to poison oak (and whatever she's picked up now), she has no self control and wants none.

It crawls up her forearms. Before she wises up it's in the hollows of her ankles where she scratched the mosquito bites, and on her neck and forehead. On hot nights it spreads down her thighs in a red wave of swollen, sweating flesh. The itching leaves her sleepless and cranky. At work she is unable to concentrate. With people, impatient and distracted. Alone at home, sorry for her miserable self.

She suffers for a week while the poison runs its course. In feverish darkness, she ponders her complicity in visiting such a plague on her body. If there are no accidents, which she believes is true at some level of consciousness, then why did she do this to herself? If there is a God, then what sin has she committed to deserve such a punishment? Is this a down payment on the price of paradise?

Unlike the apple of Eden, the mango of Kaimukī presents an opportunity to keep on sinning long after the last bite has been consumed. The mango's deepest, most irresistible temptation is not to eat but to scratch. Without hesitation she will yield. For a minute's relief in the here and now, she will willingly trade hours of future torment. She scratches her skin until it bleeds.

In the yard, mangos fall. Three or four a day, more overnight. She leaves them all to rot. She walks among her fallen, decaying crop, savoring her obstinate refusal to harvest. The air is black with fruit flies. Cockroaches the size of toy cars join worms and beetles at the sweet feast. Up in the trees, birds raise a ruckus while pecking holes in the ripening fruit. Over the fence, from her neighbors' yard, an ingenious apparatus appears and hovers in the branches, a long bamboo stalk with a wire-rimmed canvas pocket at the end, big enough to hold two or three mangos, designed to pluck them before they fall and pull them away to more eager, most likely rash-immune, arms. Rape of the mangos. Sole eyewitness declines to notify authorities.

Raw, itchy, angry, she refuses to touch another mango. Coated with a flaking crust of calamine and scabrous flesh, she stays inside. She has not been expelled from the garden, she's boycotting it. She's on strike against God.

II

A year later she's back on the job, this time with a better attitude. Armed with information and the proper tools. She has questioned her neighbors and friends at work. Searched the Kaimukī Library. Queried the Net. Learned her lessons.

It turns out the mango *is* related to poison oak. The irony does not escape. The house she last lived in was at the edge of a wood she rarely entered for fear of poison oak. Inches off the trails, easy to spot but hard to avoid, it grew everywhere in Portola Valley, a dangerous bush proliferating beneath live oak and bay laurel trees for miles at a stretch.

Even if she managed to prevent the leaves from touching her skin, she would invariably pick up the oil from her clothing or the fur of her dog. She always had a run of the rash somewhere on her body, but she never learned to live with it. She heard that as Portola led his troops over the Santa Cruz mountains way back when, some burned the shrub in their campfires, inhaled the poison and died horrible deaths.

She learns that her tree is not a "Haden" or "Pirie" (two local favorites) but a hybrid which, by an act of genetic serendipity, produces fruit as desirable as that of either variety.

She figures it's the sap that gave her the rash, that she's not allergic to the leaves of the tree, the pollen from the flowers, or the skin or meat of the ripe fruit. Blisters did not bloom on her lips after she ate it. All she needs to do, she is certain, is avoid touching the sap.

Thus her outfit: tennis shoes, old blue jeans tucked into the tops of white athletic socks, heavy-duty rubber gloves pulled over the cuffs of a long-sleeved denim work shirt. Red bandanna rolled and worn as a sweat band around her forehead, exposed skin on face and neck covered with mosquito repellent, and a baseball cap.

Her tools: an aluminum ladder to get her up on the roof, where she has access to the upper branches of the tree, and a homemade mango-picker modeled after her neighbors' stealth grabber. Getting the bamboo was not easy. The commercial fishing-rod poles weren't long enough. She ended up cutting her own, a twelve-foot stalk, in a bamboo forest on Mount Tantalus, strictly legal, with a permit from the Forestry Division to show on demand.

She's outfitted, armed and ready to go.

The harvest never comes.

Mango trees are supposed to fruit between March and October, but on hers nothing happens. Months pass, red new leaves turn to green, flowers bloom and pollen dusts the air, but no buds show. She asks her neighbors, what's the problem? They say, it happens. You never know, sometimes a mango tree skips a year or two.

III

In year three, the early signs are favorable. In January, tiny green buds appear in the tree. She goes up on the roof to get a closer look. She can't imagine what she'll do with all these mangos. There must be hundreds of them.

Early in February, the trade winds rise. They blow day and night, pummeling her thin-walled house, relentlessly clanging the neighbors' wind chimes, flapping loose gates, rolling wayward trash cans down the street, jarring the local dog network into barking fits. One night, awake after a chaotic, wind-driven dream, she hears a small object hit the roof, roll down the slope and plunge into silence.

It's not until the next night, after hearing it repeated several times, that she realizes what's making the sound. The winds are blowing the budding mangos off the tree.

The next morning she sees them scattered all over the yard. Climbs to the roof and finds more in the rain gutter. Perfect, comma-shaped miniatures the size of golf balls. She is definitely losing her mangos. At this rate, she calculates with a rush of panic, they will soon be totally gone. She feels like a woman going bald.

In the same way she used to worry about her failed marriage, she wonders if it's her fault. Are the young mangos unable to withstand the winds because she didn't water the tree enough? Because she watered too much? Should she have, as one neighbor suggested, fed the tree some fertilizer? Is there some elixir she doesn't know about, available from an obscure garden supplier, that toughens up mango stems the way gelatin fortifies fingernails? Back in India, home of the mango, is some prayer or ritual act performed during a significant phase of the tree's annual cycle?

By day, in frustration, she rakes up the fallen embryos. At night she cringes at the terrible falling sounds. But she can't stop the process. The winds blow for weeks, and finally she concedes. This year there will be no harvest. And this year is her last chance.

Uncomfortable as a talker-to-plants, she decides to write the tree a letter. She composes it on the computer, then handwrites the final draft. It is an apology *(O mango, abundantly leafy yet fruitless, forgive me if I have inadvertently or neglectfully done you harm)*, a farewell *(For I am out of here, as the house has been sold and I have been notified to vacate the premises in sixty days)*, and a warning *(I gravely urge you to prepare for a shock far worse than the still-gusting Cruel Winds of February. The landlord tells me that your new owners intend to prune you in a most extreme manner, reducing your farthest-reaching branches to mere stubs, sparing only your life, allowing you to grow back but never again to such house- and yard-dwarfing proportions.)*

She addresses the envelope "MANGO" and delivers the letter personally, affixing it to the tree's trunk with a push pin. She stores the stepladder under the house, rakes up the fallen buds a final time, and turns her attention from the tree.

She spends less time at home, leaving for work an hour earlier each morning to give herself free time for afternoon house-hunting. The effort is discouraging. She soon gives up looking only for a house with a mango tree in the yard, admits it's asking too much. But she stands firm on her refusal to live in a high-rise.

Weeks pass. A month before moving day, she is no closer to finding a new home. The winds fall. Calm is restored to the neighborhood and her dreams. On a sunny morning in mid-March, she hears a familiar sound. It can't be, but it sounds like a mango falling. She goes outside to check.

She finds the newly-fallen fruit among several others in various stages of consumption and decay. Above, the tree is filled with ripening mangos. How could this be happening? She watched this season's mangos die an early death. Are these new ones, or buds she failed to notice that escaped the winds? It doesn't matter. She has thirty days to reap the harvest.

IV

For the next month, mangos are her life. Gathering, processing and distribution take hours a day. Every morning before work, every evening before dinner, she's busy with mangos. She can't skip a day. There's gold in the yard, and she's compelled to mine it. Determined to make amends for prior neglect.

It becomes a ritual. First an Easter egg hunt in the yard, a search for the bright-colored treasures concealed in the bushy green mondo grass and under the walking lily. She carries two plastic supermarket bags, one for keepers, one for throwaways. As long as she stays on top of the situation, most are keepers.

The trick is to get to the mangos before other creatures do. Some are goners already, deeply bruised or split open on impact, perforated by birdbeaks, munched by insects, swarming with fruit flies. Some can be partially salvaged. At the height of the harvest she gathers a dozen mangos a day, just from the ground.

Up on the roof, it's a different drill: survey the tree, check on the crop, and selectively harvest. Walk along the diagonal rooftop, hand-picking the fruits, or netting them. She takes only the brightest-colored mangos, ripe and ready to fall, their stems easily broken with a quick tug. Some mornings she comes down the ladder with fifteen or sixteen mangos, the bag so heavy its handholds stretch like taffy.

Still in uniform, she sets up the home processing plant. First she washes the mangos in warm, soapy water and rubs them with a sponge to remove the hardened sap. Next she rinses them and allocates each to one of three dish drainers, sorting by degree of ripeness for later distribution to the refrigerator, paper grocery bags, or production line.

The production line is the fate of fruit that can't wait. She peels the skin and cuts most of the meat off with a knife, then takes the seed in both rubbery hands and squeezes the rest into a big bowl. She puts equal portions of slices and mash into sealable sandwich bags and transfers them to the freezer where, she has been assured, they will last for at least six months.

Every day, she eats what she can—mangos straight; sliced mangos with granola and milk; mangos blended into smoothies with banana, papaya, and yogurt. Still, she has hundreds more than she can ever use. Bagged by the dozen, she gives them away to neighbors, friends, people at work, the landlord, the new owners when they come by to see the house. In return, some bring her mango bread, mango jam, mango chutney, pickled mango, mango ice cream.

She keeps a mango count, enters it into her computer and views the data on pie charts and bar graphs. At the end of the harvest, she has collected four hundred forty mangos—an average of twenty mangos a day for a period of twenty-two days, not counting the throwaways, only two every three days. Her freezer is filled with orange baggies, room for nothing else. One shelf of her refrigerator is still occupied by ripening mangos, down from three at the peak of the harvest. Finally the tree is empty.

The night before she leaves, she writes a farewell letter:

Dear Mango:

I and others too numerous to name would like to thank you for your abundance. Your progeny were well received by all.

I have good news. The new owners, impressed by the quality of your fruit (as personally experienced) and the extent of your seasonal yield (as witnessed in my computer-assisted presentation), have decided to abandon their radical chainsaw agenda for your future. Instead, you will be trimmed only minimally, to bring your branches away from the roof and telephone lines.

I leave you in what I now believe to be good hands.
Aloha.

Her new home has no mango tree. What it has is litchi, avocado, kukui, and a big patch of banana plants.

BY CEDRIC YAMANAKA

BENNY'S BACHELOR CUISINE

enny" Akina and Denise Park met at a New Year's Eve cocktail party thrown at the luxurious Diamond Head beach house of Jules Reinnard. Monsieur Reinnard, of course, is the famous owner of Waikīkī's Silver Oyster Pub and Cafe. Benny Akina was a restaurant critic for *The Honolulu Advertiser*. Denise Park, one of Hawai'i's most respected chefs. Over spinach salads, crab cakes, fresh oysters and rigatoni, they talked about the weather, politics, sports and—the subject they shared the highest mutual interest—food. Great banquets, unforgettable dishes, secret recipes, and favorite restaurants.

A year later—after dozens of dinner dates and home-cooked meals—Benny Akina and Denise Park were married. Together, they were a happy couple. Gifted with looks, intelligence, grace, style, success, and youth. Life was as sweet and smooth as a perfect cabernet.

Three years later, they bought the Silver Oyster Pub and Cafe in Waikīkī. Jules Reinnard—after fifty-nine years in the restaurant business—retired. Benny handled the administrative affairs. Denise created amazing dishes in the kitchen. Lines formed outside the restaurant. The guest list included kings and queens, presidents, Hollywood stars, and champion athletes.

Two years later, Benny Akina and Denise Park finalized their divorce. Denise hired the finest attorney in town and got the houses, the cars, and the Silver Oyster Pub and Cafe. Benny got the shaft.

What had happened to this promising marriage? Benny asked himself the question hundreds of times.

Their union seemed to have been filled with love, respect, friendship. Denise always kept the house neat, made sure Benny's clothes were clean and pressed, prepared delicious meals. Benny brought home chocolates and dozens of long-stemmed roses, took Denise on long drives around the island on Sunday afternoons, politely endured the opera on public television with her—even though he wanted to watch Monday Night Football.

Perhaps, Benny thought, he was just not cut out for marriage. Had never been. He was a natural bachelor. And, basically, a slob. Leaving his bed unmade in the morning because at night, the sheets just got mixed up again. Leaving clothes on the floor because a shirt on a carpet was easier to find than one hanging in, say, a dark closet. Leaving his hair brush uncleaned for years until it resembled a sea anemone because hair just needed to be combed again and brushes, well, they just got dirty again.

Denise, on the other hand, was the opposite. She was a woman who liked neatness, order, and organization. Everything had its place. She arranged pots in her cupboard by size. Placed spices in alphabetical order. Made sure the television remote control was exactly perpendicular to the television set.

Maybe, thought Benny, little by little, it was these tiny differences that had disintegrated the real love Benny and Denise had shared. Like waves breaking on rocks, turning them gradually into sand.

One day—destitute and near penniless—Benny Akina walked down Beretania Street and came upon an empty shop with a "For Lease" sign taped to the window. That's when the idea hit him. A voice in the wind told him to open up a restaurant. A restaurant solely for bachelors. There must be millions of them out there, thought Benny. A place to make them feel at home. Or a place for married men to go so they, too—even for just a meal— could feel like a bachelor once again.

"What used to be here?" said Benny to the realtor.

"A dress shop," the realtor said.

"It's perfect," said Benny Akina. "I'll take it."

Thus, Benny's Bachelor Cuisine was created. The menu was enough to bring a tear to any bachelor's eye. Spam and rice. Campbell's Soup. Instant Saimin. An assortment of TV dinners. Bologna sandwiches. Vienna Sausage. Pretzels. Pork and beans, with the option to eat them straight out of the can.

And the decor. Pure bachelor gems. Laundry baskets. A weight bench. Ashtrays with coins and car keys inside. Various athletic equipment. Magazines like *Sports Illustrated*, *Popular Mechanics*, *Esquire*, an occasional *Playboy*. Black velvet glow-in-the-dark posters of panthers, dragsters, Elvis, and Bruce Lee hung on the walls.

On its first day of business, Benny's Bachelor Cuisine received no guests. Not a soul. The second day was no different. Alas, neither was the third day. Benny began wondering if he had made a terrible mistake. On the fourth day, a young man wearing a silk shirt, Angels Flight pants and Famolare shoes walked into the restaurant. He had perfect, blow dried hair. A gold tear drop around his neck. Benny thought he was seeing a ghost from the seventies.

"You look familiar," said Benny.

"You might have seen me in the movies," the ghost from the seventies said, sitting down at table five. "I was in *Saturday Night Fever*...."

"Of course," said Benny. "I should've known...."

"Remember when John Travolta wins the disco dance contest? I'm in the background, watching him do his thing. Second guy from the left...."

The ghost from the seventies became the first official customer of Benny's Bachelor Cuisine when he ordered the spaghetti with Ragu sauce. It was on the house.

Soon, word of mouth spread and Benny's Bachelor Cuisine flourished. Bachelors began gathering by the dozens. There were the young downtown professionals. Accountants, architects, and attorneys. Eating dinner before attacking Restaurant Row or Ward Centre. Thinking they ruled the world. Then there were the working class guys. Construction workers, stevedores, bus drivers. Enjoying a beer before heading off to a night of Hawaiian music. And then there were the older customers. Like the balding, sixty-year old doctor who wished more than anything he was a bachelor again. While his wife was at the symphony, he was driving his red BMW convertible up and down Keeaumoku Street, looking for the perfect Korean Bar.

"What's the secret to the success of Benny's Bachelor Cuisine?" a curious bachelor asked one day.

"I'm not quite sure," said Benny. "All I know is there's a lot of bachelors out there who are lonely. They need a place to go, a place to meet. And bachelors do get hungry...."

"But let's face it," the curious bachelor said, looking at his plate of canned chili. "The food here is kinda terrible...."

"That's part of the charm, I think. If folks want good food, they can go to thousands of other restaurants...."

Benny did it all. He bought the ingredients, prepared the food, served it, cleared the tables, washed dishes. Sometimes, he even played the role of psychiatrist. Take, for example, the case of the gloomy account executive who thought he'd never find a girl.

"Girls don't like me," the account executive said, staring despondently at his plate of canned sardines. "I'm too dorky...."

"You'll find a girl," Benny said. "In the meantime, enjoy the freedom of your bachelorhood. Think of it like, uh, like you're a caterpillar...."

"Caterpillars are worms, aren't they?"

"Have patience," said Benny. "And before you know it, you'll find the girl of your dreams and your life will be transformed. Like a caterpillar turning into a beautiful butterfly...."

"Bachelors are worms, huh?"

Sometimes, Benny performed the duty of social worker. Here is the dilemma of Ray, a fireman.

"I lost my girl," said Ray. "My life is over."

"Don't talk like that," said Benny. "There'll be others."

"Not like Suzanne," said Ray, a tear falling into his bowl of canned chunky stew.

"Sure there'll be," said Benny. "Trust me. I was married once. . . ."

Yes, bachelors gathered at Benny's Bachelor Cuisine and talked of fish that got away, waves that had been surfed, cars, deals, beers that had been drunk, and—of course—women.

"There's a girl with the best set of legs at work," said one bachelor. "When she uses the Xerox machine, I wait patiently behind her and tell her to take her time. . . ."

"There are too many wahines calling me up," complained another bachelor. "I can't get any sleep. As soon as I lie down, the phone rings. . . ."

"Listen to us," one brave bachelor finally said, standing up. "We sound like a bunch of kids in a high school locker room. Treating women like objects. Aren't you fellas ashamed of yourselves? Don't you all wanna get married? Have kids? Take on responsibility? Share your life with someone? Experience true love?"

The poor soul was booed louder than a BYU touchdown at Aloha Stadium.

As for Benny, he returned to the lifestyle he had once thrived upon before his unfortunate marriage. Sitting around the laundromat with other bachelors. Playing poker until the wee hours of the morning. Drinking a dozen different liquors in a dozen different places with a dozen different girls. Laughing, joking. While other less fortunate bachelors stood around dance floors like those statues on Easter Island, Benny Akina was the king of parties.

Secretly, though—very secretly—Benny often thought about Denise. Not only did he miss her venison, her rabbit, her souffles. He missed her. Her smile, her warmth, the way she filled an otherwise empty house.

One day—one magical day—the unthinkable occurred. The afternoon began like any other, feeding hungry bachelors.

"I'll have the hot dogs," a customer in Levis jeans said. "Three of them."

"Hot or cold?" said Benny.

"Don't ask stupid questions," the somewhat belligerent bachelor said. "Cold, of course. Right out of the refrigerator. How else do real bachelors eat hot dogs?"

"What's your special today?" another bachelor asked.

"We have a potato chip and beer combo," said Benny, somewhat proudly. After all, he had come up with the dish himself.

"Potato chips?" the discriminating bachelor said, rather disappointed. "That seems so, I don't know, boring...."

"Boring?" said Benny. "You call seventeen different kinds of potato chips boring?"

"Seventeen? No way. Get out of here...."

"Sour cream and onion, barbecue, cool ranch, extra crispy, low salt...."

All of a sudden—for the first time ever—a woman walked into Benny's Bachelor Cuisine. Jaws dropped. The insurance men turned off their calculators. Two crane operators stopped comparing tattoos. Dead silence. It was Denise Park.

"W-what are you doing here?" said Benny, not realizing he was walking backwards, moving away from Denise as if she was Frankenstein's monster.

"I'm hungry," said Denise, with a meek smile. "This is a restaurant. I'd like to order something to eat."

"C-can't you read the sign outside?" said Benny. "It says Benny's Bachelor Cuisine. You know what a b-bachelor is?"

"So?" said Denise. "Women can eat cold hot dogs and Spam and rice." She studied the menu. "The eggs simmered in Tabasco sauce sounds interesting. But let me give you a little tip. People are becoming a bit more health conscious. You should turn towards lighter, more healthier foods. That's what we're doing at the Silver Oyster Pub and Cafe. One of our most popular dishes is a linguine with asparagus and eggplant...."

"I'll have you know, Miss Smarty Pants, that our Vegetarian special is one of our most popular selections. Kim chee and rice. Dill pickle on the side...."

"May I sit down?" said Denise.

"Jeez," said Benny, throwing his hands up to the ceiling in despair. "Yeah. Sure. Go ahead."

"Thank you," said Denise, selecting table four. A popular window seat with a view of the health club across the street. Bachelors fought like rabid dogs to sit there and watch the aerobic instructors going home from work. "I think...." said Denise. "I think I'll have the Benny's Bachelor Cuisine Blue Plate Special. Cold, two-day old frozen pizza."

"Excellent choice," said stockbroker Hank.

"What did you really come here for?" said Benny.

"What do you mean?" said Denise.

"You didn't come here to eat two-day old pizza...."

"Doesn't the aging process bring out the flavor of the cheese?"

"Denise?"

"All right," said Denise, taking a deep breath. "I was worried about you. I missed you and I wanted to see you. Okay? Is there anything wrong with that?"

"I've missed you, too," said Benny.

"Oh, Benny," said Denise. "I miss rinsing your hair from the bathroom sink after you shave. I miss the way you squeeze toothpaste from the top of the tube, not the bottom. I miss the way you perspire after working out and still insist on lying on the couch without taking a shower. . . ."

"I've missed you, too," said Benny. "I miss the way you always complain about me leaving the toilet seat up. The way you arrange your CDs in alphabetical order. The way you insist on wiping your silverware before eating with it. . . ."

"Why did we fall apart?" said Denise.

"Maybe it's true what they say," said Benny. "Everything that's created is destined to fall apart."

"You think there's a chance that we could, uh, we could try again?" said Denise.

"Anything's possible," said Benny.

"Do you want to?" said Denise.

"Yes," said Benny. Then, "But what will happen to Benny's Bachelor Cuisine?"

"Leave it open," said Denise.

"Really?"

"Of course," said Denise. "There are a lot of bachelors out there who need a place to go to. A place to talk, share their triumphs, their sorrows. . . ."

"I love you Denise," said Benny.

"I love you, Benny."

And to this day, Benny Akina and Denise Park are together. Living in a three-bedroom house in ʻĀina Haina. Monday to Saturday, they work at their respective restaurants. Sundays, they spend together. Denise prepares a breakfast of waffles, eggs Benedict, and iced coffee. Like thousands of couples here in Hawaiʻi, they may go to the movies, spend the day at the beach, or stay at home with their two children.

Of course, there are still arguments every now and then. About Benny leaving crumbs in the carpet or dripping water on the bathroom floor after a shower. About Denise having to make sure the clocks in the house match the time given by the recording on the telephone. But both Benny Akina and Denise Park have learned that the love they have rediscovered is a precious gift that cannot be taken lightly, that these differences in personalities are what makes the world go around.

Yes, even for bachelors.

BY CEDRIC YAMANAKA

Oz Kalani, Personal Trainer

z Kalani was the kind of person who believed a life could be created, transformed, defined by a single moment. This was his.

Hawaii Five-O. Episode Number 21. "Aloha Means Goodbye." A pyromaniac extortionist threatens to set the entire island on fire unless he is given a priceless feather cape once worn by ancient ali'i, now under lock-and-key at the Bishop Museum. Remember that episode? There's the scene where a Lincoln Continental explodes on a Chinatown street. The extortionist guy ducks down an alley. Steve McGarrett, immaculate in dark suit and tie, gives chase.

"Which way did he go, bruddah?" McGarrett asks a young taxi driver.

"Dat way," says the young taxi driver, pointing towards Diamond Head. He is wearing a blue aloha shirt and a straw hat.

McGarrett, without another word, runs after the extortionist.

That young taxi driver was none other than the hero of our story, Oz Kalani. And *Hawaii Five-O*, Episode 21, was Oz Kalani's television debut.

"Dis is it, boys!" I remember an excited Oz Kalani saying the night the episode aired. We watched the show in the living room of his Kuhio Park Terrace one bedroom apartment. "Dis is Da One. . . ."

"Da what?" one of us asked, confused.

"Da One!" said Oz Kalani, wearing a puka shell necklace and Hang Ten t-shirt. "Da Big One!"

"Da Big What?" someone said, still confused.

That's when Oz Kalani leaned over and told us his philosophy on life.

"Lissen," he said, sighing and sounding slightly exasperated. "I going only say dis once. In every person's life, deah comes a moment wheah his life can change forevahs. One chance. Dis *Hawaii Five-O* ting, dis is it. My ticket out of heah. Oz Kalani is a new man."

Days after *Hawaii Five-O's* Episode 21 was aired, CBS Television and the Diamond Head studio where the show was taped were inundated with hundreds of telephone calls asking about the young taxi driver. Who was he? When would we see more of him? How, you may be asking yourself, would your humble narrator know the inner workings of a major television production? How would he know that producers and executives were barraged with dozens of questions about Oz Kalani? I know, dear friends, because I made the majority of these inquiries. At Oz's request.

"Eh, Oz!" someone said, that day me and several of Oz's closest friends worked the phones like a bunch of crazed telethon volunteers. "You can do me one favor, or what? You can get me Jack Lord's autograph?"

"Shoots," said Oz Kalani.

"And ask em how he keep his hair so nice. Da ting nevah get messy, you notice dat? And even when da ting get little bit messy, like if da wind blow em around, da buggah still look shaka. You notice dat? Kinda like Elvis. Oh, and ask em if I can borrow dat big, black Cadillac of his to drive around. I get one date with Sassy Nancy next week. Dat car would impress da pants off her. . . ."

"I see what I can do," said Oz Kalani.

Believe it or not, Oz Kalani's plan worked. He had created the illusion of public demand. He was asked to do another *Hawaii Five-O*. Episode 32. "Beretania Street is a One-Way Street, Ewa Bound." Oz Kalani is a down-on-his luck boxer looking for quick cash. He joins an Asian heroin ring led by the international criminal Wo Fat. You remember the menacing Wo Fat? Bald head, thin moustache. Wo Fat's first order to Oz is, indeed, an evil one. Place poisonous blowfish meat on the Governor's inaugural dinner plate. Oz's conscience, however, gets the best of him and he dutifully climbs the steps up to 'Iolani Palace and reports the vile scheme to McGarrett.

In the end, McGarrett and yes, Oz Kalani, capture Wo Fat at the old Oceania Floating Restaurant in Honolulu Harbor.

"I'll get you, McGarrett," says Wo Fat, perfectly sinister.

"Book em, Danno," says McGarrett, unruffled.

"Ho, awesome!" we said, once again watching the broadcast in the living room of Oz Kalani's Kuhio Park Terrace one bedroom apartment. We cheered and clapped and popped open a bottle of Cold Duck.

"Dis is Big," said Oz Kalani, flushed and triumphant. "Dis is Da Big One!"

"No forget us, when you famous, ah?" someone said, maybe me.

"No worry," said Oz Kalani, with a wink that was, somehow, both reassuring and confident at the same time. "I going buy one big mansion and we going sit by da pool, eat poke and drink beer. . . ."

"Legend," someone said.

"Giant," another said.

"King," still a third said.

Everyone wanted to be like Oz Kalani. Not just because he was on *Hawaii Five-O*. Ever since we were kids, growing up in Kalihi. Oz Kalani was one handsome buggah. Tall, square chin, white teeth, body tanned from years of surfing off Canoes and Kaisers, brown eyes sweet as chocolate covered macadamia nuts. But it wasn't simply because of his looks that everyone wanted to be like Oz Kalani. It was because of his drive, his desire. Unlike most of us, he knew exactly what he wanted to do with himself. He knew exactly where he wanted to go.

Let me make the record clear, ladies and gentlemen. Oz Kalani was no overnight success. Whatever triumphs life handed him, he earned through years of hard work, focus and dedication. We all saw it. Even in the very early days at Kapalama Elementary School.

While the rest of us in the fourth grade played kickball and rode skateboard at Uluwatus, Oz Kalani scripted a ghost story. One day, during class, he acted it out for us. I don't remember much about the performance except it was supposed to occur in a graveyard and once or twice, he turned off the lights and screamed. The lunch bell rang during Oz's play, I remember, but nobody moved from their seats. The ultimate compliment.

As the years went by, Oz nurtured his love for the stage. He played Brutus in a Farrington High School production of Shakespeare's *Julius Caesar*. Caesar was being played by our dork valedictorian and in the scene where Brutus stabs Caesar to death, everyone in the audience cheered and chanted Oz's name. "Oz-*zie!* Oz-*zie!* Oz-*zie!*"

At the University of Hawai'i, Oz Kalani was Tony in *West Side Story*. He was the Man of La Mancha, the King in *The King and I*, Jesus in *Jesus Christ Superstar*.

But it was television that excited Oz Kalani most, and one show in particular.

"I gotta get on *Hawaii Five-O*," he told me, one day.

That was one thing we had in common. We were both big fans of *Hawaii Five-O*. I still am. I've watched every episode, remembered all the plots, tracked the numerous guest appearances by local celebrities. I'm a walking *Hawaii Five-O* encyclopedia.

Anyway, Oz Kalani submitted dozens of photographs and cover letters to *Hawaii Five-O* executives and one glorious day, he was called in to do a reading. The rest, as they say, is history.

Now, after his first two *Hawaii Five-O* appearances, Oz Kalani's future looked as bright as the white shoes and polyester pants Steve McGarrett sometimes wore. Rumors about Oz were everywhere. The producers at *Hawaii Five-O* appreciated Oz Kalani's talent so much, they planned to offer him a role on the series as a regular. Right up there with Danno, Kono and Chin Ho.

"Da deal is dis," Oz confided. "Me and McGarrett, we going be partners. Like Batman and Robin. . . ."

Another rumor circulating around Kalihi revealed that some big time Hollywood producer vacationing on Maui saw Oz Kalani on *Hawaii Five-O* and wanted him to be the lead in a film biography about King Kamehameha the Great.

Oz Kalani hired himself a mainland agent. The agent got him a role as an extra when the *Brady Bunch* came to town. The agent also got him a cameo on *Charlie's Angels*, the two-parter when the girls visited the islands.

Now, if life was fair, Oz Kalani would have become famous, a household name, a star of stage and screen, a legend. You'd have seen him thanking God, his agent and his family at the Academy Awards, holding up the golden Oscar statue after winning Best Actor. You'd have seen his picture on the cover of *Time, Newsweek, Life, People, Esquire* and *Rolling Stone*. You'd have seen film clips of him on the news, walking hand-in-hand with beautiful starlets in exotic locations. In a tuxedo in Cannes. Climbing out of a limo in Hong Kong. Dining out in a trendy Manhattan bistro. You'd have seen him as the Grand Marshal of parades. You'd have seen him sing the Star Spangled Banner before the Super Bowl. You'd have seen his star on the Hollywood Walk of Fame.

If life was fair.

Alas, Oz Kalani was never asked to be a regular on *Hawaii Five-O*. He would not play Kamehameha on the big screen. And after awhile, the phone stopped ringing and the offers stopped coming. The letters and photographs he sent out in the mail returned unopened. The well appeared to be running dry.

"What happened to yoah agent?" someone asked.

"He trying," said Oz. "He say no worry."

Now, no one loved Oz Kalani more than Yours Truly. But I must confess to you that during this dark and frightening period in his life, Oz Kalani became a royal pain in the you-know-where. Take going to the movies, for example.

"You call dat acting?" I remember him whispering during a feature at the Cinerama one night. "I can do bettah dan dat clown. . . ." He memorized lines during the movie, leaned over to me and recited them. "How's dat? Good, ah? Bettah dan dat bastard, ah? Da buggah getting all kind awards. He one millionaire. Wahines all ovah da place. Jeez. . . ."

When we saw the *Godfather*, Oz Kalani said he could give shooting lessons to the Corleone family.

"But dey all gangsters," I said. "Dey awready know how shoot. . . ."

"You just no undahstand da acting business," said Oz, rolling his eyes.

During *Jaws*, Oz wanted to help Quint, Brodie and Hooper kill the great white shark.

"I come from a long line of fishermans," he said. "If I was on dat sorry ass boat, I'd shove my tree prong spear right into dat shark's eye. Dead meat, brah. . . ."

Oz wanted to be the first Hawaiian in space after watching *Star Wars* and *E.T.*

"Who's dis Dart Vadah clown?" said Oz Kalani. "You think he scare me? He's nothing. One panty. Half da boys at K.P.T. could knock him out. . . ."

And when we saw *Rocky*, Oz Kalani wanted to beef the Italian Stallion. "I can be da scrapping Hawaiian," he said. "I'd give dat bruddah dirty lickings. . . ."

Yes, sadly, Oz Kalani was becoming angry and disgruntled. But he had a point.

"Deah's no good scripts foah us local guys," he'd always say. "No good parts. You know dat. I know dat. My useless agent know dat. And you know why dat is? Because da big wig mainland executives, dey no care about Hawai'i. Dey come heah, go Waikīkī Beach and Pearl Harbor. But dey no really care about da Hawaiian peoples. . . ."

Sadly, Oz Kalani and I started drifting apart. I'm not sure why. It didn't happen in a day. It was a gradual thing. We just saw less and less of each other. Before I knew it, a year had passed. Then two. Then three. One day, I called his home. A recorded voice said she was sorry but I had reached a number that was vacant and no longer in service. I asked around. No one seemed to know what happened to Oz Kalani. It was as if he had disappeared from the face of the earth.

As for me, fate led me down the improbable path of Animal Medicine. I became, of all things, a veterinarian. One day, I treated a Doberman afflicted with bad breath. On top of my usual fee, the Doberman's grateful owner gave me a lifetime membership to the Ikaika Fitness Center.

I was not what you'd call a health freak. I readily admit I could have gotten a little more exercise, maybe trimmed a pound or two off the midsection. And while a number of friends and acquaintances had turned to tofu, stir fry and salads, I clung to old favorites like New York steaks, chili burgers and kalbi ribs. And while others warned me about the health risks,

I heartily enjoyed cups of strong coffee, a Chivas Regal after a particularly hard day, and an occasional Cuban cigar.

Still, I decided to check out the Ikaika Fitness Center and, yes, I was impressed. Heated pools, saunas, jacuzzis, racquetball courts, basketball courts, rows and rows of exercise bicycles and Stairmasters, dozens of fitness machines and free weights.

My first day there, I saw a beautiful girl in skintight leotards standing in front of a mirror curling tiny dumbbells, one in each hand.

"Very good, sweetie," said a huge guy next to her. Obviously an instructor. And then it hit me. The pecs were bigger, the quads more expansive, the biceps and triceps more defined but—of course—the instructor was none other than my dear, long-lost friend, Oz Kalani. But I had to be sure.

"Excuse me," I said, tapping the instructor on a massive and very hard shoulder.

"Just a second," he said, not turning around. "You wanna work out? Call me." He handed me a business card.

Oz Kalani, Personal Trainer

"Oz," I said. "It's me."

He turned around and when he finally realized who I was, his eyes opened real wide and he hugged me. After the girl's workout was finished, Oz invited me to the lounge on the first floor of the gym. The Ikaika Bar. I was looking forward to a beer. Oz Kalani ordered two zucchini and broccoli shakes. The guy gave it to him for free. That was no surprise. An autographed photograph of none other than Oz Kalani—pumped and smiling—hung on the wall, behind the cash register.

"Damn, it's good to see you," said Oz, as we sat on a terrace overlooking a jacuzzi. He sized up my body in that unique way guys who lift a lot of weights like to size up other people's bodies. "So, what you doing with yoah life now?"

"Me?" I said, touched by his interest, to be honest with you, "I'm a veterinarian."

"Oh yeah?" said Oz, very impressed. "Awesome, brah! Whoo, I admire you guys! So what? You no eat meat? How about chicken?"

"No, no," I corrected. "I'm a *vet*erinarian. Not vegetarian. Veterinarian."

"Oh," said Oz, nodding. "But what about seafood? Fish and stuff. . . ."

"No," I persisted. "You see. . . ."

"Eh," said Oz, apparently tired of the subject. "I'm glad you're working out. Shape dat body of yoahs. Sculpt it da way one artist carves art out of one slab of marble. . . ."

"Dis is my first day," I said.

"It's so easy," said Oz Kalani. "Keeping fit. Dis is da only body you'll evah have. You bettah take care of it. . . ."

Oz Kalani explained how he was a personal trainer, working out one-on-one with politicians, celebrities, and businessmen.

"Uh," I ventured. "What happened to yoah acting career?"

"Oh dat?" said Oz, waving at two girls daintily dipping their toes in the jacuzzi. "You've heard dose stories about some actor who worked as one waiter or one gas station attendant. Den one day, he's what-you-call discovered? Das what I'm doing. Only ting, I one personal trainer. I just passing time, waiting for da call to come. Da Big One. Den boom, my life going change. Das what my agent in Los Angeles says. He tell me, 'Be patient. Tings are gonna happen.' And I believe him. . . ."

During the next several weeks, I visited the Ikaika Fitness Center every Monday, Wednesday and Friday after work. Oz Kalani was always there. As I curled, pressed, squatted and benched, I watched Oz assist nubile lasses as they stretched their hamstrings and looked lovingly in his eyes. I watched him cheer on sweaty, out-of-shape executives struggling on exercise bicycles. And I watched Oz diligently take pencil to clipboard as he charted the weight training progress of young college students hoping to impress girls in Hamilton Library with the size of their shoulders and chests.

Oz had a fast, breathless, machine gun-like way of dishing out encouragement. *C'mon!Youcandoit!Pushpushpush!* And all the while, he wore a tight polo shirt—with the handsome Ikaika Fitness Center emblem, available for $29.95 at the front desk—shorts, Nikes, and shades hanging down from a string around his neck. Sometimes—on bad hair days, he explained—he wore a baseball cap sporting the insignia of a winning athletic team or the logo of a successful designer footwear manufacturer.

One day, though, Oz wore something new. Something I hadn't seen in ages. He wore the look of hope, a blissful sleepwalker enjoying the greatest dream of his life. And that afternoon, over watercress smoothies and no fat, no cholesterol energy bars, I heard Oz Kalani's familiar refrain.

"Dis is Da Big One," he said.

"Da what?" I said, not sure I'd heard correctly.

"Da Big One," he repeated. "Remembah how I used to say one moment can change da course of yoah entire life?"

"Yeah," I said, the understatement of my life.

"A producer guy just offered me my own exercise show. Can you believe dat? We start shooting tomorrow. I want you to be in my first show. You going stand right next to me. Stretching, doing jumping jacks, lunges, da works. . . ."

"Who's dis producer guy?"

"One of da students in my Tuesday, Thursday aerobics class. Dey call him Da Kid. He said we going start locally. But who knows wheah dis going lead? Maybe I can go national, have my own exercise videos. Den some big time buggah going discover me. My dreams going come true. . . ."

"Da Kid?" I said.

"Yeah," he said, with a wink that reminded me of the old, confident Oz Kalani I used to know. "You know dese Hollywood guys. Dey give each othah all kind funny nicknames."

I have to admit. I was pretty excited that night. I couldn't eat well. I hardly slept. After all, unlike the extremely photogenic Oz Kalani, I had never been on TV before. How much mousse should I put in my hair? Would I sweat too much?

Words can't describe the surprise waiting for me the next day when Oz Kalani took me to the set of his exercise show. Maybe I was naive. I was expecting us to tape at a beach or the grounds of a lush resort. Instead, Oz Kalani drove me to the employees' parking lot at the Ala Moana Shopping Center.

"Dis seems like a weird place to tape one exercise show," I said.

"You always so skeptical," said Oz Kalani, slightly annoyed. "Look at all da exercise shows on TV. Dey eithah working out in some fancy studio, or at some nice beach or golf course. Da Kid, he sharp. He like us be different. . . ."

"Whatevahs," I said, shrugging.

And, yes, words can't adequately describe the surprise when Oz Kalani introduced me to the big time producer named Da Kid. Instead of some forty-something-year-old executive type with dark glasses and a pipe, I wound up shaking hands with, well, a kid. A sixteen-year old stock clerk on his lunchbreak from an Ala Moana store.

"Are you Da Kid?" I said.

"Yes," said Da Kid.

"We going shoot Oz Kalani's exercise show in one parking lot?"

"Yep," said Da Kid. "And we gotta hurry up. I only get twenty minutes befoah I gotta go back work."

Oz took off his warm up jacket, revealing skintight bike shorts as black and glossy as Steve McGarrett's hair. Da Kid positioned Oz and me just slightly left of a Toyota Tercel and an Acura.

"If you like," said Oz Kalani. "I can sing, too. I get one good voice. I could have done duets with Frank Sinatra. I could've been da Fifth Beatle. Or you rather hear my Elvis?"

Da Kid whipped out one of those home video cameras you use at surprise birthday parties and baby luaus and Oz took us through his workout regime. A group of onlookers slowly gathered, making me quite self-conscious, as you can imagine. We got through some stretching and light aerobics when disaster struck. Several burly security guards informed us that we were on private property and just as quickly, kicked us off the aforementioned private property. Tears streamed down my face.

"Eh," said Oz Kalani, putting a consoling arm around me. "No cry for me, pal. I going be all right. . . ." I didn't have the heart to tell Oz that somehow, my cursed mousse had mixed with my sweat and run into my burning eyes. "I always thought my destiny was to be somebody," said Oz, watching a Nissan Pathfinder squeeze into a parking stall clearly labelled 'compact.' "I always thought I was going do Big Tings. Put Hawai'i on da map. Now, foah da first time in my life, I not so sure. Maybe I been wrong all dis time. . . ."

Oz Kalani was not at the Ikaika Fitness Center the next day. Nor did he make an appearance the next day. Or the next day. It was as if, once again, Oz Kalani had disappeared from the face of the earth. For a while, rumors about Oz Kalani circulated among the members of the Ikaika Fitness Center. He had received an offer to serve as Chief Trainer at the exclusive—and rival—Hawai'i Club. Others said he was in Japan, personal therapist to sumo wrestlers. Still others said he was in Hollywood, signing a contract to star in an action thriller to be shot on location in Kaka'ako.

Recently, I was at the Ikaika Fitness Center and there—before my very eyes—Oz Kalani made his triumphant return. Sort of. Actually, they were running an old rerun of *Hawaii Five-O* on the TV. And there was a much younger Oz Kalani, with so much hope and promise written on his eager face, pointing out the way a mad bomber had run to Steve McGarrett. I wanted so bad to hear Oz Kalani's voice one more time but the clanking of the weights in the Ikaika Fitness Center drowned him out, kinda like the way you lose track of sound when you stick your head underwater.

BY LOIS-ANN YAMANAKA

SUNNYSIDE UP

Twelve tiny bantam eggs all at once, all sunnyside up, until the brown lace on the edges crackles around yellow, yellow yolks. Yellower than store eggs, which Father says is because bantam eggs are fresh from the coop.

My father cooks a pot of hot rice. We put all twelve sunnyside up eggs facedown on the hot rice. Father slurps up the egg white that hangs from his fork. I cook up more bantam eggs for my mother, who likes her yolks broken; Calhoon, who likes hers over easy; and myself. I like mine sunnyside up just like Father.

The sunlight is pink on these mornings.

Last Sunday, Father took us to Jimmy Lee's to pick out new chickens. He wants Araucanas, which lay blue-and-green eggs. Then we can have Easter eggs for breakfast every Sunday.

Araucana chickens are bigger than bantams, like regular chickens without fancy feathers on their legs. And a little uglier. But the blue-and-green eggs—I can imagine them speckled in a tuft of grass, ready for finding. The Araucanas live near but not with the bantams in our yard.

Father had injected each chicken with pox vaccine. Mosquitoes had stung the red-rubbery part of their chicken faces, making them all bumpy with chicken pox. The real kind.

Father held each chicken and injected each rooster and hen with the medicine he bought from the Garden Exchange Feed Store. And he gently told them what he was doing as he poked their faces.

I saw a bantam rooster fly into the air once and spur my father on his eyelid. Blood dripped into my father's eyelashes.

The rooster that knifed him got a second chance, until the other day, when it spurred him in the ankle. Father was trying to shoo the rooster and his hens out of the garage. The cut bloodied his heel.

The rooster got this: Father, taking his wallet out of his back pocket, slowly walks up to the rooster. And WHAM! Right on the head. The rooster is stunned, so Father grabs him, ties up his legs, then hangs him upside down from the clothesline, nice leg feathers and all.

The morning turns to noon and it gets hot. The chicken tongue hangs a little out of the beak. Then it turns to night. The chicken hangs until he dies. Even in the end, Father doesn't want his chicken to die. He looks funny with the tiny Band-Aid soaked with Mercurochrome over his eye. And he walks with a slight limp for a couple of days.

Every day after breakfast my father gives his papaya rind and lots of papaya seeds to the chickens. Every day by noon the entire rind is gone. Father says one of the Araucana roosters must be pulling it off into the bushes somewhere.

This goes on for days. Calhoon finds the rinds first. Rinds, chicken bones, and pork-chop bones stuck in a hole under the aluminum shed from the Sears catalogue.

On a humid day, Father sees a huge rat, the size of a kitten, drag the rind, seeds and all, to the hole under the shed. So we set trap after trap. Nothing. Nothing kills this rat, who Father says must love chicken eggs too.

Uncle Ed tells my father, "Eh, Hubert, the fuckin' rat like papaya so much, bradda, why no poison that sucka?" So simple.

I watch my father pour grass poison all over the papaya rind and some chicken bones. I smell the poison strong and pure. Father places the rind and bones under the pua kenikeni tree. He keeps all the chickens in their coops. Later in the morning, the rind and bones are gone. Father and me never see the rat again.

The other night while watching *Combat* with Vic Morrow, we hear the coops being hit like wire pulling and loud chicken squawking. I grab the Eveready and run outside with Father. We see two white dogs, one huge and one medium, running from the coops. "Gunfunnit," my father yells, "goddam Portagee dogs. No can even chain um up nighttime, shit."

This goes on for several nights. We hear loud noises, run out there, and throw a couple rocks. The dogs run off again.

Uncle Ed suggests that we get a cage from the ASPCA and "trap those fuckas, then call the dogcatcha up and he gas those suckas by Saturday. Then you teach that damn Portagee one lesson to chain up his fuckin' dogs nighttime, Hubert." My father agrees.

We set up the cage that night. We put goat meat and some broken Araucana and bantam eggs inside the cage. And we wait. The chickens cluck low and soft inside the coops. The manure smells like sour scratch. And my father chicken-clucks to his bantams and Araucanas. He seems to say, "Nothing going harm you. Nothing."

In the morning, I wear my black rubber boots to the coops in the back. "I got something! I got um!" Father yells. When I get to the cage, it's a huge tomcat.

"You mean it was a cat, Daddy?" I say.

"No. No way. Was two dogs. The two white dogs from that Portagee's yard. Gunfunnit. He neva do nuttin' to my chickens. Let um go." The cat runs straight-tailed into the honohono.

Today, Father gathers smooth stones to slingshot the dogs to death. He goes by the lychee tree and practices. He aims for the fruit and when the big red ones fall, I gather them and peel their bumpy outsides and let the juices drip down my lip. I spit the seed Clint Eastwood style like in *High Plains Drifter*. Father practices all morning.

The dogs return at eight. Father creeps up to the anthurium patch. Then closer to the kumquat tree, then SMACK! Right in the white dog's ribs. The huge one screams and they both run off. Father dances in the backyard like an elf.

The next night both dogs return.

My father gets his pitchfork and puts a hāpu'u log near the aluminum shed. "The hāpu'u is those dogs," he tells me. "Watch this." Father raises the pitchfork above his head and hurls it at the hāpu'u log. WHOOMP! Threads of hāpu'u fly off into the grass. "Then you the backup man, okay? You stone that sucka. Here. Practice. Okay, wait." He runs to get his pitchfork.

"Okay, ready?" WHOOMP! "Stone um, stone um! Throw the rock, Lovey, you the backup man." I hurl the rock, hard as I can. We do this again and again. His pitchfork throwing gets very accurate. Always in the head.

At night, the pua kenikeni bloom. The white dogs come. Father readies his pitchfork. I hold my stones. Father steadies. He gets within range. Close. Closer. He throws.

I drop the stones to my feet.

The pitchfork breaks flesh. And a human sound of something screaming. A frenzy of legs jerking and pulling, dragging a body, and chickens squawking, hitting their bodies against the wire coops. The big white dog, brown shepherd eyes, and the concrete of the chicken yard covered with thick, purple blood. I swear, I see tears falling. I swear it.

And the sound of the pitchfork handle hitting the dog's skull. It's a small, sharp cry in the end. We never see the other white dog again.

*　　*　　*

The sky is pink.

Father has gathered the chicks of one of his bantam broods into a cardboard box. When the hen wants to leave, Father lifts the chicken mesh off of the box and puts a light bulb over the box to keep the chicks warm.

One has a crooked beak. She cannot get the mash quickly enough as the others peck away wildly. He feeds her from the palm of his hand. She gets her own papaya rind and seeds. Father carries her everywhere and strokes the dark black feathers on her back. She has no name.

He lets the one with the crooked beak roost at night in the stuffed pheasant he bought at a garage sale. "It must be comforting," he says. She greets him at the back step every morning because she belongs to no rooster strutting his hens around the yard.

The sky is pink on the morning when I watch her settle down and lay her first egg. I wash this one very carefully in the washtub outside. I carry the egg, warm in my hands, into the kitchen.

Her first egg, the one with no name, Father fries up in the big black frying pan with lots of hot Wesson oil. He fries it until the brown lace forms a crackly halo around the yellowest yolk you have ever seen. And Father eats this on hot, hot rice.

BY LUE ZIMMELMAN

END ZONE

n Sunday night the thieves came to Charlie Boyer's watch shop. Most likely kids, the cop said the next morning, glancing around with his notebook out and his dark glasses dangling from a pocket.

Ellen, Charlie's wife, showed the officer the broken cabinets, the empty drawers where the watches had been, the hole in the roof through which the intruders had come. Charlie sat at his bench, his soft shoulders hunched, his stubby hands folded in his lap, and listened to his wife and the cop talk.

She was asking what he thought, would they catch them, was there any chance they'd get their property back? And the cop, being polite, was saying they'd do their best, who knows—they might get lucky, anything was possible. Then someone else came, a short, fidgety man who carried a leather case and spread an inky dust everywhere, hunting for fingerprints.

"Find something, Jack?" the cop asked when the man was packing his tools, and Jack said he'd picked up a few around the safe and cash register, but they could belong to the owners, he'd have to check. Then the cop walked him out, and Charlie saw them talking near the blue-and-white, the small man's hands moving restlessly while the cop stared down the street.

After a while the officer came back, closed his notebook and pulled out his dark glasses. "Guess I should tell you," he said, "the chances we'll catch them aren't too good," and for the first time Charlie made a sound—one that was close to a groan yet almost a laugh.

"We've been here 40 years. Twelve times we've been robbed. Not once, not once," he repeated, raising one finger for emphasis, "has anyone been caught. Why should this time be different?"

"It's rough," the cop agreed, and avoided the old man's eyes by giving the ravaged shop one last survey. "Look, Mr. Boyer, I'll do my best. If anything turns up, I'll call you first thing."

"Thank you." Charlie felt the anger that had straightened his shoulders slide away. He rested his fingers on the edge of the workbench and raised his eyes so that they focused on the man's chest. "I know you'll do what you can."

After the cop left, Ellen walked into the back room and returned with a dustpan and broom, and a yellow sponge floating in a bucket of water. While she swept up the broken glass, Charlie tried to figure out whose watches had been taken, but found it hard to concentrate. He kept looking out the window at the stunted shade tree the city had planted in a stone box at the edge of the sidewalk. Blooming from its lowest branch was a single yellow flower, catching the morning sun.

He was still looking at the tree when Ellen pulled a wooden stool close to his bench and sat. "How much is missing?" she said, and Charlie answered, "Almost everything."

"Harada's watch?"

He nodded. "And Ching's and Maeda's. They broke the lock on the drawer and emptied it." He felt guilty, as though he'd failed her. He wanted to say something more, maybe touch her so they'd be in this together, but the firm line of her body, the tightness around her mouth that deepened the grooves angling across her cheeks, held him still. "Maybe," he said finally, "we should have bought insurance."

"How were we going to buy the insurance, Charlie? With what? You need money for insurance."

She was a small woman, thin in the face, with purple shadows under her eyes. Her hair was dark and pulled back in a limp ponytail. She wore a plain cotton dress that skimmed wide hips and hid most of her legs. Her feet and hands were tiny, delicate, and when she was young, she'd been vain about them. Now that vanity seemed incredible. When she looked at her hands it was like looking at a map of how far she'd come, barely remembering where she'd started from.

Sometimes she blamed Charlie for the clothes she wore and the way she looked. Sometimes she thought about the boys she'd dated in high school. One was a politician now. Another a doctor. Another a banker. All owned big homes—Makiki Heights and Nuʻuanu and Kāhala. Occasionally their pictures appeared in the papers, smiling, confident faces looking straight at her the way they had a long time ago, and Ellen would ask herself what if?

Sometimes, deep in her heart, she blamed Charlie for the smallness of their lives, and the stillness. Sometimes when they argued, she threw the names at him—Koga, Ikeda, Tatsumi—and felt a brief satisfaction before the uselessness.

"We should have found the money," Charlie said. "Somehow we should have found it."

"Where were we going to find it?" She waved a hand at the window. "Growing on that tree?"

Charlie followed her gesture and looked again at the butter-colored flower hanging motionless in the August heat.

"Money doesn't grow on trees," Ellen said, and when Charlie didn't answer, she waved her hand around the shop. "We work all these years and for nothing. They come in and take what they want. They want our clocks, they take them. Your tools, they take them. The watches, they take them. And they don't just steal. They break things and smash our store apart." She breathed in shakily. "What was it all for, Charlie?" and he knew she was asking about something else, something more than the theft.

Once they'd been happy. He had pictures of them young and smiling. The boy was still alive then. Eddie standing between them in front of the shop, everyone grinning at the camera, their arms laid across one another's shoulders. Or they were at the beach, sprawled on the tatami mats or on Maui where they used to go when Ellen's mother was still alive.

In his wallet Charlie had a photograph of Ellen in a shirred, two-piece swimsuit, lounging on Kailua Beach, her legs stretched forward, calves rounded and tan, one hand holding back a tumble of long, black hair. When it was taken, he was a soldier from Brooklyn, stationed in the Islands for W.W.II. She was a clerk in a bookstore on Fort Street.

Every weekend he'd hitched in from Schofield and bought books and watched her. She was quiet and serious and lovely. She didn't flirt with the soldiers the way the other shopgirls did. He sensed her pride. After a month, he made himself ask her out and was stunned when she accepted. They'd eaten Chinese food in Waikīkī and seen a movie, then he'd taken her home early. She lived with her brother, Masao, and his wife in a small white house in Mō'ili'ili.

There'd been red anthuriums in the yard, sitting in stone pots on rows of bricks. Five hundred plants, Charlie had estimated the first time he saw them. Maybe more. "My brother raises them," Ellen said as they walked along the front path. "They look like hearts," Charlie said, and she had smiled.

He'd wanted to kiss her then, but hesitated, and she'd stepped onto the porch, out of his reach. Then she'd surprised him by reaching for his hand. "Goodnight, Charlie Boyer. I hope you ask me out again."

After that they went out every weekend. Her brother wasn't happy, and Charlie's army friends made comments. None of it mattered. She listened and he listened. He wanted to own his own store; she wanted to go to college and become a teacher.

Now Charlie tried not to think too much about happiness. He was 65. If in a day he sold a watch and a few people came in with repair jobs, he counted himself lucky.

It was different years before. Then Charlie Boyer's Watch Repair was the only watch shop from Kaimukī to McCully. He'd sold birthday watches and graduation watches and Christmas watches. His repair trays had been filled, each timepiece tagged with its owner's name. Customers had come from all over Oʻahu, brought by word of mouth, brought by hearing that Charlie Boyer was honest and fair.

Now they went up the street to the new shopping mall. Parking was easier, and there was a Vietnamese there who fixed watches more cheaply than Charlie Boyer ever could. His store was full of shiny glass counters and soft carpets and plush chairs. Music played, and when the door opened a bell chimed. His wife wore silk dresses and a gold watch and a diamond ring.

"I could have borrowed the money," Charlie said. "Maeda would have made the loan."

"It's too late to talk about it. We don't have insurance. Not to replace the watches or fix the roof. What are we going to do?"

Charlie thought for a moment, then his mind grew numb. "I don't know," he said, and realized he was scared.

Getting up, Ellen reached for the broom. "Are you hungry, Charlie? I brought leftovers from dinner. I can make sandwiches."

He shook his head and sat still until she went behind the beaded curtain into the back room where they kept a refrigerator and a hotplate and a canvas cot. He heard the cot whine as she lay on it. Holding in a sigh, Charlie Boyer got up and walked out.

Traffic rushed by on King Street, sounding, when he shut his eyes, like the sea. Maybe he would go to the beach and look at the water. Years before, he'd taken the boy to the ocean. He'd taught him to float, then tread water, then swim. He'd watched Eddie slice over the waves, arms and legs churning smoothly, his body moving with sureness from here to there, and felt safe.

He was in Japan, part of the Occupation, when the boy was born. Ellen had found a place in Kaimukī, a converted garage that a Chinese couple rented out. There were roaches everywhere, she wrote. They came out at night if she left the light on, so she would lie in the dark with Eddie close to her and listen to the radio. She thought of him in Japan. She missed him, she wrote, more desperately than she'd imagined. She missed the way he touched her, and the way his eyes watched her, and the feel of his hands.

Charlie looked down the street. The storefronts burned in the summer light. There was no wind and the air was thick. On the news he'd heard that a storm was coming from the south.

He began walking, past the Xerox shop and the bicycle store and the Korean bar. He'd been in the neighborhood longer than of any them. He remembered when the Xerox place was an upholstery store owned by a man who took football bets on the side. One season nothing went his way, and he'd had to sell the business.

The bike shop had been a liquor store until the owner was killed late one night by a robber. Afterward, his wife had come and taken the beer and whiskey and wine. The place remained vacant for almost a year. People said there was bad luck in it and maybe there was. Charlie had watched one business after another come and go. Now some hotshot was selling fancy European bikes, some of them costing what cars used to. Well, good luck to him, the watchmaker thought. Good luck to all of them.

Charlie cut through the parking lot beside the Korean bar and turned down a narrow lane lined with apartment buildings. He followed the backstreet to University Avenue, then moved up to King Street and walked past a row of stores. He was headed, he realized, to the park where the stadium once stood. In the park, he picked a bench in the middle, under a shower tree.

He watched a father run slowly with his son, a white kite bobbing after them. Two babies crawled across the grass, faces raised to the sky while their mother laughed. A leaf floated down and landed in Charlie's lap. He ran a finger over it and found it soft, though it was mottled, yellow and brown.

He told himself to think about what he was going to do, how he could pay back Maeda and Ching and Harada, but his mind loped away. Leaning back, Charlie looked at the sky and the shapes of the clouds.

One summer he'd taken Ellen and Eddie to Brooklyn and showed them the apartment were he was born and the school he went to and the watch shop where Mr. Harold Begelman taught him the trade. They'd walked past the playground where he'd played football, and the carpet factory where his mother had worked, and the garage that employed his father until the Depression shut it down. He had pictures of that summer in one of the albums they kept on the bookshelf: a smiling Ellen squeezed between her husband and their handsome son.

The following fall Eddie played his last year of high school football. On weekends Charlie went with him to the school ground near the store, and they threw the football back and forth and practiced plays. Then they'd sit in the swings and talk, watching the younger kids play basketball.

"What was your best game?" Eddie had once asked, and Charlie told him about the time his team demolished Forest High from upstate New York 42–0. "We all felt pretty good that night," he said.

"Remember my first game?" Eddie said. "The one I sprained my ankle on the first play, sat out the rest of the night, and our team won by 30 points?"

Swinging forward, Charlie smiled. "You were a good sport about it, Eddie."

"I was mad." The boy grinned. "I'd been growing all these dreams about being a hero and making the big play, and that guy from Farrington—remember how big he was?—tackled me, and I was out."

"Your mother wanted to go down on the field to make sure you were okay."

The grin widened, but the boy grew quiet. After a while he said, "I was angry at first, but then I saw that it didn't matter. Only a few guys make touchdowns, but without the other guys there'd be no game."

Charlie had twisted the swing to look at his son, at the brown hair framing white and Asian features, and the skin that was gold from the summer, and the quick, bright eyes.

Friday nights, when Eddie was playing, Charlie and Ellen would walk the few blocks to the stadium and sit in the center bleachers where the high school kids sat and cheered the boy on. Eddie was fast and smart. The coach told them he was good enough to get a scholarship and play in college. They had watched their son dodge across the grassy field and felt proud. They had thought of the scholarship and felt safe. The boy could go on, be better, be more.

Eddie talked about being a teacher. In college he took history courses. He wanted to teach children, he wrote, and maybe make a difference. When Ellen read his letters, Charlie saw her pride, and it was suddenly all right, the choices they'd made, the things they'd picked up and left behind.

Across the field, the father and son had gotten the kite in the air. It was floating up and up, lifted by the light southerlies that had risen. The child was running with it and the father stood back, watching, letting the boy go.

Charlie looked at the clouds directly overhead. They billowed and exploded, plumes of white shooting off in all directions. Then, not wanting to see them, he closed his eyes.

The summer after he graduated, Eddie came home and they all flew to Maui. That year Fusae was still well enough to make the drive with them up Haleakalā.

They woke up early and dressed warmly. Ellen filled thermoses with coffee and packed the fruit and doughnuts they'd bought the day before. The mountain road was narrow, precarious in the pre-dawn light with its sharp bends and sheer drops, and more than once Charlie wondered if the journey was a mistake and if they should turn around.

Then they reached the clouds and the car was swallowed in mist, and only they existed—Ellen and her mother laughing, Eddie reaching out the window—and Charlie knew it was worth going on.

At the top, it was like winter. Wrapped in odd, rarely worn coats, they walked to the mountain's rim and looked down at the undulating land, bleak and beautiful. In crevices silverswords stretched and bloomed. A white bird dove into the harshness and disappeared. Then the sun rose.

Charlie lined them up—Ellen, Fusae, Eddie—and took their picture while the sky turned pink. Then Ellen took Fusae back to the car while Charlie and Eddie followed a trail into the mountain.

In places the earth was brittle; in others, powdery. They walked slowly, silently. By the time they reached the turning point and started back, the sky was a sharp blue and the air warm enough to unzipper coats.

Eddie picked up a black rock and tested its weight. "How long do you think it's been here?" he asked, and Charlie said he didn't know, maybe a million years. "That's long," Eddie murmured, returning the stone carefully to the ground. Then he put his hands in his pockets and said, "I'm being drafted, Dad." Charlie stopped and squinted at his son in the startling light. "I fly back to California at the end of the week. I wanted to tell you first. I'll tell Mom when we get back to Honolulu."

"All right," Charlie said. Not knowing what else to do, he began walking but quicker now as though time was short or he was running from something.

The day before Eddie left, Charlie walked with him to the park and they threw the football until the sun disappeared.

"Don't worry," Eddie said as they made their way across the basketball courts and the uncut grass beyond. "When they see how I handle a gun, they'll give me a desk job. I'll slide through the two years."

"Your mother doesn't want you to go. She's taking this hard."

Eddie nodded and broke stride long enough to pluck a stalk of pink seeds from the grass. "But she's handling it well. I mean, she's not crying or anything."

"She keeps her feelings inside. That's how she is."

"I use to wish she was different." He scraped a thumbnail along the stalk so that the seeds went flying. "More affectionate maybe. She stopped giving me hugs when I was five."

"In her own way, she cares for you."

"Yeah, I know." With a quick smile, Eddie tossed aside the stalk and ran ahead, cutting left then right, then running backwards, reaching his arms out for the ball. "Throw me a touchdown," he shouted, and Charlie had sailed the ball in a high, curving arc, whistling proudly when Eddie pulled it in.

The day the two soldiers came to the store, Charlie thought they were customers. They'd told him first, and he had gone into the back for Ellen, his heart pumping wildly. She'd looked up from the lunch she was making, listening, her face hardening, then softening unbearably.

In the distance the Ko‘olaus were a ripple of browns and greens. For a second Charlie Boyer imagined his son running across the field. For a second he could see the boy slicing across the grass, flying from here to there, over the wide white line, safe.

Then he felt someone in front of him, pulling him back. It was Ellen.

"I brought you lunch, Charlie. I made ham sandwiches, and I stopped and bought iced coffee." She was carrying two paper sacks. Sitting on the bench, she took out the cups and the sandwiches wrapped in waxed paper. They began to eat.

The wind grew stronger. Clouds moved in from the horizon, and the light grayed. The mothers lifted their babies and headed home. The boy hauled down his kite and walked off, holding his father's hand.

"How did you know I'd be here?" Charlie said.

"I knew," was all she said. She took a long sip of coffee. "Remember how Eddie used to run, right here where we're sitting?" Because they never talked about the boy, Charlie only nodded, hiding his surprise. "He was fast, wasn't he?"

"The fastest."

"He was a good boy." She was holding her cup in midair.

"Eddie was the best."

Ellen lowered the cup until it rested on her knee. Suddenly as though the words had been kept too long she said, "I should have held him that last day. I meant to hold him, Charlie. I wanted to, but I put it off and then it was too late."

"Eddie understood."

"Did he?" She turned sharply to search her husband's face. "Did he really, Charlie?" The watchmaker nodded and it seemed enough. Ellen looked toward the mountains. "We'll find a way to pay back the stolen watches. We've been robbed before and managed. We'll manage this time."

He nodded again then said, "It's going to rain. I heard it on the news."

She stuffed the waxed paper and empty cups into a bag, then crumpled the bag and carried it to the garbage can on the other side of the tree. They heard drops begin to spatter on the leaves and on the stone walkway that led from the center of the park to the street.

"I miss him, Ellen." He looked up, straight into her eyes, and there was something in them like a long time ago.

"I miss him too." Surprising him again, she stretched out her hand and waited until he took it. "Let's go home, Charlie," she said.

TEETH

1999, oil on illustration board

Contributors

Alan Aoki wishes to thank *HONOLULU Magazine* for sponsoring its annual fiction contest and Bamboo Ridge Press, especially for its continuing support of the literary arts in Hawai'i. Alan has not written anything for several years and was pleasantly surprised (nay, absolutely thrilled!) and grateful for the opportunity to appear in their publications.

Alani Apio grew up in Pu'uloa, otherwise known as 'Ewa Beach. Fished a lot. Surfed a lot. Graduated from Kamehameha. Got a B.A. in Drama and Theatre from U.H. Mānoa. Has had three plays produced so far: "Nā Keiki 'O Ka 'Āina," "Kāmau," and "Kāmau A'e". Has the best 'ohana a person could ask for.

Pamela Ball's story "The Centipede of Attraction" was an early version of what later turned into her novel *Lava*. Her second novel will be published next year.

"The story was based on an incident from my childhood growing up on the windward side of O'ahu. It's been around ten years since I've seen this version of the story, and it was fun to read—almost like discovering an old diary."

Stuart Ching is a graduate of the M.F.A. program at Colorado State University and currently lives in Nebraska, where he teaches writing at Creighton University and is writing his dissertation for the Ph.D. in Rhetoric at the University of Nebraska-Lincoln.

David Choo grew up in Hawai'i Kai, graduating from U.H. Mānoa before getting an M.F.A. in Creative Writing at The American University in Washington, D.C. "Akiko Buries Her Son" was written during a particularly cold winter in Washington.

Wanda Dial: The author of "Rom Bori" is a University of Missouri journalism graduate and a finalist in the 1998 *HONOLULU Magazine* short story contest. The story of a gypsy bride is based on extensive research of gypsy life and culture in post-World War II Hawai'i.

Marie M. Hara and *Nora Okja Keller* are co-editors of *Intersecting Circles: Voices of Hapa Women Writers,* an anthology of poetry and prose on issues of mixed race identity.

Mavis Hara: The story "Chemotherapy" is fiction. In real life, when I had a mastectomy, my relatives all visited me bringing gifts of fruit, eggs, garlic pills, teas, various health publications, and inspirational books. I appreciated them all. The story was written because Michiko Kodama-Nishimoto of the University of Hawai'i Oral History Center and Violet Murakami of the Kapi'olani Community College's Art Department encouraged me to "write it down." The story was a runner-up in 1999.

Jim Harstad: A slightly different version of "The Black and Yellow Raft" appeared in *Bamboo Ridge,* Summer and Fall 1994. Yes, dear reader, it is fiction. It is *all* fiction.

John Heckathorn began writing for *HONOLULU Magazine* in 1984, joined the staff in '85 and became the magazine's editor in 1993. He's won multiple awards for his writing from the Hawai'i Publishers Association and the local chapter of the Society of Professional Journalists. But he's best known for his restaurant criticism, which has also garnered both local and national awards.

He earned a B.A. in English from Wittenberg University and a Ph.D. in British and American literature from the University of Pennsylvania. He's taught at Penn, St. Peter's College, Rutgers and, for nine years, at the University of Hawai'i. He's published fiction and poetry, and served as managing editor for *The Berlitz Travellers Guide to Hawai'i* and *Gayot's Best of Hawai'i.* He does a weekly radio show for KHVH.

Craig Howes teaches English at the University of Hawai'i at Mānoa, and edits *Biography: An Interdisciplinary Quarterly.* He won the Elliott P. Cades Award for Literature in 1994. Without Sara Collins, *Bamboo Ridge,* the Hawai'i Literary Arts Council, and Pat Matsueda, "The Resurrection Man" would not have been written; without Ian MacMillan and Frank Stewart, it would not be the story it came to be.

Yokanaan Kearns is the literary alter ego of John Michael Kearns, Associate Professor of History and Humanities at Hawai'i Pacific University. Locally grown, he received his Ph.D. in Classical Linguistics from UCLA, then taught Latin and Greek in New England before returning home from ten years in exile. He is the author of numerous stage plays, screenplays, short stories, and a novel entitled *Death in the Eye of the Astronomer.* "Confessions of a Stupid Haole" first appeared in *Bamboo Ridge,* no. 73, 1998.

Mary Lombard once liked to fool around on an old Underwood typewriter trying her hand at stories. Then she won the 1985 *HONOLULU Magazine* Fiction Contest. Her stories have since appeared in a number of *Bamboo Ridge* issues, including *Sister Stew*, as well as *Chaminade Review, Iris, Shockbox, Mānoa, The Honolulu Advertiser* and *Hawaii Pacific Review*. She lives in Kailua with her husband Herman Mulder and now fools around on a computer, in earnest.

Georgia K. McMillen lives, works, and writes on Maui.

Wendy Miyake is a poet and a fiction writer. Her work has been published in *Taxi, Hawai'i Review,* and the anthology *Growing Up Local.* She currently teaches in Honolulu.

Jason Nobriga: From comic books to computer animation, he has always had an interest in art. After working a few years as a computer graphic artist for a local software company, a close friend introduced Nobriga to a traditional medium . . . oils.

Since then, his work has appeared in *HONOLULU Magazine, Honolulu Weekly*, HMSA's *Island Scene Magazine*, and *American Medical News*; in 1998 he received the 'Ilima Award of Excellence for Best Editorial Illustration.

Nobriga lives in Honolulu and is also an avid guitar player.

Gary Pak teaches writing at Kapi'olani Community College. He is the author of a collection of short stories, *The Watcher of Waipuna and Other Stories* (Honolulu: Bamboo Ridge Press, 1992) and a novel, *A Ricepaper Airplane* (Honolulu: University of Hawai'i Press, 1998). He is a recipient of the Elliot Cades Award and the 1993 National Book Award for Literature from the Association of Asian American Studies.

Graham Salisbury grew up in the Hawaiian Islands where his family has lived since 1820. He graduated from California State University, Northridge, and received a Master of Fine Arts degree from Vermont College of Norwich University. He now lives with his family in Portland, Oregon. He is the author of four books for young readers: *Blue Skin of the Sea, Under the Blood-Red Sun, Shark Bait,* and *Jungle Dogs.* Among the awards these novels have garnered are the Bank Street Child Study Association Children's Book of the Year Award, three *Parent's Choice* awards, three Oregon Book Awards, the 1993 PEN/Norma Klein Award, Hawai'i's Nene Award, the California Young Reader Medal, The Family Channel Seal of Quality, *Booklist* Editor's Choice, and the Scott O'Dell Award for Historical Fiction

William Steinhoff grew up in Flint, Michigan. He has traveled extensively in Asia with the U.S. military, as a student, and as a free-lance foreign correspondent. He lives with his wife, Patricia, who is a professor of sociology at the University of Hawai'i at Mānoa.

Catherine Bridges Tarleton and her husband Dwight relocated to the Big Island from Washington, D.C. in 1989. They reside in Waikoloa along with three blue and gold macaws, a prolific banana patch, and an expanding collection of Star Trek paraphernalia. She works for the Mauna Kea Resort as Executive Secretary to Managing Director, Adi Kohler.

Her essays about life in Hawai'i have appeared in *ALOHA* and *HONOLULU Magazine*, and her entries in the fiction contest have earned three honorable mentions. She is presently writing "an erotic science fiction metaphysical novel," which she will polish and promote at the Maui Writers Conference in August.

Bill Teter teaches high school English in Honolulu. He has learned to correctly pronounce Kui Lee's name.

Lee A. Tonouchi is/wuz/goin be insai *The Asian Pacific American Journal*, *Bamboo Ridge*, *Chaminade Literary Review*, *Hawai'i Review*, *riksha*, *Tinfish*, and *ZYZZYVA*. He wuz nevah insai da *New Yorker* [commercial: HRallHIsp.ed.stay_outNOW/ info4geffem/gocall8089563030] cuz he nevah sent dem nahting. But SACK3 is coming soon. SACK or be sacked. Write on, brah.

Peter Van Dyke: Shortly before this story was published in 1991, I left Honolulu for a job in a botanical garden in Captain Cook, on Hawai'i Island. While I am happily occupied here with plants, family, farm, and the nearby shoreline, I always enjoy visiting Honolulu and checking out my old haunts there. I find it somehow encouraging to see that for all its growth, Waikīkī still provides an ample habitat for the loafers and eccentrics that I like to write about.

I am currently at work on a novel. My novel's main character, I realize in revisiting this short story, is a distant British cousin of Dr. Wang's.

John Wythe White is a free-lance writer of fiction, travel literature, investigative journalism, and advertising—a dubious combination of genres which earned him a "Sour Poi" award in 1999 from *HONOLULU Magazine* for failure to disclose a potential conflict of interest. He was a theater reviewer for the *Honolulu Star-Bulletin* and a media columnist for *HONOLULU Magazine*. He has been a contributing writer and editor to *The Hawaii Observer*, *EastWest Magazine*, the inflights *Pacifica* (Continental Micronesia) and *Hana Hou!* (Hawaiian Airlines), and *Honolulu Weekly*.

One of his plays, "Biff Finds Himself In Hawaii"—a satirical sequel to Arthur Miller's "Death of a Salesman"—was produced in 1990 by Kumu Kahua Theatre.

Cedric Yamanaka's fiction has appeared in, among other places, *Mānoa, Hawai'i Review,* and *HONOLULU Magazine.* He is a graduate of Farrington High School. At the University of Hawai'i at Mānoa, he was the recipient of the Ernest Hemingway Memorial Award for Creative Writing. He was also awarded the Helen Deutsch Fellowship for Best Undergraduate Writer of the Year at Boston University, where he received a Master's Degree in English. He is a past winner of the *HONOLULU Magazine* Fiction Contest and his screenplay, "The Lemon Tree Billiards House," won a Best Hawai'i Film Award at the prestigious Hawai'i International Film Festival. He has worked as a print, radio, and television journalist for over ten years. He is currently working on a number of writing projects, including a novel.

Lois-Ann Yamanaka's most recent novel is *Name Me Nobody* for young adults. She is currently working on children's stories and her next novel in her beautiful garden in Kalihi.

Lue Zimmelman: "I'm pleased and honored that 'Endzone' was selected by *Bamboo Ridge* for publication in their *Best of Honolulu Fiction* issue."